FEVER COAST

EPIC ADVENTURE SERIES #11

COLIN FALCONER

Copyright © Colin Falconer

Cover design copyright © Colin Falconer

The right of Colin Falconer to be identified as the author of this work has been asserted in accordance with the Copyright, Designs and Patents Act 1988.

All rights reserved. No part of this publication may be reproduced, stored in, or transmitted into any retrieval system, in any form, or by any means (electronic, mechanical, photocopying, recording or otherwise) without the prior written permission of the publisher. Any person who does any unauthorized act in relation to this publication may be liable to criminal prosecution and civil claims for damages. The only exception is by a reviewer, who may quote short excerpts in a review.

This is a work of fiction. Names, characters, businesses, places, events and incidents are either the products of the author's imagination or used in a fictitious manner.

Part 1 previously published as a novella, *Blood Moon Over Africa*.

This is for Lise.
I couldn't do it without you.

PART 1

Blood Moon Over Zanzibar

CHAPTER 1

East Africa, 1750

'I can hit that hippopotamus from here,' Andzile said.

'We're not aiming for the hippo,' Lachlan said, annoyed. 'There's a white flag in the mud, there in the estuary. That's the target.'

'I hate hippos. One of them killed my uncle.'

'Not that one.'

'You can tell them apart?'

Lachlan took a breath. It had been like this since they were kids, this banter. He would give him a little latitude. But he didn't like him talking back in front of the others. They weren't children anymore and this wasn't play.

'Just aim for the flag.'

'One less hippopotamus isn't going to matter. The spirit of my uncle would approve.'

The gun crew shuffled bare feet in the sand. Some of them were grinning. This wouldn't do.

'The spirit of your uncle is not in charge of the gun. Now follow the order.'

Andzile bent down behind the cannon and checked the elevation screw. Two men stood to the side with long iron bars, ready to traverse the barrel.

'To the right, just a little bit, no more than a monkey penis! I'll blow his fat rump all over the mangroves.'

Lachlan pushed him aside. 'We're aiming for the flag, not that poor dumb beast.' He gave the order and the two young men grunted and strained at the iron levers to inch the ancient cannon back to its original position.

'You said I could aim the gun,' Andzile said.

'Stand back.'

'You promised me.'

'What I said was, you could practise aiming for the flag. If you won't do what I said, then I'll have to.'

Lachlan re-checked the sighting on the barrel and adjusted the quoin.

'You made me the gunner,' Andzile said.

'Now I'm unmaking you. Advance cartridge!'

Andzile tried to push his way forward, but Lachlan put a hand on his chest and propelled him back again. 'When you think you can take simple commands, I'll make you gunner again.'

For a moment Lachlan wasn't sure if Andzile was about to burst into tears or fly into a rage. In the end, he chose to sulk. He turned and walked away.

Lachlan knew his gun crew were watching to see how he would handle this. Best to let him go. Give him an hour or two and he would calm down. He always did.

But Andzile had to have the last word. He pointed a finger at him. 'I take orders from your father and Bwana Rory. Not from you. You're just a boy!'

'A boy that will beat you black and blue if you talk to me like that again. Now get out of here.'

Andzile retreated, picked up a handful of sand and threw it at Lachlan. Lachlan spat the sand into the dirt and ignored him. He turned to the crew as if nothing had happened.

'Advance cartridge,' Lachlan repeated.

One of the young men ran forward and handed the wormer the canvas bag with the charge. He pushed it down the barrel and the lad on his right shoved it into position with the ramrod.

'Fikani!' Lachlan shouted. 'Keep your thumb on the vent! How many times have I told you?'

When they finished loading, Lachlan bent down behind the gun and re-checked the sighting. He stepped back. 'Prepare to fire.'

A young man called Kotani was holding a smouldering linstock and he took a step forward, ready.

'Fire,' Lachlan said and Kotani touched the linstock to the match protruding from the vent.

The cannon reared back from the embrasure and a flock of parrots exploded from the palm trees in fright. The hippo burst out of the water and took off through the bush in a lumbering run. Fikani started screaming and running in circles with his head in his hands. He'd forgotten to cover his ears. The others dissolved into convulsions of laughter.

Lachlan took out his telescope and saw the cannon ball buried in the mud twenty yards from the white flag. Not bad shooting.

'Well done,' he said. He wondered if any of them could be relied on to load and fire the cannon if it came to it and there was a ship out there firing back at them.

Fortunately, he reckoned, that would never happen.

With the passing of the monsoon season, Lachlan McKenzie had celebrated his twentieth year. He looked nothing like his father, Hamish. He was a head taller, with a mop of blonde curls and his mother's blue eyes. His nickname among the local Tsonga was *Nkala* – mongoose. He had earned the name when he was a little boy and his older sister Katherine had disturbed a snake. Instead of running away like his brother Callum, he had stepped between her and the cobra and attacked it with a stick.

It had won him a reputation for fearlessness among the local people, though Hamish chose to call it recklessness, a hot temper that wouldn't be tamed.

No one in the fort had forgotten the time a few years before when Lachlan had got into a fight with two of Mohammed Daoud's crew. He said they had insulted his sister, though they denied it later. Whether or not it was true, it had been a brave thing to do. Or a stupid one, depending on whether it was his father or his sister recounting the story.

Lachlan had taken them both down, though he was only sixteen years old, and they were bigger and stronger. They were older men from Dar es Salaam, and Hamish had told him afterwards that he was lucky they had not drawn the Kris knives they carried in their belts.

Over the past year Lachlan had taken over the training of their *chikunda*, their native army, teaching the young Tsonga men what to do if the fort was ever attacked. He drilled them in how to fire their arsenal of smooth-bore Brown Bess muskets and chose a dozen of them as crew for the two ancient cannon his father and uncle had acquired. They weren't very skilful at loading and reloading yet, but at least none of them had lost a limb.

Lachlan scratched at the nest of mosquito bites behind his ear. The sun was sinking over the river, leaving a brush stroke of flame across the paling sky. He heard a hippopotamus grunting, just its nostrils and ears appearing in the dimpled mercury of the water. He wondered if it was the same one that had killed Andzile's uncle.

The argument with Andzile had been stupid. He put it out of his mind. Andzile was a hothead, but by tomorrow he would have forgotten all about it.

Tendrils of smoke from the cook fires rose from the Tsonga village outside the fort. Soon, the drums would start, as they did every day at sunset.

Most days there were a few gazelles on the far bank come down to drink, though fewer than there used to be since Sasavona's boys had started spearing them to make their hides into drumskins. Tonight, the bank was empty, and now he saw the reason. A lion had come down to drink. He watched it turn away from the river and pad into the trees. It was a battle-scarred male, one of a mating couple that had been seen outside the fort for days now. The Tsonga said it was a bad omen, but then they saw omens in everything.

Still, it made him uneasy.

He set off back to the *boma,* the main house. He had to go past the godown on the way. As he got there, he heard something that made him stop and turn. One of the heavy ironwood doors to the warehouse was swinging open. Something wasn't right.

He heard noises coming from inside. He took his hunting knife from his belt and went in.

It took his eyes a moment to get accustomed to the gloom, for there were no windows. The godown had a thatched roof like all the settlement houses, but the walls were solid, made from heavy coral stone. The family's ivory was stored in here on racks, along with copper wheels ready for shipping. It also served as their arsenal, so the doors were always padlocked.

Who was there? No reason for his mother and sister to come in here. It had to be Callum.

'Cal?'

'Over here.'

He followed the racks to the end of the building and found his brother standing over a body. A Tsonga lay on the dirt floor, covered in blood. Callum was holding a shovel and was panting hard. He must have hit the fellow more than once. Lachlan put his knife back in its sheath, wrestled the spade out of his brother's hand and pushed him away.

He bent down. Dear God, it was Andzile. He was unconscious and the wool of his hair was matted with blood. It was everywhere. Droplets of it had even sprayed onto the yellow ivory tusks in the racks. He lay on his side with his eyes rolled back in his head.

'What the hell happened?'

'I caught him stealing from us.'

'Andzile isn't a thief.'

'I caught him at it, red-handed.'

'How did he get in?'

Callum pointed to a gap between the thatch and the limestone. 'Up there, I suppose.'

There was a pulse, a weak one.

'Is he dead?' Callum said.

'Did you intend him to be?'

Andzile shuddered and coughed a froth of bubbles through his nose. There was so much blood, Lachlan couldn't see where it was all coming from.

'How many times did you hit him?'

'Only once.'

A lie, Lachlan thought. You couldn't do this much damage with one hit from a shovel. His little brother must have been pummelling him with it.

He scooped Andzile up in his arms. Although he was about the same age, he was a skinny kid next to Lachlan and light as a feather.

'Get the hell out of here,' he said to Callum.

'You can't tell me what to do.'

'You want to deal with this?'

Callum shrugged and backed off. 'What are you going to tell pa?' he said.

'Is that all you're worried about?'

'It's only a *kaffir*.'

'I'll try and forget you said that.'

Callum turned and ran back to the house.

What a mess. Blood dribbled out of Andzile's nose, one eye was a pulpy mess, and his head was so swollen he could barely recognize him.

Cal, what the hell have you done?

The native village was outside the compound, away from the river. The rondavels of the pole and dagga huts nestled among a grove of cashew and mango trees next to the salt flats. Lachlan carried Andzile through the millet gardens that separated the village from the fort. Kids and dogs appeared from nowhere, the curs yapping at his heels, the children staring at him with eyes big as plates.

What was he going to tell Sasavona? Andzile's father was their family's sergeant – the *macazambo* – their most senior and trusted man among the local people, and chieftain of the Tsonga. This was bad.

Sasavona's first wife came running out of her hut. She shrieked when she saw Andzile. Then Sasavona's other two wives ran out and crowded around, Andzile's little brothers and sisters as well. They all started wailing together.

Finally Sasavona appeared. He was a big man, broad as an axe handle across the shoulders. When he saw his son in Lachlan's arms, he pushed the others aside and took him from him. 'What happened?' he said in Swahili.

'I found him in the godown,' Lachlan said. Not all the truth, but some of it.

A muscle worked in Sasavona's jaw. 'He shouldn't have been in there,' he said. He turned and walked inside. His son was as limp as a puppet in his arms.

Lachlan looked down at his shirt. He was covered in gore. For God's sake, this wasn't right, even if Andzile had been thieving. He looked around the village. No one would look at him.

Hamish would have plenty to say about this when he got back.

Johanna McKenzie had had a busy afternoon, coping with the usual but many aggravations of domestic management in the African bush. The local fish eagle had been around again, hoping for a change to his diet. All afternoon he had been sitting on one of the topmost branches of a baobab tree, measuring the distance between himself and one of Johanna's chickens with a quick and practised eye.

She had foiled his efforts, but not so the giant and raucous crows, who had been mobbing her kitchen veranda since daybreak. They had helped themselves to at least half a dozen of the young chicks in the yard. She couldn't even scold them, let alone throw a rock or two at them. That would have been taboo in the eyes of her kitchen girls.

The first she knew of trouble was when Callum rushed in, red-faced and dishevelled. He stood in the doorway of her kitchen, pointing wordlessly toward the storehouse on the other side of the fort.

'*Godverdomme*,' she said, for even after all these years she had never learned to swear in her husband's language. 'What is it?'

He had been running hard and couldn't get his breath. With growing alarm, she saw the specks of blood on his shirt.

She grabbed him by the shoulders. 'Tell me!'

'It's Lachlan,' he gasped. 'He's done for one of the Tsonga boys with a shovel!'

CHAPTER 2

Mozambique Island

'You call this wine?' Hamish McKenzie said, raising his cup in a toast. 'It tastes like pig urine, you overblown, tatty thief.'

The Governor of Mozambique – who passed as the law in these parts - spoke not a word of English. Even if he did, he would have been unable to decipher Hamish's accent. So the insult went unpunished. He just nodded, smiled and touched his cup to Hamish's to return the toast.

The governor then turned and spoke to his fellow Portuguese. Jorge Ferreira sucked on his empty pipe and translated for Hamish.

'Now to business,' Jorge said. 'He wants twenty *escudos* on every bar of ivory and one cloth in seven on your imports. The same on beads.'

'Twenty *escudos*? Tell him he's the biggest thief in Africa.'

'I would, but he would take it as a compliment. Look, the man is a complete fool. If we cannot rob him blind before we pay the duties, what does that say of us?'

A breath of wind from the sea stirred the papers on the governor's desk, bringing with it the taint of the food market: ripe fruit and fish. They could hear a Portuguese sergeant drilling his sepoys, his native soldiers, down in the square.

There was another brief exchange of words in the damnable language Hamish could not understand and then Jorge said to him in Swahili, 'He says you do not have to pay it all in gold. You can pay half in grain and millet, of which you have plenty, and which the governor is constantly in need of.'

'So, he keeps the gold, and his garrison gets fed. What does the king get?'

Jorge shrugged. 'The king is a long way away, in Lisbon.'

And so, the deal was done. Hamish was overcharged on the duty for his ivory, which he and Jorge had outrageously under-declared. In return he would pay half of a quarter of what he should have done, mostly in manioc, corn, rice and millet, which he was given as tribute by the local tribes and cost him nothing.

The governor thus ensured that the soldiers guarding the fort for the king would not starve. He would put his own share of the graft toward the estate he planned to buy on the Douro River in Portugal when he retired.

Both men were well pleased with the result of the negotiations.

When their business was concluded, another toast was required. A black slave in a frayed, white jacket was summoned and poured more bad wine.

'May you be violated by a mongoose in your sleep,' Hamish said and told Jorge to tell the governor it was an old Scottish blessing.

Mozambique Island, known to everyone as *Ilha,* was a narrow stretch of sand, two or three miles long, covered with palm groves. The chunky grey fortress of São Sebastião sat at one end of it. Two hundred years before, countless slaves had died under the whip dragging the coral stone from the other end of the island to build it.

A wide, sandy square adjoined the fortress, and from there twisting narrow lanes ran through a warren of stucco and stone flat-roofed houses. The locals called it Lime Town. It was home to a hundred Portuguese and two hundred Indians and *kaffirs*. It was where many of the *prazeiros,* colonist farmers, had built houses, where they could stay when they came to Ilha to do business with the government.

Jorge Ferreira had supervised the construction of his villa himself, using wooden beams of almost indestructible ironwood from Matibane. The terrace on the roof afforded a panorama of the entire island. On one side, he had a view of the Portuguese warehouses near the fort, bulging at this time of year with ivory tusks, copper and tortoiseshell; on the other, he could make out the crowded mud and palm leaf huts at the southern tip, where the natives lived. It was a rabbit warren of fishing nets, cook fires and naked, squealing children. The island was so narrow, a man could throw a stone across the narrowest part.

It wasn't much to look at, but he knew the Dutch and the English would give anything to get their hands on it. The Dutch had already tried twice without success.

A pleasant offshore breeze brought with it the thick scent of spice from the godowns by the docks. It all but disguised the taint from the slave market.

Jorge invited Hamish to join him on the terrace to watch the sun set and celebrate the successful conclusion of their business with the governor. He had one of his servants bring up a bottle of square-face Hollander gin and two glasses. The first swallow made Hamish's eyes water, but it was better than the vinegar they had been served at the governor's house.

There was a roar from the direction of the square. They were whipping another poor wretch. Hamish despised the trade and would have nothing to do with it, but it was where all the money was these days.

'Now, there is just the small matter of my commission,' Jorge said.

'Ten bars. As always.'

'Twenty.'

'Twenty! You cannot be serious?'

'I have decided to calculate my commissions in a different way from now on. Twenty.'

'I can't afford that! The Nguni are fighting among themselves in Natal and there's a drought in Swaziland. There's not much ivory to be had. I'll be lucky to get twenty bars myself, this year.'

Jorge laughed and slapped the table. 'What a wonderful liar you are! You remind me of me when I was your age.' He pulled his tobacco pouch from the pocket of his tunic and lit his clay pipe.

'You'll break me!'

'Even if that were true, it wouldn't worry me in the slightest.'

'I tell you; I cannot pay twenty bars of ivory!'

'Senhor, let me remind you. This is Portuguese Africa, and you are an Englishman.'

'I'm Scottish. Don't insult me.'

'English, Scottish, you have no governor to complain to for your rights. You pay me what I ask, or you must leave Delgoa Bay.'

Hamish slammed his drink down. There was some gin left in the cup and he hurriedly finished it before slamming it down a second time. He would not go wasting good gin by splashing it over this bastard's table, even for the sake of dramatic effect. Besides, twenty bars really wasn't such a bad deal and he decided to get out while he was ahead.

'May you rot in hell,' he growled, reverting to his mother tongue. He put on his hat and got up from the table.

'Safe journey back to Delgoa Bay,' Jorge said and smiled. 'My compliments to your wife!'

CHAPTER 3

Hamish gripped the dhow's wooden rail, scanning the loom of the coast, searching for the river entrance. The estuary guarding Delgoa Bay was hard to discern among the endless ribbon of pale beaches stretching for hundreds of miles from Ilha to the Cape.

Their skipper, Mohammed Daoud, couldn't venture too close to the shore because of the turquoise shallows that were haunt to gaudy flocks of flamingos and local fishermen in dugout canoes. Occasionally there were thick forests of mangrove swamp.

Below them, the ocean ran so clear Hamish could see a hundred feet down to the seabed. Dolphins played in their wake.

I'm a long way from home, he thought, or at least, a long way from the cold, grey farm where I was born. Delgoa Bay was one hundred leagues north of the place Vasco da Gama had called Natal, and two days' sailing south of the Portuguese forts of the Swahili coast. The hinterland belonged to a Tsonga chieftain known as Mangobe and was mostly uncharted.

It was as desolate a place as any white man could come.

Mohammed Daoud shouted from the tiller and half-naked seamen dropped out of the rigging and swarmed around the massive teak boom, running it forward and back again. The *al-Shahadah* creaked and groaned as she butted against the tide, coming around agonizingly slowly. Hamish's nose wrinkled as he smelled the bilges stirring below decks.

Mohammed had seen the river mouth. How, Hamish didn't know. The man was uncanny.

If finding the river was difficult, navigating the sandbanks and coral reefs that guarded it required an almost supernatural skill. A captain had to know the vagaries of the local tides, especially if he wanted to take a hulking oceangoing dhow like theirs as far upriver as Fort Greenock.

Their skipper's beloved Allah had blessed them with a windless morning of flat, pink sky. The only sounds were the gurgle of the wash and the singsong chant of the boy at the bow as he counted off the markers on the lead line. As they entered the channel, Mohammed crouched at the tiller, his face a mask of concentration.

Was he never afraid, Hamish wondered. Did he ever doubt his own judgement? If he did, he never showed it. Hamish had seen him run between reefs during a monsoon looking as if he might fall into a dead sleep at any moment.

Hamish himself couldn't help but feel his guts churn. No matter how many times they did this, he always thought that this time Mohammed must surely be about to run her aground on the banks or break her back on the reef. Twenty years they'd been sailing together, and he would have thought he'd have learned to trust him. He was the finest pilot this side of Zanzibar.

Mohammed shouted another order, and his men scampered about the boom, hauling at the lines. It creaked and swung, and the dirty grey triangle of sail found some zephyr that only Mohammed could feel. Suddenly they were inside the reef and running past the mangroves on their port.

Hamish could make out Fort Greenock on the northern side of the river.

It had taken Hamish and Rory McKenzie almost twenty years to build it but, as he always told the Portugals, it was a statement of intent rather than a practical defence. There was a single timber palisade above a *glacis* of ramped earth. Above it, two gun emplacements faced the river, equipped with a pair of twelve-pound bronze cannon he and his brother had pirated from the wreck of a Dutch frigate that had run aground further up the coast. The guns still had the VOC monogram stamped into the greened metal, and the maker's name, *Cornelis Crans, Hag.*

Their fort would be scant defence against a modern Dutch or English warship. Their real protection was the estuary itself. It was only navigable at high tide and only then with the assistance of a master pilot like Mohammed Daoud. Their defence to the landward side was their mutually beneficial trade agreements with the *rio cafres*, as the Portugals called the native kings.

The warehouse and stables were the only other stone buildings in the settlement beside the boma. Beyond them were the thatched roofs of the barrack houses for the eighty-man *chikunda*. It was a sizeable army in this part of the world, but Hamish had always boasted that he would never need it.

Yet you could never be sure, not in Africa, and not when you had things another man might want. What was it his father had always told him? A man with a beautiful wife and a castle on the frontier must always be prepared for war. He supposed he had both.

He was close enough now to make out the bright splashes of colour from the lurid green and orange wraps, *capulanas*, that the local women had hung out to dry on the bushes along the river.

Mohammed Daoud pointed out the spray from a bloat of hippos further downstream and steered to port to avoid them. A flock of ibis rose from the mangroves on the far bank and disappeared into the morning haze.

Hamish had been almost a month from home, and he could not wait to see Johanna, Katherine and the boys again. His family had seen them now; already there was a dugout on its way out to ferry them to the shore.

Familiar figures lined the sand. He looked forward to a bath, a good dinner and a kiss from his wife.

But as he stepped out of the canoe onto the riverbank and strode up the strand, he knew straight away there was something wrong. He slapped irritably at a welcoming mosquito, as he looked at the solemn faces of his wife and his daughter. He prepared himself for a more bitter homecoming than he had hoped for.

Johanna put her arms around his neck, but he disentangled himself and said, 'You'd better tell me the worst.'

Hamish's desk was a symbol of his authority at Fort Greenock. Hand carved from ebony wood by his brother Rory, it was by far the most impressive piece of furniture in the settlement. It had a plinth base with two banks of opposed drawers lined with sandalwood. It was dressed with swan-neck brass handles and had an inset, tooled leather writing surface.

He stood in front of it now, his arms crossed, and regarded his two sons with a look of displeasure. There was a cowhide war shield and two crossed *assegai* stabbing spears on the limestone wall behind him. They had been gifts from a Nguni chieftain in Natal and only added to his fierce demeanour. There was still dried salt in his beard from the voyage and brine stains on his shirt. He was tired, and he wanted his bath. He was in no mood for this.

'I take it you both know why you're here,' he said.

'How is the *kaffir*?' Callum said.

'Andzile,' Lachlan said. 'His name's Andzile.' He stared hard at Callum, who avoided his eyes, looking down at the *kaross* of zebra skin at his feet.

'Never mind how he is,' Hamish said. 'Tell me what happened.'

'I already told Mother,' Callum said.

'I don't care. Now tell me.'

Lachlan fixed his gaze on the limestone wall behind his father's head and let Callum speak first.

'I was walking past the warehouse, and I heard the sound of a fight from inside.'

'What?' Lachlan said.

'So, I went in, and I saw Lachlan standing there with a shovel in his hand.'

Lachlan cursed under his breath.

'Carry on,' Hamish said.

'That's all. He had this wild look on his face. In fairness to Lachlan...'

Lachlan's eyes blazed.

'...the *kaffir* was stealing from us. He probably deserved it.'

'The *kaffir*, as you call him, was Sasavona's eldest son.' Hamish looked at Lachlan. 'If he was thieving then his people would have punished him for it. You should know that Lachlan.'

'I do know it.'

'So, why did you do this?'

Lachlan continued to stare resolutely at the wall.

'I'm talking to you, boy.'

'I didn't do it.'

'Your brother says you did. Have you nothing to say to him?'

'Oh, I'll have plenty to say to him.'

Hamish shook his head. 'Callum, what I want to know from you is this: if Andzile got in through the roof, how did you get in? The warehouse is locked at all times.'

'The key hangs on a hook on the wall in your office, sir,' Cal said. 'I suppose Lachlan went to get it when he heard Andzile inside. That's why the door was open when I came along. Look, Lachlan wouldn't have meant to hurt him, he was just trying to protect what's ours.'

'Is that true, Lachlan?'

'No, it isn't.'

'Tell me your version, then.'

'It's not a version. It's the truth. I didn't do it.'

'You're saying it was Callum and Callum is saying it was you. Is that it? Who am I to believe?'

'You'll believe what you always believe,' Lachlan said.

Hamish considered. There was no way of knowing what had gone on here. Andzile was still unconscious. Johanna had told him she thought he might not live through the night. He stared at his two boys, trying to divine the truth of it. He didn't like the way they were playing it, but he just couldn't see Callum doing something like this.

'Do you boys have any idea what you have done?'

They needed the Tsonga, as much as the Tsonga needed them. The tribe had come to Delgoa Bay from the south, ten years before, to escape famine and the alarming incursions of the Xhosa and Zulu. Sasavona was their headman, and in return for Hamish's protection from slavers and other tribes he paid a tribute in grain and game every year. Just as importantly, he also provided soldiers for the fort's standing army.

Sasavona was a proud man, and this kind of rough justice would not sit well with him. Hamish knew the Portuguese *prazeiros* in the north were accustomed to treating the local people with casual violence, but they had government soldiers to back them up if there was trouble. Hamish relied solely on Sasavona's good will.

Besides, he liked and respected the man. Brutality like this was something he could not condone.

'You've disappointed me, both of you. I'll speak to you again in the morning when I've had my bath and had a chance to think. Now get out.'

Lachlan waited until they were on the *stoep* before he rounded on his brother and grabbed him by the collar. He shoved Callum against the wall of the lodge and pressed his bunched fist against his throat. 'What the hell are you doing?'

'Just telling him what I saw.'

'You just lied to save your own skin! You know that isn't what happened!'

'All I know is you nearly killed the *kaffir*.' Callum was smiling even as his eyes bulged with the pressure on his neck.

The door burst open, and Hamish thundered out onto the *stoep*. 'Lachlan!'

Lachlan stood back. Callum was still smiling.

'What's this about?' Hamish shouted.

Lachlan glared at Callum, then at his father. He knew he had no way of winning this.

'Get to your jobs, both of you!'

Lachlan walked away.

'Go on, boy,' Hamish said to Callum.

'He wants me to take the fall for him and I won't,' Callum said.

'It's your word against his. Get on with you.'

Callum straightened his shirt. 'He's got a temper,' he muttered. 'I wonder where he gets that from.' He said it just loud enough for Hamish to hear then headed off down the *stoep*.

CHAPTER 4

Late the next afternoon, Katherine McKenzie found her brother lying in a hammock strung between two casuarina trees. The tide was out, leaving the *al-Shahadah* stranded in the estuarine mud. Lachlan had made a driftwood fire and the flames were fanned by a light breeze off the Indian Ocean. He had caught a fish for his supper and was roasting it in the ashes.

He must have heard her, but he did not look up.

'I see you, brother,' she said in Swahili.

'I see you, Little Sister.'

Katherine put her back against the trunk of the tree, then followed his gaze toward the littoral and the distant shimmer of the ocean beyond the sandbar. 'What happened last night, Lachlan?'

The coir rope that tied the hammock to the tree creaked as it rubbed against the bark.

'I know you didn't do it,' she said.

'How do you know that?'

'I know my brothers better than pa does.'

'It's Cal's word against mine. Who do you think he's going to believe?'

'Is Andzile going to die?'

'He might.'

'So, what are you going to do?'

'What can I do? I can't prove what really happened and you know our dad, bloody Callum is his golden boy, isn't he? He'll take his part over mine every time.' He sat up and put his bare feet on the sand. 'I just can't believe Callum would lie about something like this.'

'He's never been one to take his punishment. Even as a little girl I remember seeing him steal molasses, then telling pa it was you.'

'And he always believed him.'

'He does it because he's jealous of you.'

'Why would Cal be jealous of me? He's the favourite.'

'You're bigger, you're stronger, and you're smarter. He's grown up in your shadow and he resents it.'

'But to do something like this...'

'He chose his moment. Everyone heard you tell Andzile that you were going to beat him black and blue.'

'Heat of the moment, I didn't mean it. Him and me, we've been scrapping since we were kids, but we'd never actually hurt each other.' He put his head in his hands. 'You say I'm smarter than Callum. Well, he's smart enough. He knew when to pick his time so that I'd get the blame. The Fount of All Wisdom is not going to believe me over bloody Callum.'

Despite herself, Katherine smiled when she heard Lachlan use the nickname he had given their father. Their pa always thought he was right about everything, but being right and never admitting when you were wrong were not the same thing.

'What about Sasavona?'

'What about him?'

'He knows you wouldn't have done this to his boy.'

'I'm not so sure.' Lachlan rubbed the back of his neck, as torn as she'd ever seen him. 'At least someone believes me. I'm glad you're my sister.'

Dusk never lasted long over the bay. The sun slipped down the late afternoon sky and sunk swiftly below the horizon. Night fell dramatically, like the snuffing out of a candle.

Lachlan and Katherine sat with their own thoughts for a while. A wind from the sea stirred the thorn trees along the riverbank, and there was the plaintive yip of a jackal from somewhere in the dark. Translucent ghost crabs ventured up the sand and hesitated a moment in the firelight. They scuttled away, clustering around the frayed coir rope and the heavy piece of coral that secured one of the dugouts to the shore.

'He's going to send me away,' Lachlan said.

'Send you away, where?'

'Hindustan.'

'Because of what happened to Andzile?'

'No, I think he's been planning to do it anyway. This will just help to make up his mind.'

'He won't do that.'

'Yes, he will. Why do you think he brought Arjuna here to teach us his jabber?' He shook his head. 'He's talking about sending ivory to Malabar and Coromandel. Someone will have to go over with it. This will be his excuse to get rid of me.'

'But you're the oldest. You'll have to run things here one day.'

'No, Uncle Rory will do that when the time comes. And after that, Callum.'

'Callum couldn't find his own fingers in the dark.'

'Even so, I reckon that's the plan.'

She sighed and brought her knees up to her chest. 'Maybe it's not so bad, even if you're right. Don't you ever dream of getting away?'

'No, I like it well enough here.'

'This place isn't for you, Lachlan. You're meant for bigger things. I can feel it. You have a destiny somewhere else.'

'A destiny? That sounds grand. A destiny is something princes have, not an ivory trader's son with dirt under his nails.'

'But don't you ever think what it would be like to go to other places? I do, all the time.'

'I've been to Ilha. It's hot and it's full of Portuguese.'

'What about Cape Town? Madras?'

Lachlan shook his head and threw a leaf into the fire.

'Don't you ever think about getting married?'

He smiled. 'Maybe. What about you?'

'Who is there for me to marry out here? I'm a girl and I don't have the same freedoms as you.'

'What freedoms?' he said.

'You know what I mean. I saw one of the Tsonga girls stop by your *luana* the other night. Perhaps she was lost.'

Lachlan couldn't meet her eyes.

'Did she stop to ask directions?'

'You're imagining things.'

'I don't blame you. I'm just a little jealous, I suppose. I heard Jorge Ferreira has a daughter your age.'

'Ferreira? Father calls him a dirty little thief behind his back. Besides, he says she's cross-eyed and has bristles on her chin like a water buffalo.'

'That's not what I heard him telling Ma.'

'What did he say?'

'That she was a catch, and it would be good for business.' She stood up, brushing sand off her skirt. It was late to be sitting out here in the dark. There were crocodiles and hippos in the river. Andzile had been right about the hippos: they were far more dangerous than any lion.

'You won't stay here forever, Lachlan, no matter what you say. There's something big waiting for you out there. I can feel it.'

'Everything I want is here.'

'Mother says we can't always get what we want. She says that sometimes life has other plans for us, and there's nothing we can do about it. Perhaps that's how it will be for you. Come on, cheer up. We'd better go back.'

The family sat around the long table in the kitchen in heavy silence. None of them had touched their dinner. Katherine excused herself and went to bed early. Johanna could feel the tension between the two boys and waited for the explosion.

'Some home-coming this is,' Hamish said. Lachlan pushed back his chair and stood up. 'Where are you going, boy?'

'To the warehouse. I'll fetch a couple of muskets, shoot all the horses then pummel the kitchen staff with the wood axe.'

'That's not funny.'

'It wasn't meant to be,' Lachlan said. 'I can't sit here all night. It's giving me indigestion.' He went out and Hamish heard his heavy boots clomp down the veranda.

Hamish waited until he had gone and then turned to Callum. 'Tell me the truth,' he said.

Callum cut off a slice of kudu steak and put it in his mouth. 'I have told you the truth,' he said. 'You know what Lachlan's like. Why won't anyone believe me?'

Hamish watched Johanna douse the oil lamps in their bedroom and fuss with the mosquito nets around the bed. She went to the yellow wooden chest where she kept her private things and took out a pale blue night dress. For a moment, as she put it on, her body was silvered by the moonlight.

Twenty years they had been together now, and she stirred him as much as she did when he had first seen her. Three sons and a daughter she had given him, counting the one they had lost, and she was still as lithe as she was when they came to Delgoa Bay.

She sat on a stool, combing out her hair in the dark, and Hamish thought he would go mad watching her. A month he had been away.

'Will you not come to bed?'

She put the hairbrush back on the dresser but made no move to get up. 'What will you do with the boys?' she said.

'I don't know. What would you have me do?'

'Find the truth of it.'

'And what is the truth of it? No one saw it. Callum says it was Lachlan, and Lachlan says it wasn't him.'

'And what do you think?'

'It sounds to me the kind of thing Lachlan would do.'

'Does it?'

'If there's ever trouble he's always in the middle of it. He's arrogant, and he's got a temper.'

'So, you keep telling me, but I'm his mother and I've never seen it.'

'He's reckless.'

'He's spirited. What's wrong with that in a boy? The trouble is you're always on his back.'

'Not without cause. It was only a few months ago, he swam out to the bar on his own. Have you forgotten?'

'He's a strong swimmer.'

'And so are the sharks that patrol the river mouth. It's a miracle he wasn't taken.'

'He said Callum dared him to do it.'

'What if he did? He didn't have to rise to it. And what about those two lascars he picked a fight with?'

'He says it was the other way around.'

'It's always someone else's fault, isn't it? To hell with it, come to bed.'

Johanna got up with a sigh. As she slipped under the mosquito net, he put his arms around her and pulled her down beside him.

'I've missed you,' he whispered and tried to kiss her.

'I don't believe Lachlan would do something like this,' she said.

'I think I know my own boys well enough.'

'But do you really?'

'Let's talk about it in the morning.' He pulled her towards him a second time and tried to make love to her, but it was like trying to love a statue. She wasn't thinking about him, he realised, her mind was on her boys. Women! Couldn't she ever just leave these things to him? It was her job to look after them when they were children. Now they were men it was his concern.

She rolled onto her side and went to sleep. He put a hand on her shoulder to bring her back to his side of the bed, but she hardly stirred. Some homecoming this was.

And all Lachlan's fault.

Johanna lay awake for hours listening to the night wind. There were a thousand ways the wind could move the ragged palm leaves over their heads; the whispers, the rattles, the rustling, the creaking. It was always changing.

She kept thinking about what Hamish had said to her about Lachlan being arrogant, about his temper. It made him sound like some sort of monster, not the young gentleman she knew. She couldn't imagine that he was capable of beating Andzile nearly to death with a shovel, despite everything Hamish had said about him over the years.

But if it were true, it meant that Callum had done it and was prepared to let his brother take the fall for it, just to save himself. One of her sons was not a boy she wanted for her own. She supposed that Hamish must be thinking the very same thing. Was he right about Lachlan? He always said she was blind to Lachlan's ways and had warned her about him often enough.

When she finally rolled back towards him, Hamish was asleep. He lay still as death, exhausted by the long sea voyage back from Ilha. She had not meant to be so cold to him. She wished he would tell her again that everything was going to be all right, and that the past would stay dead.

But the past was never dead. It always came back to haunt you somehow.

CHAPTER 5

Tamil Nagar fort
Trincomalee, Ceylon

A peacock flared out its feathers with a great show of rustling. A spotted deer nibbled at the elegant flower beds. Napoleon Gagnon thought the gardens might have been an Eden, if not for the noises coming from inside the governor's bedroom. The man had no restraint. Only peasants paraded their perversions like this.

The *Het Zeventien* – the Dutch East India Company's omnipotent board of directors in Amsterdam - had declared that their employees should not have congress with the natives. Napoleon supposed this was why their interview today must take place in this tiny cottage on the far side of the Company gardens, instead of the boardroom in the Residence. He tapped his foot on the tiles and winced when he heard the girl scream again. All this grunting and shrieking was getting on his nerves.

He stared at the bright red splashes on the whitewashed path. A man might be excused for thinking they were blood - the Dutch certainly had a reputation for violence among the natives here - but it was just betel nut juice. He would never understand the natives' addiction to it. Half the population walked around as if they had suffered lung wounds, with their lips and teeth dyed bright red.

And all this spitting everywhere. It was vile. He might have been raised in Pondicherry, but his father was a gentleman of refined manners, and he had never grown accustomed to the locals' foul habits.

There it was again, another shriek. For goodness' sake, man, can't you wait until we have conducted our affairs? The girl was clearly having trouble meeting his demands. He had no idea what pleasure a man derived from this sort of thing.

But this was business. *Mijn Heer* Keyser could be having congress with a goat and a monkey in there for all he cared. If he had a commission for him and was willing to pay handsomely to see it carried out, then so be it. A standing army cost money. Soldiers had to be fed and billeted. And the way the Indies was right now, a good businessman could not allow his assets to sit around letting their swords and their muskets go to rust in the rain. The nawabs, the rajahs, the British, and the French were all at each other's throats. It was not a question of finding a war but deciding which one would be most profitable for Napoleon Gagnon.

Another year, perhaps two, and unless peace broke out between the French, the British and the local Indian princes, which seemed most unlikely, he could afford to retire. The business of making money was wearing on a gentleman's nerves, and he did not always appreciate the class of people he had to deal with.

He would like to settle in France: Paris perhaps, to ensure Adelaïde got a good education and a husband worthy of her unique gifts. He had never been there, but he thought he might find it pleasurable. His father had often promised to take him there.

His father had promised many things, but when a fever killed his mother, he hadn't stayed around long enough to deliver any of them. If Napoleon ever found him, he'd cut his damned throat.

The high-backed chair was uncomfortable. He got up and went to stand under the eaves, tapping his cane on the tiles. Adelaïde swung her legs and watched a gecko on the ceiling. Her feet still did not touch the ground when she sat all the way back in an adult chair. Adorable.

'Papa, what is he doing in there?' She sounded curious rather than frightened.

He wondered how to answer her. He never fobbed her off with easy answers, even if they were indelicate. 'He's fornicating with a child.'

'Will he be long?'

'I hope not.'

'Could he not have got this out of the way before we got here?'

'I agree. Still, we have come all this way. We should wait. I am assured it will not be a waste of our time.'

'Who is he?'

'His name is Jeronimus Keyser. He is the governor of this rather humble little outpost. He is Dutch. Ceylon is, for the most part, a Dutch island. The coast, anyway.'

'What do you think he wants?'

'I don't know, but I'm ready to be surprised.'

He returned his gaze to the gardens. A Sinhalese in a white turban got on his knees and placed some frangipani flowers at the base of a shrine to Ganesha, which was nestled at the foot of a breadfruit tree.

There was another scream.

'Why is she screaming?'

'He is hurting her,' he said.

'Why?'

'Some men take pleasure in it.'

'Do you?' she said, fixing him with her ice-blue eyes.

'I would not hurt anyone unless there was profit in it. What is the point?'

She nodded and returned her attention to her book, a translation of Homer. He encouraged her to read at every opportunity. The life he had prepared her for would require a good education.

The floorboards creaked as *Mijn Heer* Keyser finished and he shifted his great bulk from the bed to the floor. Napoleon heard him bark an order to one of his servants. A young man in a sarong and a white jacket appeared from nowhere and hurried across the room. He left the door open behind him, and Napoleon was afforded a rare glimpse of the Dutch governor, stark naked. He put out a hand to cover his daughter's eyes.

She blinked slowly and said, 'Thank you, Papa.' She returned her attention to her book.

He smiled. He could not have borne it if she had been one of those hysterical children he sometimes saw in the French quarter, always demanding and crying. Her mother had said Adelaïde was just like him: she had ice in her veins and an abacus for a brain.

She had not meant it as a compliment.

He had thrown her out soon after that. He would not tolerate anyone criticizing him in front of his daughter.

A servant hurried to close the door, and for a moment he saw Keyser's paramour sitting naked on the bed. She was very young, and her breasts were no more than buds. There was a smear of blood on the inside of her thighs. It was a wonder the Dutchman hadn't smothered the life out of her. She was so tiny, and the old governor was so fat.

A little while later, they were finally graced with his presence. The governor had dressed, after a fashion. He had put on a sarong with a ceremonial sword buckled over the top of it, along with a dress uniform jacket of scarlet brocade, which was showing signs of age. But then most uniforms rotted away after a year or two in this climate. He wore sandals on his feet, and Napoleon noted that *Mijn Heer*'s yellow toenails needed cutting.

Keyser was sweating as if he had just come from his bath. His cheeks were flushed, and his sparse blond hair was plastered across his scalp. And the belly on him! Perhaps that was why he couldn't take better care of his feet. He couldn't even see them.

For some reason, the governor had chosen to wear his medals - three enamel and diamante stars. Am I supposed to be impressed? Napoleon wondered. You can put a skirt on a pig, but it's still a pig.

He waited for an apology at being kept waiting but did not get one. In his mind, he added another twenty percent to his contract price.

'You're Gagnon?'

He bowed. 'At your service.'

'Who's this?'

'My daughter.'

'She can stay out there.'

'She goes with me everywhere.'

Keyser looked him up and down. 'Suit yourself. This way.' He led them into a large, rectangular-shaped room, something like an audience chamber.

Just as Napoleon went to follow him inside, he heard a door open behind him, and a girl ran out of the bedroom and stumbled down the veranda. She was wearing a sarong and little else. It was the child the governor had abused.

He wondered who she was. Some native of no account, he supposed. They were everywhere in the Indies, girls like that. She sobbed as she ran. He guessed she was no older than Adelaïde, and he wondered what was going through Keyser's mind, having to conduct the interview with another ten-year-old girl in attendance.

It might make him uncomfortable. Good, he could use that. Before Napoleon entered any negotiation, he always liked to have the advantage.

Keyser told himself he lived in some style, even for a provincial governor. Not like those swine in Colombo or Batavia but well enough. He had not scrimped on furnishings. There were satinwood boards on all the floors, polished till they shone like beeswax, raw silk drapes, and all the furniture was carved from ebony and sandalwood by local craftsmen.

He had paid for all of it himself. Well, not quite. It was perhaps true that not all the sapphires from the Company mines found their way into the VOC vaults in Amsterdam, but if those high and mighty bastards in Holland would not pay him his due, what was a man to do? They only had themselves to blame if they forced him to organize his own commissions.

He dabbed at his face with a handkerchief. All these years living in the tropics, and he still suffered in this accursed climate. The stone walls of the cottage were a foot and a half thick, and they were supposed to keep a man cool.

He sat down behind a massive teak desk and clapped his hands. A servant hurried in with glasses and a decanter of honey-gold Madeira.

'Do you want a drink?' he said.

The servant immediately filled two long-stemmed crystal glasses, but Napoleon held up his hand and shook his head. 'I don't drink,' he said.

Godverdomme, how could you trust a man who didn't drink? It was unnatural. 'Just one, man.'

'I never drink while I'm working.'

'Are you working now?'

'I'm always working.'

Joyless bastard! Well, that wasn't going to stop Jeronimus Keyser. He took a long swallow of the Madeira and let its warmth settle him. He leaned back in his chair. It made him sick to his stomach having to deal with men like this. This Gagnon, what was he, a frog or a native? Half of each, they said.

A strange-looking man and scrawny as a crow. From what Keyser had been able to discover, Napoleon Gagnon's father had been a captain in the *Compagnie Française,* and his mother was some sort of Indian princess. Hard to tell what he was by looking at him with his Western clothes, curled moustaches and that white turban on his head. It was almost as if he were proud of being half-nigger.

Keyser supposed there was no point in trying to conceal it, though. A man couldn't hide being spotted with the tar brush.

But Gagnon had a reputation for getting things done with no qualm about how and where. His services had been utilised by the French at Pondicherry and the Nawab at Hyderabad. He came highly recommended. A man with a private army and two serviceable warships was never going to be idle for long, not in the Orient.

Some people called him a pirate, but in Keyser's experience pirates only got their loot after a battle. Apparently, this man always asked for payment in advance.

'So, what is the commission you have for me?' Napoleon said.

'There is someone I want you to kill.'

Napoleon looked irritated. 'You brought me all the way here because you want me to murder one man?'

'Not just him. His whole family with him. It won't be easy. Like you, he has his own private army. That's why I brought you all the way here.'

'What has this man done to you?'

Keyser leaned back in his chair. 'That is my business,' he said.

'Who is he?'

'His name is McKenzie,' Keyser said. 'Hamish McKenzie.'

CHAPTER 6

The way the girl stared at him, without blinking, set Keyser's teeth on edge. Her hair was almost white and was combed perfectly straight on either side of her face. Her skin was so pale it was almost translucent. She couldn't be more than twelve years old, he supposed, and she sat in her chair as still as a china doll.

He had been told that Gagnon took her with him everywhere. It was unnatural. What man took his daughter along with him when he was on business, especially the sort of business that Gagnon engaged in? Keyser was both attracted and repulsed by her. He forced himself to look away.

'Where do I find this man?' Napoleon said.

'Africa.'

Napoleon raised an eyebrow.

'A rather large place. Can you be more specific?'

'Delgoa Bay, north of Natal. He has a trading post there.'

'And you want me to kill his whole family?'

Keyser nodded. 'He has a wife and three grown children. A brother, also.'

A shrug. 'So be it. Everything can be arranged for the right price.'

'There is a complication. He is well protected. His boma is fortified with a stockade, and he has a standing army of eighty men, natives trained to use muskets.'

'Where he lives, this Delgoa Bay. It belongs to Portugal, yes?'

'He has an arrangement with the Governor of Mozambique. He sub-leases the land from one of the *prazeiros*.'

'This will not be easy.'

'If it were easy, I should have done it myself. But my hands are tied. This part of the African coast belongs to a rival nation, and I may not use Dutch soldiers to settle a personal matter. That is why I have approached you.'

'You wish me to sail my men to the east coast of Africa?'

'I was told you could handle such an assignment. Or perhaps I was misinformed.'

'It can be done. But it will be very expensive.'

'Name your price.'

Napoleon took a weather-stained notebook from his coat pocket and a pencil with an engraved ceramic tip. He licked the end of it before making his calculations. He took his time over it and, when he had done, he leaned toward the girl and showed her what he had written.

She pointed to something. He smiled, nodded, scratched out something and added more figures.

Then he looked up at Keyser and named his price.

Keyser felt his buttocks clench. Good God in heaven.

'So, let's talk about your price,' Keyser said.

'What is there to talk about?'

'It is a devilish lot of money.'

'It is a devilish lot of work, and there is significant risk attached to it. Your enemy is on the other side of the ocean. When I arrive, I will have to knock down a stockade and kill eighty men to get to my target.'

Keyser decided not to mention the two twelve-pound cannon his spy had told him McKenzie had somehow appropriated. Let him discover that for himself. It might complicate the negotiations further if he brought it up now.

'This is not a simple assassination, *Mijn Heer*. You are commissioning a small war.'

'Perhaps I should get someone else.'

'You are of course free to employ someone else if my price is too rich for your blood. But I guarantee you will not find anyone else who can fulfil such a commission. What you ask would be impossible except for someone like me. If you wish to indulge your lust for vengeance, then you should be prepared to put your hands deep into your purse.'

'Who told you this was about revenge?'

'Am I wrong?'

'You're not wrong,' Keyser grunted.

'So, that is my price. Take it or leave it.'

Keyser didn't like being hectored, and he didn't like being told he could not negotiate a price. He was a governor with twenty-five years of service in the Dutch East India Company. He wanted to throw this upstart out of his office and have him bullwhipped on a wheel in the square for his insolence.

Instead, he smiled, reached for the bottle of Madeira and refilled his glass. He was so angry that his hands shook. Gagnon must have noticed, but if he had, he did not comment on it.

Another man would have walked away from this, Keyser thought. But he had always promised himself that one day he would make McKenzie pay for what he had done, and time was running out. He could not die peacefully until he had settled with that *zakkenwasser*.

'I want him to die slowly,' Keyser said.

Napoleon shook his head. 'I cannot contract for that. I will do it if it is possible, but if this is a requirement, I cannot agree to it.'

'I will pay you extra for McKenzie to suffer.'

'It is not a matter of money. It is about contractual obligation. I only guarantee what I am certain I can achieve. Tell me again about these others you want me to kill.'

Keyser gave him their names, and Napoleon wrote down the details in his notebook.

'I will need to go back to Pondicherry to prepare. Then we will have to wait for the monsoon. I cannot fulfil our contract for at least six months.'

'Just make sure it's done. I want you to raze the fort. I want nothing left of those bastards in the world.'

'I need a down payment before I leave. Half the contractual price. You can arrange it?'

'That is a lot of money to hand over like that. What if you fail?'

'I never fail.'

'You seem very confident. What if, afterwards, I decide your price was too high and do not pay you the other half?'

'I always fulfil my contractual obligations. If the other party does not fulfil theirs, then there is a penalty clause.'

'And what is that?'

'I kill them. Such a situation has only occurred once before. I hope it will never be necessary again.'

Keyser could not believe his ears. 'I'm the Governor of Trincomalee. You really think you can threaten me?'

'Every man has blood in his veins, no matter who he is. And spilling blood is my profession. But I always prefer money before blood.'

Keyser didn't like this man, he decided. Never mind, he thought, I will be dead soon and it doesn't matter what this poisonous little nigger threatens me with. Even paying half of what this man is asking will just about clear me out, but there is no one to leave my money to now, so why should I care?

His one regret was that he wouldn't be there to see McKenzie die. He would very much like Hamish McKenzie to know why he was dying, and that Jeronimus Keyser had won in the end. 'At least,' he said, 'tell him that it was me that sent you. Can you do that?'

'I will if it is possible.'

'I want him to die tormented. I want him to know I have evened the ledger. I don't want him to think he got away with crossing me.'

'In which case you should furnish me with the details.'

'The details?'

'Have you never considered that this man has never given you a second thought?'

Keyser stared at him. No, it had never occurred to him.

'You want to know why I want to kill this man so badly?'

Napoleon shrugged. 'It is nothing to me, personally. But if you want me to tell this man why he has to die, then I shall write the details here in my notebook and convey the information to him.'

It irked him that this half-caste mercenary should be so indifferent. He rapped his knuckles on the desk like a schoolteacher with a daydreaming pupil. 'Look at me,' he said and grunted, shifting his weight so he could sit higher in his chair. 'You think this is what I wanted for myself when I was a young man, to end up rotting in this dreary hellhole at the end of the earth? I could have been a big man in the Compagnie, if it weren't for that bastard and the stain he left on my reputation. It has followed me all my life.'

'It's a long time to hate.'

'Hate doesn't wear out. It's like wine. It just gets richer with age.' He poured himself another glass of the Madeira. 'Have you ever hated anyone, Gagnon?'

'I find it interferes with business.'

'One day, perhaps, you will know what it's like.'

'I doubt it,' Napoleon said. 'But if you have hated him so badly, why wait until now to kill him?'

'In Cape Town, I didn't have the authority or the men to go after him. While he remained outside Dutch suzerainty, I could not touch him. Then they sent me here and for a time, I tried to forget about it. I knew he was in Mozambique, but I didn't know where.

'Then two years ago, a Dutch ship ran aground just up the coast from Delgoa Bay. I received reports of an Englishman living there, trading ivory and gold right under the nose of the Portuguese governor. I made some inquiries.'

'You are sure it is the same man?'

'There is no doubt.'

'And what did he do to you that inspired such a lingering and expensive resentment?'

Keyser stared out of the window, let his mind drift back to Cape Town and that younger, handsomer, version of himself. 'Just tell him he has to die because of Johanna.'

'That is all?'

'She was mine.'

'What did he do, kidnap her?'

'He turned her head.'

'There has to be more than that.'

'He didn't just steal her. He also stole my reputation. Everyone in the colony laughed at me behind my back. People thought it was a fine joke, how he took her from under my nose and got away with it. I was never awarded a single promotion from the Board for years after that. When they finally made me a governor, they sent me here, shunted me out of the way. That man ruined me.'

Napoleon shrugged and consulted his notebook. 'And you want her to die as well?'

Keyser nodded. 'You think your men are up to this?'

'Of course.'

'But they are mercenaries.'

'The soldiers fighting for the Dutch East India Company are mercenaries.'

'They are good *Dutch* mercenaries.'

'A man needs a white skin to be a good warrior, is that what you think?'

Keyser wanted to smash his face. How dare he talk this way to him! 'How do you make them stand their ground when the cannons are turned on them?'

'I lead my men the same way you lead yours. They are like children, *Mijn Heer*. They are terrified of me when I am angry, but they love me because I reward them well when they do what I ask. They are well trained and well-armed. They will get this job done for you just as well as any good Dutchman.'

Napoleon stood up and tapped his cane on the floorboards twice. Business concluded.

'That's a fine cane,' Keyser said. 'Filigree silver on the handle. It must have been very expensive.'

'It was my father's. It is all I have of him. He left it behind with a note. If I ever find him, I shall skewer him with it.' Napoleon held out his hand to his daughter. 'Come Adelaïde, it is time to go.' She took his hand. 'I shall leave in three days with the tide. Bring the down payment, in gold, to my ship the day after tomorrow. If you do not do so, I shall assume you have changed your mind and our contract will be void.'

'Why did you bring your daughter with you?'

'This is important to you?'

'I am curious.'

Napoleon put a hand on Adelaïde's shoulder. 'I try to protect her from the unpleasantness in the world, but there is so much of it. If she must see certain things, then it is best I am there to explain them to her. I am afraid she is already old beyond her years.'

'Does she go everywhere with you?'

'Her education is in my hands. I trust no one else to do the job for me. Good day to you, *Mijn Heer*.'

Keyser watched them leave from the veranda of his office, this strange man in the turban, hand in hand with the pale girl at his side. He, like a swarthy carpet salesman in a cutthroat bazaar, she, a bloodless, delicate insect.

He went back inside, poured three fingers of Madeira into his glass and threw it down. Insolent little man. By the time the decanter was empty, Keyser was shaking with rage. It was not just the half-caste. It was the memories he had stirred up inside him.

He threw the empty bottle at the wall and shouted for his servants to bring him another.

CHAPTER 7

Delgoa Bay

Andzile lay quite still on a goat skin on the floor of Sasavona's hut. His eyes were fixed on a dark corner of the thatched roof.

The *nganga* was naked except for a cloak made from elephant hide, and a python skin which was tied around his waist. There was a necklace of bright trade beads around his neck and a paste of ochre mud was smeared onto his face. His hair was matted and wild. He crouched down beside Andzile and began to clap, chanting in Nguni, which none of the Tsonga could understand. But it was the only language that the great spirit Mamacoa could speak.

The *nganga* took two fire sticks and a small bundle of herbs from the pouch at his waist. He placed one of the sticks into a groove in the other stick and rubbed it very quickly between the palms of his hands, singing as he rocked backward and forward, summoning the fire spirits.

After a while, the vaguest wisp of smoke appeared in the fire hole. He tipped some specks of ash onto the dried herbs. He repeated this procedure several times, blowing gently on the herbs until finally a small flame appeared. He let the pile burn briefly then smothered the flames and breathed in the smoke.

When the herbs had been reduced to ash, he scattered a handful of black stones on the beaten earth floor. After consulting with them, his eyes rolled back in his head, and he fell into a trance.

A wind sprang up from seemingly nowhere, stirring the fronds of the acacia trees and spinning dust into a whirling devil in the middle of the clearing. The watchers rolled their eyes in wonder. The women pulled their *capulanas* over their noses and mouths to protect themselves from the gritty sand.

Two men brought a goat into the hut. One held it by the horns, the other by its hind legs. Sasavona followed them inside, holding a long, bright knife. The *nganga*'s eyes blinked open and he started to chant again, throwing handfuls of dust over the struggling creature. He invoked the spirits to leave Andzile and instead take up residence in the goat.

At his signal, Sasavona stepped forward and expertly drew the knife across the animal's throat. Gouts of blood spurted rhythmically over the sleeping boy. The *nganga*'s voice rose to a shrill wail. The two men held the goat over Andzile's body until the animal ceased its struggling.

A sigh passed through the watching women. The wind dropped away, and the dust devil slipped into the jungle and disappeared as suddenly as it had come.

The *nganga* gave Sasavona the pouch. Inside was a tooth from a spitting cobra. He told Sasavona to put it under Andzile's pillow. 'The boy will soon be well,' he said.

Sasavona's wife gave the old man a chicken in payment and the *nganga* walked away, swinging the bird by its legs.

Sasavona carried the dead goat far away into the bush and buried it so the bad spirits now trapped inside it could never return.

It was early. A mist hung over the river, and the long shadows were cool. A family of vervet monkeys loped along the strand.

Hamish had Sasavona line the *chikunda* in rows and he addressed them in Swahili, going through the preparations for defending the fort in the event of an attack. He didn't care that they had all heard the rules dozens of times before. In his experience, men would forget everything they knew, whether it was in a fistfight or a full-scale battle, unless they had rehearsed it so many times, they could do it without thinking.

'Should there ever be an attack on this fort, someone will ring the bell outside the boma,' he told them. 'When that happens, you must run to the storehouse. You will be given a musket and thirty rounds of ammunition. Then you must form up in the square and wait for Sasavona. He will tell you what to do.'

Each of them had a leather satchel over their shoulder. Sasavona took over and led them through the drill for firing the muskets. At his order they reached back, pulled a cartridge out of the satchel, and bit off the end. Then they spat out the paper and poured a little of the powder from the cartridge into their musket's frizzen pan. The rest of the powder and the shot went down the muzzle, the paper acting as a sort of wadding. They rodded the ball down the bore. Sasavona shouted at them to make sure they had properly seated the round in the breech. If you don't, he warned them, the barrel might explode.

Even then, after all their practice, he had to remind two of his fellows that they had left their ramrods in the barrel. Finally, they were ready.

'Cock and fire!' Sasavona shouted.

By Hamish's fob watch, Sasavona's best man could load and fire in twenty-three seconds. He had been told that proper grenadiers, such as the men the British and French had in their armies, could fire five shots in a minute.

But twenty-three seconds was probably as much as he could expect from lads like these.

Hamish had taught them that they didn't have to be accurate, they just had to be quick. There was no point aiming a smooth bore musket. There were no sights on the barrel and because the barrel wasn't rifled, the rounds could go anywhere. There was a one in five chance of a misfire, even on a good day, and if it was windy or raining the odds were probably much worse.

He thought it improbable that his *chikunda* would ever see real action, but if they did, he was convinced it would not be because of a threat from the hinterland. They were on good terms with the local native chief, Mangobe. He was more interested in trade than warring.

If they were ever attacked, it would be by the Portugals, in retaliation over lost tax moneys. Jorge Ferreira and the Governor would be found out one day. The day they do away with good honest corruption in East Africa, Hamish thought, is the day we will have to pack up and go home to England.

The musket drill finished and Hamish and Sasavona went to inspect the targets they had set up under the mango trees. Their *chikunda* had shot down most of the branches, but the targets had largely escaped unscathed.

The two men stared at each other. The tension between them was palpable.

'How is your son?' Hamish said, finally.

Sasavona shrugged his shoulders.

'He still sleeps?'

'He still sleeps.'

'I am sorry for it. I wish I could put this right.'

'He should not have been in the storehouse,' Sasavona said. 'It is wrong to steal.'

'What will happen to him if he lives?'

'I will hear what he has to say. For myself, I do not believe my son would rob from you. Why would he do such a thing and bring shame on himself and on us?'

Shame. The worst fate that could befall a Tsonga. If Andzile lived and was found guilty, he would be exiled from the tribe. It was virtually a death sentence, either from starvation or from predators in the bush.

'Only Andzile can ever tell us for certain,' Hamish said.

'I do not understand how such a thing could have happened. Nkala and my son have played together in the mud down there by the river since they were children. How many times did we scold them for it? They would not hurt each other. And my son is a good boy, not a thief.'

Hamish shrugged his shoulders.

'Some of my people saw tracks in the dirt outside the warehouse,' Sasavona went on. 'They say Andzile was hit with a weapon and then dragged inside to make it look as if he was stealing.'

Hamish was startled. The Tsonga were expert hunters and could read the ground as easily as he could read a paper contract. 'But everyone heard Lachlan and Andzile raise their voices to each other when they were drilling with the cannon. Lachlan made threats.'

'I tell my *chikunda* I will skin them and hang their hides outside my hut if they don't load their muskets faster. It doesn't mean I would really do it.'

Hamish frowned. 'Andzile is the only one who can tell us the truth of it. My wife said she would bring you medicines.'

'It is not necessary. We have our own ways.'

'Your witch doctor?'

'Last night he performed a healing ceremony.'

'Then I hope your boy is soon well again.'

As Hamish turned to go, Sasavona said, 'The *nganga* said there are bad spirits here.'

'Here at Fort Greenock?'

'Two nights ago, he saw a hyena fall from the sky and a snake with two heads. He said it's a sign that there is a strong wind coming.'

'A strong wind comes every year. It's called the monsoon.'

'This wind is different. He says it will bring thunder and death and sweep away everything in its path.'

Hamish shuddered. He had never liked the *ngangas*. Their filthy potions and black magic disgusted him. But the local people put great store by them, and he had always pretended to play along. It didn't mean he believed a single word that they said. They were all charlatans in his opinion. 'If a storm comes, we'll just batten down like we always do,' he said. 'A wind is just a wind.'

The Tsonga's village was just outside the stockade on the landward side. There were forty or fifty pole-and-dagga huts grouped around a clearing of dirt, which had been packed hard by bare feet over many years. It was surrounded by corn and millet gardens.

The drums had been playing all night, as they did when one of the villagers was sick. Johanna and Katherine crossed the beaten-earth compound to Sasavona's hut, wondering what they would find when they got there.

Villagers came out of the huts to stare. There were toothless grandmothers with white hair, young girls with babies on their hips, and flocks of wide-eyed children. The village dogs started up a chorus of yapping and howling but kept a safe distance.

Sasavona's hut was the largest in the village. It had to be, to accommodate his four wives and twelve children. His first wife, Basimbulu, was pounding grain in a giant wooden pestle in the kitchen, a small outside area of compacted mud. It was a simple affair, just one or two saucepans, a knife, and a wooden bowl. She jumped to her feet when she saw them. A young man shuffled out of the shadows in the doorway behind her.

Andzile.

'Oh, thank God,' Johanna said.

'The *nganga* cured him,' Basimbulu said. 'He sent the bad spirits in his head away in a dead goat.'

'Does he remember what happened?'

Basimbulu shook her head. 'He doesn't remember anything.'

'Nothing at all?'

'All I remember,' Andzile said, 'is that it's my turn to fire the cannon.'

CHAPTER 8

Mawuwani, the month of cool light breezes

One of Sasavona's *chikunda* ran into the kitchen, out of breath from running. He said that there was a big ship off the coast, and it was headed into the bay. Hamish was out of the door in a moment, a telescope in his hand.

Lachlan called for Callum. He told him to ring the bell and break open the warehouse, then find Sasavona and start handing out the muskets and cartridge bags.

Then he followed Hamish towards the dunes. All the time he could hear him questioning the boy in Xitsonga as he ran:

How far out is she?

How many masts does she have, two or three?

Is there one boat or two?

Is it a dhow, or a ship of the line like the Portugals sail?

He caught up with him out on the salt flats.

Hamish was standing, legs astride, looking out to the ocean. He put his spy glass to his eye. 'A frigate, by the looks of her,' he said. 'An East Indiaman. She's flying the Company's stripes.'

'Is it trouble?' Lachlan said.

'Maybe,' Hamish said. 'Maybe not. This country still belongs to the Portugals and if they meant business, they would have sent more than one frigate.' He raised the glass to his eye again. 'She has trouble with her foremast by the look of her. She's sailing bare, with no spars. She may need our assistance. Perhaps we may make a little commission out of her misfortune. We'll go out to her and take a look.'

They went out to her in a *ngalawa,* a small boat that was shaped like a canoe. It was kept steady with outriggers on each side and had a small lateen sail. The breezes were light this time of year, so Mohammed had only brought four of the local boys with him to man the oars. Even so, the muscles in their backs rippled with the effort of working against the tide.

The *Southampton* was a fine ship, as clean and trim as a man-of-war. Lachlan made a mental note of her armament as they got closer. She was carrying twelve cannons, two of them thirty-two pounders. He wouldn't want to be on the receiving end of one of those.

She was limping. It was clear though, that it wasn't an enemy that had done it to her, but the weather. Her foremast was missing two spars and not a few of her sails looked ragged, shredded by high winds.

Lachlan looked up and saw the ship's skipper watching them from the stern. The passengers lined the rails either side of him.

Hamish raised his hand over his head and waved. 'Ahoy there, *Southampton*!'

A voice broke through the hush, sharp as a musket shot. 'Well, bugger me! Hamish McKenzie!'

'We're bound for Madras,' Captain Rodron said. 'We made good time until we rounded the Cape and ran into some heavy gales that drove us off course. The storms carried off our jibs and shredded the fore topgallant as well. Thought we should lose our foremast into the bargain, so I took down the sheets. I heard there was an English settlement here and put in, hoping to make repairs. I didn't expect to see you!'

Hamish laughed and clapped him on the shoulder. 'We'll help you as best we can. We've some good ebony and fine carpenters among the Tsonga, though they're more accustomed to building rigs like the one we came out on. I'll put them at your disposal first light.'

'I can pay handsomely for the service, Hamish.'

'I'll make sure you do, Jack.' He shook his head. 'I can't believe they made you master of one of these tubs.'

'And I can't believe life brought you all the way up here.'

'So how do you two know each other?' Lachlan said.

'Oh, we go back a long way.'

Lachlan looked at them, mystified.

Hamish did not seem inclined to answer, so Rodron did it for him. 'It goes back to our days at the Cape. I was just a navy lieutenant in those days. Has he never mentioned me?' He looked surprised more than affronted.

'He never talks about the past.'

'Well, it doesn't matter. No doubt we can reminisce a little later over a glass or two of the very fine port I keep in my cabin. I insist that you stay for dinner.'

'Aye, we will, but I'll not eat the swill the Company provides. I think I can do better.'

'I was counting on it,' Rodron said.

Hamish sent Mohammed Daoud back to the fort with instructions to fetch provisions and three of his best cooks. While they waited for the party to return, Rodron introduced Hamish to several of his passengers. They were all Company people. Several of the younger men were military, Rodron said, for the Company's private army. Most of the others were going out to work as clerks – writers, he called them - in the administration.

There was also a clergyman, a doctor and just two women. They were sisters, going out to keep house for their uncle, who was a member of the council in Madras. They giggled and looked away every time they caught Lachlan's eye.

'They're really going out there looking for husbands,' Rodron whispered.

Mohammed returned just before nightfall with Hamish's three Tsonga cooks: two women and an old man called Hitsakile. They had with them cassava-leaf baskets of live prawns and crayfish, as well as rice, beans and several chickens.

Lachlan supervised the unloading, slapping irritably at the mosquitoes swarming around his head. After it was done, he went below to Rodron's cabin.

Night closed over the ship like a mist of black steam. It was sweltering in the stateroom and even with the big stern windows thrown open there was little relief from the heat. The smells of the ship were new to Lachlan. The oak wood of the cabins and the faint tint of the bilges mixed with the ripe and earthy miasma coming from the land, which was invisible now in the dark.

Rodron's cabin boy brought them a bottle of port. At first, Rodron and Hamish mostly talked about the ivory trade, and about politics in England and in the East. Twice Lachlan tried to turn the conversation to the Cape, hoping to discover more about his father's past. Rodron neatly avoided such reminiscences. Lachlan guessed his father had already surreptitiously warned him about speaking of it.

Instead, Rodron warmed to his favourite topic: Madras. 'I hope we won't find the French occupying the town when we get there,' he said.

'Is that a serious cause for concern?' Hamish asked him.

'I'm afraid so. It was captured three years ago, and we only got it back last year, but it's still under constant threat. The French have their own fort at a place called Pondicherry, to the south, and they wield a lot of influence in Hindustan now.'

Hamish drank his port, smacked his lips in appreciation, then held his crystal glass out for another. When Lachlan did the same, Hamish shook his head and shooed the cabin boy and the bottle back to the corner.

'So, the Portugals have Africa,' Lachlan said. 'The Dutch have Ceylon and the Spice Islands. If the French take Madras it won't leave much for the Company, will it?'

Rodron nodded. 'That's why it's vital we don't lose Madras. If we do, it will only be a matter of time before we have to surrender Calcutta and Bombay as well.'

They were interrupted by the arrival of their dinner. The cabin door was thrown open and their three cooks trailed in, carrying platters of grilled crayfish and steaming bowls of rice. There was also a huge dish of prawns and fresh cashew nuts cooked in a spicy stew that Hamish boasted about as if he had made it himself. Lachlan thought Rodron was going to faint. On a long sea journey such as this one, even the captain's table could be spartan at best.

All conversation was forgotten as they ate. It wasn't until their second helpings that Hamish dropped his bombshell. 'I'd often thought,' he said, 'of recommending a career in the India service to young Lachlan here.'

Lachlan looked up, startled. He'd long suspected his father was cooking up something like this, but this was the first time he had spoken of it directly.

'He could do worse,' Rodron said. 'It would hold great prospects.'

'Wait a minute,' Lachlan said. 'If everything you've just told us is right, what possible prospects could there be?'

'The best opportunities come in a crisis,' Hamish said. 'When all is safe, any fool can prosper.'

'Your father's right,' Rodron said. 'If the Company prevails over the French in Hindustan and retains possession of Madras and the Coromandel coast, then the possibilities for trade will be limitless. Fresh posts and commands will spring up everywhere. There is a lot of opportunity for young men of enterprise right now. Today's clerks are tomorrow's councillors and presidents.'

'No thank you,' Lachlan said. 'I like it well enough here.'

'There is nothing for you here, son,' Hamish said.

'There is plenty for me here. There is ivory and gold and copper.'

'What about the Portuguese?' Rodron said.

Lachlan shook his head. 'They do not trouble with us this far south.'

'That will change,' Hamish said. 'They'll not be content with getting just a share of what we make for much longer. Soon, they'll want it all. There are two things certain in this life, Lachlan, death and greed.'

'I thought we had an arrangement with Jorge Ferreira.'

'That man couldn't lie straight in a canoe.'

'Well, I'm not going anywhere. This is my family, my land.'

'Still, you should think on it,' Rodron said.

Lachlan turned to his father. 'What would you have me do in Hindustan? Work at a bench all day, crouched over account ledgers?'

'It would only be for a year or two.'

'It's what everyone does at first,' Rodron said. 'But your father says you're a lad of great enterprise. The sky's the limit.'

Lachlan stared at them both, smug as monkeys up a tree. They must have been discussing this while he was busy helping to unload the dhow. Not an hour aboard, and already they were in cahoots.

'Positions of any kind in the Company are hard to come by,' Hamish said. 'I know the current President of Madras, or at least my father did. If I wrote to him, I'm sure he could arrange something.'

'A bird has to fly its nest sooner or later,' Rodron said.

Lachlan nodded to the boy in the corner with the port bottle. This time he had him fill his glass to the brim, all the while glaring in defiance at his father. 'I am sure it would be perfectly fine for young men of a certain disposition, but it's not for me.'

'We've no need to talk about it now,' Hamish said. 'Plenty of time for that later. Now, then, Jack, let's talk about your ship. We'll have to make a list of everything you need, and we'll get started on repairs at first light. I'll put Lachlan in charge of things. It will give you both time to get to know each other better. Perhaps you can help me change his mind about Hindustan.' He beamed as if he had just laid out a royal flush at poker, then belched and reached for the port bottle, taking it right out of the cabin boy's hands. 'I'll pour again, shall I, Jack?'

Hamish stayed on board that night, sending Lachlan back to the fort with Mohammed and the cooks. He got back to Greenock the next day looking pale and liverish and nothing more was said about Lachlan joining the East India Company.

It took two days to mend the foremast on the *Southampton*. They had no canvas, but Hamish's Tsonga shipwrights stitched the sails as best they could, while their carpenters repaired the spars. Rodron was on his way on the third day. It was near the break of the season and if he missed the trades, he would have to spend the next six months in Zanzibar.

As he watched him go, Lachlan felt a shiver of unease. Hamish never mentioned their conversation with Captain Rodron, but the years were coming fast, and Lachlan knew that soon he would have to decide on his future. He had always supposed it would be in Delgoa Bay, but it was clear to him now that his father had quite different ambitions for him.

He didn't believe all this talk of things turning sour in Mozambique. Hamish wanted rid of him. It was as simple as that.

CHAPTER 9

Novo Santiago

Sofala Province, Portuguese East Africa

When Jorge Ferreira arrived at his prazo, his entire household was lined up on the beach to greet him. Once he was successfully installed on his veranda, which was shaded by purple bougainvillea, one of his slaves brought an ostrich fan to keep him cool. Another took his hat and brought him the footstool he had made himself out of bloodwood, buffalo leather and kapok. Paolo, his deputy, who had been charged with running the plantation in his absence, was given the very great honour of pulling off his boots and socks.

When he was settled, he waited for his daughter to come out to greet him. It seemed to him that she took her own good time about it. When she finally appeared, she kept her eyes downcast and her hands crossed demurely in front of her, but he wasn't fooled for a moment. She was in her one of her moods.

He shooed away all the slaves except the one with the fan. Then he wiggled his toes and examined his bare feet critically. They had not seen the sunlight for some time. He would have to get someone to work on his bunions later. He saw his daughter wrinkle her nose. Tough as nails but she could be dainty enough when she felt like it.

He was, as always, astonished that she was his. Friends often referred to him, even within his earshot, as an ugly brute. He didn't mind. What good were looks to a man? If he had ever had them, he would only have ruined them warring or hunting.

But Catia did not look like him in any way. She was dark, for one thing. An eighth part of her was Tsonga, like her great grandfather, a local chieftain. But she had hair like Jorge's grandmother, long and blue-black. And he supposed her face was pretty enough, if it weren't for all the tart looks she gave him whenever he had a drink.

The rest of her was savage; there was no help for it. She couldn't hide the *cafre* in her, even if he dressed her in the best ladies' clothes he could get out here in this Godforsaken place. He could never take her home. She would never fit in with delicate society in Lisbon, any more than he could sit in a Tsonga hut and eat maize porridge with his fingers.

'How was your trip, Papa?'

'Satisfactory. Did anything happen while I was away?'

'The drums have been beating all the time you have been gone. Three of the villagers died from fever. One was that lovely little boy who used to bring us mangoes, Vulombe.'

He stared at her. How did she know this? They all looked the same to him even after all these years.

'I suppose you've been cheating the inglês again?' she asked.

'I am not cheating him, it is philanthropy. If it wasn't for me, how would he survive? How would he know who to pay, and how much, if I didn't help him?'

'And how much does he pay for your Christian charity?'

'Not half of what I deserve. Now, why doesn't a daughter fetch her father a drink?'

Catia went into the kitchen. She returned with a bottle of square face and slammed it down in front of him. He spread his hands wide and gave her a look: Do you want me to drink straight from the bottle? She went back for a mug and threw it at him.

'On Ilha, they have Madeira and crystal glass,' he said.

'You're not on Ilha now. And I don't like you drinking.'

'A man needs a drink, living here miles from anywhere. In Lisbon...' He stopped himself. What was the use of talking to her about Lisbon? She had never been further than Ilha.

'You smell.'

He almost choked on his gin. 'What kind of daughter talks back to her father this way? Do I not get respect in my own home?'

'I had them fill the tin bath and put it under the cashew tree.'

'I don't want a bath yet. I want a drink. You haven't asked me what I did on Ilha.'

'What did you do?'

'I had dinner with Colonel Roderigo Luis.'

He waited for her to say something. She didn't.

'Don't you remember. You met him once, on Ilha. A *fidalgo* of fine manners and sophistication.'

Still nothing. Not even a sullen look.

'His family have estates in the Douro and connections at court.'

'He snorts when he laughs and his breath stinks,' she said.

'In Portugal, he would be considered a fine catch for any woman.'

'Then let him go back to Portugal and be caught.'

'I have told him that I shall bring you with me when I return to Ilha. He is most eager to renew your acquaintance.'

'No, Papa.'

'What, what was that?'

'I said no. I will not marry him. I don't care what he has told you. You are a fool to believe he is anything other than what you were at his age, an out-of-luck fortune hunter in a tatty uniform.'

The gin burned all the way down. Sometimes his daughter's tongue was sharper than a skinning knife. She was right about Roderigo, of course - he stank like a hyena - but an out-of-luck fortune hunter? Well, all right, perhaps he was once, but she shouldn't say it aloud. Who had she been talking to?

He decided it was time to remind her what was what around here. He got up, tipping the chair back onto the floor for effect. 'If I say you are to marry, you will marry. Or you will feel the back of my hand.'

Catia picked up the square face. 'And you will feel the end of the gin bottle.'

He grabbed it out of her hands. 'Careful, you're spilling it,' he said. He sat down again. Well, threats and bluster clearly wouldn't work. He hadn't really expected it to. 'What about Colonel Fernandes? You met him at the governor's house.'

'A simpleton with a limp.'

'He earned the limp honourably, fighting those bastard English.'

'I don't mind the bit that's missing from his leg. It's the part that's missing in his brain that I can't tolerate.'

'You are the heiress to one of the finest prazos in Mozambique. It is time you found an heir.'

'So you can put your feet up and order my husband around, like you do me?'

'I would not dare to order you around,' he said under his breath.

She turned for the door. 'Papa, tell me something. Did you love Mama, or did you only marry her so you could stake claim to her land?'

'What are you saying? Of course, I loved her! She was the most beautiful woman I've ever seen.'

'Beautiful and with an estate the size of Portugal. You really did well.' She went back inside.

He sighed and poured some more of the gin into the enamel mug. He would let her cool off for a while. She always got like this whenever he mentioned the prospect of marriage. She was right about Roderigo and Fernandes, perhaps even right about him, but she was wrong about her mother. He had loved her well enough.

What was he going to do with her? She had refused all the possible suitors on Ilha. Why did they only send the idiots and the socially repulsive out here? There must be some good-looking officer somewhere who could turn his daughter's head. He sent up a quick prayer to Almighty God to send him one.

Just don't send me someone too quick-witted, he thought, quickly revising his private supplication to the deity. I need someone I can manipulate. Otherwise, what would be the point.

CHAPTER 10

Delgoa Bay

Hitsakile and the cooks had laid out their breakfasts. There were enamel bowls of rice, eggs and *matapa*, woven baskets with cornbread and papaya, and a platter of cured meats. Hamish and Johanna ate alone in the kitchen as they did most mornings. Katherine and Callum were already done, as usual. Lachlan was always up at dawn. He had to start his lessons with Arjuna, his Hindustani tutor, before doing his chores around the fort.

'Did you hear the lions this morning?' Hamish said.

'I heard them,' Johanna said. 'I don't mind them, as long as they stay that side of the river.'

'They woke me.'

'No, they didn't. You were already awake.'

'How did you know that?'

'You think I can't feel you tossing and turning all night?'

He shrugged and put more eggs on his plate.

'It's Lachlan, isn't it?'

'Perhaps.'

'He didn't do it, Hamish.'

'One of them did and then lied bald-faced about it. Anyway, there's no point talking about it anymore. What's done is done.'

'Is it? You've been like a squirrel on a hot stove since that Indiaman left.'

'Aye, perhaps. There's something I've been wanting to talk to you about.'

'Well, there's nothing to stop you.' She pushed away her plate and looked at him. 'So, talk.'

Hamish toyed with his food and wondered how to begin.

'You and that Captain Rodron were cooking something up, weren't you?' she said. 'It's no surprise to me. You spent every night on his ship all the time he was here.'

'It's true we spent a lot of time talking about the boys.'

'Did you now?'

'He promised me that when he got to Madras, he would have a word for me with Channing.'

'Who's that?'

'He's the East India Company's President in Madras.'

'Where's that?'

'It's on the Coromandel coast. It's the biggest Company stronghold in India.'

'And what is your friend Rodron going to talk to Channing about?'

'I gave him a letter to pass to him. I've asked him to find Lachlan a position as a writer in the Company.'

'Without talking to me first?'

'It's just to sound him out, find out if they have an opening.'

'What's a writer?'

'It's a clerk, I suppose.'

'You want Lachlan to spend his life in a dusty office with ink on his fingers? Is that your high ambition for him?'

'Don't get excited. Everyone has to start somewhere. He's a bright boy, and he'll progress quickly through the ranks. Lachlan can make himself anything he wants to be, we both know that. There's more opportunity for him over there than there is stuck here, miles from anywhere.'

'You put Lachlan in an office and the boy will shrivel up and die.'

'He could really make something of himself there. By the time he's my age, he could be retired and living in a mansion in London.'

'It sounds like your dream not his.'

'I'm doing the right thing by him. I know I am. Look at this place. We're hundreds of leagues from any place you could call a civilized town. It's a fever coast. Rory lost his wife to the sickness. We lost a bairn, and it's a wonder we didn't lose more.'

'You can't change the past.'

'Then let's talk about the future. Sooner or later the Portugals will drive us out of Delgoa Bay. But if Lachlan is already established in Hindustan, we'll all benefit. It's the best thing for him, and the best thing for all of us.'

'That's not the real reason you want him out and we both know it.'

'It was you just told me not to dredge up the past.'

'Do you deny it?'

'It's nothing to do with it. I've made up my mind.'

'You can't do this to him.'

Hamish pushed his breakfast away, half-eaten. 'You'll not mind if I'm the judge of that.'

'I do mind. I mind very much.'

Hamish picked up his hat and strode out. The servants rolled their eyes. Better stay out of his way the rest of the day.

Hitsakile went to clear away the plates, but Johanna picked up her coffee mug and banged it down on the table. He retreated. Let the bwanas clear away their own plates then. Today looked like a good day for pretending to have the fever chills and sleeping under one of the cashew trees.

CHAPTER 11

Mhawuri, the month of the winds

The *Kusi* wind from the south blew every day, following the line of the shore. Lachlan was forever chasing his hat down the beach. The local women laughed as their *capulanas* blew about their faces.

The seasons were unlike anything Hamish had grown up with. Between April and September, the winds blew from the south and could take a ship from the Cape to the Horn, or to the Spice Islands, with no tacking. The trade winds, the Indiamen called them.

Between December and March, the winds reversed, and the *Kaskazi* blew the ships home again from the Horn down to Zanzibar, or from the Coromandel to Good Hope. The wind brought with it thunderous storms and monsoonal rains.

From season to season the rhythm of life along the river continued. Every day was much like the last. The women went to and from the wells balancing clay pots on their heads, fishermen headed across the salt flats and sand banks to their canoes every morning, and every night the village drums told their stories of births, weddings, sicknesses and deaths.

Life in Delgoa Bay revolved more around the tides than the winds. Twice every day the sea flooded the mangroves and the estuary, turning it from a series of natural swimming holes into a churning saltwater riptide that flooded the surrounding countryside. When it withdrew, it left behind a horizon of ivory-coloured sand that rippled towards the neighbouring islands and seemed to stretch halfway to Ilha itself.

The local sailors navigated tide and current in leaky dhows hacked together with mangrove wood. They bailed the seawater from the scuppers with baobab seed scoops and used pieces of coral rock tied to a rope as anchors.

It had been that way for hundreds, perhaps thousands, of years. But the relentless march of foreign armies and commerce would soon change everything.

Lachlan was in the warehouse, taking inventory of the stores, when he heard something on the wind. He stopped and listened. It was the singing of Tsonga bearers as a caravan made its way along the valley. It was faint at first, then swelled as they crested the rise. He ran outside and saw Hamish and his sister coming out of the boma at the same time.

'It's Uncle Rory,' Lachlan said.

'And about time,' Hamish said, but he was grinning.

They could see the caravan now from the western gate as it crested a rise in the distant hills. Six months Rory had been gone, visiting the fairs in Maputaland and Swaziland. This was the moment they all lived for. Fortune or disaster depended on how much ivory, copper and gold he had brought back with him from the hinterland. Hamish was about to find out if the deal he had made with Jorge Ferreira was a good one.

They watched the column snake down the hillside, the bearers bowed under the weight of green ivory tusks. Even the wagons were riding low on their axles.

Rory was riding at the back of the column on his bay stallion. He took off his hat and waved it in the air.

Hamish nodded and grinned. When Johanna came running out of the boma, he put his arms around her and tossed her into the air. 'Look at all that ivory,' he shouted. 'We're rich. If Ferreira could see this, he'd have a fit.'

That night, after the oil lamps had been lit, the kitchen cleaned, and the chickens locked away from marauding genets, Hamish and Rory sat down together on the *stoep*. Hamish had with him a bottle of square face he had stolen from Ferreira.

They listened to the sounds of the night. Though they were hundreds of miles from any large town, the nights were never quiet. The Tsonga didn't gather inside when the sun went down, as Europeans did. The night was for ceremony, gossip and courting, for dancing and for visiting, and most of all for drums. The drumming often went on long into the night, with dozens of different beats and tempos, sometimes accompanied by singing and chanting.

Tonight, the rhythms were especially frenzied. A lot of the young men who had been Rory's bearers on his expedition were finally home, so it was a time for celebration.

'Forty thousand pounds!' Hamish was saying. 'That's a lot of ivory. It's double what Ferreira thinks we're taking and almost ten times as much as I declared to the Portugals in Mozambique.'

'What are we going to do with it all?' Rory said. He held out his cup for another splash of gin. Six months in the hinterland was a long time without a decent drink.

'First, we pay off the Portugals and give Ferreira his share of the ivory, or his share of the ivory he thinks we have. I'll arrange to trade the rest ourselves, in Malabar.'

'Can we do that?'

'When I was on Ilha, I spoke with Shariff Massoud. He said he'll extend me the credit and the ships whenever I say the word.'

'It's a risk.'

'All life is a risk, Rory. You know that. But this is less of a risk than letting the Portugals get some inkling. If they ever find out how much ivory we've been trading these last few years, then the first thing they'll do is tax it. After they've bled us dry, then they'll tax us again, and soon they'll get tired of only taking a share. They'll want it all. It's taken us long enough to create our amity with Mangobe and the Nguni in Natal. I'll not do all the work so these fools can walk in and take over.'

'My worry is that the Governor of Mozambique is too corrupt, even for the Portugals,' Rory said. 'They'll replace him sooner or later and put someone else in charge on Ilha. Business will get a lot harder for us then.'

It was a beautiful night. A full moon, hovering in a velvet sky bled a halo of spectrum colours into a tattered band of cloud.

Rory pressed some shreds of dry shag from his tobacco pouch into his ancient clay pipe. He lit it with the nub of candle on the wooden rail by his elbow.

'With luck, we'll have moved on by the time that happens,' Hamish said. 'We're seeing the last of the good times. There's going to be a glut of ivory soon. Besides, it's all about the slavers now. Put some poor wretch in manacles and the market never seems to have enough.'

'A bad business, to my mind.'

'I'm glad we're agreed on it then, for I want no part of it. I saw a few of them while I was on Ilha with Ferreira. Terrible business. Even if you don't see them, you can smell them. God alone knows what conditions they keep them in. Where are they all coming from?'

'Prisoners of war, mainly. I saw a lot of them this time. All the chiefs are involved in it. Slaving's always been a part of their lives.'

'I'll wager they've never seen slaving like this. They're sending those poor bastards to the French on Ile de France for the sugar plantations. None of them live too long over there. The Portugals are turning a tidy profit, too. They don't buy a slave for life, like the Mohammedans, they work them to death for six months then go and buy another. They work the cost into their profits. That trade is going to change our life here.'

Rory finished his pipe, then tapped out the ash on his boot heel. 'Well, for now, we only have to worry about getting a fair price for this season's ivory.'

'Aye, what we'll do is this: I'll have Mohammed Daoud sail north while the wind lasts and pay off Ferreira and the Governor on Ilha. We'll keep the rest of the ivory here. Shariff Massoud won't be able to ship it to the Malabar until after the monsoon. I'll need that time to get Lachlan ready.'

'Lachlan?'

'Aye. He'll be going to Hindustan along with the ivory.'

'To what purpose?'

'I plan to find him employment with the East India Company.'

'But he's just a lad!'

'He's a young man now and he has to find his own way in the world.'

'Are you sure about this?'

'Sure as I'll ever be. The lad's clever enough. He can speak Swahili and Tamil and he has a good head for figures, when he chooses to exercise himself enough to use it. There are better prospects over there than he'll ever get here. I'll go with him to make sure he gets settled in.'

'I thought he wanted to stay here.'

'What is there for him here? Besides, soon he'll be wanting a wife, and a man has little chance of finding one here.' He splashed more gin into his brother's mug.

'What about Cal?'

'What about him?'

'Are you sending him away, too?'

'He's too young.' He saw the look on Rory's face. 'What is it?'

'You're not fair with those boys. You never have been.'

'Nonsense.'

'We both know why.'

'I don't ever want to talk about any of that again.'

They both fell silent, listening to the tom-toms and the singing from the village.

Hamish heard the lions somewhere close by on the other side of the river. Their coughing raised the fine hairs on the back of his neck. It was like nothing he had ever heard, and the way it echoed, it sounded like the pride was all around them.

He thought about the *nganga's* prophecy. *There is a bad moon coming.* He tried to ignore the uneasy feeling in his gut. He wasn't going to let himself get spooked by that crazy old man and his bag of snake bones, by God, he wasn't.

He looked up at the stars. They said that a man's future was written there if he could only read their cypher.

The *al-Shahadah* was ready to sail with the tide at first light. Half-naked seamen clambered over her, hoisting the lateen sail on her enormous sixty-foot teak boom. Mohammed Daoud's eldest son was on board, supervising the loading. There were sacks of rice, millet and dried meat. Water barrels had been lashed to her mast, ready for the voyage up the coast, along with sacks of green coconuts.

The slim, indigo ribbon of the ocean shimmered between the sandbar and the sky. The ebb tide that had trapped the dhow on the littoral mud overnight was now on the turn. It swashed through the mangroves, making the dhow buck and strain at her anchor line.

Mohammed Daoud said farewell to his other sons on the shore, while his wife waited further up the strand with the daughters and younger children. Finally, he came to bid farewell to Hamish.

'I wish you a safe journey,' Hamish said to him. 'I hope to see you safe back here before the next moon. *Safari njema! Kila la Kheri!*'

An hour later he watched the *al-Shahadah* head out to sea. He tried to shake off the feeling of unease that was haunting him. He told himself they were doing all right. Another few years and he could leave this damned fever-ridden country and set up a proper trading company somewhere in Hindustan. Then he would make some real money. Lachlan was a big part of his plans, if only the boy could get it through his head.

He turned around and saw the *nganga* standing under the trees, watching him. He was holding the bent wooden stick he carried with him everywhere. It was wrapped in a piece of lion skin. He held it up to the sky, then pointed it at Hamish. Was it a greeting, or a curse?

Hamish shrugged and headed back to the boma for his breakfast.

Dolphins played in the bow wave of the *al-Shahadah* as she made her way up the coast past empty islands with slender palms and squat baobab trees. The wind bellied the patched sail on the boom.

A turtle floated on the current, a long way from shore.

There was little to do and some of the crew had curled up asleep on the deck. On any other day Mohammed Daoud might have joined them under the awning. Instead, he prowled the deck, restless and vigilant. His sharp eyes picked out a pair of humpback whales in the rollers beyond the island's reef system.

A wave sent the *al-Shahadah* lurching, and the curved arch of the planking dribbled a little water into the deck. He kicked one of the boys awake and set him to work bailing.

He closed his eyes, letting the breeze play on his face and beard. Allah forgive me for what I'm about to do. But a man could not always count his conscience.

Not if he wanted to be truly rich.

CHAPTER 12

Musa lay on a wooden cot, shivering so hard Johanna could hear his teeth rattling in his head. She and Katherine squatted down next to him. There was so much heat coming off his body, it was like standing next to an oven. His two little brothers and three sisters crowded in the doorway, staring in with huge brown eyes.

Mohammed Daoud's wife, Hlulani, peered over their shoulder, nervously working the loose end of her head wrap with her fingers.

'Has he never had the fever before?' Johanna asked her in Swahili.

She shook her head.

Johanna peered under the cot. Sweat had soaked through the reed webbing and stained the packed earth floor, yet Musa's whole body shook as if he were freezing to death.

She turned to Katherine. 'It's the ague. Heat some stones in a fire, then bring me as many blankets as you can. We have to sweat the fever out of him.' She looked up at Hlulani. Three children already, and she was barely older than Katherine. She looked terrified. 'We'll do what we can,' Johanna said to her.

When they got back to the boma, she went to the yellow wooden chest in the corner of the kitchen. It was where she kept her jars of devil's bark, bugbane and mustard seeds, her extract of lettuce cough mixture, and Dr. Chamberlain's sovereign diarrhoea remedy.

She found the last stock of the wormwood she had brought with her years ago from the Cape. She put some of the root into a stone mortar, rolled up her sleeves and started to grind it.

Katherine watched her, a doubtful look on her face. 'We haven't much left. Papa will be angry when he finds out you've used it.'

'No, he won't. He knows how much Mohammed Daoud has done for us. Even if he is angry, he'll soon see the sense in it. When I'm done, we'll steep this in cold, clean water and make some tea out of it. Then we have to find a way of getting it into him. Don't just stand there, girl, find some more blankets and get back over there! I'll not have Mohammed come back to grieving. He's already lost one wife to the fever. I'll not have him lose a son as well.'

Lachlan stared out of the window at the village women, headed through the mangroves to the wells in their lurid *capulanas*. They make the parrots look dowdy, Katherine always said.

The Tsonga women didn't wear animal skins like the Nguni in the hinterland. Hindustani traders had brought these wraps with them as trade goods hundreds of years before, and now the local women used them for everything: as wraparound skirts, as head coverings, as towels, and as slings to carry their babies. The women measured their status by how many they owned. They wore two or three, one over the other, even on the hottest days.

He watched one of the young girls, entranced by the graceful swing of her hips, even with a clay water pot balanced on her head. She was the girl Katherine had talked about, the one she had seen slipping out of his hut.

He thought about what his sister had said to him about getting married. The truth was he hardly thought about anything else these days.

Arjuna was reading Hindu conjugations from a book. A gecko was hunting, high on the wall behind his head. It's having more fun than I am, Lachlan thought. A striped squirrel ran along the wall under the thatched eave. They're free to do what they want. Not me.

Suddenly Hamish was standing in the doorway, hands on his hips.

'Ah, *sahib*,' Arjuna said. 'I did not see you. Have you come to check on our progress? I am most pleased with...'

Hamish shook his head. 'Never mind. You can give me a full report later. It's almost time for lunch. Why don't you take an early break today?'

Arjuna nodded eagerly and packed away his books. He made a *namaste* to Hamish, then hurried out and made his way back across the compound. He was long, all elbows and knees. In his white dhoti and sandals, he resembled a rather ungainly stork.

Hamish waited until he was out of sight. 'He's been telling me how well you're doing with your lessons. He says you've already attained a proficiency. In another few months you'll be speaking Hindustani like a native.'

'I reckon I could get by.'

'Good. There's a reason I wanted you to learn it.'

'You're sending me to Madras.'

'Not only that.'

'You're going to trade our ivory in Coromandel. I heard you talking to Uncle Rory. It makes sense.'

'I'm glad you think so. It's true. Ferreira's commissions are getting a little too rich for my blood. It's the black gold everyone wants now, and I'll have nothing to do with that trade.'

Lachlan nodded. 'When do I leave?'

'At the end of the rainy season.'

'And Cal?'

'Callum stays here. You and I will be going over there together.'

'Good.'

'Don't be too pleased yet. You haven't heard it all.'

Lachlan readied himself. He knew what was coming.

Hamish went on. 'I'll be coming back alone. You'll remember that before Rodron left here, he agreed to talk to Channing in Madras about you.'

'You're still going through with that?'

'I am.'

'I told you I wanted no part of it.'

'It's not your decision.'

'This is my home.'

'Home? It's a trading post in the middle of nowhere. We have to look to the future. You'll be the vanguard for our family. Look at it that way.'

'Vanguard? That's a fancy name for a clerk.'

'Show the Company you've aptitude and you'll make your way up the ladder soon enough. We'll follow you over when the time is right.'

Lachlan didn't say anything.

'I only want the best for you, son. The world's changing. Time doesn't stand still, not for anyone.'

Lachlan slammed shut his study book of Tamil grammar. It sounded like a pistol shot in the tiny room. 'The reason you want me gone is nothing to do with the world.' He brushed past his father in the doorway.

'Where are you going? I haven't finished talking to you,' Hamish said.

Lachlan stopped and turned around. Hamish never thought he'd see one of his own look at him that way.

'No, but I've finished talking to you.' He walked away without a backward glance.

Lachlan walked blindly out of the palisade gates and down to the river strand. A clerk! Was that all his father thought he was good for? He wasn't going to spend his life with ink on his fingers in some hot and dusty warehouse.

He heard footfall on the sand behind him, thought it was Hamish and wheeled to face him. But it wasn't Hamish. It was Callum. Katherine ran up behind him.

'Get away from me, Cal.'

'I just want to know what he said.'

'I think you know.'

'I wouldn't be asking if I knew.'

'I'll wager you were listening.'

Katherine tugged at Callum's arm. 'Come away, Cal, for God's sake. Leave him alone!'

Lachlan took a step towards him. 'Why didn't you tell him the truth?'

Callum was all innocence. 'About what?'

'About what happened to Andzile.'

'I did tell the truth. You beat him with a shovel.' Callum grinned, enjoying himself. 'He's sending you away, isn't he? He doesn't trust you. He wants me to take over here when I'm old enough.'

Lachlan saw the curl of Callum's lip and realised his little brother was laughing at him. He swung, caught his brother on the point of the jaw, and down he went. Katherine put both hands on Lachlan's chest and pushed him away.

He heard another voice, louder and angrier. 'What's happening here?'

Hamish strode down the sand. He grabbed Callum by the shirtfront and pulled him to his feet, then shoved him back in the direction of the fort.

Callum had bitten his tongue when Lachlan hit him, and he was spitting blood into his hand.

'Katherine, get him out of here.' Hamish turned back to Lachlan. 'That temper of yours! Is this what happened with Sasavona's boy?'

Lachlan swallowed hard. There was no point trying to defend himself. His father always believed what he wanted. 'Hell with you,' he said and walked away into the dark. He needed some time alone.

CHAPTER 13

Mohammed Daoud's rondavel was inside the stockade. It had four rooms and an expansive garden and was built on the other side of the long hut that served as a barracks for their *chikunda*.

When Johanna and Katherine reached the rondavel, they found Hlulani waiting for them in the doorway. She had a baby in her arms and her face was all but hidden by her headscarf. She stood aside to let them in.

At first, Johanna thought the boy was dead. For the last two days he had tossed and writhed with the fever. One moment he had been shaking so hard with cold she thought his teeth would shatter, the next he was boiling up and trying to toss off the mountain of blankets on top of him.

But this morning he slept peacefully. He lay so still Johanna was almost surprised to feel the whisper of breath at his lips. There was a yellowish tinge to his cheeks, but his skin was cool to the touch and his breathing was even and deep. The first fever was always bad, but now that he had survived it she thought he might yet grow to be an old man.

'You did it,' Katherine said to her.

'God decides who lives and dies,' Johanna said.

'Theirs or ours?' Katherine said, looking around at Hlulani.

'I'm sure it's the same one. It's only men and women who speak a different language. If you ask me, He understands us all.'

She stood up, relieved to find the boy well again. Hlulani lowered her head in deference, but she did not smile. She didn't say a word.

'I don't like her,' Katherine said when they were outside, 'and I don't think she likes us.'

'It doesn't matter. At least we saved the boy. Mohammed Daoud has served your father faithfully through many years. If we helped at all, it's the least he deserves.'

CHAPTER 14

Zanzibar, three weeks later

The feathery palm groves and the slender finger of a minaret were silhouetted against the night sky. A crescent moon hung over the sombre walls of the Arab fort. Insects buzzed and clattered against the lamp that hung from the crosspiece of the awning.

There were two frigates riding at anchor, yellow oil lamps burning at their mastheads. They dwarfed everything else in the harbour. A small lateen-rigged *felucca* made its way towards them. Mohammed Daoud sat in the stern of the *al-Shahadah* and watched it come.

A native stood at the bow, holding a lamp. There was a man standing behind him, ramrod-straight, wearing a white turban. That must be him.

All his life he had found the creaking of a ship's timbers soothing, but tonight they got on his nerves. He wished he had never agreed to this, but it was too late to change his mind now.

Besides, what man could resist such an offer? If his gamble succeeded, he could live the rest of his life as a king. So why did he wish he could get under sail right away and get away from here before this Napoleon Gagnon bought his soul?

As the felucca came alongside his crew hooked on to her with chains, and Napoleon Gagnon came up through the entry port. Two of his soldiers followed, carrying a large wooden chest between them.

'Peace unto you,' Mohammed Daoud said, touching his fingers to his lips and his breast.

Napoleon Gagnon had brought a *djinn* with him. Mohammed had heard whispers about her. It was a pale creature and looked almost bloodless in the moonlight. When the Frenchman sat down, it sat beside him imitating his movement. It must be his spirit, Mohammed thought, for he did not make introduction to it, and he did not look at it or speak to it.

Napoleon sat cross-legged on the salt-crusted carpet, dressed in a robe and turban like an Indian prince. The cane and whiskers were Western affectations. He laid the cane across his knees and spoke in flawless Arabic. The *djinn* did not move, just stared deep into Mohammed Daoud's soul.

Mohammed Daoud poured tea, brewed with cinnamon, cloves and ginger, into tiny brass thimbles. Mosquitoes whined around their heads. It was deathly hot, with no breeze, not even out here on the harbour.

They exchanged pleasantries, inquiring after each other's health and families. Finally, they got down to business.

'Everything is in readiness?' Napoleon asked.

'Yes, *effendi*.'

'Tell me.'

'I have delivered a cargo of rice and millet to the Portuguese governor at the fort on Ilha. This I did one week ago.'

'When will this McKenzie expect you back in Delgoa Bay?'

'Within the next few weeks, when the *Kashkazi* blows.'

'And if you are not there?'

'He will suspect nothing straight away. He will think I have had problems, a storm perhaps. It has happened before.'

'Tell me about the defences at Fort Greenock.'

Mohammed tasted bile in the back of his throat.

Napoleon reached into his jacket and brought out a chart. It was a map of the coast between the Ilha da Mozambique and Nativity Bay. 'Show me.'

Mohammed Daoud stared at the map for a long time, then tapped a long and dirty fingernail on a spot at the southern end of Delgoa Bay. 'The fort is along the estuary here. Unless a man knows the waters, it is impossible to sail even a *felucca* along it.'

'But you can get my frigates alongside the fort?'

'With God's help.'

'I don't need God's help. I need yours. I am paying enough for it.'

Mohammed Daoud flicked away a droplet of sweat that was poised on the end of his nose. 'I know the tides and shallows better than any man alive. But you will not have long. You must attack with the full of the tide and be gone by the ebb or you will be stranded in the mud.'

'I ask you again, what are his defences?'

'He has two bronze guns, twelve-pounders.'

'Does he, now? *Mijn Heer* Keyser neglected to tell me about this. What else? How is the settlement defended?'

'He has eighty Tsonga soldiers that he has trained to use muskets. The boma and the warehouse are surrounded by a timber palisade. But his main defence is the sea itself. No one would ever think to attack so far upriver for fear of losing their ships.'

'Unless they have you on board.'

Mohammed Daoud nodded slowly.

'He will be there?' Napoleon said.

'Of course.'

'What about the rest of them? He has a wife, yes?'

'Yes. But you will not harm her?'

'I give you my word, none of the women will be harmed.'

Mohammed Daoud looked around. Gagnon's *djinn* was still staring at him with those unnatural blue eyes.

'He has two sons, both old enough to fight. The *effendi* has a brother, also. He goes into Maputaland and Swaziland every year to buy ivory and gold from the chiefs. He may already be gone by the time we return.'

'You have a map of the fort?'

He hesitated.

Napoleon held out his hand.

Mohammed Daoud produced a creased and salt-stained parchment from his robe and laid it on the carpet. Napoleon leaned forward to study it. Mohammed pointed out the cannon emplacements.

'The *glacis* allows the two cannons a killing zone just beneath the walls,' Napoleon said. 'We shall have to eliminate the guns before I land my men.'

Mohammed fanned himself harder. He was suddenly aware of the stink of the bilges and the sour drift of the slave smell from the fort. 'You promise me, *effendi*, you will not hurt the women.'

'What was that?'

'You gave me your oath.'

'What is their fate to you?'

'His wife has always been kind to us. She helped my wife when she was in labour with our third child. She sent food when my children were ill.'

'If she has been so kind, why are you doing this?'

'I have no choice.'

'Every man has a choice.'

'With this money, I will never have to work again. My sons will never have to go to sea. I can make the *hajj* to Mecca and ensure my place in Paradise and when I return, I will buy my brothers and my sons their own businesses in Oman.'

'What is it you want, then? Money or kindness? You cannot have both.'

Mohammed Daoud picked at the caulking in the decking.

'In life, my friend, you will find that sentiment is a poor substitute for money.' Napoleon looked over his shoulder. At his signal, his two soldiers brought forward a large wooden chest and dropped it on the deck. One of them took a dagger and pried open the lid, splintering the wood. Mohammed peered inside and caught his breath when he saw the silver bars inside, nestled like puppies in a bed of straw.

'Half now,' Napoleon said. 'The other half when the job is done.'

Looking at what was in the chest, Mohammed supposed this Gagnon was right. You could take all the kindness in the world and stack it in a score of godowns and it would not buy you a fine house and servants and a future for your sons. Those silver bars meant he would not have to spend the rest of his life sailing up and down the coast in a wormwood-eaten dhow.

'But there is a thought in your mind, is there not,' Napoleon said, 'that you might take my silver and then try to run with it?'

Mohammed put a hand to his heart. 'I am an honest man. I should never do such a thing.'

'An honest man would not betray his employer or the woman who nursed his sons and his wife through sickness.'

Mohammed saw two soldiers emerge from the shadows with his eldest son, Hammid. One of them was holding a knife to his throat. The other had his sword drawn to dissuade any of Mohammed's crew from intervening.

Mohammed started to get to his feet, but Napoleon put a restraining hand on his arm. 'He will come to no harm, provided you keep your bargain. I am sure you will. As you said, you are an honest man.'

'Not my son!'

'Listen to me, Mohammed Daoud. You will follow my frigates in the *al-Shahadah* as far as Delgoa Bay. From there you will transfer to my flagship and guide us down the estuary to the fort. When that is done, I will return your son and the balance of the silver. We have an agreement and I always uphold a bargain, and so will you.'

Mohammed watched, helpless, as they bundled his boy over the side and into the *felucca*. Hammid was struggling with his captors and one of the soldiers clamped a hand across his mouth to keep him from yelling.

Napoleon Gagnon stood up and brushed off his robes. He stopped at the rail and gave Mohammed an ironic salute. The *djinn* followed him down into the *felucca*.

How had this man known what he had intended to do? He supposed no man ever became rich enough to give away silver bars by trusting other men. Now there was no choice but to go through with it. The *effendi* and his sons would have to die.

As this father of *djinns* had said, no one ever got rich through kindness.

Lachlan could not sleep. He heard the wind rustling the long palm fronds in the trees outside his window. It was not quite the full of the moon. Soon there would be rain and the black billfish would be running.

The year would turn in a month or so. His last one here, before his father sent him to Hindustan, damn him to hell.

If there was such a place. He'd never had much use for religion and all the dire threats that went with it. His mother was the only one of their family who ever spoke much of God and the devil, and then only twice a year. The events were Easter and Christmas, when the whole family gathered on the veranda of their boma. Johanna would read a passage from the Bible, and they all sang a hymn. It was as close as any of them ever came to any kind of religion. Hamish only went along with it because his wife insisted on it.

The Tsonga always came along to listen. They liked the hymns, and afterwards there was a free feast with lots of beer. Of course, they didn't believe anything that was written in Johanna's black book. For them it was all as quaint as a fairy tale.

They might live simple lives, but it seemed to Lachlan that their religion was more sophisticated than anything he had ever heard in the churches on Ilha. They believed that every man and woman had two spirits. One entered the body when they were born and returned to the ether when they died. Sasavona said it was like taking a cup of water from the river, then pouring it back in again afterwards.

But the other spirit, the *ndzuti,* kept the characteristics of the dead person and did not leave the living world. In Sasavona's view, his village was filled not only with the living, but also with the ghosts of everyone who had ever belonged to his clan. The living and the dead existed as a community, side by side. So, the worst fate that could befall any Tsonga man or woman was to be exiled from the tribe. It meant not only losing their life but losing their soul as well.

It made a lot of sense to Lachlan. He was sure that, wherever he went in his life, his spirit would always be a part of this land and this family. To leave here was to leave behind not only everyone he loved, but everything that made him what he was.

He got out of bed and went outside. The ground was cold underfoot. There was a feeble quarter moon. The sun was not yet risen, and dawn was just a dirty ochre stain creeping up the distant ocean.

That was when he heard them, lions, a mating pair.

They emerged from the mangroves and came down to the river to drink. The male shook his mane and grumbled deep in his chest. Lachlan felt the vibration through his feet.

They knew he was there. The male looked directly at him for a moment, then turned and padded away along the sand, muscles rippling beneath his golden hide. He disappeared into the trees.

Lachlan turned his gaze to the sea. They had seen no more ships since the *Southampton*, but her arrival had unsettled them all. More would come sooner or later. They would be English, Dutch and French, and Hamish said most of them would be slave ships. Times were changing.

As he walked back to the boma he imagined he could still hear the lions, patrolling the far bank. They were hungry and dangerous, and looking for a way across.

CHAPTER 15

Delgoa Bay

The short rains had come and gone. One moment there was a downpour, a few minutes later the sun shone from a cloudless sky. The land was so parched it seemed to soak up every pool and every puddle like a sponge. Out in the bush, animals worried at empty creek beds. The villagers scooped muddy water from the wells for there were no freshwater rivers here, just the endless pulsing of the sea in and out of the estuary from the vast ocean.

The jacaranda tree outside Lachlan's window blossomed into a riot of lilac colour. It meant the monsoon was close.

The winds turned, coming from the north, from Zanzibar. It was the *Kashkazi* wind that had carried sailors and traders from Oman, China and India for hundreds of years. Everyone prayed for the long rains. When they finally came, they would come in torrents and the waterholes would start to fill again.

Lachlan knew this would be his last monsoon in Delgoa Bay. It would also be the loneliest. Most nights he built a fire of sagebrush on the beach and spent the evenings down there, preferring his own company to his family's. If his father didn't want him around, he thought, well he'd oblige.

Sometimes, after dinner, Katherine would come out to keep him company. But often he was alone with his thoughts until it was time for bed.

As Lachlan settled himself on the hard sand, he heard someone behind him. He looked around, expecting to see his sister. But it was his Uncle Rory. He stood in the shadows, his hands in his pockets. He stood for a long time like that, in companionable silence.

With dusk, the river glowed in the pink sheen of the sunset. The wind fell away and the mosquitoes came out in swarms, whining in a thin mist around his head. Lachlan stocked up the fire. The sage smoke would soon keep them away.

Suddenly it was dark. There were always just a few heartbeats between the sun going down and the pitch dark. The moon was already high in the sky, and it threw sharp shadows under the monkey-thorn tree. Something splashed in the river, a large fish hunting on the surface or perhaps a crocodile.

Drums beat in the background, muffled by ancient trees.

'Tell me something, uncle,' Lachlan said.

'If I can.'

'You and my father were together in the Cape.'

'That's right.'

'Where were you headed?'

'Hindustan.'

'To do what?'

'We had letters of employment to the East India Company, as writers. The same job you're going to do.'

'But you didn't get there. Why not?'

'It's complicated.'

'Simplify it for me. He met my mother on the way, right?'

'Yes, he did.'

'But he never speaks of it and neither does she. You all clam up whenever I bring it up. What's the big secret?'

'We had some trouble there.'

'What sort of trouble?'

'There's some things best left in the past, Lachie.'

'That's what he always says. Do you rehearse your lines together?'

'It's not my place to talk about these things.'

'How the hell did two clerks end up here, in the middle of nowhere?'

'We weren't clerks though, were we? We were farmers. Your grandfather gambled away everything we had. Coming here was our only choice.'

Lightning flashed along the horizon, ink-dark clouds rising toward a gibbous moon. Somewhere out there it was raining.

'Sometimes,' Rory said, 'life takes you down roads you don't expect. That's what happened with us. Perhaps things would have worked out better for us if we'd gone to Hindustan, perhaps not.'

'You don't believe that and neither does he. If you hadn't stepped off at the Cape, he wouldn't have married Mother.'

Rory took out his pipe, knocked it on his heel. He felt in his shirt and trouser pockets for his tobacco pouch, but couldn't find it, so he put the pipe between his teeth and sucked on it, unlit.

They heard Johanna calling them from the boma. Rory seemed relieved. 'Are you coming in for dinner tonight?' he said.

'I'm not hungry.'

'You have to eat.'

'I don't want to eat with *him*.'

'Lachlan, let it be.'

'Let it be? Is that what you think I should do?'

Rory put a hand on Lachlan's shoulder. 'Everything will turn out alright in the end, Lachie. Come on, lad. You have to eat, so let's eat.'

He steered him back toward the fort.

The blanketing sea mist dispersed as soon as the sun rose. Napoleon Gagnon peered through the fog and satisfied himself that the *al-Shahadah*'s dirty lateen sail was still visible behind them.

They were sailing south, tacking hard into the wind. A shoal of flying fish rippled the sea on the ship's beam, frightened by some unseen predator. His companion frigate was off the port beam, the crouching forests of Madagascar behind it.

The African coast lay off the starboard bow, its slender blue line almost hidden by the marching grey swells of the Mozambique current. Twice the rough weather of the *Kashkazi* had driven them to take shelter in one of the bays, first at Angoche, then Sofala.

It had put them behind schedule and Napoleon was a man who did not take well to frustration and delay. He hoped what Mohammed Daoud had told him about Fort Greenock was true. Forty thousand pounds of ivory, on top of his commission, would help to assuage his frayed temper.

Not long now.

CHAPTER 16

Hamish stood on the bank watching the tide swashing into the mangroves. He turned away and held up his eyeglass. There was hardly a ripple out on the ocean, not even a bubble on the reef. With luck they could get in a few hours of fishing before the weather turned.

He headed back to the fort and turfed two of Mohammed Daoud's lascars out of their beds. He sent them down to the beach to get the *felucca* ready. She was smaller and lighter than the *al-Shahadah*, with a light draft, perfect for navigating the coastal reefs and banks.

Then he went back to the boma. It was still dark enough that Hitsakile had left the oil lamps burning in the kitchen. As he walked in he smelled warm butter bubbling in one of the skillets. Both the boys were up and dressed. Johanna was helping Hitsakile cook some eggs and cured sausage.

Callum was at the long yellow wood table, eating his way through a huge plateful of eggs and potatoes, while the servant girls bustled around him. Damn, that boy could eat.

Lachlan was nursing a mug of black coffee.

'Are you coming with us?' Hamish said to him.

He shook his head slowly. He didn't even look up. He mouthed something into his coffee cup, an insult most likely.

Damn him then.

Johanna looked at Hamish, imploringly. It would be the first time he had ever gone out fishing without Lachlan, but what was he supposed to do?

'Hurry up then, Cal.'

Hamish helped himself to coffee from the pot and took it outside. Rory was sitting on one of the rails making a pipe. His tobacco pouch was perched on his knee.

Johanna followed Hamish out. She put her hands on her hips. 'How long is this going on for?'

'He doesn't want to come. He's old enough to make his own decisions.'

'Have you not made peace with the boy yet?'

'I've tried. He's stubborn.'

'Not as stubborn as you. End this now.'

He tried to put his arms around her, but she drew away.

'He'll come around,' Hamish said to her, 'in his own good time.'

'Will he? One thing I've learned in life, Hamish McKenzie, is that you never have as much time as you think you have.' She went back inside.

The coffee tasted bitter. Hamish spat out the dregs.

'Why are you doing this?' Rory said.

'Not you as well.'

'The boy wants to know what he's done wrong. Isn't it about time you told him?'

'Have you said anything to him?'

'It's not for me to tell him. But this is wrong, Hamish. What you're doing is wrong.'

'When I want you to interfere in my affairs, I'll tell you.'

'You have a prickly nature no mistake. You always did have. You don't like to think that you might be wrong about something.'

Hamish turned away. 'As I said, I'll tell him in my own good time.'

'Johanna is right. No moment like the present.'

Callum came barrelling out of the kitchen, He jammed his broad brimmed leather hat on his head and tugged at Hamish's arm. 'Are we going?'

Hamish looked at Rory.

Callum was already halfway to the boat. 'Dad!'

'I'm coming,' he said. He followed Callum out of the gates. He stopped once and looked back at the house. A greasy dawn was breaking over the sky.

Something told him to go back and talk to the boy now, like Rory said. His pride wouldn't let him. Callum called a second time and Hamish turned and headed for the river.

Johanna sat down at the long table across from Lachlan. She sent all the servants out of the room. He looked up at her, his eyes lidded and his expression wary.

'You've a right to know,' she said. 'It can't be a secret forever.'

Lachlan swallowed hard. He'd been agitating for the truth. He hadn't expected it would be his mother who would be telling it.

She took a deep breath. 'The fact is, your father and I didn't meet at the Cape. We knew each other a long time before that, in Amsterdam.'

'I thought his family came from Scotland.'

'The border country. He and your uncle Rory first came to Holland to sell their wool. Their father owned a lot of land near a place called Berwick. My father was a weaver, and he owned a very large business. The short of it, your father took a shine to me and every time he came across the Narrow Sea, he made a point of courting me. He asked my father for my hand and a date was set.'

'I don't understand. That's usual, isn't it?'

'That's not the end of it. Hamish's father declared himself bankrupt. He had accrued massive debts, gambling mainly, that neither of the boys knew about. They lost everything. That's why Hamish never talks about him. He's never forgiven him.'

'Is he still alive?'

'I don't know.'

'So, what happened?'

'My father broke off the betrothal. He wasn't having me marry a pauper. Instead, he found another suitor, an ambitious young man who worked for the Dutch East India Company. He came from a very wealthy family, and my father was delighted with the match. He thought he was perfect, but in truth he was as joyless a man as you could ever wish to meet. And he had a dark side. Violent.'

'He forced you to marry him?'

'A bride's objections are worth nothing in Holland, or anywhere else over the sea. The marriage went ahead, and soon afterwards my new husband was given a posting overseas at the Cape of Good Hope. He told me he had a bright future ahead of him. Perhaps he did.'

'What happened to father?'

'He and Rory had used their connections to get positions in the British East India Company in Madras. They hoped they would make enough money there in a few years to restore the family fortunes.'

'The same plans he has for me now.'

'It's the way of it, it seems, to inherit your father's dreams. Many sons do.'

Lachlan crossed his arms. He leaned back in his chair, taking in this new history.

'The next time I saw Hamish was when his ship stopped at the Cape for provisions on its way to Hindustan.'

'Father courted you again in Cape Town even though you were married?'

She shook her head. 'My husband was a powerful official by then. There was no courting, Lachlan. We saw each other and spoke briefly. I had to decide on the spot what I would do. I agreed to leave the Cape with him, and I've never regretted it, for all of your father's failings.'

'What did you do?'

'There was a Portuguese ship in the harbour set to sail for Ilha. We knew the Dutch would never find us there. Hamish and Rory had already negotiated passage, and I met them at the dock a few minutes before she sailed. We had to make sure my husband had no warning of our plans, or Hamish would have ended his days on a Dutch scaffold. I held my breath the whole way to Ilha.'

'What happened when you got there?'

'We'd only been there a day or two and Hamish met Jorge Ferreira. I suppose they both saw an opportunity. Ferreira had a lease on the land here in Delgoa Bay but didn't have the resources to exploit it. He and your father came to an arrangement. We came here and built Fort Greenock.'

'And Ferreira gets a percentage of everything we earn.'

'Quite a handsome one. But if your father paid that man everything he asked for, we'd starve. That's why he dreams of India. You're his chance to get out from under Ferreira's thumb.'

It was too much to take in. Lachlan's mind was a fog. 'What happened to him?' he said. 'Your husband.'

'I don't know, and I don't care. In that short time we were married, I had grown to hate him. Even the few months we had lived in the Cape he'd earned a reputation as a brute. He had one of our house slaves flogged to death for talking back to him. Have you ever seen a flogging, Lachie?' She closed her eyes to try to push the memory from her mind. 'It took hours for the poor boy to fall silent and even longer for him to die. I begged him to stop, but I think he enjoyed the whole thing.' Her eyes blinked open. 'There, now you know the truth of it.'

Lachlan reached across the table and took his mother's hand. She was trembling. 'Thank you for telling me.'

'I should have told you a long time ago.'

'It still doesn't explain why Father acts the way he does towards me,' Lachlan said. Then he saw the expression on his mother's face. It told him everything. 'I'm not his, am I?' he said. 'That's why Callum is his favourite.'

'Hamish is still your father. He raised you and he has been there for you every day of your life since you were born.'

'But I'm not his real son.'

Johanna looked down at the table.

'What was his name, the Dutchman?'

'He's called Jeronimus Keyser.'

Hamish and Callum waded into the shallows and jumped into the *felucca* the two lascars had dragged out from the shore. Hamish grabbed the tiller. The lascars got in behind and took their place at the oars.

They headed toward the mouth of the estuary. Hamish stood on the thwart to get his bearings on the sandbanks, staring into the shifting patterns of shadows thrown by the rising sun. He kept the tiller rope wrapped around the big toe of his right foot, then leaped back to his place at the stern when they reached the first of the sandbars.

It was easy work for the lascars, running with the tide.

They were not alone on the sea. They were soon joined by local fishermen heading out in dugout canoes, some with flimsy patchwork sails. As the sun rose, he made out dozens of boats on the golden, sun-flecked water, among the lagoons and shallow coral reefs.

The fishers stood at the bows of their boats, poised like herons. To be out here so early some of them must have camped on the low-lying islands overnight. Some fished in groups with a shared net, others tried their luck alone with a simple hook and line or bow and arrow. A few of them had ventured to the very edge of the reef, bobbing and bouncing on the breakers.

As they tacked through the second of the sand banks, headed toward the reef, Hamish looked back at Fort Greenock. The Tsonga children were playing on the beach amidst the washing the women had hung on the bushes and rocks to dry. An oil lamp still burned in the boma. He imagined Johanna there, pummelling dough on the bench top as she worked, her cheeks rosy with anger.

He shouldn't have left like that.

He still couldn't shake this uneasy feeling he had. He fought an urge to turn the tiller and head back to shore. But he couldn't do that. They would all think he'd gone soft in the head.

'Lachlan says you're sending him to Hindustan,' Callum said.

'At the end of the season.'

'Will you send me there as well?'

'We'll see how things are with Lachlan first. I'd rather you stayed here and learned how to run things.'

Callum grinned. 'I'd like that,' he said.

The two lascars knew the waters off Delgoa Bay almost as well as Mohammed Daoud. They could find the best reefs for fishing with the same uncanny certainty that a bushman might find water in the desert. On the leeward side there were stretches of shallows and sand, where fishermen and flamingos waded among shimmering thickets of red and white mangroves. They nosed the felucca through reefs and shoals, heading out to the deeper waters out of sight of the shore.

They reached a drop-off, northeast of the estuary. Hamish could make out sea urchins on the coral heads below and dense shoals of bright-coloured reef fish. It was the perfect place to catch predators. He knew the depth plummeted here from less than ten fathoms to over two hundred, and with the full moon waxing, they would be feeding.

At this time of year, the sea writhed with creatures. Even before they started their first drift, a sailfish erupted from the water in an explosion of silver.

Hamish shouted to Callum and pointed over the starboard gunnel. There were stingrays stacked in a tower below them, five or six circles deep. Callum leaned over the side and watched them, laughing with excitement.

Even before they had a line in the water, a reef shark and a barracuda came spiralling from the deeps, curious about this newcomer on their territory.

Callum speared a grey mullet from the bait bag onto a steel shark hook, eager to be first to catch a fish. He fixed it to a cod line with a leader of chain. He swung it overhead several times and released it.

Hamish watched it streak over the surface before streaming down into the water. The rope skipped and jumped over the deck. As the lead sinker hit the bottom, Callum coiled the slack rope as Hamish had taught him to do.

They settled down to wait. One of the lascars started bailing with a baobab-seed scoop. The tub was as leaky as a rusty bath.

Hamish scanned the horizon. It was a bright, clear morning with few clouds.

On the windward side, dry sand spumed from the dunes of deserted islands. He could make out the ripple of wind blowing across the channel.

A good day to be alive. Nothing amiss, he told himself. You shouldn't have let that stupid witch doctor get into your head. You must be getting old.

CHAPTER 17

A lone frigate bird flew high above them, riding the thermals. Occasionally it spiralled down toward the waves before resuming its vigil. Standing at the tiller, Hamish altered course to follow it. He thought it was likely there were feeding fish beneath it.

The offshore breeze had died away and the indigo waters were slick as the surface of a lake. Only the gentlest of swells lifted the bow. What a fool he would have looked if he had gone back to shore this morning. It was a perfect day to fish.

They had a good catch: three red snapper, two good-sized steenbras and a bag of parrotfish. Hamish himself had hooked a monster grouper. But it was getting on toward midday now and he reminded Callum that they shouldn't be greedy. They would have to head back in soon to catch the tide. The weather could turn quickly in the afternoons. Already there were dense, white clouds mushrooming up the sky to the north. Perhaps it would finally rain.

'One last drift,' Callum said.

Hamish nodded. 'Alright, just one more.' He cut some belly fillets from a big bonito and carefully folded them onto the hooks. He squinted against the glare of the ocean at the spread of baits skipping in their wake.

Shoals of fish swam to the surface, curious. The lascars reefed the sails and they drifted toward them, hoping for a strike.

'There!' Hamish said.

The electric-blue dorsal of a large sailfish broke the filmy surface in a chaos of white water, followed by the sweep of a black sickle tail. Then it was gone.

Callum twisted around. Fish were darting everywhere in confusion, looking for refuge beneath their hull.

'Where is she?'

'She'll be back,' Hamish said.

Sure enough, he saw the beak appear behind one of the belly-shine strips he had set for it, tapping at it inquisitively with its bill.

Callum picked up the coil of cod line and fed it gently over the side between his thumb and forefinger. 'Here, my sweet,' he murmured.

'You've not got gloves,' Hamish said, and at that moment the water boiled and splashed. Callum was almost pulled out of the boat by the weight of the strike. He jammed his knees against the gunnel, but the line tore through his hands, and he screamed in pain.

'Gloves!' Hamish shouted to one of the lascars and grabbed the line to help his son.

The sailfish exploded out of the water and tail-walked across the surface. Hamish threw his weight onto the line but could not stop the run. He looked at Callum. The palms of his hands were a bloody mess, but he threw on the pair of heavy leather gloves the lascar had tossed him and tried to muscle Hamish out of the way.

'I have it,' Hamish said.

'It's my fish!' Callum shouted back and Hamish stepped back and let him take the line.

The sailfish jumped out of the water in a series of head-shaking jumps and the loops of line snaked across the deck. Hamish thought they would lose him. One of the lascars wanted to help Callum with the line, but

Hamish shook his head. Callum had never taken a fish this big before and he wanted him to have his chance.

Finally, the running line slowed, and Callum put the sole of his foot on the gunnel and started to haul her in. He was drenched with sweat and every muscle in his torso was bunched with the effort.

Hamish itched to grab the line and take over. His willpower broke, and he bent to take the loop of line behind Callum's heel.

'No!' Callum shouted. 'I can do this!'

Callum dragged the sailfish back. Hamish coiled the line onto the deck. Three times, it coiled out again, working a furrow into the gunnel, but each time the run was shorter. Hamish wondered whose strength would give out first. He would have had her in the boat by now, but Callum was only half his size.

He realized they had drifted into shallow water. One of the lascars signalled that they were in less than three fathoms and directly over razor sharp pinnacles of coral. Unless he got that line in soon, Callum would lose it.

He was so close. Hamish could see the fish hanging in the water, trying to dive into the sea canyons. He waited for the line to snap, or shred on the sharp coral, but the brass leader held.

Callum gave a shout of triumph as the sailfish struck the surface, one huge black eye staring up at them, gill plates pumping. Hamish fetched the billy and brought the heavy lead club down on its head. There was another explosion of seawater and then it stiffened and turned onto its back, its white belly exposed to the sun.

Callum pulled her in, grabbing the beak and the line in one hand, and hooking his heel around the body of the fish as he hauled her aboard. The damned thing was almost as long as he was. He collapsed onto his haunches on the deck, dripping with sweat and seawater, the fish cradled in his lap like a lover. He tore off the gloves, grimaced as blood dripped from the ends of his fingers onto the deck.

'Well done, son,' Hamish said.

Callum beamed at him. 'You see,' he said. 'I'm every bit as good as Lachlan.'

A chill went through Hamish then. There was a look on his son's face - he had never seen it before - a look of cunning and desperate hunger.

One of the lascars gave a shout. There were two sets of sails on the horizon, cutting down from the north, flying with the breeze. They had all been distracted by the struggle with the sailfish and none of them had seen it.

Hamish ran to the transom to fetch his spyglass, his laughter at the catching of the fish dying in his throat.

The *nganga* hobbled into the compound and left a small clay pot in between the roots of the ancient baobab tree. Inside it, there was a hair from the bwana woman, that he had found in her kitchen, a tortoiseshell comb from the bedside table of the white-haired boy, the one they called Nkala, and a tobacco pouch from the second bwana. He tied two scraps of cloth to a branch with some strands of banana palm.

Lachlan sat in the schoolroom and watched him, wondering what the old man was doing. He saw Mohammed Daoud's wife put something in his hand. Payment, perhaps. Then she hurried off in the other direction, towards the Tsonga village, her *capulana* pulled tight around her face.

CHAPTER 18

There were two frigates bearing straight down on them under full sail. The wind had swung around to the land, and they had the nor'easter right behind them.

'What are they doing?' Callum said. 'Haven't they seen us?'

'They've seen us,' Hamish said and lowered the spyglass. 'They're not flying colours.' He vaulted the sailfish and jumped to the tiller.

'Who are they?'

'I don't know, but they're coming straight for us.'

He shouted to the lascars to unfurl the lateen and help Callum get the flying sail sheeted home.

'Can we outrun them?' Callum asked.

'We'll soon find out.'

The wind filled the lateen like a musket shot. They started to get under way, but slowly, much too slowly. Hamish looked over his shoulder. The mass of canvas on the first warship seemed to fill the entire sky. It was five boat lengths clear of the others. The bows cut through the water straight at them. Already it was so close that he could make out the scarlet paint on the gun ports.

'Who the hell are they?' Hamish brought up the spyglass, holding the tiller with his other hand. He saw soldiers lining the rails. They were wearing uniforms, but not like any he'd seen before. They weren't Dutch and they weren't Omanis. They looked like Canarins, like Arjuna. But what would they be doing here, so far from home?

And why had they no colours at mast or stern? Pirates, then.

It was Hamish's habit to carry a musket and shot with him everywhere he went, even on the ocean. He kept it wrapped in waterproof oilcloth. Callum pulled it out of its stowage place under the stern thwart. He loaded it with his back braced against the transom, not an easy thing to do under full sail. He measured a powder charge from the flask, rammed the wadding down the barrel, fumbled for a ball from the shot bag. He rodded it down the bore with his legs braced against the mast.

He checked the pan and reclosed the frizzen.

Hamish watched him, fascinated by the lad's composure. But what good did he think that would do against a warship and a company of soldiers here on the open sea?

He looked up again. They must have seen their *felucca*. There was no chance that this was a mistake. The warship's intentions were clear. They intended to crush them under their hull.

Hamish fumbled again for the eyeglass. He made out a man standing at the bow, leaning on the forward rail with the casual air of a gentleman out to take the sea air. He was holding something, a musket perhaps.

As Hamish refocused the spyglass, he finally made out what it was. 'A cane,' he said, aloud. A pirate playing at being a dandy. Who the hell was he and what was he doing in Portuguese waters? And why was he headed for the bay? Everyone in this part of the world knew the waters here were unnavigable for big ships.

They were so close now Hamish could see the man's black curly beard and the white trailing sash of his turban.

Callum braced himself against the mast. He brought the musket to his shoulder, swinging the muzzle effortlessly up to aim, just as Hamish had taught him. Impossible to get a good shot off on a pitching boat, but he admired the boy's guts.

'I'll shoot his damned turban right off his head,' he shouted and fired. The recoil knocked him sprawling backwards into the scuppers. Hamish looked over his shoulder. The man in the turban gave him a mocking salute with his right hand.

The ship loomed over them. It was so close now he could hear the wind drumming in its sheets and the creaking of her timbers.

'Why the hell are you doing this?' Hamish screamed. He didn't mind the dying, even on a day as fine as this. He just wanted to know why. And not Callum, that was not fair. He was just a boy.

One of the lascars looked up at the three-masted monster bearing down on them, his eyes wide. 'What do we do, *effendi*?'

Hamish searched the horizon, but the land was a distant dun smudge on the sea. They would never be able to outdistance the warship. He stared at Callum's sailfish. Its eyes already milky with death. The hunter had become the hunted, but perhaps their prey had a lifeline for them.

He remembered how the fish had dived into the chasm, trying to break the line. The reef that had almost saved the sailfish might yet save them. 'Bring her to port!' he shouted.

Callum grabbed the halyard, bringing the gaff upright, and the lascars released the sheets. Hamish turned her off the wind, and for a moment the *felucca* rocked alarmingly in the water. He heard the whip of bamboo as the lateen snapped from port to starboard. Callum fastened the sheets then secured the halyard and stays. Hamish took her across the wind, gibbing hard to take her round.

'What are you doing?' Callum shouted.

'The reef! We have shallow board, and we can navigate it, but it will tear their hulls out if they try to follow.'

'How far?'

Hamish stood, his fist gripping the tiller, squinting against the glare of the ocean. He guessed they had drifted perhaps five cable lengths from the reef. He thought he could see spray jumping from one of the outcrops. He tried to gauge the distance between the first warship and themselves. With a favourable wind they might just make it.

He realised that it wasn't just their lives at stake anymore. The only lure in these waters for men like this would be Fort Greenock. A man didn't bring a small army of soldiers to drown a man and a boy. If he let this bastard get the better of him, there would be no one to protect his family.

But if this privateer knew about the fort, then he must also know he could not navigate the estuary that protected it.

A sickening thought occurred to him. He focused the eyeglass again, followed the lines of the leading frigate to the wheel at the stern of the ship. 'Mohammed Daoud,' he murmured under his breath. Dear God, that was him beside the helmsman.

'What is it?' Callum said.

'Look for yourself.'

Callum took the eyeglass, focused on the leading frigate. 'Dear God save us,' he said.

That was why this bastard was sailing into his bay with impunity: he had a man at the helm who knew every wind, every bank, every reef, and every tide. They had not come here on a whim or by accident. Now he knew why the *al-Shahadah* was late back from Ilha.

He could hear the soldiers on the deck cheering now, as if this were all a game. If he could lead these bastards onto the reef, they would not think it was so funny. Let's see them laugh when the coral chews out the bottom of their ship.

But as soon as he thought it, he realized it was no use. Mohammed Daoud knew these waters better than any man. If that really was him at the helm, he would never let that happen.

The wind shifted. The sail started luffing. Hamish tried to bring her closer to the wind, but then the breeze died away completely.

'*Inshallah,*' he murmured under his breath.

One of the lascars went down on his knees and took out his prayer beads. His fellow did the same.

'Andzile,' Callum said.

Hamish spun around. 'What?'

'It was me,' Callum said. 'It wasn't Lachlan who beat Andzile with the shovel. It was me.'

Hamish stared at him. All these years, he thought, I had it all wrong. And now it's too late.

They were in the frigate's shadow now and Hamish took a moment to admire their nemesis. She was a beautiful ship, two-decked, with over fifty cannons. Fifty paces bow to stern, he reckoned, and freshly painted, too.

Nothing to do now but brace himself. The bow wave lifted them, so that they were surfing on the crest of it. The pressure wave drove them forward.

The shadow of the bowsprit blotted out the sun. For a moment, the only sound was the hissing of the bow wave. He watched the lascars' faces. Their eyes almost rolled back in their heads as the warship rose out of the water above them.

Hamish leaped from the tiller just as their *felucca* went under, grabbing Callum by the arm. 'Take a breath!' he shouted and leaped over the side. The dhow exploded into splintered planking as the frigate's bow ripped her in two.

He didn't break for the surface straight away. He swam down to avoid the barnacle-encrusted hull that could strip the flesh off a man as it passed.

The undertow drove them even deeper, cartwheeling them into the deeps, and held them there until Hamish thought his lungs would burst. He felt Callum punching out as he struggled in Hamish's arms. He couldn't hold him any longer. He let him go then swam for the surface after him, his chest pumping.

He didn't know which way was up. He knew he had to stop swimming and let his body's buoyancy take him up. He fought the instinct to struggle. There were black spots in front of his eyes.

He hit the surface and sucked in one raking breath after another. He trod water, retching and choking, searching the bright water for his son.

Where was he, how did he lose his grip on him? He twisted around, kicking hard with his legs, trying to rise far enough out of the water to see over the waves. 'Callum!'

The boy was a strong swimmer. They could not have been under longer than a minute. He couldn't have drowned.

'Callum!'

Flotsam from the *felucca* bobbed to the surface. The bow of the warship had turned her into firewood. He saw a body and swam toward it. One of the lascars. Hamish rolled him over and grimaced. The hull of the warship had turned his head into jelly.

The sharks would come soon.

'Cal!'

And then he saw his beautiful boy, floating face down. He dived under him, put his arms around his shoulders, kicked hard back to the surface.

Callum's head lolled back, half-lidded in death, his face pale and bloodless. Hamish tried to breathe life back into him, clamping his mouth on his, praying as he had never prayed in his life, willing him back. But it was hopeless.

The frigate was turning slowly, scything a wide arc in the water. He had hoped to see her break on the reef, but Mohammed Daoud was too clever, too skilled, to allow that.

He watched her turn about, reefing sail, while the soldiers crowded the gunwales, searching the water for him. The other frigate had veered away out to sea now that the chase was over.

'I'm sorry, Cal,' he whispered. 'I'm so sorry.' It was his fault. He shouldn't have let go of him. If he'd held on his boy would still be alive.

He let his son's head dip below the water as he let him go for the last time. He watched him sink under the oily surface into the everlasting blue.

He felt for the knife in the back of his belt. He would stick it in that turbaned bastard's guts if it were the last thing he did. He started to swim, striking out with strong, steady strokes.

CHAPTER 19

Hamish knew he had no chance. He supposed the soldiers would shoot him dead in the water long before he reached the warship. Or they could just sail away and let him drown. He was miles from the shore.

Yet he had always found a way to survive before, no matter what life had thrown at him. It might be too late for Callum, but Johanna, Lachlan and Katherine were back at the fort, Rory too. He was their last hope. To kill a snake, even one many feet long, you only had to strike off the head. If he were to save his family he had to get aboard that ship and kill the man with the turban, whoever he was, whatever he was.

The ship drifted closer, fully reefed. One of the sailors threw a rope webbing over the side for him to clamber up. The soldiers were beckoning to him, cheering him on and laughing. There was a carnival atmosphere. Nothing like killing a man's son for some fine sport on a bright morning.

He clambered up the webbing. The sepoys reached out for him, shouting at him in a language he didn't understand. As soon as he was close enough, he reached into the back of his belt and brought out his knife. One swipe and he felt warm blood spray across his cheek. That wiped the smile off their bloody faces.

He leaped over the gunwale and into them. One of them lay on the deck howling, clutching his face. Another sat on his haunches, blood pulsing from his wrist. Where was the bastard in the turban?

The crowd of soldiers surged back and formed a ring around him. He heard someone shout an order from the mizzen. He didn't even see the musket, but he felt the pain as the lead ball hit him in the back of the leg.

As soon as he was down, they leaped on him. They stamped on his knife arm, another slashed at him with a bayonet. But he was beyond pain. He kept fighting. They would have to kill him to stop him now.

'I'll kill the lot of you, you bloody heathen! You killed my son!'

His leg was numb, and he couldn't move it. The press of them was crushing the air out of his lungs. Someone tried to prise the knife from his grip. He wouldn't let go, so they took a knife to his fingers.

Eventually they had him roped and trussed, his arms behind his back. They dragged him into a sitting position against the transom. It was only when they had him secured that they retreated, leaving him shouting defiance, his blood smeared over the deck.

The crowd parted and there he was, the bastard in the turban. He was swinging a silver-topped cane, which he tapped impatiently on the deck. He frowned at the two soldiers still writhing in the scuppers, stepped carefully over them to avoid an inconvenient puddle of gore. He gave a nod, and the two men were carried below still screaming.

He smoothed his moustaches and regarded Hamish with something like regret. He leisurely unwound the turban. He had long black hair to his waist, with a single white streak through the centre of it. He had different blood from the soldiers. His features were almost angular, and his skin was the palest Hamish had ever seen in an Oriental. Mixed race, then. He was tall and thin as a poker. There was a ruby on his finger the size of a walnut.

'You must be Hamish McKenzie,' he said in heavily accented English.

'Who the hell are you?' Hamish shouted at him. 'Why have you done this?'

'My name is Napoleon Gagnon. I have been sent to kill you. It is a commercial exchange. There is nothing personal in it.'

'Who sent you?'

'His name is Jeronimus Keyser. He is the governor at Trincomalee Fort. Is the name familiar to you?'

It was as if he had dashed a bucket of ice-cold water in Hamish's face. Keyser! Surely not, after all these years. That was twenty years ago. 'Keyser?'

'He hoped you would remember him. Apparently, your feud goes back many years, but *Heer* Keyser has not forgotten it. He was quite explicit in his instructions. He wants you to suffer before you die.'

He stared at the bayonet wounds on Hamish's arm, two missing fingers, his leg shattered by the musket ball. 'But I see you already have.' He shook his head with regret. 'I told *Heer* Keyser that I would bring you pain, as he asked, but it was not part of our contract. Frankly, it was a lie. I do not like *Heer* Keyser, and I admire your spirit. So, I will make your end as quick and easy as possible.'

Hamish spat at him. Napoleon grimaced with distaste and took a step back.

'Fight me like a man!' Hamish shouted, struggling with the ropes.

Napoleon smiled. 'That would be unseemly and foolhardy. Besides, even should I take up your challenge I do not think you would be able to fulfil it. Look at your leg and your hands.'

Hamish followed his gaze. The musket ball had passed straight through his thigh, shattering the bone, which was protruding through the tear in his breeches. Christ, he was right, the bastards had sawed off two of his fingers. He couldn't even feel any pain, not yet.

'They don't pay me to fight, do they, Adelaïde? They pay me to kill.'

Adelaïde?

The last thing he expected to see on a warship was the blond angel who stepped out from behind her father's white robes. She was a wisp of a thing, pale and pink-eyed, and looked as fragile as a porcelain doll. She had straight white hair combed around her face. She wore an ivory-coloured silk dress, her black shoes polished to a shine. She stood quite straight with her hands loose at her sides and regarded him with an intensity he found unnerving.

She cocked her head to one side. 'You're bleeding,' she said.

The man with the turban held out his hand and she slipped hers into his. Their fingers interlocked.

'Please, Daddy, may I?' the little girl said.

Napoleon looked down at her and frowned. 'I'm not sure you're old enough yet, my sweet.'

'But you promised me.'

'I said *perhaps*. I made no promises.'

'*Please.*'

Napoleon considered. 'Do you mind, McKenzie? It has to happen one way or the other. I would consider it a personal favour.'

He took a pistol from his jewelled belt and cocked the hammer. He handed it to the little girl. 'Now aim it straight, like I showed you. Make sure you do it correctly, the first time. We do not want this brave man to suffer more than he already has.'

Hamish thought he saw her smile. But there was no answering smile from Napoleon Gagnon, not even a flicker of the eyes. She took the pistol from her father, raised it so that she could sight along the barrel, holding it straight-armed.

She aimed at Hamish's chest and fired.

CHAPTER 20

Lachlan looked out of the window. Mohammed Daoud's boy, Musa, was sitting on the *stoep* outside the schoolroom. He had been there for almost an hour by Lachlan's reckoning.

'*Lachlan-ji*, shall we continue?' Arjuna said.

Lachlan stood up. 'Just a moment please, Mister Arjuna.' He got up and walked out onto the *stoep*.

Musa leaped to his feet. '*Effendi.*'

'What are you doing here?' Lachlan asked him in Swahili.

'They have all gone, *effendi.*'

'Who has gone?'

'My family. They have left.'

'Where have they gone?'

'I do not know. One of my father's men came early this morning. I heard him whispering to my mother. When he left my mother packed up everything and told us we must leave.'

'Then why are you still here?'

Musa stared at the ground. 'I could not run away like that. I was too ashamed. Your esteemed mother saved my life.'

Lachlan took the boy by the shoulders. 'Do you know why they left?'

Musa shook his head.

'Oh my God,' Lachlan said aloud, for in that moment he knew, but it was probably already too late.

Mohammed stood beside the helmsman, as they drifted through the banks, and heard the chant of the boy at the bow who was taking the soundings. A flock of egrets rose into the air from the mangroves on the port side. At the turn, he slatted the canvas on the jib. It filled again, with a sharp crack, when they were around the bank.

He reminded himself that his family were safe. There was nothing to worry about. He needed only to get through this day, and he would live the rest of his life as a wealthy and important man.

When Johanna saw the look on her son's face, her heart sank. 'What is it?' she said, wiping her hands on her apron. 'Tell me.'

'Warships,' he said. 'There are two frigates heading down the river.'

'That's impossible.'

Lachlan shook his head. 'Mohammed Daoud has betrayed us.'

She threw down her apron and followed him outside. It was true. Two ships, sails furled, were drifting upriver with the burgeoning tide.

Lachlan seemed eerily calm. 'They are not flying colours,' he said to her. 'They're certainly not Dutch or British, and the Omanis don't have ships like that.'

'Where's Rory?'

'He's out hunting. I've sent a runner for him. He should be back soon.'

'Is your father still out there?'

'He is. Callum too.'

'He should have been back by now.'

The first ship turned broadside and let down two longboats off the davits. Soldiers in blue and grey uniforms poured over the side and into the boats.

'Sound the alarm, Lachlan,' she said. He ran to the bell in the centre of the compound and yanked hard on the rope. It was like kicking over an ants' nest. The sound of it set men running everywhere.

But it's too late, Johanna thought, looking back at the two warships. There's nothing we can do to stop them now.

Even as he was pulling the bell rope, Lachlan was making plans in his head. He was thinking about lines of fire and staged retreat, rehearsing everything he had ever taught Sasavona's *chikunda*. He saw the big man running toward him from the other side of the compound. He had Andzile with him.

He wondered how many of his men were out with Rory. It didn't matter. They would have to make do. The fort was lost. All they could do was hold the attackers off for as long as possible while they got Johanna and Katherine away. Then they would try to slip away into the bush after them.

If only there had been more warning.

CHAPTER 21

Sasavona's men came from all directions. Lachlan yelled at them to hurry. He grabbed the key to the storeroom from the boma, then ran across the compound and threw open the doors. He went to the racks, handing each man a musket. Andzile stood next to him, passing out the leather satchels with the paper cartridges. When they were done, Sasavona led his *chikunda* across the compound to the palisades.

'Where the hell's Uncle Rory?' Lachlan said.

Just at that moment he saw him loping in through the gates. His men were in a ragged line behind him. His face was flushed with sweat, and he could barely draw breath. 'What's happening?'

'We're under attack. Two frigates.'

'I'll get the gun crews,' Rory said. 'You make sure that Johanna and Katherine get away. I'll see you up there.' He ran toward the stockade.

Lachlan went to the stables and told the boys who looked after their horses to get the two Arab mares and a bay stallion saddled up. 'Can you ride?' he asked Andzile.

'A little. I mean, I know how.'

'Good. Find my mother and my sister. Ride with them to Mangobe's *kraal*. Ask him to shelter them until we come for them. Will you do that for me?'

'My place is up there on the stockade with my father.'

'This isn't your fight anymore. We owe you a life.'

'You owe me nothing, Nkala.'

'Just look after my family. Please.'

Andzile nodded and headed off across the compound.

The sun was bright on the water and Lachlan had to put up a hand to shield his eyes. The first frigate was alongside the fort. He saw the gun ports drop open. Rory was still getting their own gun crews to their places.

'Are Johanna and Katherine safe?' Rory said.

'Andzile has gone to find them.'

'Advance cartridge!' Rory shouted to his first crew.

Lachlan went to the second cannon. Fikani was ready with a twelve-pound shot, but as Lachlan shouted the order to load, he panicked and dropped it in the dirt. When they finally loaded, the young lad on the fuse was shaking so hard he couldn't hold the makeshift linstock.

Lachlan took out his telescope and watched the first of the warships come abreast. Two ancient twelve-pound cannons against two frigates with two batteries of guns at starboard and port. This was madness.

'It's like trying to fight an elephant with one of my mother's rolling pins,' he said to Rory.

'We just need one lucky shot, Lachie.'

Rory's crew had the first cannon loaded just as if it was a drill. His lads were so excited by the chance to fire their cannon at a real target they had forgotten to be afraid. They were laughing and chattering like children.

Rory worked the elevation screw, while two of the crew levered the barrel with heavy iron bars. 'Left, left,' he shouted. 'Left, God damn it! Another hair left!'

Rory nodded to one of the other men. He had brought a copper bowl with ashes from the kitchen and some lengths of fuse wire. He stepped up and held the fuse to the vent.

'Clear!' Rory shouted. Two of the *chikunda* had coir ropes tied around the cascabel to delay the recoil. When the shot fired, the rope fizzed through their hands. They both fell over and curled up on the ground, yelling in pain.

'Where are your gloves?' Rory shouted at them.

Lachlan saw their ball hit the water and bounce across the surface, twice, three times. A plume of water spouted from the river as it finally sank, well short of its mark. One of Rory's boys stood to one side, holding a rammer with a piece of goat's fleece wrapped about the end. He plunged the fleece into a clay pot of water and was about to plunge it into the barrel.

'How many times have I told you?' Rory said. 'You don't need that much water. You'll soak the powder.' He found a rag, squeezed it out, rammed the barrel and stood back.

'Advance cartridge!' he yelled at his crew, but the boy with the shot just stood there, his mouth hanging open.

He had seen what Lachlan had seen. The leading frigate had its guns turned out. Suddenly, the hull disappeared behind a cloud of white powder smoke. The ship heeled in the water as the broadside from her upper starboard battery rocked her back on her beam.

The sound of the discharge echoed through the mangroves. The first salvo kicked showers of sand from the beach, falling well short. Then there was another flash of smoke and flame, followed by a second thunderclap, as the second deck opened up.

This time the second salvo went over their heads. The barracks and Mohammed Daoud's hut erupted into flame. The gunners were still finding their range. The next salvo, or the one after, would land right on the palisade.

'They're going to blow us to heaven,' he said.

Lachlan went to the quoin, raised the elevation on his own cannon another five degrees. There was a deafening boom as it fired. Lachlan saw the water spout fifty yards from the frigate's bow.

Rory seemed encouraged. 'We're getting closer,' he said.

Lachlan shook his head. What was the use? It was like throwing marula berries at an angry lion.

'Steady lads,' Rory shouted to his crew.

Another of the *chikunda* primed the barrel with powder and a wad of coconut fibre. They loaded their iron ball and two of the younger lads stepped in with long pieces of ironwood. They levered the barrel while Lachlan knelt down and sighted it. He waited until the second frigate came into view.

He nodded to Kotani, who held the linstock to the powder hole. The gun roared back on its wooden wheels. The stench of sulphur from the gunpowder made several of them retch. Lachlan peered through the telescope. He saw their round throw up a huge fountain of water just twenty yards from the second frigate.

So close.

Johanna went to the refectory, took Hamish's two heavy elephant guns down off the wall and started loading them. It was a laborious business, nothing like the muskets with their paper cartridges. She needed to prime the pans from a powder horn and the buckshot had to have its own wadding to keep it snug in the barrel.

Finally, it was done. She gave one of the guns to Katherine and went outside. There was a thunderous boom as the first salvo from the frigates landed inside the fort. The *stoep* shook so violently it knocked them both off their feet.

One of the cannonballs blew a hole in the thatched roof of the barracks on the far side of the compound. The concussion sent Andzile flying backwards through the air. He opened his eyes for a few moments, just long enough to see that the bottom half of his body was gone. He stared in utter astonishment then looked up at the bright blue sky and died.

CHAPTER 22

Johanna stood up. Her knees were shaking so violently she had to hold on to the veranda rail. The barracks was an inferno, and there were blackened bodies lying everywhere in the dirt.

'Katherine?'

Katherine was crouched against the wall of the boma, her hands over her ears. She couldn't stop screaming.

Johanna slapped her, then slapped her again, harder, to make her stop. She shook her by the shoulders. 'We have to get out of here. Do you understand?' She pulled her upright. She scooped up the double-barrelled elephant gun and the powder horn and dragged her towards the stockade.

Where was Hamish? Had the privateer found him out there on the open sea? No, it was impossible. Hamish couldn't be dead. She couldn't bear it if the last thing she said to him were those few angry words on the *stoep* this morning. She had slept with her back to him all last night. That mustn't be the way they said goodbye.

But why wasn't he here? Even far out to sea he would have seen the smoke and heard the cannon fire. There was nothing he could do to stop this, but she knew Hamish. He would have come back for them, no matter what.

One of the frigates fired another broadside and the sound of the discharge rolled along the river. The ground shook and the air itself seemed to shake. A round landed behind them on the boma, then another on the palisade. The stockade exploded. Splintered timber and earth mushroomed into the air.

Johanna saw Sasavona run across the compound towards them, Musa stumbling behind him. Their big sergeant had a musket in his right hand. There was blood streaming from a head wound.

'You should not be here,' he shouted at her.

'I won't leave my family.'

'I'll send Nkala and the bwana Rory after you. It's finished. Please leave!'

'I won't go without them!'

'Just get to the horses. They'll be there right after you! Musa, go with them!'

The first long boat, packed with infantrymen, was already headed for the beach.

This was no ordinary privateer, Lachlan thought, not with pretty uniforms like that and their artillery so well drilled and coordinated. Besides, the pirates on the Swahili coast were all Arabs. They had dhows, not ships of the line. If these men were from Hindustan, why had they crossed an entire ocean to attack this little outpost in the middle of nowhere?

The soldiers jumped from the boats and waded through the water with their muskets and packs held over their heads. They assembled in platoons high up the beach.

Professionals, Lachlan thought, with a chill. He could hear their officers shouting orders as the boats returned to the frigates for the next wave. Was all this just for the few thousand pounds of ivory they had in the warehouse?

Smoke and flame leaped from the gun ports of the second frigate and the salvos burst one after another along the walls. Earth and pieces of lumber rained down around him. He heard a woman screaming.

He looked over his shoulder and saw his mother and sister running across the compound. 'Get away from here!' he shouted.

He ran down the earthworks to get them, just as one of the frigates fired another salvo. One of the rounds landed behind him with a deafening roar. He kept running. He didn't hear the second ball land, but he felt the concussion. It lifted him by the seat of his pants and threw him into the air.

He blacked out for a moment. When he came to, he was lying on his face, covered in dirt. He pulled himself up onto his knees. He spat wet sand out of his mouth and looked around. Their gun emplacement had taken a direct hit. Rory was gone, the guns were gone. The ships' cannons had turned the palisades on either side to matchwood.

The smell of burning hung over everything.

'Rory!' He scrambled back up the embankment. One of the gun barrels protruded from the sand and the gun carriage lay in pieces. The claw of a man's hand lay half-buried in the earth beside it. Lachlan pulled on it as hard as he could to try to free whoever lay buried there. He suddenly found himself sitting on his haunches, holding a severed limb. The rest of the body was gone.

It was white flesh, not black, and he recognized his uncle's wedding ring.

Sasavona found him and made him drop his grisly find, then dragged him down the embankment by the shirt. 'You must get out of here,' he said.

The first longboat had beached, and a dozen soldiers leaped into the shallows. They started running up the strand.

'My *chikunda* cannot stop them, bwana. We will hold them as long as we can. You must gather the women and get away.'

Lachlan stared down the beach through the jagged holes in the timber palisade. 'Who are they?' he said.

'Canarins, or Sinhalese, perhaps. I have never seen such soldiers before.'

'But who sent them?'

'What does it matter? You must get away. Musa is with your mother and sister. They are waiting for you at the stables.'

'Where is Andzile?'

'Go, just go!'

'Come with me. They will take you to Ilha as a slave if they capture you.'

'That is why I will not let them capture me. Me and my men will cover you as long as we can, then run into the mangroves. They will never find us there. Now go, Nkala!'

What remained of Sasavona's *chikunda* had already taken up positions among the smouldering wreckage of the palisade. They were busy reloading their muskets. As the first wave of soldiers came up the beach, a volley of musket fire cracked along the makeshift barricade and scythed them down.

The training hadn't been wasted on them.

Lachlan saw the mercenaries' officer point to the wreckage of the fort in consternation. He had not been expecting resistance. He ushered his men toward the rocks at the end of the beach. Sasavona's men reloaded, and another volley of musket fire raked the second boat while it was still in the shallows.

Lachlan turned and ran towards the stable. He stopped to pick up a fallen musket and took a cartridge bag from the body of one of the men. He felt numb. Even as he ran, it was as if he was watching himself from a distance through Hamish's spyglass: a gangly young man, running crooked, his eyes glazed, and his shirt covered in someone else's blood.

As the last echo of the frigate's thirty-two pounders died away, Johanna heard the trumpeters on the beach sound the charge. The infantry emerged from behind the rocks and started to flood up the strand toward the walls. The first wave was cut down before they could even reach the *glacis*, but there were too many of them to hold back for long.

Sasavona was right. It was hopeless. The fort was in flames, the stockade had been turned into firewood by the guns, and the *glacis* was a mess of shell holes. Clods of earth from the gun emplacement and shattered timbers from the palisade littered the compound. Most of the buildings were ablaze. Burning sparks had ignited the thatch on the storeroom, and now that was alight too.

The grooms were trying to lead the horses out of the stables, but they were panicked by the fire. One of the young Arab mares looked ready to bolt. The smoke was so thick it was making Johanna choke.

She couldn't even see the beach now.

Where was Lachlan?

Finally, she saw him, silhouetted against a burned-orange sun, stumbling through the smoke. He was headed in the wrong direction, towards the *boma*. He didn't seem to know where he was.

'I'll get him,' Katherine said and went after him.

Johanna felt Musa's hand on her arm. 'No, we have to go.'

She could not go without Katherine and Lachlan. But as she struggled with Musa, a blue-coated soldier appeared through the smoke. He raised his musket and aimed.

'Musa, look out!'

It was too late. Musa's eyes went wide, and he toppled forward.

Johanna fumbled with the elephant gun. She brought it up to her waist and braced the stock under her arm. She could not remember if it was already primed. The soldier stared at her in shock. He had never seen a woman with a gun before.

The hammer snapped shut. The recoil threw her three paces backwards, and the gun flew out of her hands. For a moment she was blinded by sparks and white smoke.

She stood up slowly and stared in disgust at what she had done. The shot in the musket had been intended to take down an elephant. She had never dreamed what such a weapon could do to a man.

Sasavona raised his musket and fired. The sepoy was less than ten paces away, and the musket ball slammed into his chest. He reeled back from the force of it.

Beside him, one of his *chikunda* had finished reloading his spare musket. He handed it to Sasavona. He saw another blue coat appear out of the smoke and aimed, then changed his mind. The soldier was walking aimlessly up and down the beach, his arm hanging uselessly at his side. It had been half-severed at the elbow. He wouldn't waste ammunition on him.

Sasavona peered through the cloud of smoke rolling along the bank. He couldn't see or hear anything. His ears were ringing from the battle noise.

He wiped the sweat from his eyes and waited for the smoke to clear. When it did, he saw bodies littered up and down the strand. His men had halted the first wave, but there were more sepoys splashing into the shallows all along the beach. In a moment they would come again.

His *chikunda's* musket barrels were overheating. They couldn't reload as quickly now, and they were all running out of ammunition.

He turned to one of the men squatted beside him. 'We need more cartridge bags!'

The man nodded and ran off toward the storehouse. Sasavona felt the earth shake, The spare powder in the storehouse had caught fire and exploded.

No more ammunition, then. It was time to run.

The explosion knocked Lachlan off his feet. He got up, unsure of where he was. The storehouse was an inferno and he put up a hand to shield his face from the heat. He saw soldiers in blue and grey uniforms standing at the landward gate. How in God's name had they got there? Mohammed Daoud must have landed another body of men further up the coast, a few hours' march away. He knew there was only one way they might escape. His betrayal was complete.

One of the soldiers saw him, raised his musket to his shoulder and aimed. Lachlan dived to his left. He heard the musket ball whizz past his head and crack into the wall of the warehouse behind him.

He looked up. The man was reloading, but now his two fellows had seen him as well and they had their muskets ready. Lachlan leaped back to his feet and ran. He heard two more shots and felt the lead balls whistle past his face. He threw himself around the corner of the burning building and lay there, blinking at the sky.

He looked back at the beach. The next wave of militia was streaming toward the palisade, leaping over their own dead and wounded on the cratered sand. They clambered over the splintered timbers of the palisade, firing their muskets as they came on.

Lachlan put his back to the stone wall and waited. What in God's name was he going to do now?

He heard Katherine's voice.

He looked around the corner of the boma and saw her running through the smoke, calling his name. He knew what was about to happen, but there was nothing he could do to stop it. He shouted a warning, but it was too late.

There were two more shots and she fell to her knees. Bright blood blossomed over the front of her white blouse. She looked at Lachlan in blank surprise, tried to say something, then pitched forward on her face.

An officer appeared out of the smoke. He had a navy cutlass in his right hand and a scarlet sash around his waist. There was a smoking pistol in his other hand. He didn't see Lachlan coming at him until the last moment and didn't have time to use his sword.

Lachlan knocked him down in blind rage, using his fists and his boots. As the man fell, he dropped his sword. Lachlan picked it up and stabbed down at his throat. He felt the man's blood spray over him. He didn't wait to see if he was dead.

The soldiers at the gate had almost finished reloading their muskets.

Lachlan went at them with the cutlass. One of them fired at him point-blank, but somehow the ball missed him. He thrust the cutlass into the man's chest. As he fell forward, Lachlan stepped back to release his sword, but it had stuck fast. He had to use the heel of his boot to pry it free.

The other one was still trying to get shot into the muzzle of his Brown Bess, but his hands were shaking so hard he dropped the ramrod. He fumbled for his bayonet, reaching for it on the wrong side of his belt. He looked into Lachlan's eyes and knew it was too late. He dropped the musket and put out his hands in supplication, shouting something in his own language. Lachlan realized that he understood. It was Hindu: *Please, have mercy. I have a wife and children.*

'I had a father and a sister,' Lachlan said. He brought his sword around in a perfect arc and took him head high. The soldier was dead before he hit the ground, blood spurting from his neck.

Lachlan threw down the cutlass in disgust. Katherine was sprawled face-first in the dirt. He knelt and cradled her in his lap, holding her face in his hands. Her eyes were open, and her face was white as chalk. Already, she didn't look like his sister anymore. There was blood everywhere. Her dress was sopping with it.

He was suddenly aware of the clamour all around him. He heard a roar as the ceiling of the warehouse collapsed, and another wave of heat seared the side of his face. There were even sparks in his hair now. Through the drift of smoke, he saw soldiers clubbing at wounded men with their muskets or stabbing their writhing victims with bayonets.

There was a strange, tall creature in a white turban marching through the carnage, shouting orders. He must be their leader, Lachlan thought, the privateer who had started all this carnage. He scrambled to his feet, picked up the bloodied cutlass and charged at him. He had taken no more than a few steps when another of the soldiers appeared in front of him, raised his musket and fired.

Lachlan fell backwards, blood pouring from his head. The soldier looked down at him, satisfied that he was dead, and moved on.

There was a small hole in Musa's back just below his shoulder. A little blood oozed out of it.

Johanna turned him over and cradled his head in her lap. 'Musa?'

He was unconscious. He was too big for her to carry, so she dragged him across the stable and laid him against one of the thick ironwood posts.

We nursed him for days, she thought, and now he's almost dead again, just like that. She looked around for her daughter. 'Katherine!' She couldn't see anything. 'Kathy! Lachie!'

The smoke hid everything now.

The soldiers were inside the fort. She could hear them shouting to each other in a language she didn't know.

Four of them appeared in the doorway. Johanna scrambled in the dirt for the other elephant gun, but they were too quick for her. One of them casually knocked her senseless with the stock of his musket.

CHAPTER 23

When Johanna came to, she was lying on her back, her legs spread and her skirts around her hips. She rolled onto her side and retched. There was blood on the straw underneath her, and she realised it was coming from her.

The four soldiers stood over her. They were pleased with their booty. Their leader had his thumbs in his belt, grinning. He was a scarred brute with a luxuriant moustache. He said something and the others laughed.

Johanna had no doubts about what they planned to do to her. Well, she would teach them a lesson about McKenzie women.

As he knelt between her legs, she reached for the dagger in his belt. But the knock on her head had taken away her strength. She closed her fingers around the ivory handle, but she couldn't pull it free. The world started to spin, and she groaned. Her head fell back onto the straw. The soldier suddenly realised what she had tried to do. He jerked back, shocked at her defiance.

There was no more laughing after that. One of the men grabbed her arms and held them above her head. The other two took her ankles, forcing them apart so she was spread-eagled on the dirt. The one with the moustaches shucked off the belt with the knife and pulled down his breeches. He was erect already. As he bent over her, she spat in his face.

Napoleon Gagnon picked his way through the smoking wreckage of the fort, holding out a hand to help Adelaïde across the worst of it. Once they were inside the compound, the going became a little easier. He manoeuvred her delicately around a body, or what was left of one. He warned her to step carefully so that she didn't dirty her shoes in a puddle of blood.

He produced a perfumed handkerchief and held it to his nose. He gave a spare kerchief to his daughter.

He looked around, disgusted. What a waste! Shelling this damned fort had eaten into his profits. Who would have thought these damned niggers would have put up such a fight? He had taken at least twenty percent casualties and used more than he had budgeted for in powder and shot. He had hoped to defray some of his costs with ivory and slaves, but he only had a handful of prisoners so far and the warehouse was an inferno.

He saw his men lining up a few women they had found hiding in the mangroves, together with some Tsonga who were too badly wounded to keep fighting. His captain asked what he wanted him to do with them.

'Get the doctor to them.'

The captain looked surprised.

'If we can get some of them to the slave blocks in Zanzibar it may reimburse us in some measure for the capital we have lost storming this pigsty.'

The heat from the burning storehouse was so intense he could get no closer than twenty paces. Mohammed Daoud had given him a rough estimate of the inventory. He had said it was creaking with ivory, zebra skins and gleaming copper wheels. Napoleon had reckoned on another small fortune in teak and ebony.

The gunnery captain would pay for this. He would whip him raw.

He heard screams coming from the stables. He strode across the compound and found four of his men bent over a woman. They had spread-eagled her in the straw in front of one of the horse stalls.

He tapped his cane on an ironwood post to let them know he was there. The men jumped back, terrified. The one on top of her, a sergeant with a thick black moustache, scrambled to his feet, fumbling with his breeches.

The woman sat up. She clutched at her torn shirt and pulled her skirts back down over her legs. From the looks of it they had not gone too far with their amusements, though there was blood in her hair where one of them had hit her.

'I apologize for the behaviour of my men,' he said to her. 'Straight out of the gutter most of them.' He took his pistol from his belt and pointed it at the sergeant with the moustaches. 'You know my orders about abusing women,' he said in Hindi. 'I will not abide it.'

'You can't stop us,' the man said. 'This is part of our wages. You don't pay us enough as it is.'

Napoleon shot him through the heart. The other three, knowing they would receive little mercy either, drew their swords. One of Napoleon's officers appeared at his shoulder, but he waved him away. He drew his sabre and asked Adelaïde to please stand back so that she was not inconvenienced.

As he suspected, they did not know how to properly use their weapons. Fodder for the cannons, these types. The first one tried to rush him. He knocked aside the intended blow and, with a flick of his wrist, opened the man up from breastbone to groin. The man fell to his knees, trying to hold his insides from spilling on the floor.

Napoleon let the other two see what lay in store for them and then engaged them.

Even though it was two against one, he quickly had them backed into a corner. He slashed one man on the arm then took off a piece of his ear, playing with him. Really, he would have to have a word with his sergeant-at-arms. Without their muskets these men were all but useless.

One of them started to weep, begging for his life. Seeing the way of it, the other threw down his sword as well.

Napoleon called his officer over. 'Take them back to the ship. Fifty lashes for both of them.'

Johanna heard the pistol shot and saw the soldier who had tried to rape her fall dead. It came to her through a daze of pain and shock. She thought for a moment that she was dead, because there was an angel standing over her.

'Hello,' she said.

'Hello.'

'What's your name?'

'I'm Adelaïde.'

Johanna tried to sit up. She saw a flash of steel, and a thin, dark man in a white turban and robes killed another of her attackers with his sword. She felt numb and dazed. It came back to her slowly: the ships, the bombardment, Katherine running away through the smoke. This wasn't heaven at all. She had woken up in hell.

The man in the turban appeared at the girl's side. There was a smear of blood on his sword. 'I am very sorry for this. I cannot abide the abuse of women.'

'My daddy says that's not part of his job,' Adelaïde said.

'May I ask your name, *madame*?'

'Johanna,' she whispered.

'Your husband is Hamish McKenzie?'

She nodded.

Napoleon held out his hand to one of his officers. The man took the pistol from his belt and passed it to him. Napoleon cocked it and aimed it at her chest.

'Not in front of the girl,' Johanna said.

Adelaïde gave her a curious smile. 'It's all right,' she said. 'I don't mind.'

'Mrs. McKenzie, I am required under the terms of my contract to end the lives of you and your family.'

'What?'

'My services have been paid for. There is nothing I can do for you. I am to advise you that this is done at the request of Governor Jeronimus Keyser. He wants you to remember what you have done and repent of it before you die.'

'Jeronimus? Dear God.'

'I am afraid God is not here. Only me.'

'You'll never get Hamish.'

'That was the easy part.'

The way he said it left no room for doubt. Hamish was gone then and Callum too. So, what was there to live for?

'Does Jeronimus know he fathered my oldest boy?'

Napoleon's eyes flickered with interest, but his aim did not waver. 'I think that would be news to him.'

'Just do it,' she said and closed her eyes.

She didn't feel anything. He shot her through the heart, making it as quick and painless as possible.

CHAPTER 24

The soldiers were everywhere. Sasavona could hear them shouting to each other, in their strange language, over the sound of the screams. The acrid stink of smoke and gunpowder made him nauseous. He retched into the dirt. When he had finished, he tossed aside his musket. No good going back to the *senzala*. These bastards would burn it down, and anyone they found alive would be taken away as slaves. He hoped his wives had had the sense to escape into the mangroves with the goats and the children.

He started to run blindly through the smoke and tripped over a body. The dead man sat up and groaned. It was one of the bwanas. He couldn't make out who it was straight away as his face was a mask of blood.

Ah, it was Nkala.

He tried to stand him up, but he was too heavy. When Lachlan was a child, Sasavona used to carry him around the compound on his shoulders. Now he could barely drag him ten paces through the sand.

He looked around. Hard to see anything through the smoke but it also meant the soldiers couldn't see them. They didn't have much time. They couldn't go back to the river through the stockade, or what was left of it, because the beach was still swarming with soldiers. The smoke cleared for a moment, and he saw a gaping hole in the palisade on the landward side. He glimpsed a grove of mango trees and the mangrove swamp beyond.

'Can you walk?'

Lachlan could stay on his feet if Sasavona supported his weight. Together they staggered over the smouldering ruins of the eastern stockade. Sasavona heard a shout, and a musket ball zipped past his head. One of the soldiers had spotted them making their escape. But then another curtain of smoke billowed across the compound. By the time it had cleared, they were through the wreckage of splintered timber and churned earth and into the mango grove.

Sasavona leaned Lachlan against a tree trunk and stopped to get his breath. He winced in pain. He had burned his bare feet on the burning timbers. He saw a dugout canoe beached on the sand, left behind by one of the local fishermen. It was their best chance.

'Leave me here,' Lachlan mumbled. 'Save yourself.'

'I'm not leaving you, Nkala. Now lean on me.'

They stumbled through the trees to the water's edge. He manhandled Lachlan into the boat, pushed it into deeper water, then jumped in after him. He picked up the oar and started to row. If they could reach the mangrove swamp on the other side of the river, the soldiers would never find them.

He looked back at the fort but couldn't see much, just the orange glow of the fires through the haze, and the shadowy figures of the soldiers as they moved about the beach. A pall of smoke hung low and greasy across the green river. He spared a glance at the two frigates anchored midstream. If anyone on the ships had seen them, he doubted they would think them important enough to worry about.

The bilge in the dugout was dark with blood. Where was it coming from?

Lachlan tried to sit up.

'Stay down.'

'Where are we going?'

'We're going to hide in the mangroves.'

'Can't they see us?'

'I don't think so. There's too much smoke. Even if they can, what are they going to do about it? They won't waste their time for one *kaffir* in a boat, right?'

One of the African slaves was trying to fight the soldiers with his bare hands. He was an old man, and frail. His men thought it was comical and took it in turns to prod him with their bayonets as he yelled and flailed at them with his fists.

Before Napoleon could shout an order to stop, one of the soldiers got tired of the game and shot the old man in the knee.

Napoleon hated waste. That man would be no good for the slave block now. But that was the mentality of the common soldier. They were too stupid to understand that there was no point in shooting a man unless there was profit in it.

He walked up to the soldier who had fired the shot and cut off the end of his nose with a flick of his sword point. The man gave a high-pitched scream and dropped to his knees, cradling his face in his hands. Blood wormed through his fingers. With his other hand, he scrabbled in the dirt for the tiny piece of flesh. What, did he think he could tie it back on?

The *kaffir* was writhing in the dirt, clutching his knee, howling. That his Adelaïde should have to witness such stupidity. Still, it was a lesson for her. She should never underestimate the idiocy of the ordinary soldier.

'What's your name?' he asked the slave. He had to shout to make himself heard over the sound of the boma as it burned.

The man continued to shriek and writhe.

Napoleon put a boot on his neck to keep him still and leaned over him. He took out his pistol and showed it to him. 'Answer my questions, and I will put you out of your misery,' he said in Swahili. 'Do you understand?'

The man nodded, gasping through the pain.

'What is your name?'

'Hit... Hitsakile.'

'All right, Monsieur Hitsakile, tell me where I can find Lachlan McKenzie.'

The man shook his head.

'I've looked all over this damned fort, and I can't find him, living or dead. Where is he?'

'You fucker of goats,' Hitsakile said in Xitsonga.

Napoleon stood on the black bastard's leg where the lead ball had gone in. Hitsakile shrieked.

'Where's Lachlan McKenzie?' he repeated.

Hitsakile spat in his face.

Napoleon sighed. He had four definite kills and a probable. The youngest of McKenzie's two sons had drowned under the keel of his flagship and McKenzie himself had died right in front of him. He had eliminated the wife and he had seen the body of the daughter. His men had pulled what was left of another white European from the wreckage of the gun emplacement. Was that the last of them? He would like to be sure.

He had them rope the old man up by his thumbs on the baobab tree and had one of his captains take the stock whip to him. Thirty strokes. Fifty. They laid the man's back bare to the bone. Still, he wouldn't say anything, except to curse them all in his own gibber. He died hanging there in the ropes.

One of his officers brought him Mohammed Daoud, who fell on his knees in front of him wailing that one of his sons was dead. Well, what did he expect him to do about it? Napoleon ignored him and told his infantry captain that he wished to return to the frigate immediately. He would like his prayer mat and a glass of French brandy, served in the crystal, if you don't mind.

He had had enough of dirt and unpleasantness for one day.

The Tsonga believed there was something magical about the mangroves. Everyone claimed to have seen the women-fish who lived there, what the bwanas called manatees. It was common knowledge that if you stayed there too long you would fall into a charmed sleep.

It was true, Sasavona thought, as he paddled the canoe through the tangled lattice of roots, because he had to fight to keep his eyes open. It could be exhaustion from the battle, or perhaps it really was the spirits of the forest working a spell on him.

He looked up and saw egrets and pelicans nesting in the high branches. Flocks of them rose into the air, startled by his arrival. He supposed the soldiers could follow his passage from the shore easily enough just by watching the birds, but he didn't expect them to follow him in here.

It was like no other forest he had ever seen. The overhanging branches of the mangroves formed gloomy tunnels and there were barnacles encrusted on the trunks right up to the high-tide mark. The tree roots formed palisades of arched stilts and air roots thrust up through the sand in knobbly spikes.

He shuddered. He had always avoided coming to this place. He had heard so many stories about the restless ghosts who lived in the mangroves, but today the choice was to hide in here or become a ghost himself.

He threw down the oar and slithered into the warm, waist-deep water to push the canoe further up the bank. The mud was slippery, and sticky as honey. It didn't smell like honey, though. It stank like a dead animal. He heard something slide into the water close by, perhaps a crocodile. He was too exhausted to care.

He curled into a ball, protected by the writhing arms of the tree roots and stared into the shallows, a breeding ground of prawns, lobsters, starfish and crabs. Shoals of tiny silvery fish leaped in and out of the water.

He could still smell the smoke from the burning fort. Now and then he heard the solitary crash of a musket as the soldiers chased one of his brothers through what remained of his village. The soldiers could not stay there very long, he thought. The frigates would have to make their way downriver and out to sea again with the turning of the tide. Then he and Nkala would make their escape.

He thought about his wives and Andzile. Had any of them survived?

He remembered that this was what the *nganga* said would happen. Then he fell asleep.

CHAPTER 25

Sasavona woke with a start to the call of a screech owl. It was dark. Fish like tiny sparks lit up the water, and he heard the scuttling of a thousand crabs all around them.

He sat up. 'Nkala, are you awake?' He supposed what he meant was, 'Are you alive?'

Lachlan mumbled something. Sasavona was relieved and more than a little surprised. Why was he not dead, with such a wound?

He put his hand outside the canoe and realized there was only mud underneath them. The tide was on the turn. 'Nkala, we have to get away from here now.'

He slithered down the bank, sinking to his knees in the mud. It took all that remained of his strength to drag the canoe to the water line. The mangroves were silent and ghostly in the moonlight. On foot he could never have found his way out of here, but in the dugout, they could just let the tide take them through the water channels. Once they were out in the bay they could make their escape. He would row all the way to Sofala if he had to. He wasn't going to end up on a slave block on Ilha.

Lachlan came to, as the bow of their canoe crashed into the surf.

'Hold on!' Sasavona shouted, raising the oar from the water as another huge wave broke over them, soaking them through. Their dugout swung wildly as it danced over the break line.

Lachlan's head hit the bulwark. The pain jolted him fully awake, and suddenly he was covered in a greasy, stinking sweat. He leaned forward and retched into the bilge.

Sasavona was braced in the stern, smeared with blood and muck.

Where were they? Lachlan couldn't remember anything. 'What happened?'

Sasavona didn't answer him. He was too busy trying to guide the canoe through the reef.

And then it came to him in a sudden shock. 'Where's my mother?' Lachlan said.

'She's saved, Nkala. I saw her riding away on a horse with Katherine and the boy, Musa.'

'Katherine's dead. Tell me the truth.'

'That is the truth, Nkala.'

'I saw Katherine die.'

'Alright! I don't know what happened to her. I don't know what happened to Andzile or any of my wives either. For now, we are alive. Let that be enough.'

Their little boat shuddered as they broached another of the breakers.

Lachlan twisted around. The moon was low in the sky and soon it would be completely dark. All he could make out was a froth of surf on the reef and the orange glow of the still-smouldering fires from the fort upriver. 'You should have left me there,' he said.

'So the soldiers could kill you?'

'It would have been better.'

'How is it better to be dead?' Sasavona picked up the oar and paddled furiously towards the north star.

'There's no one left. I have nothing left to live for.'

'You have everything to live for. You must find the man who did this and destroy him. Only then can the ghosts of your family rest in their graves. Never forget that Nkala. Promise me you will not give up until it is done.'

Lachlan stared at the lights on the mastheads of the two frigates on the bay. The strange crow in the white turban and Mohammed Daoud were on one of those ships, so very close. But there was nothing to be done about them for now.

Sasavona was right. He could not give up. His job now was to find the men who did this and make them pay.

'Promise me!' Sasavona repeated.

'I promise,' Lachlan said.

CHAPTER 26

They drifted under a blazing sun. Sasavona used seawater to clean Lachlan's wound. The water loosened the crust of blood from his face and hair. When it was done, he started to laugh.

'What's so funny?'

'Now I see why you are not dead.'

'Why?'

'The lead ball could not penetrate your thick head. It has gouged a big crease in it, but your brains are still inside. If you have any!'

Lachlan supposed at any other time he might have laughed too. But not today.

Sasavona lay down the oars, unable to struggle any more against the current. They were somewhere in the middle of the bay. The coast was a thin dark line on the horizon. The riding lights of the privateers' frigates were already far behind them and almost invisible now.

'Try to sleep,' Sasavona said. 'Tomorrow is another day.'

The morning brought with it new torments. A pitiless sun rose quickly up the sky. They had no shade and Lachlan felt his skin crisping like a buck roasting over a fire. He could not stop retching and the pain in his head was unremitting. It felt like his skull was about to crack.

All he could think about was water. He could not remember the last time he drank anything. He even thought about taking a handful of brine from the side.

Just to wet your lips, some crazed voice in his head whispered. *Just a little.*

But even half-mad and half-dead he knew that if he did that, it would truly be the end.

His thoughts tumbled end over end inside his head. He remembered his father coming into the kitchen – was it really only the previous morning – and asking him to come fishing. Had that been the stubborn old bastard's way of saying he was sorry? He would never know.

Then he thought about the half-breed with the tail of his turban flying as he ran through the stockade gates. He promised himself he would not rest until he found him.

The sun beat down. He tossed in delirium. Life, or the prospect of it, drew further and further away.

Lachlan woke to a droplet of rain on his cheek. His eyes blinked open. It was dark, yet a moment ago they had been baking under a midday sun. Another drop of rain spattered onto his forehead, and he stirred himself awake.

Sasavona lay sprawled near the stern, mumbling in his own language, talking to his gods perhaps.

Lachlan nudged him with his foot. '*Tsonga malume!* It's going to rain!' His tongue was so swollen that he could barely form the words.

Sasavona groaned and opened his eyes.

Anvil clouds, the colour of slate, hurried from the north. The air felt eerily still.

In the distance, Lachlan saw lightning arc across the sky followed by a distant growling of thunder. 'Do you see?' he said.

Sasavona nodded.

A single gust of wind shook the boat. 'This is not good for us,' Lachlan said.

He watched a squall race across the ocean towards them, dimpling the water. Within minutes it swept over them, soaking their burned and blistered bodies and whipping up the waves. The shock of the icy cold sea spray after the hot wind took his breath away.

He cupped the rainwater in his trembling hands, snuffling like a dog as he sucked the moisture with cracked and bleeding lips. Another gust of wind came from nowhere and rocked their canoe so violently he thought they were going to keel over.

He looked around. This storm seemed to have come from nowhere. For weeks now, they had all been praying for the monsoon. Well, now it had arrived.

The waves rose and a breaker swarmed over the bow and spun the little boat like a top. Sasavona scrambled for the oar and tried to bring the nose into the wind, but it was hopeless.

Wave after wave crashed on top of them, and each time they went under Lachlan expected to find himself in the sea. He clung desperately to the sides of the dugout. As they dropped into the trough between each swell, he got onto his knees and tried to bail with his bare hands.

The pounding seemed to go on for hours. Finally, he gave up bailing, too exhausted to continue. It was hopeless. He was vomiting seawater through his mouth and nose, and his body ached with chill. His eyes burned from the salt. He could barely see and the howling of the wind deafened him.

He looked at Sasavona and saw his own desperation mirrored on the other man's face. This must end soon. A mountainous sea rose ahead of them, its crest turned to foam by the force of the wind. They rode it to the peak and as they descended into the swell, he decided that this time they must go under.

Lachlan was flung forward, and the two men clung together in the scuppers. He was sure that they were going to die.

'Goodbye, Mongoose, my friend!' Sasavona shouted over the crash of the waves.

As their tiny canoe plunged into another massive swell, Lachlan heard something over the hiss of the wind. It sounded like cannon fire. He peered into the raging dark, but he couldn't see anything, the wave peaks were too high.

A breaker passed underneath them and sent them into a deep trough. When they rose out the other side Lachlan was afforded, just for a moment, a dizzying glimpse of a beach and a line of palm trees. The palms were bent almost to the ground by the violence of the wind, and a line of surf marched towards them.

Then he saw where the cannon fire was coming from. There was a froth of white water where the storm waves threw themselves on a submerged wall of coral reef. If they came down on top of that, their bodies would be stripped and pounded into mincemeat.

Their little canoe skidded down the face of the next wave so steeply he was sure they would drive straight under. Sasavona flailed with the oar, trying to turn the bow away from the reef, but it was hopeless. The dugout had been built to navigate the rivulets of the estuary mangroves not the open ocean. Yet another wave broke over them and all but swamped them. For a moment, their canoe wallowed in its wake.

The sound of the reef was thunderous now. Above them the sky seemed to peel apart as a lightning fork arced across the sky. He saw the jagged teeth of the reef exposed as a rip trailed out from the beach.

Sasavona shouted with terror and redoubled his efforts with the oar. But there was no way out of it. Still Sasavona would not release the oar, searching for a passage through.

They were so close now that Lachlan could see gouts of foam rise into the air from the rocks. He remembered a Dutch ship of the line sinking off the coast here a few years before. He and Hamish had found countless bodies of the sailors drowned on the beach and it hadn't been pretty. Coral could strip a man's flesh off his bones quicker than a shark. It was not the way he would have chosen to die. But God never gave a man that sort of choice, as his uncle Rory had once reminded him.

He and Sasavona put out a hand and gripped each other's arms.

'If we do not see each other again in this world,' Lachlan said, 'I will see you in the next.'

'Forget the next world. Find the crow in the turban. Do it for all of us.'

Lachlan kicked off his boots ready to swim if he survived the reef. 'Look out,' he said.

A king wave reared over Sasavona's shoulder, foaming at the crest. It picked up their dugout and spun it around. Sasavona fell backward off the stern, sending the oar flying.

It hit Lachlan a glancing blow on the head, opening his head wound again. He went sprawling into the scuppers. He felt the boat tip, and then he was in the sea.

He was helpless, cartwheeling under the water, and he braced himself for the impact on the reef and for the pain. Bright lights flashed behind his eyes, and his chest felt like it was about to burst.

He bobbed to the surface briefly, choking and coughing, and gulped in one precious lungful of air before the breakers dragged him under again.

It was like being shaken in a giant fist.

He came out of the maelstrom a second time, coughing seawater through his nose. His eyes burned from the brine, and his lungs were on fire. He kicked furiously, looking for the shore.

Another breaker picked him up and carried him, tumbling, through the surf. Suddenly he felt soft sand under his feet, and he tried to stand. He fought desperately against the rip as it streamed back from the strand.

The backwater rushed past him. Another wave took him and tossed him on the beach like driftwood. He lay in the in the shallows, retching.

He crawled as far as he could up the shore until he was beyond the tide line and then he collapsed, unable to move.

It was still raining.

'Sasavona,' he said, but he had no strength left to look for him, or even to raise his head.

CHAPTER 27

Dawn came bright and clear. The sky was a washed blue, and the lagoon was flat, but the wind was still gusting, and Lachlan had to shield his eyes from the blown sand.

He raised himself on one arm. 'Sasavona?'

The swell was still booming on the reef, but the tide had dropped back, leaving the strand strewn with flotsam and palm fronds. Everything was covered in a thick scum of foam from the waves.

A gull fished above the lagoon. It splashed into the water and then flapped back into the air a moment later with a silver fish wriggling in its beak. Lachlan's own belly growled with hunger. And water, he needed water.

But first he had to find Sasavona. He tried to stand, but he was too weak. He could barely raise himself off his knees.

He saw something further along the beach. At first, he thought it must be a big fish thrown up on the sand by the retreating tide, but it was too large for that. Besides, a beached fish was white or grey. He dragged himself towards it on his belly.

As he got closer, he realised it was Sasavona.

One brown arm was flung out from his body. The rest of him lay face down, half-buried in the sand. Lachlan heard the clicking of crabs hurrying back to their holes, angry at being disturbed in the middle of their feast.

He winced as he rolled him over.

There was not much left that he could recognise. The waves had smashed him against the coral and the crabs and sea lice had done the rest. He closed his eyes and said a prayer to his gods, wishing his friend an easy passage in the world to come. Then he rolled his body over again so the seabirds could not get to his eyes. He did not have the strength to bury him. He hoped Sasavona's spirit would forgive him.

He lay there, his head rested in the crook of his arm. It would be so easy to stay where he was, to just give up. He was so tired, and every little movement required a massive effort. But then he thought about the crow in the turban, and Mohammed Daoud, and his promise to Sasavona. He forced himself to keep moving.

The first thing was to find water. His lips were cracked and swollen from salt, and he could barely swallow. He looked around. The beach was littered with shiny green coconuts. If he had a machete, he could have split them open and drunk the liquid inside. He searched Sasavona's body but could not find the bone handled knife he always carried with him. He must have lost it when they hit the reef.

He made out a sand bar two or three hundred paces away. That meant a river with fresh water. If he was going to live, he had better get there.

He started to crawl through the sugary, brown sand. Two days ago, he could have crossed the distance in a hundred strides. Now it took him the better part of an hour. A family of rock rabbits watched his progress with startled interest before scampering back to their holes.

There were times he didn't think he was going to make it, but then he imagined Sasavona's voice in his head, urging him on, and he kept going.

He slid down the sand bar. He guessed the sea must cross the breakwater every time there was a storm, like the one the night before, flushing it clean.

He cupped a handful of river water and brought it to his lips, then sniffed at it. He groaned with relief and plunged his head in, drinking until his belly was bloated. He drank so much he retched half of it up again.

Other animals had come down for a drink. A kudu with massive, spiralled horns stared at him in astonishment when it saw him, then fled back up the bank with water still dripping from its muzzle. He realised he could not stay down here long. There would be crocodiles living on the banks, and lions and hyenas would come down for water sooner or later.

Already he felt the river water crusting on his skin and the sun burning his blistered back. He had to find shade. There was a sweet thorn tree a hundred paces away, further up the bank.

He started to head towards it.

Even a hundred more paces was too far. The shade tree might as well have been Cape township. He couldn't do it. He didn't have the strength.

'Don't you dare die,' a voice said.

He looked up, thinking it was Sasavona, but it couldn't be.

'Father?'

Hamish stood there, a rifle over one shoulder, his thumb tucked in his belt. His mop of salt-and-pepper hair was dark with sweat, like he'd just come back from a hunt. 'I'll not have a boy of mine give up like this.'

'I thought you were dead,' Lachlan said.

'What kind of a son did I raise? You see why I wanted to send you off to clerk in an office. You're soft.'

'I did my best at the fort...'

'You let me down. Where's your ma, boy? You should have died before you let anyone lay a hand on her!'

Lachlan put out a hand, hoping Hamish would help him up, but then he was gone. No one was going to save him now. He had to do this himself.

His head was bleeding again. He felt blood trickle down his face and drip off his chin into the sand. Nothing to be done about that. He raised himself on his elbows and set off toward the tree.

He leaned against the rough bark and slid down onto his haunches, exhausted. He had water but no food. and he had lost a lot of blood from the head wound. That would account for his fatigue. He felt feverish. He might have an infection as well. If he didn't get help soon the wound would kill him long before starvation.

He put a hand on the bark of the tree to steady himself and tried to get back on his feet, but his legs wouldn't hold him.

He wondered how far up the coast he and Sasavona had drifted in the dugout and how far he might be from help. He knew he couldn't survive out here very long on his own. He was badly knocked around and he didn't have a weapon. The bush was unforgiving. It was just a matter of what predator would find him first.

A shadow flickered across the sun. He looked up and saw a vulture circling overhead. It glided in to land, its great black wings outstretched. It settled on some rocks twenty paces away.

It didn't take long for them to spot you out here.

The vile bird twisted its head on its scaly red neck and peered at him. It was enormous. He had never seen one this close before and it terrified him. It watched him impassively, like an undertaker measuring him for his last suit.

'Damn you!' he shouted. 'Get away from me!' He searched around for a weapon. He found a smooth river pebble and hurled it in the bird's direction. The stone clattered into the rocks. The bird hopped back a few paces but remained watchful.

He could smell it. Like rotten meat. He found a large branch and used a stone to knock off the long, silver thorns. He practised hefting the branch like a club, left-handed. It made him feel a little better. The bird preened its feathers and watched him. Occasionally he tossed another pebble at it. Once he hit it, high on its body. It squawked and flared its wings, but then settled back into its hump-backed vigil, unperturbed. It could afford to be patient.

Lachlan knew he had to get himself moving. There were few settlements around the bay. The closest was Ferreira's place up near the old fort at Lourenco Marques. But it would take a fit man more than a week to get there on foot from Greenock. He would be dead long before that.

He didn't think he and Sasavona could have travelled very far in the dugout. He guessed that Delgoa might be around the point of the bay he could make out to the south. There was no sign of the frigates, and once the soldiers were gone, the Tsonga would return. They would help him.

If he could get himself moving again, he would follow the coast south. If he had to divert inland, he would use the termite mounds to navigate. The very tips of the nests always pointed north. Hamish had told him once that they were God's compass.

But he was loath to leave the water, and out of the shade the heat was stupefying. He decided to rest through the heat of the day and then strike out when it was cooler.

After a while he felt his head lolling forward. He told himself he mustn't fall asleep. He had to stay alert for predators. But inevitably fatigue got the better of him, and he woke with a start to see the vulture hopping toward him, its talons spread. He yelled and ducked out of the way of that terrible beak then scrambled in the sand for the sweet thorn branch and struck out at it, landing a swipe across its wrinkled, red neck.

It hopped away out of reach again. He screamed at it and, unable to find another pebble, he threw a handful of sand at it. The bird settled back to wait again, roosting on a piece of driftwood.

It was then he thought he heard voices.

He kept quite still and listened. There it was again. He was about to call out then checked himself. No, it couldn't be. He was hearing phantoms.

I'm losing my mind, he thought. I have to get myself moving.

He pulled himself upright. He would leave the water and the shade behind and take his chances. He struggled to get to his feet.

Hamish stood in front of him, his hands on his hips. 'Don't you give in,' he said. 'I forbid it. You will keep walking. You won't die here.'

Lachlan clawed at the trunk but couldn't pull himself upright a second time. He slipped slowly to his knees.

Two other vultures planed their wings in the sky, circling. One of them angled down into the branches of a fever tree. Lachlan knew they were cowards and they only ever approached like this when it was almost over.

'Get away,' Lachlan said and pitched forward on his face.

CHAPTER 28

'What, in the name of all that is holy, was that?'

Jorge Ferreira pulled on the reins and shouted at his *voorlooper* to stop the wagon. Catia pointed to the vultures circling over the Mfele river. It could be a buffalo or lion kill, but that was unusual so close to the river. Crocodiles dragged their kills under the water and took them to their mudholes. They wouldn't leave carrion on the bank.

'We should take a look,' Catia said.

'I'll send one of the boys.'

'It's only over the hill there,' she said and jumped down from the running board.

'Come back here,' Jorge said.

'I'll do it.'

Jorge shook his head. Well of course she will. This daughter of his thought she could do everything. 'What's the point?' he shouted at her.

'The point is that I want to,' she said. She reached around behind the transom and took out the Charleville musket. She checked that it was primed and fully loaded. 'Are you coming with me?'

'You're not going anywhere. You'll do as I say.'

'*Sim*, Papa,' she said and headed towards the river. He asked himself again why God had made women. Was it just to torment all decent, God-fearing men? He left the wagon with his *voorlooper*, grabbed the spare musket - she'd left him the fowler, for God's sake, a woman's weapon - and went after her.

Catia heard the surf pounding on the other side of the sandbar. The swell was still up after the storm the night before. As she got closer to the river, she moved more cautiously. There were always animals down here, mostly springbok and gazelle, but sometimes lions as well. She stopped when she saw something lying under a sweet thorn tree.

It was a man.

Holy Mother of God there were vultures as well. She shouted at them as she ran up the sand, and they raised their wings and fluttered off. But they only retreated a short distance, still unwilling to give up their prey. Catia didn't want to waste good shot on a bird, so she threw a rock at the nearest one and it retreated again. There were three of the revolting creatures.

Catia laid the heavy musket on the ground and knelt down beside the man.

What a mess.

Whoever he was, he was a European. He was very young, not much older than her, despite the pelt of stubble on his cheeks. But he had the body of a man sure enough. Stand him upright and she guessed he must be well over six feet tall.

He lay prone. He was still partly conscious, God help him. He was in a bad way. The damned birds had torn strips of flesh off his back and shoulders and the skin had been burned off his face by the sun, leaving raw pink patches. She rolled him onto his side. *Santa Mãe de Deus!* There was a massive, seeping wound in his temple, a crease the width of her forefinger. Hard to tell how much damage there was with so much blood everywhere.

His face was crusted with gore. Underneath, his skin was the colour of chalk.

She heard her father stumble up the slope behind her. Two of their *chikunda* followed.

He put his hands on his knees, out of breath from the long trudge uphill through the sand. Out of condition these days, she thought. Too much Hollander gin and not enough healthy exercise.

Jorge took one look and shook his head. 'He's not going to make it.'

'He looks strong enough to me.'

The man moaned and tried to move. Catia held his head in her hands. 'Give me some water,' she said.

Jorge handed her his canteen. She wet the man's lips and his eyes flickered for a moment. Then they rolled back in his head again.

'Who do you think he is?' she said.

'My guess, it's one of the inglês from Delgoa Bay. He must have survived the attack on the fort. But the runner who brought me the news told me the pirates hadn't left anyone alive.'

'Well, he was wrong, wasn't he? I wonder how he got here?'

'By boat, I suppose. It's too far to swim.' He bent over him. 'That's a musket ball did that.'

'I know what a musket wound looks like.' She cradled him in her arms. 'But the ball didn't go into his brain. If he gets some proper care, he'll be able to tell us what happened himself.'

'The vultures have been at him, and he looks like he's been cooked. He's as good as dead. If it were a horse, you'd shoot him.'

'But he's not a horse, is he?'

The young man mumbled something, and his hands scrabbled for the water. She dribbled some more onto his lips. They were cracked and blistered and were seeping watery blood. He must have suffered a lot.

'He needs a doctor,' Jorge said. 'Even then, I wouldn't give you five *escudos* for his chances. Look at him. You don't know how long he's been lying here like that.'

'It can't have been too long, or the vultures would have finished him off.'

'Finishing him off would be the kind thing. I wouldn't want to live if I were in that state.'

'Really.'

'Not after the vultures had been at me. Have they taken his eyes? They go for the eyes first.'

'He has both his eyes.'

'How can you tell? There's blood everywhere.'

'What do you think Mama would do if she were here?'

'But she's not.'

She glared at him.

'Every time you don't get your own way you bring your mother into it!'

'If that's what it takes to remind you of your Christian responsibilities.'

'He won't last the night. Why should we waste our supplies on him?'

'I'll make a bargain with you. If he's still alive in the morning, you give me a day to nurse him well again.'

'What?'

'It's a deal then?'

'We can't afford an extra day. It's the monsoon. We're a day away, maybe two, from their *fortaleza*. Once the rains set in, we won't be able to get the wagon back to the prazo. Then what will we do?'

'A man's life is worth more than a wagon cart.'

She saw that her father seriously disagreed with her valuation but didn't want to say so.

'I'm your father. You'll do as I say.'

'Is that the best of your arguments, Papa? If it is, then let's get him back to the wagon and I'll get him cleaned up.'

'Impossible.'

'Isn't the inglês a friend of yours?'

'He's a business associate. Not the same thing at all.' Jorge scratched his earlobe.

'I don't care what you say, I'm not leaving him.'

Jorge clenched his fists and looked at the sky. No help there.

Catia nodded at the two *chikunda*. They spoke not a word of Portuguese, but they knew abject defeat when they saw it. They grinned at her and lifted the young man easily between them. The larger of the two hefted him across his shoulders and they made their way back to the wagons, Catia following.

Jorge swore and looked around for some way to vent his frustration. He saw the vulture preening its feathers on a piece of driftwood, levelled his musket at it, and blew it into blood and feathers.

Catia had them lay the young man on his left side in the back of a wagon. She had to make space for him among the rows of iron hooks with their rattling pots and pans. By the time Jorge came grumbling back from the river, she had him settled on a lion-skin *kaross,* out of the sun at last, with a blanket under his head. She fetched a bar of soap, a clean towel and a bowl of tepid water.

He was naked, apart from the torn rags of his trousers. She took a pair of steel scissors from her medicine chest and was about to cut them off.

At that moment Jorge tore aside the long sail curtain and stood on the afterchest, aghast. 'What do you think you're doing?' he said.

'If I am going to nurse him, I have to undress him. He has to be washed and I must check for other wounds.'

'Well, you can leave his damned trousers on.'

'I have seen men naked before.'

'Cafres!'

'God made white men no different to black men, did he?'

'I'll have one of my *chikunda* undress him. You can wait out here with me.'

'He's unconscious. What are you afraid of?'

'You are not taking his trousers off and that's final!' He grabbed her by the arm and pulled her outside.

CHAPTER 29

Jorge had brought two dozen of his *chikunda* with him on the expedition. That night as they made camp, he gave his sergeant the instructions for the night watch. They were to keep a fire burning, to keep away the lions and jackals, and have the men patrol with loaded muskets to guard the pack mules and the oxen. He told him the animals were to be kept within sight of the wagons, but he should put knee halters on them so they could graze.

He went to check on Catia's patient. She had put him in one of the spare wagons. The canvas was waterproof, more or less, and would keep off the worst of the sun during the day.

The inglês was in a sorry way. Catia had cleaned and dressed the wounds on his back as best she could, using some of his best gin, but they were sure to become infected.

The musket wound in his forehead was deep, but it had not penetrated the bone and she had declared it would not kill him. He was lucky. Another inch to the right and the lead ball would have blown out his brains.

His body was raw with sunburn. There were cuts all over his arms and legs, which Jorge guessed were from the coral reef. What would probably kill him were the wounds on his back where the vultures had been at him. Their beaks were razor sharp and rancid. Jorge reckoned he'd get a septic fever and be dead inside a day.

Catia was determined to keep the young bastard alive though, he'd give her that. She had found some fever root bark in her mother's old medicine chest and boiled up a tea with it. She had tried to make him drink it, but the boy couldn't keep anything down, probably because of the sunstroke.

All a waste of time and good medicine, in his opinion.

Catia held out as little hope for her patient as her father, though she would not let Jorge know that. The next day, as she expected, the fever came. The boy tossed and moaned in the back of the wagon, thrashing around with his arms and legs, and crying out at ghosts. He started to burn up. Catia stayed with him, cooling him with damp cloths.

'I told you,' Jorge said.

'The fever will break,' she said.

The inglês suddenly sat bolt upright, startling them both. 'Katherine, look out!'

She eased him gently back onto the *kaross*.

'What's he saying?' Jorge asked her.

'I don't know. It's English.'

He shook his head. 'Some of the boys found the wreckage of a boat on the beach,' he said.

'Do you think he was alone?'

'There was a dead *kaffir* down there. They said he stank to high heaven. They buried him in the dunes. I'd like to know what happened at the fort. Some of the inglês' ivory belonged to me.'

'Damn your ivory,' she murmured under her breath, but he didn't hear her.

'He's a dead man.' Jorge said cheerfully and jumped off the afterchest.

Catia made a face at her father's back. She didn't care what he said, she wasn't going to let the boy die. She had seen too many graves dug in this unforgiving African dirt. Her mother, for one, and her little brother, his infant body lying under a stone back at the prazo. And her nanny, Mama Vutlhari, that beautiful lady with the big laugh who had wasted away to nothing in a few weeks from the sickness.

She changed the dressings on the inglês' back. The skin around the wounds was swollen, angry-red and hot to the touch. Scabs had formed and she could smell the corruption underneath them. She would have to lance and clean them again. She wouldn't be sparing any of her father's square-face gin to do it, either. He drank too much of it anyway. Her patient needed it more than he did.

Evening came, but despite Jorge's grim predictions the young man was still alive. Catia nursed him through the second night, persisting with the fever tea, making sure there was a never-ending succession of damp towels to keep him cool. She sent two fellows from their *chikunda* down to the river with clay pots, again and again, for more water.

The inglês thrashed and shouted into the early hours. She remembered this was how her mother had died. She had taken sick early one evening and the next morning she was gone, just as the sun rose. Death was a quick-fingered thief. He picked your pocket of everything you loved and then disappeared back into the shadows. She could almost feel him, lurking in the dark, waiting his chance.

Her mother had died while she was asleep in the next room. Catia still told herself that if she had stayed awake, if she had only gripped her mama's hand tightly enough, she could somehow have pulled her back from the edge. She could have prevented her from leaving them.

This time she would not make the same mistake.

CHAPTER 30

Sometime during the night Catia fell asleep. She woke with a start and found him staring at her. At first she thought his eyes had opened in death, but then he blinked.

She put a hand to his forehead. His skin was cooler to the touch. She lifted the bandage on his shoulder and sniffed at the wound. It did not smell as bad now and some of the heat had gone out of it.

'Water,' he murmured.

She lifted his head and let him sip from the canteen of clean water she kept beside her.

'Who are you?' she said.

But in moments he was asleep again.

It was light, but the sun had not risen. She heard Daniso, their cook, rattling pots and pans in the kitchen tent, boiling water in the black iron kettle, and grinding coffee beans in the mortar. Jorge was shouting for someone to fetch him his boots.

She stroked the inglês' blond curls and traced the outline of his cheek with her fingertips. 'We showed him, didn't we?' she whispered.

There were footsteps outside the wagon, and she saw the glow of a lantern on the canvas. Jorge pushed aside the canvas flap. 'I brought you coffee,' he said and handed her an enamel mug.

'I need a razor,' she said. 'I want to give him a shave.'

'He's still with us, then?'

'He's strong. I told you I could save him.'

'We need to get going. I don't want to still be out here, giving him manicures, when the monsoon comes.'

He stamped back to his tent, muttering to himself, but he fetched his razor and shaving brush anyway. She took them from him without a word, then went to work. She lathered some shaving cream onto the boy's face then scraped the stubble off his cheeks, dipping the blade in a mug of water between each stroke.

Jorge watched her and felt again the stirrings of his misgivings. This was more than Christian charity on his daughter's part, he thought. The boy looked a lot different without that brick flush to his cheeks. Those damned blonde curls made him look almost angelic. 'Has he been awake?'

She nodded.

'Did he tell you his name?'

'He asked for water, that's all. Then he fell asleep again.'

Jorge watched her fussing over him. He put his hands on his hips and reconsidered. It seemed the lad wasn't going to die after all. If that was so, then he'd have to work out a way to make a profit out of this.

Lachlan slept most of the day. He was so peaceful now that she could hardly hear him breathe and continually put her cheek to his lips to check that he was still alive.

Her father stamped about the camp, irritable at the delay. He kept jumping up onto the afterchest to check on his progress. Finally, he took his *chikunda* and half a dozen Long Land muskets and went off hunting. She heard shots echoing around the plain all morning. He came back just after noon with two springboks. Four of his lads carried them in strung on long poles.

Partly mollified by the success of the shoot, he went looking for his supply of square face and seemed shocked to discover how much she had borrowed to treat the inglês. Good *genever* gin, he said to her, and she'd splashed it over the boy's cuts and bruises like it was holy water. He retired to his wagon for the rest of the afternoon to sulk and woke up just on sunset in a sour mood. She heard him shouting at the cook and the *voorlooper.*

When he finally reappeared, he threw aside the after-clap as if he were an actor faced with a particularly unruly audience. 'Well, how is he?'

'He's sleeping.'

'We're leaving at first light for the inglês fort.'

'You said we had to hurry back to the prazo because of the monsoon.'

'To hell with the monsoon, I want to get my ivory. And if he's not well enough to travel, we leave him behind.'

'He'll be ready.'

CHAPTER 31

They were breakfasted and loaded as soon as the sun appeared over the eastern horizon. Jorge had his *voorlooper* inspan the oxen, a dozen bullocks to the team and yoked in pairs. He planned to set off a hundred paces ahead of his *chikunda* so they would not be eating his dust. His six pack mules took up the rear.

He jumped into the back of the wagon. 'What are you doing in here again?' he said.

'I'm looking after our *inglês*.'

'You said he's well enough to travel, so he doesn't need a nurse anymore. You can travel on the running board with me.'

'You'd let a suffering man lie here on his own?'

'Damn right I would. What does he want, a feather bed and a man with a violin?'

'I said I would take care of him, and I will.'

Jorge swore under his breath. He realised with a jolt that he was jealous that this interloper had so much of his daughter's time and attention, but he was too proud to admit it. So, he climbed through the fore-clap and shouted at his *voorlooper*, taking out his bad mood on him. The lad was accustomed to being yelled at and ignored him. Jorge sat down on the running board, pulled his tobacco pouch from his jacket, and filled his clay pipe. He decided to take a nip of gin as well, just to spite his daughter.

Still, he reminded himself, the boy might be useful in the long run. He would just have to be patient. He flicked the trek whip, all twenty feet. It sounded like a musket going off. The oxen stirred themselves and they got under way.

'Who are you?' she asked him in Swahili.

He did not answer her. He was awake. His eyes were fixed on the canvas roof of the wagon. She knew he could hear her.

'My name is Catia,' she said. 'We are Portuguese. My father is a hunter and trader. We have a prazo, south of Lourenço Marques.'

He blinked, but he did not turn his head.

'My father knew an inglês. Hamish.' She made an attempt at 'McKenzie' but found the name too difficult to pronounce. 'They made much business together.'

Lachlan nodded. 'He was my father.' He turned his head and fixed his clear blue eyes on her. For a moment she thought he was about to say something else. But he turned away again and continued to stare at nothing.

They bumped over mile after mile of veldt. The wagon rocked and swayed.

She didn't ask him anything more. She would be patient for now. He was in shock, she supposed. He looked a little like her father after her mama died, like all his insides had been hollowed out. When you visited the land of death, you didn't come back straight away.

CHAPTER 32

Delgoa Bay

'*Santa Maria, Mãe de Deus!*' Jorge said.

The stockade was down on three sides and charred and splintered stakes lay everywhere. All that remained of the boma and warehouse were the stone walls. Tendrils of smoke still rose from blistered, fallen beams. The pirates had torched the *senzala* as well. The gardens had been pillaged and the compound was littered with the rotting bodies of a few dozen dogs.

The stench of smoke and burned flesh was hideous. The soldiers had not bothered with burying any of the dead. Wild animals had taken advantage of the feast. When they arrived, a pack of hyenas and some scavenger storks were fighting over the remains.

Jorge put a handkerchief across his nose and mouth and went into the warehouse, or what was left of it. His boots kicked up clouds of hot ash as he crossed the *stoep*.

'*Joder,*' he muttered under his breath. A few days ago, it would have been stacked to the ceiling with ivory, furs and wheels of copper. There was nothing left now but some charred and blackened splinters of elephant tooth. It had been a wasted journey. He went back to the wagon.

'Who did this?' Catia said.

'I don't know. I was told two frigates flying the Dutch flag appeared a few days ago in Sofala. The captain spoke French, said they were headed for the Cape and had called in to make repairs. That was all I knew of them until the runner came and told me about the attack on the inglês *fortaleza*. How did they get upriver? Only McKenzie's pilot knew how to do that.'

'Perhaps they bought him off.'

Their *voorlooper* shouted a warning. He pointed to an old woman who was standing under the mango trees, watching them. When she knew they had seen her, she scuttled away.

Catia ran after her and caught up with her easily. The woman cowered, terrified, her back against the tree. Catia spoke to her in Swahili, but she didn't seem to understand, so she tried Xitsonga. She guessed the woman had come here to scavenge and thought they were going to punish her.

'It's all right, mother,' Catia said to her. 'We are not going to hurt you. We have come here looking for the rest of the inglês. Is there anyone left? Did anyone survive?'

'The soldiers came and burned everything. They killed our men and took the children and young women for slaves. Then they left.' The woman looked over Catia's shoulder. 'So, you have found Nkala. I was right. I told the others. You can't kill the Mongoose.'

Lachlan had climbed out of the wagon and was leaning against the rear wheel. It was all that was holding him upright. He was staring slack-jawed at the devastation - reliving everything that had happened that day, she supposed.

'You know him, mother?' Catia said.

'Of course, I know him. He was son to the bwana, the white chief.'

They went over to him, and the old woman took his hand. Lachlan stared at her, his face blank.

'You must tell him I am very sorry,' the old woman said. 'They died a long way from home and now their spirits will wander endlessly. Tell him we did our best for them.'

'I will,' Catia said. She tried to help Lachlan back into the wagon, but he was too heavy for her. Two of the *chikunda* ran to help her. 'Get him back to bed,' she said to them.

As they passed him back through the after-clap, she turned back to the old woman. 'What did you do with the bodies?'

'We washed them, closed their eyes, and wrapped them in white cloth. Some of us kept them company the night before they left the earth. We buried them under the sacred baobab tree and helped them on their way with prayers and with drumming.'

'Can you show me this baobab tree?'

The old woman pointed out the ancient tree. It stood close to the blackened remains of the *senzala*. Catia thanked the old woman and gifted her some of their antelope meat.

'The old woman said the Tsonga who escaped came back and buried his family over there,' she told Jorge. 'They will not settle here again. They are frightened of the soldiers and the bad spirits they left behind.'

'Not much information for quite a lot of meat,' Jorge grumbled.

Catia went into the forest. There were three mounds of earth under a huge baobab. She said a quick prayer and hurried back to the wagon.

The next morning, Catia sat on the running board with her father as they broke camp. It was early and the sun was low and molten over the veldt. There was still a glimmer of stars in the west, but the sky over the sea had lightened to a dirty ochre stain.

'Aren't you glad now that you didn't abandon him?' she said.

Jorge grunted and offered no opinion.

'So, what are we going to do with him?' she said.

'Eu não sei, petite. I don't know. But I do know this: he's on his own from here. I've done my Christian duty.'

'No papa, I did your Christian duty for you.'

'God understands why I do the things I do.'

'Then God is a genius,' she said, but decided not to fight him. They would have plenty of time to battle over the fate of Lachlan McKenzie when they got back to the prazo.

CHAPTER 33

Novo Santiago

So this was Novo Santiago, Lachlan thought. The dazzling white walls of the *luana*, the large and rambling farmhouse, were shaded by waving palms and almost hidden by trees of purple bougainvillea and frangipani. The fenced *quintas* of Jorge's retainers were clustered around it. The settlement was protected by a fortified stockade, similar to Fort Greenock. Her father had built it in the early days, Catia told him, but there had not been any trouble from the Dutch or from the local Tsonga chieftain for many years.

There were vast green fields of sugar cane, rice and maize spread along the coast as far as he could see. Millet fields rippled like the surface of a lake. It was the wet season now and everything was lush and green.

Catia told him the plantation was almost a hundred years old. It had originally been built to export the gold that the early traders bought at the native fairs in the hinterland. Now the goldfields were exhausted, so most of their trade came from what they could grow and the ivory they could hunt or buy from the Tsonga.

'It has been my home for as long as I can remember,' she said. 'It is your home now for as long as you want.'

A few days later, the monsoon season began in earnest. Torrential rain flooded the compound for hours every afternoon and lasted until evening. Jorge had given Lachlan a small hut on the very edge of the compound to sleep in. It was behind the quarters reserved for the servants, and as far away as possible from the lodge he shared with Catia.

At night he was invited to the main house to have dinner. The dining room reminded him of the refectory at Fort Greenock. It had high stinkwood beams with kudu and antelope skins decorating the floors and walls. There was a long dining table made of blackwood, which had been polished to a mirror shine with beeswax by the houseboys. It could comfortably seat at least a dozen people.

Jorge always sat on a carved chair at the end. Catia sometimes sat next to him, depending on her mood. If he'd upset her, which was not infrequently, she very purposely chose a seat as far away from him as possible, so that he almost had to shout to make conversation.

Despite the imposing dining table, it was still a working kitchen, with sausages and hams hanging on hooks, and brimming woven baskets of sun-dried maize. After dinner Catia played the harpsichord, while Jorge drank copious amounts of Cape brandy and smoked his pipe.

It seemed to Lachlan that Jorge had warmed to him a little. He had been cold at first, but now he even spoke a few words to him in Swahili occasionally.

Once, when Catia was not around, Jorge told him how she had thought they should put him out of his misery that day they found him. 'But I said to her, big strong lad like this, we must do our best to save him. Besides he's the son of my good friend, Hamish.' He patted him on the shoulder. 'And look, I was right, you're still here!'

Jorge Ferreira had revised his opinion of the inglês. He might not be the well-bred Portuguese officer he had planned on having as a son-in-law, but he was good with a rifle, and he could speak Swahili and Xitsonga. He wasn't even that stupid, not for an Englishman.

Jorge was starting to feel his years and Catia would need someone to help her run the prazo. When he was gone, it would pass to her, and she couldn't run it on her own.

Catia wasn't a bad looking girl, perhaps a little strident at times. He had noticed how she and the inglês exchanged hurried glances whenever he passed her in the kitchen. Admittedly, when he had first seen it he had thought about blowing the lad's balls off with his elephant gun, but recently he had reconsidered. This might be a good thing if he managed the situation properly.

The English were a cold lot. He had heard most of them preferred little boys. But he took the precaution of telling his manager, Paolo, to sleep outside the inglês' door. If she did manage to tempt him, he didn't want him tasting the fruit before he bought the orchard.

CHAPTER 34

The moon threw an aura on the tattered edges of the clouds. It finally emerged, huge and brilliant. The air smelled of frangipani.

Lachlan lay in his cot, staring at Orion's Belt through the small window of his room and listening to the lapping of the waves on the beach. The air was thick as soup. He sat up, put his head in his hands. His body was still weak, and his back ached unmercifully from the wounds the vultures had left.

He couldn't sleep. It was too hot in the room and there was a mosquito buzzing around the netting over his bed. It might as well have been a seagull, the noise it made. He jumped out of bed, pulled on his shirt and trousers, and slipped outside. He had to step over Paolo who lay on his back by the door, snoring. He headed for the beach.

The wind had ruffled the waves to a dark indigo. It flipped spray into his face as he walked along the hard sand. The moon had risen late. It was a blood moon, riding low in the sky and tinting the clouds a watery magenta.

A whole life waiting for something to happen and now his world had been torn apart in a few weeks. He looked up at the stars and thought about the crow in the white turban and about Mohammed Daoud. Wherever you are, you murderous bastards, I am going to find you. Both of you.

He didn't hear her over the sound of the wind, didn't know she was there until she was almost at his shoulder.

'It's beautiful, isn't it?'

He turned around, startled. 'Catia.'

'I thought I could see you out here. Why aren't you asleep?' When he didn't answer, she said, 'You're thinking about your family.'

'I hardly think about anything else.'

'I can't imagine what you're going through.'

He couldn't think of a thing to say to that. The fact of it was that he felt mostly numb. It was as if his mind still refused to believe what had happened and was waiting for Katherine or Hamish to step out from behind a tree any moment. It was letting the pain leak in a drop at a time, so that it didn't overwhelm him.

'What are you doing out here?' he said.

'My father is snoring like a warthog, full of Cape brandy. The whole house is shaking.' She lifted her long skirt around her ankles and walked ahead, scuffing at the sand with her toes. He followed her.

The sea churned and waited. Before the moonrise it had been so dark it was impossible to go very far from the *stoep* without walking into a tree. Now the full moon was so bright it was light enough to read a book.

'How are the wounds on your back?'

'They're healing. Thank you.'

'Let me see. Take off your shirt.'

He did as she said. He felt her fingers trace the tender new flesh on his back, where the raw, pink skin had started to knit together. Her touch made him shiver, despite himself.

'Does that hurt?'

'No,' he said. He could smell the soap she used.

'You're lucky to be alive,' she said.

'I know. I can't make sense of it.'

He turned around. She smiled up at him. The moonlight threw half her face into shadow. He felt the heat from her body and her breath on his face. He heard two voices in his head, one saying this is not right, you are supposed to be grieving. The other drowned it out, urging him to take refuge from all the pain.

Her lips brushed his cheek and his neck. Then she took his face in her hands and kissed him so hard he could not breathe.

Afterwards he lay there, listening to the hiss of the sand in the wind and the lapping of the waves. The blood was pounding in his ears. She wrapped her arms around him.

He rolled onto his back.

'What's wrong?' she whispered.

He shook his head. 'Nothing,' he said. 'Thank you.'

She smiled.

He could not tell her how he really felt in that moment because there were no words for it. A part of him felt as if he had betrayed his family by forsaking his grief, if only for a moment. Another part of him wanted to cling to her like a drowning man reaching out for rescue.

'You have to go on living,' she whispered.

'That's what Sasavona said.'

'Who is Sasavona?'

'Your *chikunda* buried him on the beach. He saved my life.'

They padded back through the dunes, hand in hand, the soft sand squeaking under their feet. When they reached the trees she kissed him and ran back to the main house. He went back to his own hut, stepping carefully over Paolo on the way in, and lay down on his cot.

Sleep came no easier than it had before.

Lachlan had settled into the rhythm of his new life. But it was an interlude, nothing more. He would let his body heal and regain its strength and wait for his moment.

As soon as the wind turned, his life and his fate would be back in his own hands.

CHAPTER 35

The kitchen girls bustled around the long, mahogany table with dishes of fiery curry made with chicken and chilis. There were antelope cutlets with *rabandas*, that Jorge had taught the cooks to make personally, as well as *bacalhau a bras*, made with salt-dried cod, eggs and potato. Afterwards there was a special sweet made from coconut milk and ginger.

The girls giggled among themselves and gossiped in a dialect Jorge did not know. He glanced up irritably and growled at them to hurry. He stirred a generous splash of Cape brandy into his coffee and regarded his daughter with suspicion.

There was something wrong, but he couldn't make out what it was. His daughter's mood had changed. For months she had been unusually cheerful, had had a certain glow about her, but tonight she was unusually subdued.

He looked up the table at the inglês. Hard to know what the lad was thinking. His moods were unpredictable. He would spend some days on the beach just staring at the waves; other days, he would sit on the back porch laughing with Catia.

She said they had to be patient with him. He supposed he had been through a lot. He didn't know how he would have acted in his place. He had never had much use for family himself. His own father was a loveless bastard and Jorge was just one of six brothers. He had left home as soon as he could.

The only thing he had ever cared about was Catia's mother, and when she died, he dealt with it by trying not to think about her ever again. A man had to get on with things. It was the way of it. People died all the time. You couldn't rely on them to stick around.

He had put Lachlan to work and had been pleased with the results. Running Novo Santiago was not much different from running the inglês place in Delgoa Bay, and the lad had often been in charge of things whenever Hamish went to Ilha on business. He would make a perfect husband for Catia. Jorge had decided to put the proposition to him in the next few days. He could hardly refuse.

'Catia says she is teaching you Portuguese,' Jorge said to him in Swahili. 'Show me.'

'Senhor?'

'*Dizer alguma coisa em Português.* Say something in Portuguese.'

Lachlan took a deep breath. '*Eu ainda não sou muito bom. Eu preciso de muito mais aulas.* I'm still not very good. I need many more lessons.'

Jorge made a face. 'He talks like a three-year-old,' he said to Catia in Portuguese.

She shrugged.

'I may not be able to practise for much longer,' Lachlan said to Jorge in Swahili.

'Why not?'

'I cannot stay here, senhor. You have been more than kind to me. But I have to go to Ilha.'

'What's at Ilha that's so damned important?'

'There is a man there I must see. An Arab merchant called Shariff Massoud.'

'That flea-bitten thief.'

'He did a lot of business with my father. If anyone knows who was behind the attack on Fort Greenock it will be him. And he will also know where I can find Mohammed Daoud.'

'And what good will that do you?'

'I am going to kill him,' Lachlan said.

Por Deus, he means it, Jorge thought. The inglês has a dark streak in him just like his father.

'But before I kill him, he will tell me the name of the pirate who murdered my family.'

'And then what, you're going to kill him, too? Whoever he is, he has two warships and a private army.'

'That won't save him.'

Jorge wanted to laugh, but the look on Lachlan's face stopped him. He was deadly serious.

'Now that the monsoon is over you will be sailing to Ilha.'

'How do you know that?'

'Catia told me. She says you go every year, at the end of the monsoon, to sell your ivory and copper to the governor. I want to come with you.'

Jorge lit his pipe and leaned back in his chair. He rapped on his glass for the girls to bring him the brandy bottle. Before he answered, he waited until the rank Turkish tobacco he was smoking had sufficiently fouled the room.

He had to put a stop to this. His own plans were far more important.

'Before you go running off on this fool's errand, there's something I think you should consider.'

'My mind's made up.'

'Now hear me out. I got some news last week from Ilha. There's talk that Lisbon is going to make Mozambique independent of those pen pushers in Goa. If that happens, things could change a lot around here. I need to talk to the governor and find out if this is true and make sure our interests are looked after.'

'I don't understand,' Lachlan said.

'You see, the governor and I understand each other. If they let us run things our way down here, there's real money to be made. I can see that you're your father's son. I'll be needing someone who can speak to the natives and knows how to run a place like this. And now you're learning some Portuguese, you'll soon be able to deal with the governor as well. You could have a big future here.'

'I can't.'

'Come on, McKenzie. I'm offering to teach you everything I know.'

'What he means,' Catia said from over her father's shoulder, 'is that you have to know how to cheat and lie if you're going to deal with the government, and my papa is the biggest liar and the best cheat this side of the Zambezi.'

Jorge beamed at this high praise. 'That's right. I am.'

'All my life,' Lachlan said, 'I wanted to live the way that my father did. Having a farm like this, being master of my own destiny, having a beautiful wife...' He glanced at Catia. 'It's still all I want. But I can't do that until I've avenged what has been done to my family. I am going to find those two men and make them pay for what they did. There is no place they can hide from me, and I won't rest until it's done.'

CHAPTER 36

Mozambique Island

The native women were awake before dawn. They hitched their children onto their hips and set about the serious business of collecting kindling for the morning cook fires. They all wore a white paste of pulverised *mussiro* bark on their faces to protect them from the sun. In the dirty, grey light before sunrise it made them look ghostly and a little sinister, despite their broad smiles.

With the sun came the familiar scents of daybreak: frangipani, wood smoke, bougainvillea, brine. Salt spray drifted over the beach and the fishermen's shacks. The only sounds were the seabirds and the shush of the waves.

Lachlan hailed one of the lascars mending his fishing nets and negotiated a price for the short trip to Sancul on the mainland. He gave the man some coins and jumped into his dhow. He watched the dolphins play in the wash as they made their way through the channel. From the bay he could see how misshapen the island was; one end was far lower than the other, as it had served as a quarry for the fortress. God alone knew how many young native men had died digging out those rocks.

Away to the north he could make out people moving on the causeway, heading to market. It was low tide and there were islanders foraging for shellfish on the reef below the small fort at the other end of the island.

His gaze moved to the mainland. Already he could make out the village of Sancul. The ruling sheiks of Ilha had long ago moved to the southern shores of the bay, away from the comparative hurly burly of the island and, more especially, away from the Portuguese.

His lascar beached the dhow in the shallows.

Lachlan jumped out. There was a long beach, with straw-thatched huts nestled among the palm groves. He heard the wail of muezzins from a Mohammedan church. Boys in white caftans and girls in black *bui-bui* robes scooted along the laneways to attend their morning prayers.

He left the beach and set off down a sandy lane to find Shariff Massoud.

The sheikh was an important man on the coast. Without him, his father and Rory could not have carried on their trade. He had arranged lines of credit for them, as well as ocean dhows for their fledgling trade in Malabar and the Coromandel.

It was not as hard as he had feared to find him. He had been there once before, with his father, and he remembered the way. He passed a straggle of mud huts and found the house nearby. It was surrounded by a large fence and was only just visible through a garden thick with citrus trees and coconut palms. There was a flock of goats and a few chickens. They ran clucking and fussing into the bushes as he approached.

For all his wealth and reputation, the sheikh lived simply. Lachlan thought he would be challenged by a guard or at least one of the servants, but instead Massoud himself burst out onto the veranda and came running down the steps towards him. He wore a white robe, in the style of the local Swahili men, with an embroidered skull cap.

He was strong for such an old man and nearly knocked him off his feet in his enthusiasm. He wrapped his arms about him. 'But they said you were all dead!'

'Not all.'

Massoud held him by the shoulders and shook him, as if to satisfy himself that he was real. 'You are alive. I cannot believe it.'

'You know what happened?'

'Up and down the coast it is all anyone has talked about. What about your father, the rest of your family?'

Lachlan shook his head.

'God help you in your sorrow. May the men who did this to you die a thousand terrible deaths.'

'I thank you for your condolences.'

'Your father was a man of great renown. We all weep for him. Come, boy, come and sit. We must talk.'

The sheikh led him to a shaded courtyard at the rear of his house. He sat down, cross-legged, on a thick Bokhara carpet in the shade of a palm tree. A canvas screen afforded them shelter from the salt spray drifting up from the beach. He clapped his hands for servants to bring them coffee and a *hookah*.

'When you came here with your father, may Allah keep him, you were just a boy. You did not even have a beard.'

'It was no more than two years ago.'

'Yet so much has happened.'

The last time he had been here with Hamish, they had smoked the perfumed Turkish tobacco for hours, exchanging pleasantries while the water bubbled in the pipes. It seemed much longer than two years since then.

Never hurry the conversation with a Mohammedan, his father had always told him. Show respect. Observe the formalities, always, no matter how urgent your business is.

But today the sheikh had no time for the usual etiquette. He went straight at it.

'Thanks be to God that you are here. Now tell me everything. I was told that you were all killed by the pirates. How did you get away?'

'The sergeant of my *chikunda* helped me. He saved my life. He was a brave man and loyal, and he deserved a better death. I was unconscious. He found me and put me in a boat.' Even as he said it, he wondered if anyone believed him; or did they all think he was a coward, that he'd run away and left his family behind?

'Where have you been hiding since that terrible day?'

'A Portuguese trader found me. He has shown me great kindness and nursed me back to health on his prazo.'

'What trader?'

'His name is Jorge Ferreira.'

The sheikh spat impressively in the dirt. 'Kind? He's a cheat and a thief.'

'Yet he took me in when he could have left me to die.'

The water pipe bubbled, and Massoud exhaled a long stream of smoke through his nose. 'I have wept a thousand times a thousand tears for your father. You must pray to God for strength to bear this great suffering in your life.'

After they had finished the *hookah,* they drank coffee from tiny brass thimbles. A droplet of sweat fell from Lachlan's nose onto his lap. A servant with a palm leaf fan attempted to keep away the flies.

'What will you do now?' Massoud said.

'I have given no thought to the future. All I know is I must avenge my family and I will move heaven and earth to do it.'

'It will not be easy. Do you know the names of the men you seek?'

'I know one of them. His name is Mohammed Daoud.'

'He served your father since he was a boy.'

'Two warships found their way along the estuary to our fort. There is no other pilot on the Mozambique coast who knew the banks and reefs like he did and no other captain who would have attempted it.'

Massoud nodded and looked grim. 'Is that why you are here?'

'Yes,' Lachlan said. 'Because you will know where I can find him.'

Massoud sighed. 'Men far wiser than me have said that the best revenge is to be happy. If you kill Mohammed Daoud will it bring your father back to life, or raise your family from their graves?'

'My mind is set on this.'

The old man sipped his coffee while he considered. At last, he nodded. 'I can only tell you this. At the beginning of the last monsoon Mohammed Daoud appeared on Ilha, behaving like a prince. No one knew where his new-found wealth came from, though everyone knew it must have something to do with the pirates who attacked your fort. He has told people he is building a fine house in Oman.'

'With blood money.'

'One day, he will answer for his sins to God.'

'I cannot wait that long.' Lachlan stared into the old man's face. There were long creases in his cheeks and the strands on his once golden beard were now all turned to grey.

Massoud looked suddenly very sad. 'He is not hard to find. Perhaps you even walked right past him in Stone Town.' He looked over Lachlan's shoulder towards Ilha.

'He is there?'

'I am told he is reinvesting his dirty money in black gold,' Massoud said. 'If you wait beside the slave block inside the fort, today or tomorrow, you will surely see him there. You may not recognise him straight away. I am told that these days he wears clothes of much refinement.'

'I thought he would have hidden himself away,' Lachlan said.

'Why? He believes all his enemies are dead.'

'So now he buys and sells slaves?'

'It is a very profitable business. Why are you surprised? He did not become rich by following his conscience.'

'He is as rich as he is ever going to be. As he will soon find out.'

Massoud put out a hand and laid it on his arm. 'Start on the road to revenge and it crumbles away behind you. There is no way back.'

'Then I shall say farewell,' Lachlan said, 'because I intend to walk down that road as far as it leads.'

CHAPTER 37

Slaving was an unsavoury business, Mohammed Daoud thought. After all he had done in his life, it surprised him that he still had the capacity to be sensitive to these things. He went over to the auctioneer and used his cane to point out one of the young girls. What had they done to her? She was all bones. She looked as if she had not eaten for a week. They were no good to anyone like that.

The heavy iron collar had formed a sore around her neck. Sometimes those things formed lifelong scars. If he bought her, he supposed he could hide the marks with a cheap necklace when he offloaded her.

He asked the trader to open her mouth and he peered inside to look at her teeth. She was fourteen or fifteen he would guess, and she had no scars on her face. He reconsidered. If he put some flesh on her bones she would fetch a nice price for one of the Egyptian or Arabian harems.

Another troop was led in and lined up against the wall in order of size. They were all males, so nothing for him there. He watched as one of the men was led to a post in the middle of the market and lashed to it, his arms above his head. The slaver started to whip him with the branch from a thorn tree, while some French traders looked on. It was customary practice, done to test their strength and endurance. Every time they cried out the price went down.

The French were new at this. They wanted slaves for the sugar fields they had recently planted in Mauritius. They were changing the trade and driving up prices. Once there were three female slaves to every male. Not anymore.

Mohammed had never imagined himself standing here like this. After he had made his bargain with Napoleon Gagnon, he thought he would take his money and leave Africa. His plan had been to build a house in Oman, where he could grow fat and lazy and watch his children grow. It hadn't worked out that way. Money, he soon discovered, was an addiction like opium or sex. Once you had a little, you wanted more. Now he had money to invest in black gold, he realised he could make a lot more.

He agreed a price for the girl and signalled to his lascars to take her back to the dhow with the rest of his day's purchases.

'Feed them,' he said to the captain. 'There's no profit in putting them over the side to feed the sharks before we even get to Oman.'

'Yes, *Sayeed*,' the man said and led the livestock back through the wrought iron gates to the beach.

Yes, he was a *Sayeed* now. He commanded respect wherever he went. A rich man.

Somehow he thought it would feel better than this.

Lachlan barely recognized him, just as Massoud had warned him.

He had put on a lot of weight. His long white tunic – *dishdasha* – and the richly embroidered open robe that he wore over it looked expensive. He had on a dark red *massar*, in the traditional Omani manner, instead of the plain white headcloth he used to wear.

Lachlan followed him as he headed out of the market towards the fort. Of course, Lachlan thought. He has to pay the governor his commission.

Heat radiated from the whitewashed walls of the Lime Town, and the humidity left him soaked in sweat. Old men sat in the lanes, their faces as coarse as peach pits, and barely spared him a glance as he went by. Women crouched in doorways and fanned themselves with their headscarves, their hennaed hands fluttering like butterflies. A fat tree bulged into a shaded lane.

Mohammed Daoud made his way across the open square in front of the fort. Lachlan veered away. He didn't want to be seen just yet. He heard the familiar tick-tock of hammers and axes. Some local men were building a dhow on the sand in front of the San Antonio chapel. Swahili boat-builders had been doing this, using the same five tools, for thousands of years. He remembered how he used to watch Mohammed Daoud at work on the beach below Fort Greenock. Mohammed had laughed and made jokes as he clambered over the skeleton of the *al-Shahadah*. Lachlan used to call him uncle in those days.

He watched Mohammed speak to the guards at the main gate and then slip inside.

Lachlan waited by the shore, watching the fishermen mending their nets on the green-slimed beach. Naked children ran laughing through the shallows. Women harvested seaweed.

He had never killed a man in cold blood, and he hoped his nerve would not fail him. But he couldn't hurry this. He had no plan to make Mohammed suffer, even though he deserved it. But before he finished him he had to know the truth. What had happened to his father and his brother? A part of him yet hoped they were still alive.

Most of all, he had to know the name of the thin man in the turban.

Lachlan stared at the curtain walls of the fortress. There were bright flowers growing through the rocks, surviving in the unlikeliest of places, against all odds. Like me, he thought.

The sun edged its way down the sky and slipped beneath the parapet.

Mohammed Daoud reappeared right on sunset. Lachlan watched him leave the gates and followed him into the stone town. The first stars appeared and bats flew out of the trees, as big as gulls. The night was warm and perfumed with frangipani, roasting maize and the sea.

Mohammed hurried through the dark and narrow streets. Lachlan felt for the knife in his belt.

He was still thirty paces behind, when Mohammed heard him or perhaps just sensed him there. He stopped and turned around. When he saw Lachlan, his knees almost gave way under him. He staggered and reached for the wall to steady himself. 'Are you a *djinn*, a ghost?' he said.

Lachlan showed him the knife. 'I'm very real.'

Mohammed turned and ran for the beach. He splashed into the shallows, frantically shouting for help. Lachlan heard answering shouts from one of the dhows riding at anchor in the bay. Lanterns bobbed as Mohammed's lascars jumped into a rowing boat.

Lachlan knew they wouldn't get to the beach in time.

Mohammed stumbled and fell into the water. He struggled back to his feet, but his long robe was sopping wet now and was hindering him. He had a ceremonial dagger at his waist, but he hadn't even reached for it. He turned around and waited, his hands on his knees, trying to get his breath.

Finally, he remembered his dagger and pulled it from its sheath. His hands were shaking so violently he could barely hold it.

'Why did you do it?' Lachlan said.

'I'm sorry.' Mohammed started to cry. 'I'm so sorry.'

'Didn't my father always treat you fairly. My mother nursed your son when he was sick!'

'He promised me he wouldn't hurt the mistress or the lady Katherine!'

'That makes what you did better?'

Lachlan took a step closer, and Mohammed slashed at him with his knife. It was half-hearted and Lachlan dodged the blade easily.

'I'm sorry,' Mohammed repeated.

'What did any of us do to deserve this? Was it just for the money?'

Mohammed's hands fell to his sides. His face twisted. 'What other reason is there for anything, Nkala?'

Lachlan heard shouts behind him from Lime Town. The soldiers were coming. Either someone had alerted them, or they had heard Mohammed's cries for help at the bastion. There wasn't much time.

'Who was the man in the white turban?'

'I don't know. He came from Hindustan. His men called him *Sahib*.'

'Where will I find him?'

'I told you. I don't know!'

This was the moment. Do it, Lachlan, he heard Hamish whisper. *Do it*. He hesitated.

He had killed three men at the fort with a cutlass, had taken off a man's head with a single stroke. But that was different, it wasn't done in cold blood like this. His sister had been lying dead at his feet.

Mohammed fell to his knees, his shoulders heaving, weeping into the sea.

'Fight me,' Lachlan said.

'Just do it,' Mohammed said and dropped his dagger into the shallows. 'I deserve it.' Mohammed lurched to his feet and embraced him.

Lachlan felt the man's arms go about his neck and felt a moment's resistance against his knife hand as the blade went into Mohammed's chest.

'I'm sorry, brother,' Mohammed whispered.

Lachlan stepped back. The knife had entered just below Mohammed's breastbone, right to the hilt. He watched the dark stain blooming down the front of his *dishdasha*. He caught him before he fell face first into the water and dragged him up the beach by the arms.

By the time the soldiers arrived with their muskets and lanterns, Mohammed Daoud was already dead. He lay on his back, his eyes wide, staring at the stars.

CHAPTER 38

The *Fortaleza da São Sebastião* had stood for almost two hundred years. The Dutch had laid siege to it twice without success. The thick walls, protected at each corner by a squat and forbidding bastion, had withstood months of naval bombardment on both occasions. The Portuguese garrison could have held out until their beards turned grey, thanks to their unlimited supply of fresh water. It came from two massive rainwater cisterns that had been built a thousand years before by Arab invaders. The place was now considered impregnable.

The office assigned to the Governor of Mozambique was on the top floor of one of the fortress's corner bastions. It faced away from the water, a precaution against unwanted cannonballs finding their way inside from a passing Dutch frigate. The windows overlooked the parade ground.

Jorge Ferreira took a moment to admire the view while he waited for the governor to finish signing the documents his secretary had brought him. The customs house dominated the square. Its entrance was decked with two massive anchors, which were decorative, and two cannons that weren't. The shore behind it was covered with ivory and ambergris ready for loading onto Portuguese ships. There were two baroque churches on the other side of the vast parade ground, where native soldiers in immaculate white uniforms were half-heartedly going through a drill.

A previous incumbent had planted some orange and lemon trees in the cloister below, perhaps to remind himself of Lisbon.

The governor was in full fig. Jorge was nursing a hangover, and the reek of the other man's pomade made him bilious. The tricorn, along with the gold braid, epaulettes and cuffs, was overmuch for his eyes so early on this bleached, hot morning.

The governor laid aside the quill and handed the papers back to his secretary. The man left, closing the door softly behind him.

'Is it true?' Jorge said. 'The rumours?'

'Which rumour are we discussing?'

'That Mozambique is about to become independent of Goa.'

'News travels fast for such a large country.'

'No one has anything else to talk about.'

The governor preened himself, reminding Jorge of his pet macaw. 'My new title will be Captain-General. I will responsible directly to Lisbon.'

'The council in Goa will no longer have a say in our affairs?'

The governor nodded towards the window. 'That will be the only customs house in all of East Africa. The new authorities will come into effect next year.'

'I trust it won't affect our arrangements?'

The governor shrugged, as if he had not thought about this until now. 'Well. It may affect them slightly. The more efficient running of government may increase the expenses incurred by my administration.'

'Did you have a figure in mind?' Jorge said.

'Twenty per cent.'

Twenty per cent. He could be robbed by bandits and have more left in his pockets. He supposed he would have to under-declare a further twenty per cent next year in order to turn a profit. Plead hardship; droughts in the interior driving the elephant herds further north.

'Will it affect the slave trade?'

The governor raised an eyebrow. 'The slave trade is illegal. I won't allow it.'

'Have you been to Lime Town recently?'

'It's hard to crack down on it completely. I am sure anyone you saw engaging in such activities has been forced to pay hefty fines.'

'To you?'

'To the Crown.'

'Does the Crown know about that?'

'What is your business here this morning, Senhor Ferreira?'

Jorge took out his pipe and knocked the bowl on his heel. He took out his tobacco pouch. 'I think you know.'

'Ah, the little matter of the inglês.'

'Yes, that little matter. I'm sure he didn't mean to kill him.'

'If he didn't mean to kill him, then he shouldn't have stuck his knife through the gentleman's vitals. That can have a deleterious effect on anyone's health. Did he not know that?'

'It must have been self-defence.'

'He followed him from the gates of the *Fortaleza* to the beach. Hardly the actions of a man trying to escape his adversary.'

'He can be headstrong.'

'What do you want me to do about this?'

'We're men of the world, you and me. How long have we been friends now?'

'We have been business associates for three years. Since my appointment.'

'For the sake of our fr... smoother commercial relations, I was hoping his indiscretion could be overlooked.'

'You want me to overlook murder?'

'The dead man was involved in the illegal purchase of slaves. Not a man of sound character. And, of course, a Musselman. Not Portuguese.'

The governor gave Jorge a thin smile. 'I suppose a fine might be appropriate then, in this instance.'

Jorge pulled out his drawstring purse and handed it to him. The governor tested the weight and frowned.

'What's wrong?' Jorge said.

The governor gave an apologetic shrug.

Jorge sighed and reached inside his waistcoat. He took out another purse, wincing in pain as if he were pulling out his liver. He tossed it on the desk. The governor untied the strings and peered inside.

'He's free to go,' he said.

Jorge got up to leave.

'One more thing,' the governor said.

Jesu Christi, Jorge thought. He's not going to gouge me for more?

Instead, the governor held out an envelope. It had a wax seal. Lachlan's name was written on the front in bold, copperplate writing.

'This was given to me by a British naval captain. Rodron,' he said, rolling the r's in the name expansively. 'A week or so ago his ship called here for supplies and to drop off two sick men at the hospital. He had heard about the pirate raid in Delgoa Bay. He said that if any of the McKenzie family were alive and made their way to Ilha, then I was to give them this.'

Jorge took the envelope. 'I'll see that it gets to him,' he said. He slipped it into his pocket. 'Consider it delivered.'

Lachlan had slept only fitfully through the night. There were no windows in the cell where they had put him, deep under the fortress. It was dank and airless, and he had been tormented all night by mosquitoes.

As the early morning light leeched in under the doors, he realised he still had Mohammed Daoud's blood all over him. It had stained his shirt and breeches, even his leather boots.

He heard the guards coming down the steps and the rattle of keys. The door flew open, and two soldiers came in. Without a word, one of them bent down and unlocked his ankle chains. They dragged him to his feet and frog-marched him out.

They led him up the stone stairs to the main yard. He shielded his eyes from the glare. The sun was only just up, but already it was blindingly hot.

Jorge was waiting for him, his pipe between his teeth and his hands in his pockets. 'Look at you,' he said. He took a step closer.

'Why are you here?'

'Catia told me to bring you back with me. She insisted.'

'I'm not coming back until I find the man who murdered my family.'

'You've done all you could.' Jorge shrugged his shoulders. 'He's long gone. Come back to *Novo Santiago* with me. You've killed the man who betrayed you. Let that be an end to it.'

The south wind rattled the coconut palms lining the beach, and spray leapt the seawall below the fortress. Jorge's villa groaned and creaked. He sat on the roof, sheltered by a bamboo screen. The Jesuits had built a large hospital next door, that buffered them from the worst of the weather. It looked for all the world like a Greco-Roman palace, with its fluted pillars and balustraded roof terrace.

Sick Portuguese soldiers and sailors were sent there from as far away as Macao and Goa. Even the British Indiamen, who often stopped off for fresh water and provisions to and from the Cape, left crew and passengers to the priests' tender mercies.

Captain Rodron had left three of his crew there on his last visit to Ilha. He had also left behind the letter Jorge now had in his jacket pocket.

Jorge splashed some square face into a glass and took out the envelope. He broke the seal with his knife. There was no salutation. It read:

> I don't know if this letter will ever find its way into the right hands. I find myself astonished that I am writing it at all, as everyone believes you are all dead. If any of you escaped this atrocity, then I cannot imagine how you are faring.
>
> I can think of no words of consolation for you. So, I shall keep this brief and tell you what I have learned so you might make some sense of this.
>
> A few months ago, two frigates called in at Angoche on their way down the coast. They had sailed form the Coromandel in Hindustan. I believe these were the same ships that later attacked Fort Greenock. I have heard their commander described to me by two separate accounts. This man's singular appearance leaves me in no doubt that his name is Napoleon Gagnon. He is a mercenary of French and Hindu blood.
>
> He is well known in the Coromandel and harbours his ships under the white ensign of the French navy at Pondicherry. He has powerful friends there.
>
> I cannot tell you why he attacked Fort Greenock. He must have been paid a king's ransom to do so.
>
> What will you do now? If you are without hope, then know that if you can find your way to Madras, you will find help there. I gave Hamish my word that I

would ask Channing, the President, to find Lachlan a position with the Company. I kept my word and spoke very highly of him. He has been anticipating his arrival. Well, he was, until news of this affair reached him.

Whichever of you reads this, and I pray at least one of you shall, then know that if you find your way to Madras you will find succour there. Good luck to you. I hope we will meet again someday.

If you have survived this ordeal, then I can only think that God has kept you for a purpose. I hope you will find some comfort in that and that the future is as kind to you as the past has been cruel.

Sincerely Yours
James Rodron, Captain, HMS Southampton.'

Jorge refolded the letter and returned it to its envelope. He wondered what he would do in McKenzie's position. If anyone ever hurt Catia he'd hunt him down to the ends of the earth. But this wasn't Catia, so he could afford to be objective.

It was probably best to burn the letter. If McKenzie ever found out about it, he'd only do something stupid. He needed him at the prazo, and Catia needed a husband.

He heard him coming up the steps and quickly slipped the letter back into his jacket.

Lachlan threw himself into a chair.

Jorge poured a conservative measure of brandy into a glass and handed it to him. 'What's wrong, inglês? You got your vengeance. Evened the score.'

'I thought I would feel different to this. Relieved or proud, perhaps. Easy in my mind at least. But I don't feel any of those things.'

'Who gives a damn about your feelings. You did what was necessary.'

'What about the bastard in the turban who did all the killing?'

'Forget him.'

Lachlan swallowed the brandy and held out his glass for more.

'I pay a fortune to get you out of prison and now you want to drink all my good brandy.'

'You'll make me pay you back, one way or the other.'

Jorge nodded. He was right, he would.

He had been giving some thought to the way things had turned out. The pirates may have destroyed the fort, but the land in Delgoa Bay was still leased to him. He would have to turn a profit on it somehow. McKenzie might be foolhardy, but he admired him for what he'd done. It showed he had backbone. It might not be a bad thing to send him down there to rebuild the fort. He had initiative and he knew the local chiefs. He could turn things around and start to make the place pay again within a couple of years.

He splashed some more brandy into their glasses. 'To the future,' he said. '*Saúde!*'

The chapel of *Nossa Senhora do Baluarte* perched on the easternmost tip of the island between two beaches of white sand. It could be reached only through a gate in the wall.

Sunlight slanted through the cross-shaped openings, illuminating the worn floor crypts of the conquistadores who had died of fever and wounds in God's service. The muffled sound of the waves beating on distant rocks susurrated in the vaulted chamber.

The wedding was spoken in Latin, and no one present, aside from the Dominican friar, understood a word of it.

Jorge had shaved for the occasion and had found a moth-holed frock coat and hose in his chest. They were the same ones he had worn to marry Catia's mother in this very church, twenty years before. He could not button the coat, and he was beet-red in the face from the heat, but he had insisted that on this day, of all days, he would attend to all formalities.

Catia wore her mother's yellowed wedding veil. Lachlan stood beside her at the single limestone altar, in a shirt and breeches he had been forced to borrow from his new father-in-law. He and Catia held tight to each other's hands.

The only other witness to the marriage was the Governor of Mozambique.

Afterwards, Jorge handed the friar a small purse of *escudos* and it was done.

They were borne in a palanquin to Jorge's crumbling villa in Lime Town, where Jorge's servants had prepared a wedding feast of lobsters, prawns, grouper and baby goat, which they roasted on coals on the roof. After the governor had eaten his fill and departed, Jorge, Lachlan and Catia sat together, watched the evening stars and toasted the marriage. Jorge insisted that Lachlan spend his wedding night drinking Cape brandy with him.

As Catia got up to go to bed, Lachlan took her hand. '*Tô apaixonada,*' he whispered. 'I love you.'

She nodded. 'Your pronunciation needs work.'

CHAPTER 39

Novo Santiago

Jorge crouched in the shade of a stand of mango trees. He brought out his telescope and peered through the branches into the distance. Herds of zebra and wildebeest were grazing together on the savannah grass, their shapes rippling in the heat mirage. They often banded together for safety: the zebras were the eyes, the wildebeest the ears.

The eyeglass focused on a giraffe chewing on the leaves of an acacia tree. It was of no interest to him. He swung the lens further to the right.

It was the elephants he wanted.

There were around two score in the herd. Young calves played in the dust around the legs of the cows. Several males stood apart, massive dark shapes with enormous ivory teeth.

There was only one that interested him. He was a huge bull, the leader of the herd. He had stopped under an umbrella thorn tree, his huge grey body half-hidden by the canopy of interlaced branches. As Jorge watched, he reached down with his trunk, gathered up the dust around his feet and tossed it back over his rump in a pale cloud. He spotted a marula tree and lumbered toward it, making barely a sound.

Jorge snapped the telescope shut and nodded to Chiyiza. Today was going to be his day. He could feel it.

Chiyiza loaded the shotgun with powder and wadding and rammed the ball down the barrel. It was the size of a walnut and big enough take a man's head clean off his shoulders. Jorge took the gun from him and carefully drew back the steel hammer to full cock. Steady now.

His hands were trembling with excitement. He was already calculating the price he would get on Ilha for those teeth. But that wasn't what was giving him the shakes. It was years of heavy gin drinking that had done that. Catia had warned him about it, and it looked like she was right, damn her.

He stepped out of cover and felt the heat of the sun on his back, fierce even this early in the day. A thick droplet of sweat ran down his cheek from his temple. He flicked it away with a finger.

He was across the clearing in a few strides and ducked into the shade of the thorn trees, downwind from the tusker. He took a deep breath.

Meu Deus! The size of it! He was no more than ten paces away. Its left eye seemed to be watching him through the twisted branches and waxy green leaves. But experience told him it was just his imagination: elephants were famously short-sighted. They relied mostly on sounds and smell. Its trunk constantly tapped the air, feeling for vibration. He was so close he could see the bristles quivering in the pinkish tip.

While he kept still, he was invisible.

Tears from its tiny eye had stained its grey and wrinkled cheeks and attracted a little cloud of midges. Its ears were as tattered as battle flags. As it shifted its weight, he could make out its shoulder-blades rippling beneath the creased grey hide.

He was still too far away. Five paces would be better than ten, but he dared not get any closer. The greenish light dappled and shimmered, and the sound of the cicada beetles was deafening. He heard a sound like rolling thunder. It was the elephant, making a deep rumbling in its belly, talking to the rest of the herd.

Jorge braced his feet apart and raised the gun. The wooden butt nestled against the notch in his shoulder. His chest felt tight. He was too frightened to even breathe.

He sighted the barrel. There was a crease of skin at the base of the bull's trunk, midway between its eye pouches. A four-pound ball entering there would shatter its brain.

He took a deep, calming breath. Relax Jorge. Squeeze the trigger, gently now.

He braced himself for the recoil.

Now.

The hammer hit the flint and there was a click and a puff of white smoke. Then nothing. A false fire.

That was it, then. All the tension went out of him. He whispered a brief goodbye to Catia, the one good thing he had ever done in his life.

The old bull squealed in rage and charged. He watched it coming over the barrel of the gun.

One of the massive tusks took him in the chest and hurled him out of the thorn trees and halfway across the clearing. Chiyiza heard Jorge's bones crack as his body hit the earth. The elephant gun spiralled end over end through the air and landed in a patch of arrow grass.

The elephant stamped on Jorge's body. He sprung open like a ripe peach. After that Chiyiza couldn't bear to look. Was his boss already dead when he hit the ground? He hoped so. He didn't make any other sound if that was any indication.

The elephant worried the corpse long after it had disintegrated. Jorge had intended to saw off its teeth and leave the rest of the old bull for the birds, so Chiyiza supposed there was justice in this appalling retribution. If not for the vagaries of gunpowder and the bwana's fancy gun, it would all have ended very differently.

He hid among the trees until the bull had finally spent its rage and lumbered away. He didn't go to inspect the remains. There were some things even an experienced hunter couldn't manage on an empty stomach.

He headed back to the prazo. He only looked back once. Already the vultures had begun to wheel through the pale blue morning sky.

CHAPTER 40

Lachlan followed Chiyiza back along the game trails to retrieve what was left of Jorge. He stitched the remains in a linen sheet and brought them back to the prazo. Because of the heat they buried him that same afternoon. Lachlan fashioned a cross out of tambooti wood and carved his name on it. They would get a proper marker, marble or coral stone, when they next went to Ilha.

There was no priest their side of Ilha, so Lachlan spoke a few words from the Bible over the grave. Later that evening, on sunset, he saw the local *nganga* at the grave site, blowing ashes over the grave and dancing with his spirit stick. The villagers kept up their drumming all night.

Catia didn't cry. She just sat on the *stoep*, clinging to Lachlan's hand. Later he carried her to bed. She lay there, staring at the shadows in the rafters, not saying a word. He lay beside her with his arms around her. He could think of nothing to say.

When he woke the next morning, Catia's side of the bed was empty. He got up and went outside. Paolo said he had not seen her and neither had any of the kitchen girls. He finally found her sitting on the floor of Jorge's office in the main house.

He had never been inside. It was much as he had imagined it - littered with gin bottles, contracts of sale, and boxes of homemade paper cartridges. There was even an elephant tusk propped in the corner.

The door of the iron safe was open, and the contents were strewn around her on the moth-eaten *kaross*. It contained the detritus of Jorge's chaotic life. There were several boxes of uncut gems, and a locket with a miniature of a woman that he supposed was Catia's mother. There was also an almanac for 1738, a tinder box with flint and steel, a handful of rubies, a flintlock pistol dressed in fine silverwork, a small fortune in silver cruzados, and a dagger with a handle of rhinoceros horn attached to a well-used leather belt.

Catia picked up a cross on a leather thong and held it out to him. It was made of silver and had a baroque pearl set into it.

'It belonged to my mother,' she said. 'I didn't know he still had it. I never suspected that he was sentimental.'

He handed it back to her and she looped it over her neck.

She had a letter in her right hand.

'What's that?'

'Read it. It's for you.'

He took it from her.

> I don't know if this letter will ever find its way into the right hands. I find myself astonished that I am writing it at all, as everyone believes you are all dead. If any of you escaped this atrocity, then I cannot imagine ...

He felt numb the first time he read it through, couldn't take it in. He read it again. He felt her watching him.

'When I found it in the safe, my first thought was to burn it,' she said. 'But I couldn't. That wouldn't be fair.'

He read the letter a third time and slid down the wall, as if he'd been shot. He let the paper slip through his fingers to the floor. 'Do you think he intended me to ever have it?'

She shook her head. 'Who knows what he was thinking? I spent my whole life trying to understand him. No. I think he intended to burn it and just couldn't bring himself to do it. He knew it was the wrong thing.'

> His name is Napoleon Gagnon. He is a French mercenary.

'You have to go after this man,' she said. 'Or you will not rest.'
He nodded.
'Do you know, some nights you cry out in your sleep? Even when I shake you, you don't wake up. You see this bruise?' She pointed to her cheek. 'I told you I walked into a door. It was you, you lashed out in your dreams.'
'Why didn't you tell me?'
She shrugged. 'I thought it would pass with time. But it won't, will it? Not until you find the man in the turban.' She picked up the letter, read through it again. 'But how can you go up against a man with his own army?'
'I'll wait until his army is looking the other way.'
Her eyes were swollen and red. She must have been crying all night. 'This is not a joke,' she said.
'I don't know what or how I can do this. The first thing is to find him. As it says in the letter, this Captain Rodron has already spoken to the President of the British East India Company in Madras about hiring me

as a clerk. Once I am there, I will find out more about Gagnon and work out a plan.'

'That's it?'

'For now.' He picked up the letter and put it in his shirt. 'Would you come with me?'

She shook her head. 'What do I know about Hindustan? This is my life, here at Novo Santiago.'

'I will only be gone for a while. I promise you I'll come back.'

'Don't make promises you can't keep.'

'When it's done, I will come home to you.'

'Come home like my father did, in little pieces and wrapped in a shroud?'

He reached for her. 'I have no choice.'

She gripped his hand. 'I know,' she said, but there was a catch in her voice.

CHAPTER 41

A lone cormorant patrolled the reef, looking for prey. A flock of gulls squabbled and shrieked over the fish scraps the lascars had thrown into the lagoon from the back of the dhow.

It was not long past sunrise and the water shimmered in the early light, so clear Lachlan could see tiny fish shooting past. New sandbanks had formed in the bay overnight. It was low tide and wavelets lapped around them.

She was a veteran of many crossings. Her teak and mahogany hull was weathered to a silvery grey by sea and sun. The dirty white lateen sail had been furled along the boom.

Two houseboys waded into the water with his trunk and hoisted it to the lascars waiting at the stern. Everything he had left in the world was in there. Most of it had been gifted by Jorge or Catia: a brass telescope, a shaving mirror, razor and strop, a tinder box with flint and steel, pens, writing paper and ink. There were also a dozen bottles of Dr Chamberlain's sovereign diarrhoea remedy. The captain of the dhow, an ancient Mohammedan with a wispy grey beard, told him he would need it.

The only clothes he had were those he had begged or borrowed from Jorge. His most precious possession was Jorge's gun, a silver-mounted Dutch sporting rifle with *'Penterman Utrecht'* engraved on the stock. Lachlan had coated it liberally with whale oil and beeswax and wrapped it in oilcloth to keep out the salt during the crossing. He also had some of

Jorge's first-class sporting gunpowder in a tin can and a leather pouch with ammunition.

There was a shout from one of the lascars. He pointed up the beach. Catia made her way down the dunes in breeches and a wide brimmed hat.

He walked up the beach to meet her.

'Did you change your mind?' he said.

She looked over her shoulder. Two of the houseboys were struggling down the sand with a wooden chest. 'I won't let you do this *loco* thing on your own. You know what happened the last time you tangled with this man. You ended up on your belly with your back a bloody mess.'

'*Tô apaixonada,*' he said.

She shook her head. 'You still can't pronounce it right.'

/

The wind whipped the lateen sail as they cut through the sandbanks toward the open sea. Once they were out of the bay, they would head towards the Madagascar straits and set a course across the great ocean for the Coromandel coast, the south-west monsoon behind them. The timbers creaked and groaned as they hammered through the chop, the lascars frantically working the boom. Their dhow had seen better days, but the skipper knew what he was about.

Lachlan sat among the ropes and baskets on the deck. Catia stood at the stern rail staring at the dun line of the coast until the prazo disappeared from sight over the rim of the sea.

PART 2

Full Moon Over India

CHAPTER 42

Madras, on the Coromandel coast of India

During the day, they sat on a cargo of mangrove poles, their lips chapped dry by the sun and wind. The skipper had built the dhow himself, and it was held together using coir. Like many of the Mohammedans, he thought that magnets deep under the sea would suck any iron nails straight out of the hull, so he had built her without any metal parts at all.

Lachlan felt the churn of the sea beneath him and listened to the creak of the ancient timber and the wind whipping in the great lateen. With every day, Africa receded further beyond the horizon.

Shearwaters and terns rode the currents above their heads, and sardine shoals darted in quick shadows through the water. A dragonfly landed on one of the halyard blocks.

Madras finally appeared from the haze early one morning. A fish jumped off the bows, and gulls shrieked and circled.

There was a heavy chop as they got closer to the land, and the deck was soon wet and slippery with spray. A thicket of masts and a church spire rose above the walls of a fort.

Their captain informed them that there was no proper harbour at Madras, and they would have to anchor well offshore because of the shallows. Long native rowing boats – he called them *masulas* - were heading out to ferry them to the land.

Lachlan stared at the huge surf crashing on the beach and shook his head. He had seen smaller seas wreck a three-master with a fifty-man crew.

There were half a dozen near-naked local men on the *masula*. They heaved to alongside and reached up to help them down into the boat. The captain himself handed down Lachlan's canvas-wrapped flintlock rifle. They were assured their two chests of luggage would follow on the next boat.

The rowers were all lean, wiry young men. They shouted warnings and instructions to each other in what Lachlan recognised as the local Hindu language he had learned from Arjuna. As they got close to shore, they appeared watchful but unconcerned. Just beyond the break line they decked their oars and waited. The steersman pointed as a giant wave passed under them and then, as one, the oarsmen struck their paddles into the water and rowed hard. They were launched on the crest of the swell for one breathless and exhilarating moment, before crashing down into a spray of white foam.

Moments later they were on the strand.

There were ropes lashed to the bow and stern. Two of the men grabbed them and jumped out into the surf. They swung the boat around until it was broadside to the waves. The next breaker smashed into it and drove it further up the beach. The men tied it to wooden posts in the sand. Then they ran over to Lachlan and demanded *baksheesh*.

Lachlan brushed off the wet sand. He had lost his hat somewhere between the boat and the beach, and his breeches were soaked through.

He looked over at Catia. She had a colour to her cheeks. It was the first time since Jorge had been killed by the elephant. She was even laughing.

'I like it here already,' she said.

He looked up the beach. There was a young man watching them. He was wearing a scarlet Company uniform, complete with a powdered wig and tricorn hat, and he had with him an escort of sepoys.

He came down to meet them, his hand extended. 'My name's Charlie Mathieson,' he said. 'I'm an ensign with the British East India Company.'

'You're the Customs House.'

He grinned. 'Something like that.'

'My name's McKenzie. President Channing is expecting me.'

Mathieson nodded, still sizing him up. Then he looked at Catia, and his expression changed from confusion to consternation as he took in her breeches and her long black hair. His face turned the colour of boiled lobster.

'Oh, my word.'

'May I present my wife, Catia.'

'Your wife?' Mathieson said. He took off his hat and bowed his head. 'Madam.'

Catia looked amused. 'Should I curtsey?' she said in Portuguese.

Mathieson didn't wait for the translation. He was looking over Lachlan's shoulder and frowning. 'Oh, that's bad luck,' he said.

The other *masula*, that had their two chests of clothes on board, had capsized in the massive surf. Some *peons*, who had assembled on the shore for just this eventuality, splashed into the waves to rescue what they could. They tied ropes around the chests and used bamboo poles to lift them on their shoulders. They staggered up the beach with them.

'Don't worry,' Mathieson said, 'it happens all the time. We'll wash off the salt, and the sun will soon dry everything out. Welcome to Madras.'

Lachlan and Catia followed Mathieson up the strand towards the water gate. A British East India flag, its colours faded by the relentless tropical sun, whipped and rattled in the breeze. Gulls roosted on the barrel of a bronze cannon protruding from one of the gunports.

A horde of local people were waiting in the shade of the fortress gates, mostly hawkers selling rice cakes and bananas. There was also an army of beggars: ancient grandmothers, and skeletal women with babies clinging to their necks. Mathieson shoved his way through them with the aid of their escort.

Inside the fort lay another world. There were acres of green, tropical parkland shaded by banana palms and tall tamarind trees. The broad avenues were lined with graceful mansions. It was quiet after the raucous hubbub at the gates. The only sounds were the chatter of myna birds and the muted roar of the surf from the beach. It made Lachlan think of his father's stories about England.

'White Town,' Mathieson said.

There was another, inner, fort. A native sepoy saluted as they went through the gate. Inside it was like the Portuguese fort on Ilha, but much greener. There were well-swept brick pavements, and thatched huts lined the fortress walls. Mathieson told him that they were warehouses.

'And what's that?' Lachlan said, pointing to a stately mansion that dwarfed the fort's pepper pot bastions.

'That's the President's Residence,' Mathieson said.

'I thought it might be home to the Maharajah.'

'The President represents the British East India Company on the Coromandel coast. He's far more important than the Maharajah.'

'Ask him where we're going,' Catia said.

'I'm escorting you to the President's office,' Mathieson said, when Lachlan translated for her. 'He'll want to see you straight away.'

'We're wet,' Lachlan said.

'He won't mind.'

'I mind.'

'Sorry,' Mathieson said and gave them both a winning smile. 'But they're my standing orders. All new and unexpected arrivals have to see President Channing immediately.'

Inside the Residence they crossed a vast black and white marble-tiled foyer. A staircase swept up to Channing's office on the first floor. Two more sepoys stood on guard either side of a pair of carved rosewood doors, their bayonets fixed to the barrels of their muskets. They attempted a ragged stamp of their feet and pulled back the doors.

Mathieson led the way into a vast and sombre room. Punkha-wallahs squatted in the corners, working the woven bamboo fans on the ceiling. From the windows there was a commanding view of the ships in the gage roads. Portraits of past Presidents glowered down at them from the panelled walls.

Channing looked up from the vast expanse of his desk. His grim demeanour was emphasised by his black coat and newly powdered wig. 'I'm busy,' he said to Mathieson. 'What is it?'

'This gentleman has just arrived, sir. He said you would be expecting him.'

Channing stared at him.

'Lachlan McKenzie,' Lachlan said. 'I believe Captain James Rodron has spoken to you about me. He said you might have a position here for me.'

Channing took a fob watch from his silk embroidered waistcoat and stared at it. 'That was months ago,' he said. 'You're late.'

Channing regarded the sunburned man standing in front of his desk, then glanced at the extraordinary creature beside him. They both looked as if they had stepped straight out of the jungle. The young man was bare-headed and had on salt-encrusted breeches and a dirty linen shirt. His wife, if that was what she was, was dressed as no gentlewoman he had ever met. And what was she? More than a touch of the tar brush, by the looks of it.

Extraordinary.

He leaned back into his chair.

'I'm sorry I was delayed,' Lachlan said.

'There is no need to dissemble. I know what happened to you and your family. You have my condolences.'

'Thank you.'

'Do you still wish to take up a position here?'

'With all my heart.'

'Well, fortunately for you I have much use for good young men. You should both sit down.' He spared another glance at the woman in her loose riding trousers and boots. He half rose from his chair and gave her a stiff bow.

'May I present my wife, Catia.'

'Does she speak English?'

'Very little. Her father was Portuguese.'

Channing gave him a sharp look. If he'd known the young pup would be bringing a foreign wife with him, he might have reconsidered, but it would be dishonourable to renege now.

He resumed his seat. 'Captain Rodron spoke to me about you,' Channing said. 'I knew your father, you know.'

'I didn't know that.'

'Years ago, in England. It was why I agreed to take you on. I didn't expect to see you here. My information was that Hamish and his family were all dead.'

'I was lucky.'

'You seem alright. An experience like that, it would have turned most men's minds.'

'I'd rather not talk about it if you don't mind.'

Channing didn't like it. Something about this wasn't right. But he had given his word. 'I don't suppose you know any of the local jabber?'

'My father employed a tutor. I am reasonably fluent in Tamil.'

'Good. Any other languages?'

'A little Xitsonga, Swahili and...' Lachlan glanced at Catia. '...Portuguese.'

Channing pursed his lips, impressed despite himself. 'Some of the local traders speak Portuguese, so that could be useful. Though I have to warn you, they are not popular here among Company people. They took the side of the French against us in the recent conflict. Your wife may find life a little lonely.' His interest was piqued. 'What else can you do?'

'I can turn my hand to most things.'

'What I need is someone who knows their way around an accounts ledger.'

'I kept them for my father. Someone had to. The Governor of Mozambique would steal your boots if you didn't tie your laces.'

Channing allowed himself a smile at the boy's colourful turn of phrase. He had spirit, at least. 'How much do you know about the politics of the Coromandel?'

'Not very much.'

'Then I'll enlighten you. You couldn't have come at a worst time. The situation here is parlous. The truth is the Company holds Madras and Fort

David to the south. We are hanging on here by our very fingernails. A year ago, this fort was still in French hands. Our government made peace with the French in Europe, and by the terms of the treaty, they had to give it back. But my guess is we'll be at war with them again before the year's out.'

'We?'

'The Company. We have our own army, and the French *Compagnie des Indes* at Pondicherry has theirs. Our wars aren't about politics or land or religion. They're about something far more important. Money.'

'I see.'

'No, you don't, not yet. But you will. You see, Hindustan was a single great Empire once with one Maharajah. But now it's breaking up and all the local despots are scrambling for a share. Our policy is to try to back the right horse. We'll help some jumped-up nawab grab a princedom for himself and, in return, we'll demand a monopoly on their trade. The French have the same strategy.'

'But it's not going well for us?'

Channing shook his head. 'We don't have enough men or enough money.'

'A red coat and a sword might be better suited to my temperament, sir. Not being stuck away in a dusty warehouse with ink on my fingers.'

'You want to be a soldier? The rank and file of our army are the dregs of England, pure rabble. You won't find any of them worthy of your company or your abilities. Even if I were misguided enough to make you an officer, there is very little hope of advancement compared to what I'm offering you. You'll start off as a writer. Not much to it at first but prove to me what you can do, and promotion can be very swift.'

Channing picked up his goose quill and drew a piece of paper towards him. 'For now, we have to find you somewhere to sleep. All the other writers sleep in the single men's quarters. As you're married, there's a bungalow I can make available to you, but it's not been used for a while. It will need some work. In the meantime, there's an apartment that you may use.'

'Thank you, sir. We'll make do.'

The governor raised an eyebrow. 'Good luck,' he said, bent over his papers and went back to work.

Mathieson led them across a parade ground to a two-storey building. A staircase led to the upper floors. A shaded veranda encircled the first storey. Halfway along was a small furnished apartment that Mathieson said was maintained for visiting dignitaries.

Someone had brought up their luggage. Most of it had been draped over the veranda rails to dry. Ruined anyway I suppose, Lachlan thought. Mathieson was staring at the gun case Lachlan had refused to part with ever since they climbed out of the surfboat. It was still wrapped up in its oilskin.

'Is that your gun?'

Lachlan nodded. He unwrapped it, checking it carefully for water damage.

'Beautiful piece,' Mathieson said.

'It has a rifled barrel. It can bring down a kudu at four hundred paces.'

'A kudu?'

'It's a large antelope.'

Mathieson whistled softly, impressed. He turned back to the rooms. 'Hope you'll be comfortable here. It's not much but it's the best we can offer at short notice, I'm afraid.' He clapped his hands together. 'I'll leave you to get unpacked. They'll be serving lunch downstairs when you hear the bell. You'll get the chance to meet everyone.'

After he'd gone, they looked around their new home. Mathieson was right, it wasn't much. There was a large living room with grubby, white-washed walls and a hardwood floor covered with dusty Bengal rugs. The bedroom was cramped and the mosquito net over the bed was torn. At the prazo they had a view of the Indian Ocean from their bed. Here, there was just a single opaque window, glazed with tiny panes of oyster-shell. Everything was covered in a fine layer of sand.

They went out onto the veranda. It looked out over the parade ground. Banana palms thrust their huge leaves against the bars of the balcony rails.

'It's not exactly a palace,' Lachlan said.

'I didn't expect one,' Catia said. 'What did your new employer say about me?'

'He was curious.'

'The way he looked at me! He didn't know whether to invite me to be his concubine or have me sweep his floor and empty his night jar.'

'He said the Portuguese aren't well liked here. Your people sided with the French in the last war.'

'Did you tell him about Napoleon Gagnon?'

'No, I didn't.'

'Why not?'

He shrugged his shoulders.

'Because you don't want people thinking you're *loco*.' She put a finger to her temple.

'Do you think I'm mad?'

She put her arms around him. 'My papa was crazy. I am too, a little. So, I wouldn't have you any other way.'

Through the open window, he saw a red-jacketed sepoy climb a small platform and strike a large brass bell with a mallet. The sound reverberated around the fort's walls.

'Lunch,' he said.

'We should go and meet our new friends. Well, *your* new friends. I shall sit there quietly and try not to look too Portuguese.'

The dining room was breathlessly hot, despite the best efforts of the punkha-wallahs working feverishly in the corners. It was panelled in dark teak, with an imposing portrait of George the Second hanging on one wall and a gilded coat of arms of the East India Company on another. A long wooden table ran down the centre.

President Channing took his position at the head of the table, then assigned everyone else to their seats. As new arrivals, he placed Lachlan and Catia next to him. The factors – the Company functionaries who did all the buying and selling for the Company - were seated down either side in order of seniority, with their wives. The writers were seated further away. Lachlan thought he recognized several of them from the *Southampton*. The children were assigned to the foot of the table.

Their quarters may have been spartan, but the dining arrangements were nothing short of lavish. Lachlan couldn't believe his eyes. There was a silver dining service and a small orchestra playing chamber music. And no one was dressed for the weather. The men all wore heavy brocade and had sweat pouring down their faces from under their powdered wigs. They were as red as the sepoys' jackets, but the faces of the Company wives were deathly white, caked with heavy cosmetics. It was partly fashion and partly as protection from the sun.

'They all look like sides of boiled pork,' Catia whispered to him.

Native servants rushed around with basins of water so that everyone could wash their hands. Then lunch was brought in. On the prazo, lunch meant some dried meat and fruit, washed down with a swig from a leather canteen. This was pure extravagance, like one of the Tsonga wedding feasts. The main course was roasted peacock and venison stuffed with raisins and almonds. This was how they ate every day, it seemed.

The florid-faced man on Lachlan's right had clearly not missed a single lunch or dinner in his whole period of service. He was wide as he was tall, with bad teeth, and hairs sprouting from his nose. His cheeks were blotched with tiny red veins, a sign of a lifetime of heavy drinking. He introduced himself as Dunning, the Company doctor in Madras.

'I hear,' he said without preamble, 'that you have come here straight from the African jungle.'

'Hardly a jungle, Doctor Dunning. Catia and I run one of the largest plantations south of Mombasa.'

Dunning raised his eyebrows. 'This lady is your wife?' He looked at Catia as if he thought Lachlan had rescued her from either a brothel or a mud hut.

'Her father built the farm. We grow sugar cane, rice and maize.'

'I am told Africa is mostly jungle, inhabited by savages.'

'The reports have been vastly exaggerated. Where we live, the local people only boil people up when the maize crop fails.'

Dunning gave him a look, unsure whether Lachlan was making fun of him. 'May I ask what brought you to these shores?'

'It was my father's wish that I take up employ with the company.'

'You have experience of clerking?'

'Not much. But I can haggle in English, Swahili and Portuguese. And I can fire a cannon as well as I can shoot a hunting rifle. It could be useful if the Company goes back to war with the French.'

'Let us hope it doesn't come to that.'

'What is life like here, Doctor Dunning?'

'No doubt your father has told you that it is a place where an ambitious young gentleman might accumulate great wealth in just a few short years. I do not know if he also told you that the climate here is not conducive to long life. Death is commonplace and I see far too much of it. A young man dies here, and his friends stand over his coffin and weep. The next day they are trying to outbid each other for his horse.' He gave Catia a long and lascivious look. 'Does your wife speak English?'

'Very little.'

Dunning leaned across Lachlan and said, in a loud voice, as if speaking to an imbecile child, 'Very hot, Madras!' He waved a hand in front of his face.

Catia raised her eyebrows. Lachlan tapped his glass with a finger to let her know that Dunning had been drinking all through lunch. She nodded and returned her attention to her food.

The servants brought pineapples, apricots and grapes, but the younger men at the end of the table seemed to care more for the claret and the *arrack* punch. They were already well in their cups.

'Look at them,' Dunning said. 'Would you believe the oldest of them is nineteen years old? They gamble and drink and spend all night with the Hindu dancing girls. They give no thought to their health or their morals. Here, have a little more shiraz.' Before Lachlan could answer, he had refilled both their glasses to the brim from the decanter. 'The Company brings it down from Persia. Never mind the water, you're in Madras now.'

By Lachlan's count, Dunning drank three glasses to every one of his. Finally, the good doctor's head slumped to the table, half-way through telling Lachlan about a scheme to trade cardamom on his private account.

He was carried from the hall, snoring.

CHAPTER 43

Catia slipped off her soft leather boots, rolled down her hose and kneaded the soles of her feet. She dabbed water on her neck, shoulders and between her breasts, then put on her nightshirt. She climbed into the bed, pulling the mosquito net as tight as she could. There was a large rent in it. A seagull could fly through it, Lachlan thought, never mind a mosquito.

He blew out the candle and climbed under the netting. It was too hot even for a sheet. They lay there, listening to the deafening sound of the crickets and the whine of the mosquitoes. It was hot and breathless in the room. They were both bathed in sweat.

'All the Englishmen we have met today,' Catia said, 'are either schoolboys or act like them.'

'I'm starting to understand why my father and Uncle Rory left England.'

'Who was that awful old man you were sitting next to?'

'He told me he's the Company doctor.'

'I wouldn't want him near me, even if I was mortally ill.'

'Oh, I don't know. His breath could raise the dead. With any luck we won't be here long enough to require his services.'

'Who knows how long we will be here, *meu amor*. The French are a hundred miles away inside a fortress, and you don't know if the man you are looking for is even there.' She put her arms around him. 'I don't care how long it takes. Just don't come home wrapped in a sheet, like papa. I couldn't stand it. Promise me?'

'I promise,' he said, though they both knew it was a lie.

They woke to the smell of a new country. Lachlan went onto the veranda and looked out over the castellated walls. He could make out a grey, oily sea melding into a suffocating sky.

A servant prepared their breakfast: fried fish and rice with an omelette. Soon after they finished eating, Mathieson appeared. He was dressed in a grubby white suit with sweat patches under the arms. His cheerful demeanour was somehow depressing. Lachlan greeted him at the door and invited him in.

'How do you find this heat?' Mathieson said. He produced a voluminous white handkerchief and mopped at his forehead. 'You're probably used to it. Thought I'd die when I first got here.' He saw Lachlan's rifle lying on the table, still in its oil cloth, and gave it an envious glance.

'You like shooting?' Lachlan said.

'Spent most of my life at a boarding school in London. But I spent the summers at home in Scotland, did a bit of shooting on the moors. Nothing like you, of course. Only thing I've ever bagged was grouse and a few rabbits. What's the biggest thing you've ever shot?'

'A lion.'

He saw Mathieson's jaw drop.

'It's nothing to be proud of. I had a gun, the lion didn't. I'd hardly call it a fair fight. He sprang at us from the undergrowth, there was no choice.'

'I'm afraid you're going to find all of us pretty dull fellows.'

'I never find people dull, Mathieson. Everyone has another side to them.'

'Call me Charlie,' he said.

'What can I do for you, anyway? Are you here to make sure I get off to work?'

'The old boy said you can start tomorrow. Today he wants me to show you the ropes. Ready to see Hindustan?'

Ilha was the largest town Lachlan had ever seen in his young life, so Madras left him stunned by its size, its grandeur, and its utter unsuitability as either a fortress or a trading post.

For one thing it had no useful harbour. The heavy surf they had encountered when they arrived was quite usual, it seemed. It pounded the beach below the fort on the ocean side day after day. The other side of the town faced a salt-water lagoon. Mathieson said that it flooded the plain around the fort during the monsoon. There was no natural drinking water within a mile and the soil was so sandy that nothing would grow in it.

Why the Company had chosen it as their base on the Coromandel defied belief.

The rust-red bastions of the fortress were still being rebuilt after the French siege three years before. But the walls of the wealthy residents' houses inside the 'White Town,' as Mathieson called it, were hardly touched. They gleamed like marble.

'*Chunam,* they call it,' Mathieson said. 'It's a kind of plaster they make from powdered fish bones and shell. Looks very grand, almost like the real thing. The problem is, we could be going to the expense and bother of building all this just for the French to come in and take over again.'

'Do you think they will?'

'Channing thinks they can take back Madras anytime they want.'

'Why don't they?'

'Apparently, they're only waiting for an excuse.'

'But haven't France and Britain signed a peace treaty?'

'That's in Europe, and Europe's a long way away. What happens over there doesn't have much to do with politics in Hindustan. All the local princes are jostling for power, and they're using us and the French to fight their wars for them. The Company can't stay out of it, but we have to choose the right side. There'll be more fighting soon enough. Don't look so pleased about it.'

'I'm not one for pen-pushing.'

'Well if it's warring you want, you've come to the right place. It could all blow up again any day. Two of the local nawabs are at each other's throats and we've thrown in our lot with some fellow called Ali. He's been pinned down in his fortress at Trichinopoly by some other warlord.'

'What's his name?'

'Chanda Sahib. He has the French backing him. It will be full scale war before the year is out.'

They made a quick tour of the fort. Inside the godowns, large calico-wrapped bales of muslin cloth were stacked to the rafters, waiting to be sent to England. Native porters were carrying even more of them in for weighing.

Mathieson opened the door to a large and dusty room. A punkha-wallah sat at the very end, moving a fan on the ceiling with a rope-and-pulley contraption that he operated with his toe. The young men Lachlan had seen at lunch the previous day were working in shirtsleeves at high wooden desks, long lines of them scratching figures into thick ledgers. Pages of bills of lading and stock inventories were piled in front of them. An Indian boy walked around with a kettle, refilling small glasses with chai.

'This is where it all happens,' Mathieson said.

As Lachlan looked around the hot and stifling room his heart sank. I'll go mad in here, he thought. Give me one day of this and I will start frothing at the mouth. I would rather be in prison. I would rather be dead.

'It's not so bad when you get used to it,' Mathieson said, reading his mind.

'This is what I am to do all day? Fill up the ledgers while the Company takes all the profit?'

'Only while you're learning the ropes. Someone with your experience, you'll soon be promoted to a job as a factor. Then you can do some private trading on the side, turn a profit for the company and take a percentage for yourself. There are fortunes to be made here.'

'You just told me that the French are about to take back Madras.'

Mathieson shrugged. 'Nothing's certain.'

'Tell me about Dunning,' Lachlan said.

Mathieson looked surprised. 'What do you want to know?'

'Is he of any use?'

'Hard to say. To be honest, I'm not even sure he's really a doctor. The word is his family paid a good deal of money just to get him out of England. One of the fellows heard that he was drinking and gambling too much, and then some money went missing from his father's accounts. It's only a rumour, mind.'

'And they put him in charge of the hospital?'

'It's not really a hospital. Just somewhere to put people while they're digging a hole to throw them in. Only the poorest of the Company soldiers ever go there and few of them ever come out.'

Lachlan looked up at the Company flag hanging limp in the suffocating grey of the morning. Below it, a carrion bird roosted like a gargoyle on a limed wall. Lachlan remembered one of its fellow black-eyed bastards watching and waiting for him to die on the beach in Delgoa Bay. He still had the scars from where its claws had torn strips of flesh off his back.

He picked up a stone and threw it at the hellish creature. The stone struck it a glancing blow to its breast. It screeched, flapped its wings, and soared away into the grey sky.

'Wouldn't make a habit of that,' Mathieson said. 'You'll wear out your arm if you throw rocks at every one of those things you see here.'

What a place, Lachlan thought. He had to find a way to do what he had come here to do quickly and go home.

'Lachlan. Lachlan!'

It was Katherine's voice.

She was running towards him through the smoke, and he tried to shout a warning, but he couldn't get the words out in time. All he could do was watch as the soldiers raised their muskets. Two bright red stains spread across her white blouse, and she crumpled onto her knees.

'Katherine!'

His hands were wet. He stared at them. There was blood everywhere.

A tall, thin man in a white turban appeared through the billowing clouds of smoke. Lachlan picked up a Claymore and ran towards him, but no matter how fast he ran, he couldn't reach him. It was like running through sand.

'Lachlan. Lachlan!' He opened his eyes. Catia was shaking him. 'Wake up! It was just a dream, *caro*.'

The sheets were soaked in sweat. He couldn't get his breath. 'Katherine,' he said.

Catia put her arms around him. Lachlan blinked, trying to remember where he was. He stared at the halo of the moon through the oyster shell windows. He heard the buzzing of a mosquito and the boom of the surf.

Madras. He was in Madras.

'I can feel your heart,' Catia said. 'It's like you've been running up a mountain.'

'I'm sorry I woke you.'

'Was it the same dream?'

'Yes,' Lachlan whispered.

The same dream, every night. Every night the man in the turban killed her again.

CHAPTER 44

Early the next morning, there was a knock on their door. Lachlan opened it, expecting to see Charlie Mathieson, but it was Dunning, flushed and mopping at the sweat on his face with a handkerchief.

'Doctor. Everything alright?'

'I heard you need a servant girl.'

'Where did you hear that?'

'Mathieson told me. Someone to wash and clean and make chai, that sort of thing.'

Catia came to the door. 'What does he want?' she said in Portuguese.

Lachlan told her.

'Tell him I can manage,' Catia said.

'You know you're entitled to one,' Dunning said, when Lachlan told him they would be fine without one. 'The Company are obliged to pay for one. Didn't Channing tell you that?'

'Why are you telling us all this?'

'I had a girl working for me up until last week. She'd be perfect for you. Good cook, hard-working, no trouble.'

'Why did you get rid of her?'

'She couldn't speak word of English. Just the local jabber and Portuguese, like a lot of the niggers in Black Town. No good to me, but she would be company for your wife when you're out working all day.'

Lachlan told Catia what Dunning had said.

'Where do we find her?' she said.

'She lives in Black Town,' Dunning said, 'in the *ganj*. Come on, we've a couple of hours before you have to start work. I'll take you there.'

Madras was actually two towns; there was the White Town for the Europeans and the Black Town for the local people.

While the European quarter was confined within the walls of Fort Saint George, the Black Town spread for miles beyond, with the sea and the esplanade road on one side and the river on the other. It mostly comprised drab clay cottages with thatched roofs. The only buildings to break the dreary panorama were the pagodas of the Hindu temples and the minarets of the Moors. The dun-coloured streets were wide and dusty, laid out in a grid pattern, along with some newly planted mango and coconut palms. There were small incense-choked temples everywhere.

The bazaar – they called it the *ganj* - was in the heart of the Black Town. When they got out of the *tonga,* they were overwhelmed by the smells, the colours and the noise. Frankincense billowed from a dark and ancient shrine. One moment they were walking through clouds of sweet smoke, the next they found themselves breathing in a stench foul enough to knock a man from his horse.

Dunning led them through the warren of laneways. There were women everywhere, some bowed under the weight of the baskets on their heads, others squatting on the ground hawking piles of chapattis or fist-sized mounds of onions. They all wore brilliant-coloured *saris.* They reminded Catia of the wraps the Tsonga women wore. But here even the poorest of them had gold plated bangles on their wrists and ankles, and studs in their noses and ears.

Everything was for sale: paper, gingham, swords, forks, thimbles. Catia was surprised to discover that most of the native traders spoke Portuguese as well as the local language, just as Dunning had said.

A cow, with a garland of marigolds hung around its neck, shouldered past them, its bony pelvis almost knocking her off her feet. It began munching cheerfully on a shopkeeper's lunch, eating the rice as well as the palm leaf plate. He stood to the side shouting at it and waving his arms.

'Why doesn't he just push it out of the way?' Catia said to Lachlan. 'Is he frightened of it?'

There was a hurried exchange between Lachlan and Dunning. 'He says a good Hindu cannot harm a cow,' Lachlan said. 'In the Hindu scriptures the cow is a sacred symbol of life. He is not frightened of the cow. He is frightened of something called karma.'

'What's that?'

This time the conversation was prolonged. At the end of it, Lachlan looked bewildered. 'The Hindus believe that everything we do has a consequence whether it's a good thing or a bad thing. He says it's like an invisible and eternal ledger book. And a debt can carry on not just across one lifetime, but many lifetimes.'

He turned back to Dunning. 'So according to karma, if you kill someone, that's a bad thing. You will have to pay back that life one day.'

'It's not whether something is bad or good, old boy,' Dunning said. 'It's simply consequence. Kill, be killed in return. It all keeps on and on until someone says enough and stops the karma wheel.'

'What about if someone deserves to die?'

Dunning smiled. 'I don't think there's exceptions to the rule. Not in Hindustan. Anyway, what are you worried about? You don't believe all that mumbo-jumbo, do you?'

He stopped outside a crumbling hole in the wall. There were calico bags full of peppercorns stacked outside and an awning hung over the entrance to keep out the worst of the sun.

He went inside and they saw him talking to the shopkeeper. The man had a wiry beard and curly grey hair under his skull cap. His white robe was threadbare.

'This is Senhor Antonio do Mendes,' Dunning said.

Catia spoke to him briefly in Portuguese, but it was as if he hadn't heard.

Dunning shrugged apologetically. 'He doesn't like the English,' he said.

'I'm not English.'

'But you're with two Englishmen.'

Mendes summoned someone from inside the shop. A young girl came out. She was rail thin. She had dark skin, large brown eyes and a gold ring in her nose.

'Você fala português?' Catia said. *Do you speak Portuguese?*

'O mestre diz que eu falo muito bem.' *The master says I can speak it quite well.*

'Where are you from?'

'I was born in Ceylon. My mother married a Tamil man, here in Madras, but he died. There are ten of us now. We have to work.'

'Do you want to come and live with us inside the fort?'

'If you think I might be of service, I would like that very much.'

Catia turned to Mendes. 'We'll take her.' She looked back at the girl. 'What's your name?'

'Ammani,' she said.

CHAPTER 45

Life at the British East India Company was every bit as bad as Lachlan had imagined. He worked in the godowns from dawn to dusk, taking stock of calico bags of spices and bales of muslin, and recording all the trades in massive ledgers. He wasn't allowed to do any trading himself, though he spoke the local dialect better than some of the factors. He had ink stains on his fingers instead of the red dirt of Mozambique under his fingernails.

The heat was appalling. There was no respite, even at night. Catia and Lachlan tossed restlessly in their beds for hours, dozing off towards morning only to wake a few hours later to the sound of the crows. Mathieson told them that the monsoon would arrive soon and bring some relief. In the meantime, Channing had given them two *bhistis*, or water servants. They hung woven screens made of scented grass over all the windows and doors to try to cool the air.

One evening, they went down to the water gate, braving the beggars and hawkers, and walked outside. Once, the native settlement had clung to the fortress walls on the north side. But when the French besieged Madras four years before, they had used these houses as cover for their soldiers. After they captured the fort, they had ensured no one could ever use the same tactics against them by razing the maze of hovels and shacks. This cleared a field of fire for four hundred yards around the fortress walls.

The British preferred to call this wide-open space 'the Esplanade'. In the evenings it provided some relief from the suffocating heat inside the White Town.

An elephant trundled past them, its trunk and flanks painted with mysterious symbols in ochre and white. It was smaller than the massive tuskers Jorge had been obsessed with. Whenever Catia saw one she couldn't help but think of him, and how horribly he had died. Lachlan had not even let her see his body.

The sun dipped below the sea. The surf crashed on the shore, the swell running ahead of another storm. The twilight was tinged with green, and the salt wind carried grit from the beach.

'Have you made friends with any of the Company wives?' Lachlan said.

Catia shook her head. 'They can't speak any language but the one they were born with. Even if they could, what would we talk about? None of them can skin a kudu or stitch a leg wound or load a musket. I think the conversation would soon dry up. Ammani says all they do is sit around on their verandas complaining about the heat and the servants and gossiping about each other.'

'I don't think I can stand it here much longer,' Lachlan said. 'I have to find a way to get to this man.'

'But how?'

'I'll think of something. Do you think I'm crazy doing this, Catia?'

She stopped and reached for his hand. 'If it was me, I couldn't go on as if nothing had happened. Sometimes, yes, I think about what a nice life we could have together if not for him. But you can't just forget.'

'It's not only revenge, Catia. I have to know *why*.'

'Do you think that will be the end of it? I have been asking Ammani about this thing they call karma. I worry that even if you find him, and make him pay, that it will still not be over. Ammani says that if you do it, you will make yourself a bad karma, too. Just as he did.'

'You've told her about Gagnon?'

'I have to talk to someone. I'd go mad if it wasn't for her.'

He put an arm around her. 'It will be over soon. Then we'll go home. I promise.'

Dusk fell, and the mosquitoes started to swarm. They headed back inside the fort. The air was heavy with frankincense. Clouds of it floated along the verandas and courtyards, as servants went around lighting copper bowls to keep away the insects.

Hundreds of fruit bats glided into the banyan trees to roost. The night was clamorous with the boom and tonk of frogs and the buzz of cicadas.

There was also another sound, one that sent chills through them: the eerie yowling of jackals. In Africa they only came when there was fresh meat around.

'Do you hear them?' Catia said.

'I hear them.'

'I walked around White Town yesterday after you went to work. I found the European cemetery. Some of the tombs were quite grand. They had spires, pyramids and angels to let God know they were important people, like your President Channing. Writers had a stone slab, but the soldiers only had a plain wooden cross. Not enough to stop the wild animals digging them up.'

Lachlan shuddered.

'We cannot stay too long in this place, *meu amour*,' Catia went on. 'I looked at dates on the gravestones. Most of them weren't any older than us when they died.'

'Are you having second thoughts?'

'Perhaps.'

'We'll be gone by the time of the next monsoon,' Lachlan promised her. She was right. He didn't come here to count peppercorns in a warehouse. If Napoleon Gagnon wasn't going to come to Madras, he'd have to go to him.

Channing was dressed formally even in the enervating heat. He sat at his desk in a heavy woollen coat with silver buttons, white silk breeches and stockings. He wore his usual powdered wig. His face was so red he looked parboiled.

He looked up from his papers as Lachlan walked in.

'Mister McKenzie. You asked to see me. Come in, sit down. Are you settling in alright?'

'Ensign Mathieson has taken us under his wing. He's been very generous.'

'He tells me you have a good head for figures.'

'It's not difficult work. I could barter before I could walk.'

'I think I know why you're here. It's about the apartment. It's the best I can do at this stage, I'm afraid, but we'll get you sorted out with a bungalow as soon as we can.'

'It's not about our living quarters. They're quite adequate.'

Channing put down his quill, folded his hands in front of him and sat back. 'So, what is it?'

'Do you know of a man called Napoleon Gagnon?'

'What about him?'

'He's a mercenary, French I believe.'

'Not quite French. A little bit of everything, I'm told. A cur with French pretensions.'

'He's a thorn in the Company's side.'

'You could say the same of anyone who works against us.'

'Would it help the Company's cause if he was dead?'

'Why, what have you heard?'

'Would it?'

'Yes, it would be a very serious blow to the *Compagnie des Indes*. He has a considerable private army and great tactical acumen.'

'I'd like to volunteer to go to Pondicherry and assassinate him.'

Channing's jaw dropped open. Then he remembered himself and assumed his usual steely demeanour.

'I could disguise myself as a Portuguese trader,' Lachlan went on. 'I have good working knowledge of the language. Once inside the city, I will find a way to get myself next to him and kill him.'

There was a long silence. A muscle worked in Channing's jaw. 'Are you quite mad?'

'I would need your assistance, of course.'

'What possessed you to even think about such a thing?'

'I have my reasons.'

'I cannot begin to imagine what they might be.'

'I could do it.'

Channing picked up his quill. 'Go back to work.'

'Sir?'

'Go back to work and stop wasting my time. '

'I could do this if you...'

Channing pulled his papers towards him. 'It would be suicide to even attempt such a thing. I will not have your death on my conscience.' Channing pointed to the door. 'Go.'

Lachlan got up to leave. He stopped on the way out, his hand on the door. 'I am not like these other young men you have working for you. I was raised in Africa. I can shoot. I can track. I can hunt. I have killed three men, hand to hand. I am not proud of it, but it's a fact. I am not wasting your time. If the French lost Napoleon Gagnon, it would be a huge blow to them and a massive coup for you personally. And for the Company. It's a good plan.'

'Your plan, such as it is, has already been considered and acted on. We have an agent in Pondicherry, Rabiot. He's posing as a French spice merchant. So far, he has been unable to find a way of eliminating Monsieur Gagnon. If he can't do it, then you certainly wouldn't be able to. Good day to you, Mister McKenzie. Shut the door on your way out.'

When he got home, Lachlan found Catia sitting on the veranda, staring at the ghats. Sheet lightning flashed around the horizon, and he could hear the rumble of thunder.

The light outside the window was beginning to fade and Ammani went about the room, lighting candles and placing sticks of frankincense in earthenware pots to keep the mosquitoes away.

'What did he say?' Catia asked him.

'He said no.' He went to the brass bowl on the nightstand in the corner of the room and splashed some of the tepid water onto his face, then he joined Catia on the veranda. Ammani brought two glasses of chai and put them on the table between them. Catia thanked her, and she slipped away.

'Apparently, there's already a British agent in Pondicherry assigned to get rid of him,' Lachlan said. 'A fellow named Rabiot.'

'So, what will you do now?'

'I'll just have to be patient. I won't leave here until Gagnon's dead.'

There was nothing more to say. They listened to the surf pounding on the beach, and the jackals howling as they scavenged in the cemetery on the other side of the walls.

CHAPTER 46

Pondicherry

Away from the French quarter, the native city was a teeming warren of hovels, shops and temples. It reeked of dust, dung, rotting fruit and incense smoke. Goats chickens and pi-dogs fought with each other over the choicest morsels of garbage and offal.

Napoleon picked his way through the twisting, narrow lanes, using his cane to fend off any beggars who ventured too close. Adelaïde walked in step, holding a white parasol to keep off the worst of the sun.

They passed a man with testicles the size of watermelons that he carried around in a wheelbarrow. He was haggling with a butcher over a haunch of goat lying on the bare brick shelf outside his shop. A boy with a shaved head, his deformed legs twisted up behind his hips like a giant spider, squealed at them from a niche in a wall. A prostitute with a club foot and bare breasts grabbed at Napoleon's arm from behind a canvas awning. He flicked her hand away as if it were a fly.

Another filthy, bandaged hand clawed at the hem of his robe. He was wearing the stained uniform of one of Napoleon's own sepoys. '*Sahib*,' he said. 'Don't you remember me?'

Napoleon frowned. 'Take your hand off me.'

'I was a soldier in your service.'

'Not a very good one by the look of it,' he said, but nodded to Adelaïde. She opened the drawstring purse at her wrist and took out two copper coins. She tossed them at him, and they walked on.

There were entire alleys in the bazaar given over to butchers, blacksmiths, carpet salesmen and copper merchants. Napoleon and Adelaïde made their way to what the locals called Spice Street. There was stall after stall with pyramids of cloves, ginger, cinnamon and bright orange turmeric. He stopped outside one of the shops. It was larger than the others in the street, and there were rows and rows of hessian sacks lined up outside filled with shiny carob sticks and black peppercorns.

It took a moment for his eyes to grow accustomed to the gloom. A man with a luxuriant black beard appeared from the shadows. He was clearly not a native, though he wore Hindu clothes.

'Franco,' Napoleon said.

Solomon Franco had done well for himself, trading in Golconda diamonds. His family were Paradesi Jews, had lived in Madras for over two hundred and fifty years after they fled Portugal. He had been instrumental in helping the *Compagnie* against the British four years before, but when Madras had been handed back, he had hastily removed to Pondicherry. He still had many contacts inside Black Town and in the small community of Dutch Jews in Ceylon.

His connections were what Napoleon paid him for.

'Senhor Gagnon,' Franco said. He looked down at Adelaïde. 'Young lady.'

She folded the parasol and sat down on a sack of peppercorns, her hands in her lap.

'Would you like chai?'

'I don't have time,' Napoleon said. 'Do you have news?'

'The Britishers have sent out a new officer. His name is Douglas. He fought in the British Army. He is going to take over the defence of Madras.'

'Is he of any use?'

'He comes with a reputation. He isn't anything like the one they have now. He means business.'

'When does he arrive?'

'In the next week or two, they say.'

'Anything else?'

'Yes. I have the name of the British spy you were looking for.' He reached into his pocket and handed Napoleon a folded piece of paper. 'And one other thing. It is, well, unusual.'

'Tell me.'

'My fellow in Madras. He has a Sinhalese girl working for him. He got her a job inside the Britisher fort, so she could report to him on the mood of the soldiers and the Company officers.'

'That was enterprising of him.'

'She speaks a little English. Not much, but enough, and she has not told anyone this. So, the Britisher she is working for, she overheard him talking to his wife about his plans to come to Pondicherry and kill you.'

Napoleon laughed. 'Half the world wants me dead. He'll have to line up with the rest of them. What's his name?'

'His name is McKenzie. He has recently arrived from Mozambique. Does this name mean anything?'

Napoleon narrowed his eyes. 'The name means nothing to me at all. Report to me again next week.' He turned and left the shop.

'What are you thinking, papa?' Adelaïde said, as they walked back through the market.

'I am wondering how the young pup managed to escape. I had supposed it was his body we found among the wreckage of the embrasure. It seems I was wrong.'

'What will you do about him?'

'Nothing for the moment. I'm still waiting for that fat Dutchman to pay out the rest of my fee.'

'Are you worried?'

'Only about the money.'

They stopped outside a large, whitewashed building with plaster flaking off the walls. A leper sat outside the gate with a tin cup. One of her arms was no more than a stump and she had a long strip of skin flaking off her shin, revealing the raw pink flesh underneath it.

'Take two *budgerooks* from your purse and drop them in that old woman's cup,' he said.

Adelaïde did as he told her. He waited for her on the other side of the street. Then they walked on.

'Who was she, papa?' she said, as they walked away.

'It was your grandmother,' he said.

CHAPTER 47

Madras

Work began early in the mornings. A line of porters in white *dhobis* and turbans came through the gates and filed across the compound to the godowns. The factors came out to examine the trade goods and haggle with the merchants. When a price was agreed, Lachlan and the other writers weighed the bales of cotton and muslin on massive scales suspended from the rafters. They wrote up each transaction in thick, leather-bound ledgers.

The work was mind numbing and made worse by Lachlan's factor, a man called Hodges, who kept up a constant barrage of criticism. If Lachlan smudged a figure or was too slow to the weighing station, he upbraided him mercilessly.

It was as much as he could do to keep from sitting him on his pants. He promised himself that before he left Madras, he would settle with the weasel. But for now, he would have to keep his thoughts to himself and toe the line.

Work ceased after lunch, and during the heat of the afternoon the fort was uncannily quiet. Lachlan returned to his apartments and he and Catia lay on *charpoys* on their veranda while their *bhistis* did their best to keep them cool.

He and the other writers re-emerged at around four o'clock, when the faintest breath of breeze came in off the sea and the afternoon became a little cooler. They worked for another few hours, until dark, and then the Company men and their wives and children repaired to the garden. Lachlan usually changed into the evening clothes Mathieson had lent him - a loose linen coat and baggy cotton trousers.

One night after dinner, Mathieson asked him to meet him the mess hall for a cigar and a game of billiards. He almost refused, but afterwards he was pleased he didn't. Because it was Mathieson who finally gave him the first reliable news of the man he had come all the way to Hindustan to find.

Hodges clicked his tongue when Lachlan walked in, and there were glowering looks of disapproval from some of the older hands. It had been made clear to him early on that they didn't like the way Catia dressed and behaved, or the fact that she was Portuguese.

The younger lads didn't seem to know what to think. Should they ignore him, as their bosses did, or treat him as one of their own? They never seemed quite sure, so most of them did both.

Mathieson was the only one who seemed oblivious to the stares and muttering. He took a cue from the rack. 'Most of these blowsy old drunks in here, tutting at us like vicar's wives, are jealous of you.' He said it softly, so only Lachlan could hear.

'Why?'

'Because you have a pretty wife.'

'Who says so?'

'Everyone.' Mathieson broke first and his white ball nestled softly on the baulk cushion. 'If she wasn't Portuguese, those old fools would be trying to charm her.'

'Half Portuguese. Her grandmother was a princess. From the Macua.'

'I take it they're an African people. I'm afraid that kind of royalty won't cut much ice with the Company wives.'

'That's been made plain.'

'Well, you know what the English are like. Anyone born south of the Isle of Wight is a nigger. Including the French. So, what were you doing in Africa?'

'My family had a trading post. I was raised on the banks of a river south of the Ilha da Mozambique.'

'I didn't think even the good Lord ever dared to venture that far.'

Lachlan chalked his cue and lined up his first shot. 'We didn't have many visitors.'

'If you've come looking for civilization and balmy weather you won't find it here. You're a good player for someone who grew up in darkest Africa,' Mathieson said as Lachlan cannoned his ball off the white and reds.

'Africa is only dark at night, the same as here. As for billiards, my father had a table shipped in from Cape Town. My brother and I would play any chance we could.'

'And where are your family now? Are they still in Africa?'

Lachlan straightened and leaned on his pool cue. He gave Mathieson a hard stare. 'Are you Channing's spy? You ask a lot of questions.'

'Just curious, by nature.'

'What is your job here?'

'Officially, I'm President Channing's aide-de-camp.'

'And what does that mean?'

'Hard to say, really. I keep an eye on things for him.'

'Make sure new arrivals like me aren't going to cause any trouble.'

'You make it sound sinister.'

'Is it?'

Mathieson smiled and didn't answer. He bent over the table and completed two more cannons. 'My game, I think. Shall we have another?'

The windows were open. The murmur of insects was clamorous in the trees in the courtyard. As Mathieson leaned over the baize, he paused his shot to slap irritably at a mosquito that had landed on his neck. His cue ball kissed the red and clattered into the net pocket.

Hodges looked up from his game of seven card loo and muttered something to one of the players. They all looked in their direction and laughed.

'Ignore them,' Mathieson said, out of the corner of his mouth.

'I intend to,' Lachlan said. 'For now.'

'I heard you went to see Channing the other day.'

'Did Channing tell you about that?'

'No, that would be improper. But you can't sneeze inside the fort without someone in Black Town bringing you a handkerchief.'

'What else did you hear?'

'That you showed a great deal of interest in a French gentleman by the name of Napoleon Gagnon.'

'You know him?'

'Well, of course.' Mathieson potted the red and re-spotted it. He missed his next shot, and his cue ball kissed the cushion at the baulk. 'I know, for instance, that he's a very dangerous man. What's your interest in him?'

'I'd rather not say.'

Mathieson frowned and leaned on his cue. 'My, you are a mysterious fellow.' He took a glass of shiraz from the moustachioed butler, while he watched Lachlan take his shot. 'You told our President that you would volunteer to smuggle yourself into Pondicherry and kill Gagnon.'

'Yes.'

'He refused your kind offer. Why was that?

'I don't know. It was a sound plan.'

'Was it?'

'I could easily pose as a Portuguese trader. I would have the freedom to move about, discover where he was and find a way to get near him. It was a reasonable enough proposition if he'd heard me out.'

'There's nothing at all reasonable about it. You are a writer in the employ of the British East India Company, and he is a professional private soldier and military adviser to one of the most powerful princes on the Coromandel Coast. You wouldn't get anywhere near him.'

Mathieson won the next two games. He put his cue back on the rack. 'Let's take another glass of shiraz and go outside.'

They went out onto the veranda. The night clicked and hummed. Mathieson offered him a cigar. They lit them.

'Tell me about this Napoleon Gagnon,' Lachlan said.

Mathieson folded his arms and leaned against the balustrade. 'Five years ago, he was an obscure partisan. Now he is the head of a disciplined force of at least ten thousand infantry with a well-equipped train of artillery. He has two frigates anchored off Pondicherry, so he has a navy as well as an army. A man to be reckoned with, don't you think? And you're going to stroll into Pondicherry and... what?'

'I have my reasons for wanting him dead.'

'And they must be dire ones for I can see you're determined to try it. But let me tell you it's a doomed endeavour before you even set out.'

'You seem to know a lot about this man.'

'I've been on the Coromandel for a long time.'

'How long is that?'

'Four years. Longer than most. You know what they say here: the life of a man is two monsoons. One in three of those young men you see over there, playing cards and drinking brandy, will be dead in two years from the fever.'

'So, you're an old hand.'

'Practically.'

'So, what else can you tell me about Gagnon?'

'He's a half breed. His father was French, his mother was a *bibi*, his father's Hindu mistress. The French are as fussy about bloodlines as the English, so they'll never treat him as an equal. But they tolerate him as long as he fights on their side. They say he's as ruthless a bastard as ever walked the earth.'

'There must be some way to get to him.'

'You see what I don't understand is this: you have a beautiful wife and land of your own in - where was it?'

'Mozambique.'

'Any of those young men over there would give their right arms to have what you have already, and you're scarcely older than any of us. What could be worth risking all of that?'

'I'll not leave Hindustan until I've stood over his cold, dead body.'

'What's very much more likely is that he'll end up standing over yours. You do understand that?'

'My mind is made up.'

Mathieson let out a sigh. 'I'll make some enquiries for you, see what I can find out.' He finished his shiraz. 'It's getting late. I'll be saying goodnight.' He stopped at the door and turned around. 'Oh, and McKenzie. If you're as good an assassin as you are a billiards player, you should order your tombstone now.'

CHAPTER 48

Pondicherry

A torrid night. There didn't seem to be enough air.

Napoleon, Adelaïde beside him, made his way through the *Ville Noir*. His cane tapped on the ground as they passed one of the innumerable Hindu temples. Pilgrims milled about, carrying garland offerings of marigolds and jasmine, in the glow of thousands of candles. A path opened for them among the crowds. His reputation had preceded him. Or perhaps it was something about the look in his eyes.

They crossed the canal to the *Ville Blanche*. Suddenly there were wide boulevards and well-tended parks, but Napoleon took care to keep to the shadows under the trees. He had no reason to announce his presence, not for this commission.

Crossing from the native town to the French quarter was like entering another world. Little France some people called it, though he would have to take their word for that. He had never been there.

They made their way along the Rue Labourdonnais, past villas with ornate iron balconies. High walls were set with arched gateways, and bougainvillea cascaded over whitewashed walls. They turned onto the Rue St Martin and stopped outside one of the houses. He told Adelaïde to wait for him in the shadows and pulled a bell next to the gateway. A white-turbaned servant appeared on the other side of the gate.

'*Sahib,*' the man said, and then in French. 'Who are you wishing to see?'

'Monsieur Rabiot,' Napoleon said.

'He is expecting you?'

'No one expects me.'

'Your name, *Sahib*?'

'*Le mort,*' Napoleon said. He reached through the gate and took the man by the throat with his left hand to hold him upright. His other hand, the one holding the knife, slid through the bars. The tip of the blade entered below the man's sternum and sliced upwards into his heart, shredding it instantly.

The gatekeeper dropped to his knees. While he was dying – it took no time at all – Napoleon cut the bunched keys from the looped cord around his waist. He used one of them to open the gate and dragged the dead man into the bushes. He folded his hands in an attitude of prayer and closed his eyes.

'I'm sorry,' he said to the gatekeeper. 'But it was necessary.'

Adelaïde appeared beside him. She took a white linen handkerchief from her purse. He handed her the knife, and she wiped the blade clean. She put the handkerchief back into her purse.

'Thank you,' Napoleon said. 'Wait here for me.'

Napoleon kept his back to the wall, listening to the sounds of the house. The servants in the ground floor kitchen were talking to each other in Tamil over the clash of pots and dishes as they cleaned up after the evening meal. No one else seemed to be about.

There was a courtyard at the centre of the building, surrounded by greenery. Tall, white columns, faced with white pilaster, supported carved wraparound balconies. Ornate wooden stairs led to the first floor. He followed them up, paused a second time at the landing and looked around.

He knew which room he was looking for. The door leading to it was ajar. He pushed it open with his cane, stepped inside and shut it.

Rabiot was sitting at a heavy wooden bureau. He looked up from his papers and his face turned white. 'You,' he said.

Napoleon took the pistol from his coat. It was already primed and loaded. He moved the hammer to full cock. 'You know why I'm here.'

'How did you get in?'

'I have a key. A very sharp one.'

Rabiot was younger than Napoleon had expected. He didn't even look like a spy. He looked like a clerk, down on his luck.

The man swallowed hard and, to give him his due, squared his shoulders. 'Please don't hurt my family,' he said.

'I have no orders to hurt your family,' Napoleon said. 'The contract is for you, and you alone.'

He raised the pistol and held the barrel to Rabiot's temple. His finger tightened on the trigger.

There was a scream.

A young woman stood in the doorway, her mouth open. But the scream had not come from her. It had come from the girl beside her. She was around the same age as Adelaïde. She had long, fair hair and pale skin, and wore a pink dress. Her cry was high and ended with a sob.

It made him hesitate, something he had never done before.

'What's happening?' the woman said to her husband. She didn't take her eyes off Napoleon or the pistol.

'It's all a mistake,' Rabiot said.

'There's no mistake, madame,' Napoleon said. 'Your husband has been spying for the English in Madras.'

The woman looked at her husband. 'Is this true?'

'Tell them the truth,' Napoleon said to Rabiot. 'They at least deserve that.'

Rabiot nodded.

'Please don't hurt him,' the woman said.

Napoleon fired the pistol. Rabiot's brains splattered across the escritoire. The girl screamed again. It upset him, the girl screaming. It was a piercing, high-pitched wail that seemed to go on and on. She only stopped when she fainted. Madame Rabiot went down on all fours and cradled her in her arms.

'*Desolé*,' Napoleon said. 'I'm sorry.' He bowed to her and left the room.

The servants had gathered in the courtyard. They took one look at Napoleon and scattered. He ignored them.

It was still choking hot outside. He took Adelaïde by the hand and they set off on the short five-minute walk to their home. They didn't go directly there. He wanted to go to the Promenade on the beachfront first, to try to clear his head. He felt shaken. He didn't know why. He had never had such a feeling before.

Curious.

CHAPTER 49

Madras

The rains finally came late one afternoon, slamming down in torrents and pouring from the roofs in waterfalls. The palms on the esplanade bent almost to the ground in the teeth of the gale, and the Company's red and white striped flag cracked in the wind. Spume from the breaker tops rolled across the sand.

Even the *masula* boats disappeared from the beach. The mountainous surf made it impossible to ferry goods out to the ships at anchor in the gage roads. The Krishna River flooded its banks and the land around the fort turned from dun to a vivid green overnight.

When Catia looked in their trunks, she found that many of their clothes had been ruined by the damp and humidity. She showed them to Ammani, who sent them off to be laundered, but even the best of the local *dhobi's* could not wash away the thick white mould.

Everything was rotting away before her eyes.

With the monsoon came the mosquitoes, and with them the fever season. One day Lachlan heard seven separate volleys of musket fire from the cemetery, one for each of the Company soldiers who had died of ague overnight.

At sunset, he heard the blood-chilling cries of the jackals worrying the new graves, looking for meat.

The year before, from a population of twelve hundred Europeans, four hundred had died during monsoon season. The biggest celebration held every year was not Easter or Christmas, but the thanksgiving banquet Channing held at the end of the monsoon to celebrate their survival.

I can't die here for nothing, Lachlan thought.

The fort was alive with rumours: they were going to attack Pondicherry, the French were going to attack Madras, the Company was about to abandon the Coromandel and retreat to Calcutta.

Mathieson was the only one who seemed to know what was happening outside the fort. One night, after he and Lachlan had played two rounds of billiards, they took their glasses of shiraz out onto the veranda. Mathieson said he had news for him.

'I hope it's good news,' Lachlan said.

'It's mixed. Did you hear what happened in Pondicherry two nights ago?'

Lachlan shook his head. 'They don't tell us clerks anything.'

'Our agent there was murdered. In his own house, so they say. Killed in cold blood in front of his family.'

'How?'

'Shot dead. Channing thinks he was betrayed. He believes the French have a spy, here in Madras.'

'And the good news?'

'Colonel Douglas arrived today from Calcutta. The devil of a job getting him ashore. Two of the *masula* boatmen drowned.'

'Dear God.'

'He's going to take over the Company forces here in the Coromandel. Channing's been dithering about what to do, but we'll see some action now. Douglas is the sort of man who doesn't like to let his sword get rusty. I'd say there's going to be another war.'

'And that will be my chance.'

'Not much of one. You can't take on the whole French army to find one man.'

'Douglas will need as many able men as he can get.'

'Are you sure you want to do this?'

'I've never been as sure of anything.'

Mathieson sighed and shook his head. 'Alright, I'll talk to Channing about it. See what I can do.'

They went back inside. In the corner, Hodges and three other senior men were playing cards. There were the usual mutterings as he and Mathieson walked past them.

'You shouldn't be here,' Hodges said.

Lachlan looked around. 'Did you have something to say?'

'You keep a loose household, sir,' Hodges said. 'If I were Channing, I should not allow an enemy spy to live inside the fort.'

'Are you referring to my wife?'

'The Portuguese are on the side of the French, as everyone knows.' He looked at his playing companions. 'I believe she has some nigger in her, too,'

'She has royal blood. Her grandfather was a king.'

Mathieson shot Lachlan a warning glance. It was too late.

'A king with a bone through his nose,' Hodges said.

Lachlan pulled him to his feet by his collar and knocked him down with his fist.

'I will have satisfaction!' Hodges shouted as he got to his feet. His collar was awry, and blood dribbled from his nose.

'Swords or pistols,' Lachlan said. 'It's all the same to me.'

'Don't be stupid,' Mathieson said. 'Channing will never allow this. It's against all Company rules.' And then in a whisper to Hodges. 'You are no match. He will kill you.'

'Tomorrow morning,' Hodges said, 'pistols on the maidan. At dawn.' He and his cronies walked out together.

'Well,' Mathieson said, picking up an overturned chair. 'You can say goodbye to your plans to find Napoleon Gagnon.'

'What do you mean?'

'Hodges couldn't hit an elephant with a watermelon if he was standing next to one. You told me you've spent your whole life training with firearms. So, when you shoot him dead in the morning, though it will be no loss to anyone, Channing will have you thrown in prison. I might be able to persuade him not to hang you, but he won't let you stay in Madras. You'll be back to Africa on the next boat.'

'I won't shoot him. I'll aim high.'

'It won't matter a damn. Duelling is duelling.'

'I can't back out of it now.'

'Only one thing for it, then,' Mathieson said. He walked out of the mess, strolled over to the President's residence, and told Channing about the proposed duel. Lachlan was arrested by two of the President's sepoys as he left the mess and was escorted to the prison. They threw Hodges in the cell next to him.

The next morning, Lachlan was ushered into Channing's office. The President had a face like thunder. Hodges was already there, looking like a schoolboy who'd been caught cheating on his exams.

'Sit down, McKenzie,' Channing said. Lachlan sat. Channing gathered his coat tails and resumed his position behind the vast mahogany desk. 'Last night I was informed that the two of you had intended to fight a duel this morning.'

'McKenzie challenged me,' Hodges said. 'I had no choice but to accept.'

'I don't care who proposed this foolishness.'

'Sir,' Hodges said, 'if you will allow me...'

'No, I will not, Hodges! I do not want to hear justifications or excuses from either of you. You should both consider yourselves fortunate if I do not put you on the next ship out of Madras. This is not the conduct of gentlemen, nor of officers of the Honourable East India Company. Duelling is expressly forbidden on any Company lease. You are both in flagrant violation of the rules.'

Channing let the moment hang. Finally, he said, 'I want you both to shake hands on this matter and there it will end, or woe betide the two of you!'

Hodges got slowly to his feet and extended his hand. A muscle rippled in his jaw. Lachlan thought about Napoleon Gagnon and what Mathieson had said about being sent back to Africa. He took the proffered hand in his own steely grip.

'Now get out,' Channing said. 'I don't want any more trouble from either of you. I have enough to deal with right now.'

They walked out. The morning was still. Sparrows fluttered in the eaves. A muezzin called the Mohammedans to prayer from the minarets in the Black Town.

'I still say that wife of yours is a French spy,' Hodges murmured before he walked away.

CHAPTER 50

Pondicherry

There was an empty lot inside the native quarter, where Napoleon had set up a practice range for his sepoys. Adelaïde had asked to go there for target practice and Napoleon had ordered one of his new recruits to take her.

'I'll show you how it's done,' the soldier said. 'Then you can try.'

Adelaïde watched him and said nothing.

He loaded the musket, a fourteen bore with a swan neck. It was a beautiful piece - a sporting rifle made of polished ash stock, with a brass butt and a foliage scroll lock plate. It was engraved with the maker's name: *Probin*.

'This is very expensive,' he said to her. 'It was made in a place called Birmingham. That's in England. It's a country next to France.'

'I know where Birmingham is,' Adelaïde said.

He took his time loading the gun, explaining each action to her in some detail. He put a charge of gunpowder into the barrel, followed by some wadding to hold it in place. Then he took a tiny lead ball from the satchel at his hip and dropped it down the muzzle, with some more wadding. He tamped it with the ramrod. Then he opened the frizzen pan above the trigger and added powder from the flask at his belt. When that was done, he brought the rifle up to his shoulder.

The target was a few mangrove poles piled against an ancient brick wall. A white circle had been painted on them.

'Get ready, mad'moiselle,' he said. 'You'd better stand behind me and put your hands over your ears. It makes quite a bang when it goes off.'

Adelaïde did as she was told. The soldier squeezed the trigger. There was a flash and a deafening bang followed by a puff of white smoke. The sound of the shot echoed around the empty parkland.

The sulphur smell of the gunpowder was putrid.

Adelaïde followed the soldier across the uneven ground to see the result. There was a hole in the outer edge of the white circle.

The soldier seemed quite pleased with himself. 'Your turn, mad'moiselle,' he said, and they trudged back across the sandy lot to the firing position.

He handed her the rifle. 'Don't worry, it's not loaded. I want you to get used to the weight of it first. It's surprisingly heavy. Be careful, the barrel's hot.' He handed her a roll of cloth. 'It kicks back hard when it goes off, so this will stop your collar bone getting bruised. Remember, you must hold it tight into your shoulder.'

She put the stock to her shoulder and sighted along the barrel.

'I know it's heavy but try not wave it around too much. We don't want to kill anyone.' The soldier put his hand underneath it to lift the muzzle. 'It takes a bit of strength. You'll get used to it over time. Here, I'll load it for you.'

'I can manage,' Adelaïde said.

She took the powder horn from the soldier's belt and poured some of the powder down the muzzle of the rifle. Then she took out the ramrod and tamped it down with some wadding. It was not easy, as the ramrod was as tall as she was. She poured some more powder into the flash pan, then reached over and took a silver ball from the leather satchel on the soldier's hip. She put it in her mouth and spat it down the barrel.

She tapped the stock twice on the ground, swung the stock up to her shoulder and fired in one fluid movement. The soldier stared at her in shock. As the white smoke drifted away across the lot, she handed him the musket and started marching across the empty lot towards the target.

'Be careful,' she said. 'The barrel's hot.'

He followed her. The ball had taken the bull's eye cleanly. He put his finger inside the hole. 'Fuck me,' he muttered and realising what he'd said, he coloured to the roots of his hair. He saluted her, not knowing what else to do. 'Excuse my language, mad'moiselle.' He pointed to the hole in the target and said, in wonderment. 'When did you learn to shoot like that?'

'Before I could walk,' she said. She held out her hand. 'Now give me the powder horn and the satchel. I need to practise.'

Away from his godown, Franco dispensed with Hindu clothes. He settled himself across the desk from Napoleon, in his powdered wig and tailored blue coat. He sipped the chai one of the servants had brought him. 'Keyser refuses to pay out the other half of the contract,' he said.'

Napoleon sighed. 'Does he say why?'

'He believes that his stipulations were not followed. He has heard that one of those named in his contract is still alive and living in the Saint George fort at Madras. Is this true?

'Even if it were true, there were six parts to the contract. I fulfilled five of them, at considerable expense. Yet he is withholding half of my fee. That is not acceptable. I find his attitude insulting.'

'My agent protested on your behalf. He says he is immovable on this.'

Napoleon brooded for a while. A peacock flapped into the lower branches of a citrus tree. He considered shooting it and having it for dinner.

Franco leaned forward. 'You should have told me this before. My man has a girl in his employ. It would be a simple matter to arrange. Then you can claim the rest of your fee.'

Napoleon considered this. Money was not immutable, he thought. When he was a young man, it was a desperate means to survival. Nothing else mattered. Later, it became a source of esteem, something to brandish in the faces of those who once despised him. But lately it had lost its currency.

It surprised him, but he realised that he had reached a time in his life when he cared about points of principle.

'The girl is Sinhalese?'

Franco nodded.

Napoleon called for one of the servants to bring him paper, pen and ink. He quickly penned a letter, sealed it with wax and handed it to Franco. 'I have a commission for her. Tell her if she fulfils it, she will never have to cook a white man's dinner ever again.'

CHAPTER 51

Napoleon made his way across the lot, his cane tapping at the mud. He kept a hand on the curved sword – a *talwar* - in his belt. He had on a knee-length coat made from ruby red silk brocade, with a gold lining. Together with the diamonds glittering in the scabbard at his waist, it marked him out wherever he went as a man of note.

He had a bevy of servants following him. It was a hot day and he had brought them in case he felt in need of refreshment. One of them carried a flask of iced sherbet, another had gold cups, and a third carried a massive fan of peacock feathers.

He found Adelaïde at her practice. The sepoy who had been consigned to ensure her safety snapped to attention and saluted as soon as he saw him. Napoleon told his daughter to wait for him in the shade of a nearby cashew tree. He thanked the man for his service and handed him a small gold coin. They spoke briefly and then he went to join his daughter.

'My sergeant is impressed,' he told her. 'He says you are the best shot in his entire regiment.'

'He treated me like a child.'

'You should forgive him. Technically, you still are one.'

'He's not even a very good shot.'

'I don't hire snipers. I want men who are desperate enough to risk their lives for a handful of rupees every month.'

'He thought I'd never fired a musket before.'

'I wanted you to surprise him.'

Napoleon signalled to his servants, and they brought two cups of sherbet.

'Have you been to see Chanda Sahib?' Adelaïde asked him.

'Not yet.'

'When you go, can I come with you?'

'Not this time. I will only be gone a short while, and it means a lot of hard riding to get to Trichinopoly. I want you to stay here and continue with your lessons.'

'Is there going to be a war?'

'If you can call it a war, my sweet. In many ways it is already over before it has begun. Should Chanda Sahib take Trichinopoly, he will kill the other pretender to the Carnatic throne, and then the British will be finished here in India. I may have to look elsewhere for work.'

'Will that be difficult?'

'There is no chance of peace breaking out in the world anytime soon. I am sure I shall find employment somewhere.'

'What does Chanda Sahib want with you?'

'The siege has stalled. I imagine he wants extra men for a final assault.' He finished the sherbet. 'It will be easy money. The English troops inside the fort are badly trained and ill prepared. I will see you in a few days.'

He lifted her up by the shoulders and kissed her on the lips. '*Au revoir, ma petite.* Keep up the practice. You never know when you may need it.'

CHAPTER 52

Madras

Lachlan was bent over his desk, scratching figures into a ledger, when he heard the news. It rushed through the godown like a grass fire: Channing's new colonel, Douglas, had ordered an assault on Karimkot, Chanda Sahib's capital. They weren't going to sit on their hands any longer. They were going to take the war to the French and their puppet prince.

He threw down his pen, knowing his days as a Company writer were done. He ran down Church Street, his heart thumping. He passed one of the Company's offices, ironically still shot-pocked from the French siege three years before. On that occasion, Channing had accepted a truce. This time there could be only one winner.

Not that Lachlan gave a damn about the politics. The French weren't Lachlan McKenzie's enemy. There was only one man he was at war with.

Mathieson came running out of the building. 'McKenzie, you've heard the news?'

'I want to volunteer. I'm going to see Channing now.'

'I'll come with you.'

They headed across the parade ground. A motley force of mercenaries and volunteers had already begun mustering there, preparing to save Hindustan for the Company.

'This new colonel that's arrived from England,' Lachlan said. 'He's certainly shaken things up.'

'He told Channing that if he didn't do something now, he was going to lose the whole Coromandel coast to the French. That finally lit a fire under the old boy.'

'Why Karimkot? I thought the rest of the army was besieged with Ali at Trichinopoly.'

'Douglas wants to draw Chanda Sahib's army away from the siege until Channing can get reinforcements from Calcutta. He plans to take the initiative away from the French. If we can capture Karimkot, it will show the other warlords in the Carnatic that Chanda's not as powerful as they think he is, and nor are his French masters. It will make some of them think twice about supporting him. Some of them might even come over to our side.'

A sepoy standing at the gate outside the Governor's Residence stood aside for them. They bounded up the stairs.

The President did not seem surprised to see Lachlan. He nodded to Mathieson and pointed to the two chairs on the other side of his desk. They sat down. Despite the punkha-wallah's best efforts, it was as stifling in the Council Rooms as it was in the godown. Lachlan pulled at his high collar. He felt as if it was suffocating him.

'I suppose you're here to volunteer,' Channing said.

'Yes, sir.'

'For a young man with a pretty wife and a bright future, you seem damned keen to get yourself killed. But I'm sure Colonel Douglas will be happy to take you.'

'He has quite a reputation.'

'Indeed. He seems very sure of himself, though I harbour grave doubts about the outcome. I hope I am not sending you to an early grave, McKenzie.' He turned to Mathieson. 'Look after him. Try to keep him out of trouble.' Then he said to Lachlan, 'Go and see the quartermaster. He'll get you a uniform and a musket.'

'I have my own rifle.'

'A musket loads faster. And you'll need a hanger as well, for the hand-to-hand business. Good luck. You're going to need it.'

Colonel Henry 'Blinker' Douglas was well over six feet tall, a giant of a man with muttonchop whiskers and a face that looked as if it had been carved from weathered Yorkshire granite. He stood ramrod straight in the breathless heat, his calf muscles bursting out of his white silk hose. Sweat poured down his face in rivulets from under his powdered wig. Behind him, his sergeants were forming the ragtag army into regiments on the parade ground. Bugles called the assembly.

Douglas put his hands on his hips and studied his new recruit. Lachlan understood now why they called him Blinker. He had a gaze so penetrating it was as if he didn't blink at all.

'You look a likely young fellow. Well, we need all the help we can get. Been working as a clerk, have you?'

'One day with the books and I was ready to kill, sir,' Lachlan said. 'After four months I consider myself well primed.'

'Do you now. Have you any experience of soldiering?'

'I have trained with weapons my entire life, not only sporting rifles, but drilling native troops with Brown Bess muskets. I know how to command a gunnery crew in the firing of a nine-pound cannon. I have fought in a pitched battle, when my family's stockade was attacked by mercenaries and pirates.'

Blinker's eyebrows went up. 'Is that so? And were you victorious?'

'No, we were slaughtered almost to a man.'

Blinker cleared his throat and took a step closer. 'Well, best not let anyone else know that.' He looked at Mathieson. 'What do you think?'

'Ensign material, sir.'

'I agree. I'll not put you with the scum I have for infantry. I'll give you a company of sepoys to look after. Think you can do it?'

'Yes, sir,' Lachlan said.

'Good. The two of you attach yourself to my staff. I want both of you in my line of sight at all times, d'you hear? Ah, Hodges. All kitted out, are you?'

Lachlan looked over his shoulder. He was surprised to see his factor standing in the doorway in an ill-fitting uniform. He had also volunteered his services, or more likely had been pressed into it.

Hodges gave him a venomous look. Lachlan took note. He would have to watch his step there.

CHAPTER 53

There was thunder during the night over the western ghats. It sounded like cannon fire. When dawn finally broke, the swell was still up on the ocean. Lachlan could hear the rollers crashing onto the beach, sending a salt mist drifting over the parade ground below their window.

Catia put an arm around him in her sleep, nestled her face into his neck. He felt himself stir, kissed her open-mouthed. She came awake and knelt astride him. She took off her nightdress and made love to him with savage desperation. Afterwards they lay in each other arms as the sweat cooled on their bodies. He couldn't think of what to say to her.

She watched him while he dressed. She smiled briefly when she saw the uniform they had given him, the threadbare red jacket and tricorn hat, but the laughter died in her throat. She picked up his Brown Bess musket and sighted down the barrel before handing it back.

'My father would use a gun like this to stoke the fire on a cold night.'

'It will do at close quarters,' he said. 'But I'll take the Penterman your father gave me as well.' He reached for her.

She put her arms around his neck and kissed him fiercely. Then she put something into his palm and pushed him towards the door. 'No long goodbyes. Just come back to me.'

He did not look at what she had given him until he got outside. It was her mother's silver cross. He looped it around his neck under his uniform jacket and made his way to the parade ground.

They set out on foot an hour after sunrise. Douglas had only five hundred men with him to get the job done: two hundred Company men and three hundred sepoys. They were armed with swords and flintlock muskets and had just two field guns, to take and hold a city of fifty thousand people.

Lachlan admired Douglas's daring but privately he agreed with Channing. He reckoned they were all doomed. He didn't care whether they took Karimkot or not. If the Honourable Company was thrown out of Hindustan by the French, he didn't care about that either. There was only one battle he needed to win, and just one Frenchman he had to kill. Blinker Douglas's mad and magnificent endeavour was the best chance he had to do it.

Trichinopoly

Napoleon stopped outside Chanda Sahib's encampment and looked towards Trichinopoly. The fortress was built atop a pinnacle of rock that soared three hundred feet above the surrounding plain. It had double walls, more than twenty feet high, and a moat thirty paces wide. It was considered unassailable.

Chanda Sahib had decided to starve Ali and his garrison into surrender. Everyone in Pondicherry believed that it was merely a matter of time before the city fell to Chanda, and with it the whole of the Carnatic. The warlord and his French sponsors were just weeks away from total victory.

As he rode into the encampment, Napoleon took note of the festive air. Everyone here thought the war was over as well. He saw a rabble of wild-eyed tribesmen and ragged cannon fodder wandering through the bazaars that had sprung up around the camp. They were clearly more proficient at fighting and whoring than soldiering. Unfortunately, they outnumbered the Hindu regulars, who were smartly turned out in black tricorn hats and red jackets. They had been trained by a former French infantry major, in the pay of the *Compagnie des Indes,* Louis Petit. They would give his own sepoys a run for their money in a fight.

Only I pay my boys better, Napoleon thought.

Chanda Sahib's royal tent was surrounded by the lesser pavilions of his noblemen. Napoleon dismounted and was escorted through the crush of men and horses into the *shamianah*. He looked around. Silk screens and draperies divided the interior into separate rooms. There were fretted wooden screens where the great man's wives could watch the proceedings. The entrance flaps were secured with jewelled ribbons.

It was crowded with the usual hangers-on found in every palace: scribblers from Persia, and turbaned warlords fresh out of the mountains looking for babies to skewer. He supposed it was their camels he had been forced to negotiate on his way in.

Like all military men made good, Chanda Sahib kept himself in some style. There were thick layers of carpets underfoot, and sandalwood incense burners moderated the stink of unwashed tribesmen and the taint of hot grease from the pierced brass lanterns.

Chanda Sahib wore a *jama*, a long-skirted tunic gathered at the waist with a sash. There was a jewelled dress dagger and a heavy *talwar* on his left side. He sat cross-legged on silk cushions, surrounded by officers and advisers. Turbaned boys cooled him with their plumed fans.

He wasn't quite the perfumed degenerate Napoleon had been expecting. There was still a toughness about him, despite his recent rapid ascent through the political ferment. He looked hard-eyed and practical. Someone I can do business with, Napoleon thought.

'*Salaam aleikum,*' Chanda Sahib murmured.

'*Aleikum salaam*, Highness.'

Chanda Sahib motioned for him to sit.

Napoleon lay back against a silk bolster. A peon brought rosewater for him to wash his hands, another handed him a chilled sherbet in a gold goblet. He went through the usual court etiquette, asking Chanda Sahib about his health and that of his family. He spoke in Persian, the language of all the Mughal courts.

Finally, they dispensed with the pleasantries. Chanda Sahib sucked on the long flexible tube of his water pipe and blew the smoke out through his nose. 'I have need of your services,' he said. A hot breeze rippled the fine muslin screens at the door of the tent. It brought with it the scent of the rosewater that had been used to dampen them and cool the air. 'You have heard the news?'

Napoleon nodded. 'The British plan to besiege Karimkot. Sound tactics, for once. It is unlike them.'

'If they attack my fortress, I will have to respond.'

'How many soldiers did you leave behind to garrison the town?'

Chanda Sahib looked evasive. 'They are not my best men.'

In other words, you have not paid them for months, Napoleon thought. 'And you want me to support them,' he said.

'The *Compagnie des Indes*' senior officer, Major Petit, has sent field guns and cavalry to intercept the Britishers before they reach Karimkot. He has asked for reinforcements. I cannot afford to take troops away from this siege.'

'How many Britishers are there?'

'No more than five hundred, and two field guns.'

'The Britisher soldiers are all rapists and drunkards. If they weren't taking Company pay, they'd be in prison. A rabble. They cannot take Karimkot with only two field guns.'

'I cannot afford the risk.'

No, you can't, Napoleon thought. Every warlord in the Carnatic is watching you, looking for signs of weakness that will play to their advantage.

'So, *feringhee*. You will do it?'

Napoleon smiled to disguise his anger. These natives called him foreigner; the French treated him like a native. He could bear it from the Europeans because he despised them, but these people were his mother's blood.

He compensated himself for this humiliation by doubling his asking price. Chanda Sahib winced but agreed. He must be desperate, Napoleon thought.

'It is agreed then,' Napoleon said. 'I shall return to Pondicherry and march to Karimkot immediately.'

'Do not fail me,' Chanda Sahib said.

'With respect,' Napoleon said. 'I never fail.'

CHAPTER 54

Pondicherry

Napoleon sat in his favorite cane chair in the courtyard and waited as the servants brought him his breakfast. It never varied: strong black coffee in a silver pot, a slice of pineapple and an orange, quartered.

Suddenly there was a piercing scream. It startled him. He spilled his coffee on the table. He looked up. The noise had come from one of the peacocks in the branches of a mango tree. He caught its eye and it was admonished to silence, or so it appeared. The garden was quiet again except for the dribbling of water in the marble fountains.

He stared at the coffee stain spreading over the white linen cloth on the table. It wasn't like him to react like that.

Adelaïde came down the stairs from her bedroom. She had on a white dress and white shoes. His angel. She stopped to pick a sprig of bougainvillea from one of the boughs that overhung the patio and put in her hair. She sat down at the table.

'Bonjour, papa.'

'Bonjour, mon ange.'

'When did you get back?'

'Last night. It was late.'

'You didn't come in to say goodnight.'

'I didn't want to wake you.'

'How was your meeting with Chanda Sahib?'

'Satisfactory. He wishes me to help him fight the British at Karimkot.'

'May I come with you this time?'

'Of course,' he said.

They stopped talking as a servant brought her breakfast. After the girl had gone, she said to him, 'You look tired.'

Napoleon closed his eyes. He saw Rabiot's daughter, with her white ringlets and white nightdress, and the look of utter desolation on her face. Rabiot's brains and blood were spreading across the fine panelled escritoire. The peacock screamed again. His eyes jerked open.

'Are you unwell, papa?'

'It's nothing. Eat your breakfast. As soon as you're ready, we have to leave.'

'Can I bring my rifle?'

'Of course.'

'I'd like to kill something.'

'I'm sure an opportunity will arise.' He looked up at the hot, blue sky. Rabiot's daughter was still screaming. An aberration. He was sure it would pass.

It was hot and dusty. Out on the plain there was no sign of the storms that had battered Madras all week. The uniform they had given him was impossibly heavy. An hour after daybreak his scarlet jacket was already dark with sweat. His throat was parched, and he felt light-headed from the heat.

Douglas finally stopped the column near the river to refill their water bottles. Lachlan looked back at his platoon of native sepoys, and the sight of them lifted his flagging spirits. They looked likely in their red tunics, white cross belts and haversacks. They had been well drilled and carried their muskets upright with their bayonets pointed to the sky above their cocked hats. He fancied them better than some of the jailbait among the English regulars.

After a short rest, Douglas urged them on again. They followed a wide river for hour after hour. There were jade-green rice paddies on either side, where native women in bright saris laboured under the burning sun. Water buffalo wallowed in mud hollows, waiting out the heat of the afternoon.

They camped that first night near a grove of plantain trees. Lachlan was exhausted. He ripped off his serge jacket, filled his helmet with river water and emptied it over his head. He lay on his back in the shade and felt like he could sleep for a week. But there was no time to rest. He had to set pickets and see to it that the campfires were lit.

Mathieson told him that they had another three days' hard marching ahead of them.

The next morning, they woke to the sounds of Mohammedan prayers coming from a mosque in a nearby village. The wails of the *muezzin* echoed over the river. Lachlan's nose twitched at the taint that he had already come to associate with the march, a pungent mix of woodsmoke, sweat, urine, and tobacco.

He pulled his boots on and took his jacket off the tent post. The garment would have been fine, he supposed, on a cold day in England. Here in Hindustan it was an instrument of torture.

They marched on, under a milk white sky. All colour seemed to have been leeched out of the landscape. The long line of scarlet tunics looked gaudy against the drab dun of the plain. If the Frenchies or Chanda Sahib's boys are out there, Lachlan thought, they will see us coming from miles away.

They tramped on past endless rice fields, clusters of thatched huts, and dry ditches the natives called *nullas*. Scrawny villagers in white turbans and *dhotis* coaxed their bullocks and ploughs across dusty fields. A thin haze veiled the horizon, making the disembodied trunks of the palm groves and guava trees appear to ripple against the sky. Occasionally, a colony of monkeys would scamper across the trail in front of them, screaming and fussing in dismay at this invasion of their territory.

Just after noon, they were forced to pitch canvas and take refuge from the worst of the sun. Douglas paced and fumed at the delay. They were making barely fifteen miles a day. But there was nothing to be done. Some of the English recruits were dropping from heat stroke.

'What have we got ourselves into?' Mathieson said, his face beet red. He slapped at a mosquito. It left a bloodstain on his arm as if an artery had been cut. 'Look at that! The damned things are the size of bats.'

'Once we're in the fight, you won't even notice the mosquitoes,' Lachlan said.

'I suppose you would know. What was you said to Blinker, about the battle you fought in? You've never told me about that. Did you make it up to impress him?'

'I never make anything up, Charlie. When it's over I'll tell you the whole story.'

'It feels like this will never be over.'

Lachlan shrugged. 'Everything is over sooner or later.'

After three days tramping under dull skies, they saw the black spires of Conjeeveram in the distance. Douglas told his scouts to find a route around the place, rather than through it, worried that the column would be caught up in the press of ox carts and people that choked the centre of the holy city.

There was a festival taking place, and thousands of pilgrims were pouring in from the surrounding countryside. They were all dressed in white and wore the distinctive red 'V' stripe of Vishnu painted on their foreheads.

Lachlan and his platoon stopped at a tank near the road, took off their helmets and haversacks, and ducked their heads into the pale greenish water to cool off. Then he and Mathieson threw off their boots and soaked their blistered feet on the stone steps of one of the *ghats*.

They barely had their feet in the water when they were summoned by Douglas's aide-de-camp. He was holding a hurried conference with the other officers and ensigns in the shade of a mango tree. One of the senior men was insisting that he and his men needed to stop and rest. It was Hodges. Mathieson had told Lachlan that Hodges had been seconded to Douglas's staff by Channing himself to look out for the Company's commercial interests. Every musket ball cost the Company money and would one day have to be accounted for in one of the precious ledgers.

'I know your men are tired,' Douglas said, 'but I have just received news that a French mercenary force of almost one thousand men has been sent north from Pondicherry to try to stop us reaching Karimkot. We cannot afford even a moment. We must press on if we are to take the city.'

'Take the city?' Hodges said. 'It was my understanding that our expedition was merely a diversionary tactic. We can't capture Karimkot with two field guns and this rabble we have with us. There is a garrison of over a thousand men inside the fort.'

'Ensign Hodges, you were aware of the risks attendant on our mission when we left Fort St George. I make the decisions here. Now have your sepoys ready and in good order to march within the half hour.'

'Colonel, I must object.'

'Objection noted. Anything else?' Douglas said.

Hodges' face looked like thunder. But he knew better than to argue with Douglas.

As the afternoon wore on, leaden towers of cloud rolled in from the north. By the middle of the afternoon it was as dark as twilight. The air was dense, and sweat poured from the tip of Lachlan's nose and the ends of his fingers. He had only filled his water bottle a few hours before, and already it was almost empty.

He sensed the charge in the air. There was a big storm coming. He looked over his shoulder and saw the terrified looks on the faces of his sepoys. They started like children at every rumble of distant thunder. Mathieson said that the local boys wouldn't fight in the rain. Superstition, he said. They believed that a thunderstorm was the god Indra doing battle in the sky with a dragon, and that to stay outside was to invite being caught in the crossfire.

But there was to be no respite. With French reinforcements on their way, they would have to march by night as well as by day.

Evening fell and clouds scudded across the moon. Lightning flickered on the horizon. Lachlan heard a crack as a huge palm frond snapped and fell in the gathering wind. It drove leaves and grit into their faces. A curtain of warm rain hissed towards them and in moments they were all drenched through. The dirt road they were following became a glutinous bog.

Hodges lost his tricorn. Lachlan saw it blow off his head and could have bent to retrieve it but didn't. Someone – Mathieson perhaps – stepped on it and drove it into the mud with his boot.

They kept their heads down against the wind and rain, so miserable and preoccupied with the storm that they mistook the first French cannonade for thunder.

There was a moment of desperate uncertainty. Everyone threw themselves to the ground. The men in Lachlan's squadron who survived the first salvo dragged themselves to the edge of the road. Others were screaming from their wounds and had to be helped clear by their comrades. Behind them, the road was littered with dark shapes: bodies and pieces of bodies.

They had walked into an ambush.

Douglas vaulted from his horse and ran back down the line, pushing men into the *nullah* beside the road. 'Get under cover, now!'

Lachlan drew his sword and turned to his sepoys, pointing towards the trees on their right. 'They're in the orchard!' He started counting, *'Aarru, aezhu, addu, onpathu!'* One, two, three, four!

Every Company sepoy understood what the numbers meant. They had been drilled over and over and knew how many seconds it took for a cannon to be able to fire between reloading. Any man not lying flat on his belly in the ditch after the last count was a dead man.

Lachlan looked around for Mathieson. He was frozen to the spot about ten paces away, turning around and around, gasping in shock. Lachlan grabbed him and dragged him bodily towards the *nullah*. He threw him in and jumped down after him, just as another cannonade of flame erupted away to their right. He peered over the bank and counted the muzzle flashes. Four of them. He saw an ensign called Harris running one of the field guns along the track, trying to haul it into position to return fire.

He reached the end of his next count and shouted, 'Get down!'

Too late. Harris and his team were caught in a hail of grapeshot and when Lachlan looked back they lay like butcher's meat across the road. The gun rumbled on. Its spoked wheels bounced over the lip of the *nullah* and tipped onto its side.

Some men were firing their muskets at the French guns. It was pointless at this range. The rest of his squadron still lay on the road. Every salvo of French grapeshot raked their dead into offal.

Douglas was hunkered down with Hodges and another of his senior officers about fifty yards further down the ditch. He shouted for Lachlan to join him. When he got there, the colonel had his spy glass to his eye. Hodges was shaking him by the shoulder, wide-eyed with panic. 'Their guns are tearing us to pieces! We have to retreat!'

'Not yet, Mister Hodges,' Douglas said. He sounded as calm as if he were contemplating a chess move. 'There is a path to our left that cuts through a grove of trees towards their flank. With a determined attack we could work our way behind their position. Ah, there you are McKenzie. I shall need you in a moment.'

Lachlan threw himself down beside him.

Behind him, he heard Mathieson shout '*Anpathuh!*' Fifty seconds.

Another salvo shattered the dark. Someone started screaming. He saw two sepoys drag one of their fellows along the road, leaving a dark trail of blood behind them. There were just rags of flesh and cloth where the man's legs should have been.

Douglas was talking in a conversational tone, as if he were at the dinner table. 'Mister McKenzie, I should like you to take your command and go to those trees there, do you see where I mean? At the double, please. Stay out of sight until the last. It's dark enough now that they won't see you. Capture that battery for me, intact if you please.'

Lachlan set off in a low, crouching run. Moments later the ground seemed to shake under his feet, and he thought it was another salvo from the French battery. But it can't be, he thought, I've only counted to nine. Then a jagged three-pronged fork of lightning streaked across the sky, the flash blinding him for a moment.

Shouting broke out along the line. He looked over his shoulder and saw dozens of the native sepoys throw their muskets and their packs into the mud. They were about to run. The French artillery and the thunderstorm had broken their morale. Someone had to do something.

Aarru, aezhu, addu, onpathu...

Lachlan drew his hanger from his scabbard and scrambled up the bank. The sepoys cowered in the creek below him.

'Men of Indra do not be afraid! Yes, the gods are making war tonight, but they are making war for you, not against you! They have come to help you vanquish your enemies. Look at me, am I afraid?'

He raised his sword above his head.

'I am not afraid because the spirit of Indra is inside me! And it is inside you, too!'

His last words were drowned out by a deafening crack. He thought he had miscounted, and it was another salvo from the French guns. Instead, a lightning bolt struck a banyan tree twenty paces behind him. There was a blinding flash as the branches were briefly engulfed in flame and smoke.

The sepoys cheered.

Lachlan jumped down into the *nullah* moments before the next cannonade, which would surely have blown him apart. He strode along the ditch, shouting for the sepoys to follow. The men almost trampled each other in the haste to join him.

The deluge was coming down harder, plastering his hair across his face. The bottom of the *nullah* had turned into a porridge of mud that clung to their boots and made running impossible.

He could just make out the line of trees ahead. He should have been afraid, but there was only a surge of anticipation. Let the men on the other side of this field be the pirates who attacked our fort, he thought. I want to find Napoleon Gagnon and finish this tonight.

There was another deafening cannonade. He felt the sound of the concussion through his boots. He and his men crouched down instinctively, though there was no need. The cannons were aimed away to their right, towards the road, where the rest of their column was pinned down.

He could see the French artillerymen, the dark silhouettes of the field guns, the horses' silver trappings glinting in the moonlight.

He left the ditch and led his men through the trees. They were behind the French now and he could hear their artillery captains shouting commands to the gun crews.

'Fix bayonets,' he shouted to the sepoys behind him.

It would be an alley fight, face to face, eye to eye. It was going to be bloody. The French battery was no more than thirty paces away. He could see the guns. There were four of them. They looked like nine pounders, same as theirs. He wanted to see the crow in his white turban, though he knew it was a vain hope.

'Aim,' Lachlan said.

His sepoys raised their muskets. It wouldn't do much good. There would be a lot of misfires in a storm like this. A panicked voice shouted an alarm in French. They had been seen.

'Fire!' Lachlan shouted. There was a ragged fusillade as his sepoys fired into the unprotected batteries.

Lachlan raised his hanger and led the charge. He raged into the fight, slashing blindly with his sabre, urging the sepoys to form up behind him, though he supposed none of them could hear him anymore.

A French soldier came at him, his bayonet held in front of him. Lachlan was almost impaled on the point of it. He managed to swing aside only at the very last moment.

One of the artillery captains strode out to meet him. Even in the dark Lachlan could make out his epaulettes and the silver buttons on his uniform. He thought he was about to draw his sword, but instead a pistol appeared in his right hand. He held it straight-armed, pointed at Lachlan's chest.

Lachlan would have thrown himself aside, but he was hemmed in by the men fighting around him. He stared at the black muzzle of the pistol and knew he was going to die.

Sparks flew from the firing pan, but the weapon must have been primed hours ago and the rain had ruined the powder. Lachlan roared with anger and relief and slashed down with his sword. He took off the captain's hand at the wrist. The man went down onto one knee, blood gouting from his severed right wrist. He tried to draw his sabre with his other hand. Lachlan was astounded at the man's courage. He could have finished him but instead he knocked him aside with the hilt of his sword and ran on.

In minutes, the gun emplacement had been overrun and the crews slaughtered. Some of them hung like stringless puppets over the spoked wheels or the barrels of their own cannons. His sepoys were mercilessly dispatching the wounded with their bayonets or clubbing them with their musket stocks.

But not all of them were done with. A big fusilier with a bushy, black beard came at him from the dark. Lachlan charged at him, chopping down again and again with his hanger. But the Frenchman was up to it and each of his blows was turned aside.

Suddenly he felt a blinding flash of pain in his upper arm, as the fusilier flicked his sword up and across him, slicing through his uniform jacket. I must finish this quickly, Lachlan thought, use all my strength to overpower him. This man is a far better swordsman than me.

He scythed down again. The fusilier parried the blow against the hilt of his own weapon, turning it easily aside. His sword flashed. Lachlan fell back against one of the guns and lost his balance. As he went down, the Frenchman moved gracefully in for the coup. Lachlan's fist closed around a handful of mud, and he tossed it into the other man's eyes, blinding him for a moment. He kicked out with his right boot.

The Frenchman screamed and staggered backwards. Lachlan thought he had him. He scrambled to his feet and moved in to finish it. Instead the Frenchman swapped his sword hand and lunged upwards. In that moment Lachlan knew he was finished. There was no way to sidestep the strike.

He felt a searing pain in his side as the sword point went past his guard and through his tunic. It drove him back into a tree, and for a moment he couldn't move. He tried to twist aside but it was hopeless. The fusilier wrestled with the sword, trying to withdraw it for a second strike. But it was stuck fast.

I thought dying would hurt more than this, Lachlan thought.

Their eyes met. The Frenchman put his boot on Lachlan's chest to try to free his sabre. Lachlan lunged forward with his own sword. The fusilier realised his mistake too late. He jumped back, clutching at his belly, trying to hold everything in.

Then the man's head exploded, and Lachlan was showered in his blood.

It was Mathieson. He was holding a pistol. Lachlan could smell the sulphur stink of the burned powder.

'Are you alright?' Mathieson said.

Lachlan looked down. The dead fusilier's sword had gone right through his jacket. There didn't seem to be much blood, at least, not as much as he would have expected. He couldn't move.

Mathieson was about to pull out the blade.

'Wait,' Lachlan said. 'If you pull it out, I'll bleed to death.'

The fight was over. He could make out the shadowy figures of the French gunners bolting out of the copse and dashing for the horse lines, pursued by the red coats of his sepoys.

'Get them back here, Charlie,' he said to Mathieson. 'It's enough for one night.' He felt faint, but there was still no pain.

Mathieson tore Lachlan's jacket open and called for a lamp. A sergeant hurried over and shone a light on the wound.

Mathieson's face split into a grin. 'The gods really are on your side today,' he said.

Lachlan looked down. The sword point had gone straight through his jacket and shirt, scoring a gash along his ribs, but it hadn't pierced his chest. The sergeant prised the blade out of the tree trunk, and he was free.

Blood dripped from the tips of his fingers, where the fusilier had slashed his arm.

'We did it,' Mathieson said. 'You did it.'

Lachlan looked at the bodies littering the ground around the guns, recognised the silver buttons and blue jackets of the regular *Compagnie des Indes* uniforms, and realised that his quarry was not here.

He stumbled back through the trees to find Douglas.

Douglas turned around to see what his junior officers were staring at. There was a wraith standing behind him, his jacket ripped and bloody, his hair matted from the rain and loose about his shoulders. There was gore dripping from the tips of his fingers.

Douglas looked him over, head to foot.

'Where's your helmet, McKenzie?' he said. 'An officer should never approach a commanding officer with a bare head. You have a lot to learn, young man.'

CHAPTER 55

The sun rose on a palm-fretted horizon. The jungle steamed. The muddy pools of water from the previous night's storm were starting to burn away. Crows and carrion birds were feasting on the grisly banquet laid out on the road and among the trees on the other side of the rice field.

Douglas had sent a detail to collect the dead. Their orders were to cremate the sepoys and bury the French and English. Unfortunately for the burial parties, it was often difficult to make out the difference. When you got right down to it, Lachlan thought, flesh was just flesh and grapeshot didn't care to differentiate between caste, religion or flag.

Sparks and black smoke danced into the sky from the corpse fires, but the burial parties couldn't work fast enough to keep the vultures from the feast. There was the occasional crack of a rifle as a soldier took a shot at one of the birds. But there were too many of them to scare away. They rose in black clouds whenever they heard a shot and then, with leisurely flaps of their wings, settled down again to continue their grisly breakfasts.

Stacks of captured French-pattern muskets had been thrown in a heap beside the road, ready for collection by the baggage train. If they were going to assault Karimkot, they would need all the weapons they could get.

The screaming of the wounded jangled the nerves. The company surgeon, Thomas, had been kept busy through the night. He had given opium to those too badly injured to treat in the field. Few of them were likely to survive the long journey to Karimkot on the back of the ox carts.

Thomas had taken one look at Lachlan, lathered some *ghee* on his arm, together with a herb extract the sepoys swore by, and sent him on his way. Compared with the rest of them, the wound seemed no more significant than a grazed knee. Whatever he had smeared on the wound stank to high heaven, but it kept the flies away.

Douglas gathered the remains of his officer corps under a banyan tree. Lachlan leaned against the trunk while he listened to their orders.

'Where's Mister McKenzie?' Douglas looked around and settled his gaze on Lachlan. 'There you are. Without this young man, gentlemen, we would have been pounded to mince by those guns and all would have been lost. You showed fine leadership McKenzie, and I intend to put your skills to proper use. You said you know how to command cannon, is that right?'

'I know how it's done.'

'Well, we have five guns now. One of ours and the four you captured last night. The captain formerly in charge of our artillery was careless enough to get himself killed, so now you have his commission.'

'But Colonel,' Hodges protested.

Douglas rounded on him, daring him to say more. Hodges bit his lip and kept his silence.

'You can pick your own adjutant.'

'I'll have Charlie Mathieson, sir.'

'And what unique talents does he bring to the job?'

Everyone looked at Mathieson. 'I shot a grouse once.'

'That will do,' Douglas said. 'Get yourselves cleaned up. We have a long day ahead of us.'

For the next twelve hours, Douglas force-marched them along the river. Lachlan had his crews manhandle their newly acquired guns across plains that had been turned into a quagmire by the drenching storm.

By the time they reached Karimkot it was dark, and a full moon shivered above the Mysore ghat. As they approached the city walls, news quickly filtered back along the line: Chanda Sahib's garrison, struck with panic, had fled. Who would face an enemy that could march through thunder, lightning and torrential rain in their eagerness to fight? Who wanted to face a golden-haired giant who claimed to be the son of Indra?

So that evening, with a purple haze shrouding the turrets and domes of the old city, they marched unopposed through the ancient gates to take possession of Karimkot.

They hadn't fired a single shot.

The sound of their boots echoed eerily off the walls as they marched through the red sandstone gateway. The crooked streets were so narrow they could only march two abreast and they had to leave the five field guns under guard inside the gatehouse. The city seemed deserted, but Lachlan spotted countless pairs of eyes staring out at them from windows and doorways.

They climbed up through the citadel until they reached the fortress itself.

Once inside, Douglas ordered them to raise the barred red and white flag of the Honourable Company and set about preparing the defences.

'Have your men see to their duties,' Douglas said to Lachlan. 'The French will be here soon.'

'Good,' Lachlan said. With luck, Napoleon Gagnon would be with them.

CHAPTER 56

Karimkot

Taking Karimkot had been surprisingly easy, but it was soon clear that keeping it was going to be much more difficult.

The fort was ancient and in a poor state of repair. The walls were ruinous in places and many of the ramparts too narrow to allow for a gun emplacement. None of the towers could accommodate more than one cannon. Even parts of the moat had dried up.

The high western wall was the most easily defensible. There were places on the east and south walls scarcely higher than the top of a man's head. If an attacker could get across the moat, they could almost leap over the ramparts.

Lachlan positioned his four captured field guns in the only places he could, on top of the main gatehouse and the Beggar's Tower, and on the widest sections of the southern ramparts. Their one remaining field gun he left in the citadel courtyard, in reserve.

For two days they worked themselves to exhaustion to get everything ready. It was as well they did. Mathieson woke Lachlan early on the third day. 'You'd better come and see this,' he said.

Lachlan followed him up to the ramparts.

'There,' Mathieson said.

Lachlan took out his spyglass and peered through the heat haze to the flood plain below. It was a sight to catch the breath. Chanda Sahib's army had encamped during the night - a vast city of ill-sorted tents crowded together haphazardly. Green pennants hung limp from a thousand spear points, glittering in the haze of the morning cook fires. Squadrons of horsemen in spiked helmets, the sun flashing off their fish scale armour, galloped across the plain. Cavalry horses grazed on the pastures along the banks of the river, tails flicking idly in the sun, alongside great herds of pack camels.

Something caught Lachlan's attention. There was a separate encampment on the left flank. It was quite different from the main camp and had been set out with an almost geometric precision. At first, he thought they might be French regulars, but then he saw one of their *jemadars* conducting an arms drill.

He studied the soldiers' cross-belted blue jackets and green turbans. The last time he had seen these uniforms, they were storming the beach at Delgoa Bay. He swung the spyglass back towards the centre so that he could make out the command post at the rear. A tall man in a white turban disappeared inside one of the tents.

Lachlan snapped his telescope shut. 'Got you,' he said.

Douglas gathered all his commanders in the room above the western gatehouse, which he had chosen for his command post. Despite the stifling heat, he still wore a freshly powdered wig and a heavy red frock coat.

'Well gentlemen,' he said. 'As you can see, our efforts have had the desired effect. We have made Chanda Sahib a laughingstock. While he headed south in his glorious pomp to besiege our forces at Trichinopoly, we have taken his capital. The rest of the Carnatic will be watching intently to see what happens next. The local warlords will hold back from choosing sides until they know the outcome of this. The future of southern Hindustan now relies on us.'

'What now?' Hodges said.

'Our purpose is to stay them as long as possible. To make the invincible Chanda Sahib look exceedingly...' Douglas searched for the right word. 'Vincible.'

'We have less than five hundred men,' Hodges said. 'I estimate their number at five thousand, perhaps more.'

'Their native troops are mostly peasants, cannon fodder,' Douglas said. 'They are an ill-disciplined rabble, who will be mustered into suicidal charges by their officers. As long as we have enough ammunition, which we do, our only concern is that we do not grow fatigued from shooting them all.'

'Wait,' Hodges said. 'They are not all peasants and tribal madcaps. I saw the blue and white of *Compagnie* regulars down there.'

'I am told that Chanda Sahib has released a hundred and fifty French troops from the siege at Trichinopoly. Not a great number.'

'Do they have artillery?' Lachlan asked him.

'My scouts say it will be at least another two days before their siege guns arrive.'

'And then we will be outgunned as well as outnumbered,' Hodges said. 'We have done glorious work to take this fort. But now we should face the facts of the situation and return directly to Madras. There is no disgrace in that.'

'No disgrace?' Douglas said. 'In retreat?'

'Mister Hodges is right,' one of the junior ensigns said. 'We can't expect to hold this fort against an army almost ten times our size.'

'Does anyone else think we should run away?' Douglas turned his unnerving gaze around the room. 'What about you, McKenzie?'

'He's a clerk,' Hodges said. 'His opinion is of no account.'

'This clerk won us the battle against the French outside Conjeeveram while you were hiding in a ditch, Mister Hodges so I am very much inclined to consider his opinions. Besides, he is not a clerk, he is the captain of my artillery. What do you say, Mister McKenzie?'

Everyone in the room looked at Lachlan.

Lachlan weighed his words. 'All I know is this,' he said. 'A man never wins anything, be it a war or a woman's affections, unless he is bold. There is always a way to triumph. You just have to find it. A brave man once told me that a man should never give up, ever. I agree with him. I say we steel ourselves for a proper fight. If we turn tail now, we will never be able to hold up our heads among other men, for we will have made a habit of looking down.'

'I do believe I hear the sound of thunder,' Douglas said.

Lachlan felt a pang of guilt. Would I have been so eager for a battle if Napoleon Gagnon wasn't out there, he thought. Still, I suppose every man has a different reason for being here. For some it's the glory, for others the money, and for one of us it's revenge.

Douglas looked around the room. 'Then we are agreed. If Chanda Sahib wants a scrap, he has one. I will bid you a good evening. I believe tomorrow may be a very busy day for all of us.'

They spent the rest of the day preparing their defences. When the sun set, the lights of the enemy camp were spread along the plain as far as they could see. I have to find a solitary star in an entire firmament, Lachlan thought. One of those pinpricks of lights is throwing a shadow on that bastard's face. He is so close I can almost smell him.

CHAPTER 57

The gas lamp hissed as rain seeped through the canvas and dropped onto the glass. Napoleon scratched at the mosquito bites on his neck. This damned weather. The monsoon would slow the progress of their siege guns from Trichinopoly.

The *Compagnie* staff officers and Chanda Sahib's general, and eldest son, Mustapha Sahib, clustered around the French surveyor's map on the camp table. Servants and guards crowded at the tent entrance.

Major Petit was briefing them on his plans for an assault on the fortress. It seemed to consist of using their entire army as Forlorn Hopes, throwing them at the walls and hoping for the best. Napoleon's own highly trained and well-disciplined troops were to be sacrificed as if they were some rabble he had sandbagged from the bazaars.

'So that is your tactical master plan?' Napoleon said when Petit had finished.

'We are opposed by a handful of badly trained British soldiers and no more than three hundred native auxiliaries. What do you propose, a network of underground tunnels and a Trojan horse?'

There was braying laughter from the junior French officers, eager to curry favour with their commanding officer. Their animosity to Napoleon was palpable. He had a French father, like they did, and they were being paid to fight, as he was. But they didn't like the way he dressed, they didn't like his mixed blood, and they didn't appreciate the fact that he was for hire.

Napoleon was careful not to let his smile slip. 'You're right. If it had been left to me, I should have attacked them on the road with an insufficient force and I would have done it at night, so that my cavalry would be rendered useless. Then I would have let them sneak around behind me in the dark and make off with my field cannon. That would have been a much better plan.'

There was a deathly silence.

'Do not seek to question my judgment, Monsieur Gagnon.'

'Why not? I'm not a junior member of your staff. I'm a professional, as you are.'

'What happened at Conjeeveram was a miscalculation by one of my junior officers!'

'Who was under your direction. If you had waited for just a day, you would have had the advantage of overwhelming numbers. You knew Mustapha Sahib was on his way with five thousand men. Instead, your rashness encouraged them to a night march which meant they arrived here at Karimkot before us. Now you want me to throw my men at the walls as fodder for your own cannon!'

'You have another suggestion?' Petit said.

'Yes. We wait for the siege artillery to arrive, then we blow a breech in the wall and assault it. Meanwhile we can take up positions in the town, here to the east, where our snipers can thin their numbers.'

Mustapha Sahib shook his head. 'Every day we hesitate is a blow to my father's prestige. A concerted attack will finish this quickly. After that, we will march on Madras.'

'Suicide,' Napoleon said.

Petit ignored him. He turned to Mustapha Sahib and stabbed a finger at the chart on the campaign table in front of him. 'You will attack the east and south walls. My men will take up sniper positions in the city, as Monsieur Gagnon has suggested.' He turned to Napoleon. 'Meanwhile you will attack from the west. We will begin the assault at dawn. Is there anything else?'

Napoleon shook his head. He shoved his way through the crowded tent without another word.

Napoleon had kept his own army encamped separately to the main force. His men stood at attention as he made his way through the camp, and he was gratified to see it in good order.

A guard saluted as he reached his tent. He ducked through the flap. Adelaïde sat at a folding table, wearing a long, white muslin dress, with a veil over her hat as protection from the mosquitoes. She was reading a book. She was teaching herself Farsi.

He set aside his turban and shook out his mane of long dark hair, revealing the curious grey streak along the centre of it. He took off his sword and buckler and hung them on the post by the door.

'French bastards,' he said.

'What has happened, papa?'

'They want to use my army as cannon fodder,' he said. 'What do they care? My boys aren't French so they will throw them at the walls to try to buy a cheap victory. It doesn't matter that they are better trained and better disciplined than the *Compagnie* infantry. Who paid to have them trained? Who recruited them? Who bears the cost if I lose them taking one stinking little town, that none one but Chanda Sahib cares about?'

'We could leave, papa. Chanda Sahib has not paid you yet.'

'And then I have spent two months idle, without return. No, there is a third option, my sweet.' He summoned the guard. 'Tell the jemadar I want to see him,' he said.

Lachlan could not sleep. The wound on his arm throbbed mercilessly and every nerve was on edge, anticipating the coming battle. He abandoned his *charpoy* and went up to the battlements to inspect the gun posts yet again.

The moon had set, but there were still two or three hours before sunrise. The sentries told him they had heard sounds coming from below them on the *glacis*, although they could see nothing. All the men had been recalled to their posts. Douglas did not think Mustapha Sahib and the French would begin the attack before morning, but he was taking no chances.

Lachlan paced the battlements, ensuring his gunners were alert and ready and that his cannons were primed for action.

Just before dawn, there were shouts of alarm from the main gate. There was a crash as a detachment of Mustapha Sahib's irregulars rushed the studded metal doors with a battering ram. But Lachlan had been expecting this and had one of his nine-pounders lashed, chocked and loaded. The barrel was depressed twenty degrees, ready to fire grapeshot straight down to deter their attackers from so obvious an assault.

'Fire!' he shouted. The priming powder fizzed, and the gun roared, rearing off its carriage for a moment before slamming down again. There were screams and moans in the semi-darkness.

'Another round, as fast as you can, please!'

The gunners knew their business and had already unlashed the chocked carriage and hauled the cannon away from the battlement. A rodder shoved a wet sponge far down the barrel to douse any smouldering wadding still inside, while one of the crew brought another canvas bag of grapeshot.

There were torches bobbing around the walls now, sentries shouting the alarm as the attack got under way on all sides of the fort.

One of the gunners screamed and pitched forward over the cannon. A musket ball had hit him in the back.

Lachlan swung around. 'Charlie! Tell Douglas we're taking fire from the city. He has to get some men up the Beggar's Tower to return fire.'

He ran along the rampart to check on the other gun. There was the clatter of wood on stone, and a scaling ladder appeared above the ramparts. He drew his cutlass and shouted the alarm. He hacked at the first white turban that appeared above the merlons. The man blocked the blow with his own *shamshir* sabre. At that moment one of his own gunners ran up and put his ramrod in the middle of the man's chest and shoved. The man screamed and toppled backwards fifteen feet into the moat. Lachlan and the gunner twisted the ladder away from the wall and hurled it into the darkness below.

Musket fire crashed along the walls. He saw the answering flashes from the windows in the city below.

Time and again he joined his sepoys in hurling down the scaling ladders. Grapeshot from the captured French field cannon in the tower scythed the attackers down on the *glacis*, scores at a time. Any that did make the top of the wall were immediately cut down with muskets.

Dawn leeched into the sky. He heard someone shouting his name. Mathieson was gesticulating wildly at him. He grabbed Lachlan by the arm and dragged him towards the western gate.

'What's happening, Charlie?'

'The west wall. Quickly!'

Lachlan followed him along the rampart. Mathieson pointed towards the plain. A regiment of mercenaries in blue jackets and green turbans were drawn up in three squared formations. They had their spiked muskets at port and their lines geometrically precise. The sun glittered on the gold tape on their white hose.

'They've been standing there the whole time,' Mathieson said. 'They haven't made a move.'

'What are they waiting for?' Lachlan said.

'I don't know, sir,' Mathieson said.

Sir. Well, that was new. He had never called him that before.

There was a sudden trumpet blast. The three regiments performed a perfect about face and marched from the field, withdrawing in perfect formation, in step to the beat of their drummer.

'What the hell are they doing?' Mathieson said.

'I don't know,' Lachlan said. 'But they've left a gap in their line. A bloody great gap.' He turned and ran back to the main gate. He could hear Douglas's voice booming even over the chaos of the battle and roar of the cannon. He had his sword drawn and had taken a hand at hurling back the scaling ladders himself.

'Sir, Ensign McKenzie, permission to speak!'

Douglas turned, his wig askew, blood on his frock coat. 'What is it, Mister McKenzie?'

'Permission to borrow your cavalry.'

'What?'

'How many horses do we have?'

'Two squadrons - two dozen horse at most. What do you want with them?'

'The enemy has withdrawn their regiments from the western flank and left a clear gallop to their command post. I am going to slaughter the bastards.'

Douglas stared at him as if he were speaking another language. 'You want to do what?'

'My father used to say about snakes: Never mind the tail, just cut off the head.'

Douglas called for his bugler. He told him to go down to the courtyard and sound the assembly for his cavalry. He hurried back to the ramparts, shouting orders as he went.

Lachlan went back to the western wall. He reached into his belt for his eyeglass, removed the brass lens cap and focused on the enemy encampment. The orderly lines of green turbans were still marching back to the rear. As the sun rose, it flashed on their polished silver buckles.

Perfect. The sun would be in those bastard's eyes when they rode down on them. He tucked his spyglass back in his belt pouch and turned to Mathieson. 'Can you ride, Charlie?'

'Not very well, sir.'

'Then stay here and take charge of the gun crews for me until I get back.'

'What are you going to do?'

'I'm going to pay their headquarters a visit. And then I'm going to kill the bastard who murdered my family.'

CHAPTER 58

Douglas's equerry had a roan mare saddled and waiting for him in the courtyard by the western gate. The cavalry lieutenant, Hayden, looked startled to see Lachlan leap up onto the horse and ride up beside him.

'I thought Douglas put you in charge of the guns,' Hayden said.

'I received another promotion in the field, lieutenant.'

'By God, next thing you'll be Chairman of the Company Board.'

The squadron had formed up in the shadow of the gatehouse. The horses were skittish from the battle noise and their hooves clattered on the cobblestones.

Lachlan drew his sword and turned in the saddle to face the cavalry squadron grouped behind him. 'The enemy have left their flank exposed and a fast ride will take us through their lines to their command tent. It is dangerous work and none of you are obliged to follow me. But if we ride true and if we ride hard, we may finish this siege today. Now who is with me?'

They all drew their swords as one.

Half a dozen redcoats ran to the gatehouse, unbarred it, and hauled back on the massive iron studded gates. Lachlan led the charge down the ramp, the horses splashing through the stagnant green pool - all that was left of the moat. They galloped hard across the plain. He could see the blue silk of the enemy's command tent in the distance.

If they could get there before the French realised what was happening, they would have a clear run at the heart of Chanda Sahib's army and the man he had crossed an ocean to find.

They had not even deployed pickets. These bastards thought this was going to be so easy, Lachlan thought. As easy as it was at Delgoa Bay.

The rising sun behind their backs made them invisible until the last moment. The first shouts of alarm from the French camp only came as Lachlan thundered through the first line of tents and rode down two French soldiers who were trying to aim their muskets. Then he leaped from his horse, drew his cutlass, and went searching for the crow in the white robe and turban.

The rest of the cavalry thundered through the camp behind him, laying about them with their swords and torching the tents. Some jumped from their horses to follow him into the headquarters pavilion.

Two Frenchmen ran out, one of them still trying to fasten his sword belt. He was cut down on the spot. Lachlan ran inside. There was a handful of officers gathered around a chart table. Three of them were French, the rest had turbans and beards. They stared at him in astonishment. He finished two of them before they had the chance to draw their own weapons. Hayden and his men crowded in behind him and laid into the others.

When it was done, Hayden kicked over the map table for good measure and took the senior officer's sword from him as a souvenir.

'Let's get out of here,' Hayden said.

'Where is he?' Lachlan said.

'Where is who?'

'Gagnon!'

'Who's Gagnon? Come on, we have to go!' Hayden grabbed his arm and hauled him out of the tent. Lachlan shook him off.

Where was he? He couldn't see the bastard anywhere. But if he stayed and kept searching, he was a dead man.

A bugler was sounding the alarm and French soldiers were streaming back from the lines, alerted to the incursion. He had run out of time. He found his mount and jumped into the saddle. A musket ball fizzed past his head. He bent low and spurred his horse into a gallop, following Hayden and the rest of the cavalry out of the camp.

A subedar appeared out of nowhere and raised his musket. Lachlan ran him down before he could loose a shot. A French picket ran in from the side and threw himself at him, hanging to the trappings with his left hand while he reached for his sabre with his right. Lachlan knocked him aside with the hilt of his cutlass and followed the red-coated cavalry in their helter-skelter charge back to the fort.

As soon as they were out of range, Lachlan reined in and looked back over his shoulder at the enemy line. He caught a glimpse of a tall, thin man in a white turban, standing with his hands on his hips, watching their retreat.

The man raised a hand in mock salute.

For a moment he was tempted to go back after him, but then Hayden shouted at him to hurry, and it brought him back to his senses.

The attack on the fort was still underway. Puffs of white smoke billowed along the walls, as his cannons scythed through the knots of infantry still surging up from the plain. There were hedgerows of dead below the southern wall. Some of them were trying to wade through the moat, holding their scaling ladders above their heads. If only they knew, he thought. If they tried the west wall, they'd find the gates wide open.

He galloped after Hayden and the others. They overtook a platoon of Mustapha Sahib's infantry running in the same direction. He spurred his horse on and rode through the gates just as the sentries were dragging them shut again.

He reined in next to Hayden in the courtyard. The lieutenant was red in the face, flushed with excitement and bloodlust.

'How many did we lose?' Lachlan said.

Hayden looked around, made a quick count of heads. 'Three.' He pointed to Lachlan's head. 'You're wounded.'

Lachlan felt something warm and sticky on the back of his head. A musket ball had sliced through his scalp and his hair was matted with blood. He hadn't even felt it.

'Are you alright?' Hayden said.

Lachlan nodded.

Hayden slapped him on the shoulder. 'We did it!' He stood in the stirrups and raised his sword to the sky. 'The Honourable Company!' he shouted, and the chant was taken up by the other survivors of the charge.

CHAPTER 59

Napoleon stood in the middle of the tent as the last of the staff officers was carried out. There were half a dozen colonels and subedars laid out on the grass outside, covered with blankets. Gore was sprayed on the silk flaps, and the ground was thick with blackened blood and mud. He picked up the folding map table and righted it.

It was sheer luck that he had not been at the command tent when the British cavalry squadron broke through. When Petit saw Napoleon's regiments marching away in perfect order, from the west wall, he had screamed in Napoleon's face, 'What are they doing? Bring your men to order!'

'I'll see what's going on,' he had said and gone outside, as if he was going to ride onto the field and remonstrate with the subedar of his infantry. It was just theatre because he had known precisely what was going on. He knew, because his subedar was doing exactly what he had told him to do, which was keep his troops out of range of the British cannons.

He had had a grandstand view of the audacious British cavalry charge. Although his troops had left a gap in the lines, he had not believed that the British would be so bold or tactically astute to take advantage of the opportunity. It didn't matter, because he had not been entirely displeased to see Petit and his toadies slaughtered.

Sometimes, a man made his own luck.

Two of Mustapha Sahib's own subedars and an officer from the French infantry now stood at the tent flap, staring in consternation at the bodies of their officers and then at him.

Mustapha had appointed no second in command. Of the *Compagnie* regulars, the highest officer rank was now a captain. The British had not only sliced them off at the knees with their cannon, but they had also decapitated them with one simple cavalry thrust.

The French captain stepped forward. He looked uncertain of himself. Probably his first campaign, Napoleon thought.

'Who is to lead us now?' he said.

'I will,' Napoleon said.

'But…' The captain looked around at his fellows for support. 'You are not French.'

'I am half-French. Will that do?'

'It is highly irregular.'

'I agree. So, who will lead now, you? You may be fully French, but you are only half grown.' He retrieved the maps from the grass. One was soaked with Petit's blood, and he tossed it aside. 'Bring me a cloth,' he said.

The captain hesitated, then did as he had ordered. Napoleon wiped the blood off his hands and looked at the two subedars standing at the tent door.

'Let me explain things to you gentlemen. Mustapha Sahib is dead and so is Major Petit. Petit's adjutant is at this moment gurgling away his life in the hospital tent. The British also killed two staff officers and four of your fellow subedars. There is no one left with any campaign experience aside from me. I will happily lead you, not for the glory of France, or because I wish to add to the profits of the *Compagnie Francaise*, but because if I do not, I will not be paid. Money is the greatest spur to valour that there is for me, though I see from your faces that you find that distasteful.'

'Why did your men not join in our attack,' the young captain had the effrontery to ask. 'You were the only one not to sustain losses.'

Napoleon smiled. 'What is your name?'

The young man threw out his chest. He was a sharp-nosed fellow with no whiskers and a weasel's eyes. 'Fourget'

'Well, Fourget, it is like this. My subedar, a fellow named Ram Singh, disobeyed my orders. Major Petit had ordered me to attack the western gate and even though it was the stoutest and best defended of the four walls, and even though such an assault amounted to gross stupidity, I always follow commands.'

'So where is this Ram Singh fellow?' Fourget said.

'He is unavailable. But I assure you he has been severely punished.'

'Punished, in what way?'

'That is none of your business, since my army is not answerable to the *Compagnie des Indes*. However, let me say I tended towards leniency, since if he had not disobeyed me, he and the rest of his men would have been slaughtered. And all because of Major Petit's stupidity, may God rest his soul.'

'But what...'

Napoleon drew back his hand and slapped Fourget hard across the face leaving a red welt on his pale skin. 'Do not question me again or it will be the worst for you. Do you understand me?'

Fourget stared at him in shock.

'I said, do you understand?'

He nodded.

'Good. Now, we have been resoundingly defeated today. We must regroup and plan a new strategy. I will tell you what that strategy is this evening. You are all dismissed.'

They all looked at each other. Having no other option, they saluted him and filed out.

In another three days, Napoleon thought, the siege guns would arrive. In the meantime, he would send a rider to Trichinopoly to inform Chanda Sahib of the grievous loss of his son in battle and advise him of Major Petit's blunders. He would tell him he had assumed command of the campaign and demand an increase in his fee.

Once he had taken Karimkot, he would negotiate a new agreement with Chanda Sahib to lead his army against Madras. The French would have to send a replacement for Major Petit, to take command of the *Compagnie* troops. There would be more haggling, but that was of no consequence. As long as he was paid.

When they took Karimkot, Douglas had cleared out a storeroom to use as a field hospital. Already the room was scarcely big enough for all the wounded from that day's action. Men lay groaning on tables or on benches on the floor. Some were even propped up on the stairwell. A few of them were moaning in delirium, others lay still and pale.

It was gloomy and oppressively hot. There was only a single half-moon window, high in the cellar wall, that gave a glimpse of blood red sky. It was near sunset.

An orderly began lighting the lanterns. They threw long shadows on the whitewashed walls.

Lachlan looked around for the surgeon, Thomas. He found him slumped against a pillar, exhausted.

'Where's Colonel Douglas?' Lachlan said.

Without even looking up, Thomas pointed to one of the tables on the far side of the room.

'Is he dead?'

'Close to it.'

'What happened?'

'Sniper. Took a musket ball in his chest, another in his leg. I doubt he'll still be alive in the morning.'

Douglas was as pale as the corpses around him. There was a stained bandage on his upper chest, and the sheet covering the lower half of his body was sopping with blood.

Lachlan bent down, put his lips close to the colonel's ear. 'Colonel Douglas?'

He opened one eye. 'Young Mister McKenzie,' he said. His voice was no more than a rasp. 'I am told we carried... the day.'

'It was a comprehensive victory, sir.'

'Your sally. Resounding success.'

'My father said that all a man needed in life was a stout heart and a good horse.'

Douglas laughed, then started to choke. Lachlan sat him up until the spasm passed and he could breathe again.

'Very brave thing. You did.'

'Thank you, sir.'

'Have to rest up. Day or two. D'you understand?'

'Not too long, I hope, Colonel.'

'Putting you. In charge.'

'Me, sir?'

'My other captain, Talbot. Damn fool. Got himself shot.' The effort at talking was exhausting him. He took a moment to catch his breath. 'Don't surrender. Agreed?'

'Wouldn't dream of it.'

'Never. Never!'

He made Lachlan swear to him. Then he passed out.

CHAPTER 60

Lachlan gathered the officer corps in the western gatehouse. The only officers still standing were Hodges and two subalterns, Jones and Lennox. Their force was virtually being held together by Company sergeants and the jemadars.

Hodges was white lipped with fury at being overlooked as provisional commander. But Douglas had signed the order when he regained consciousness on the surgeon's operating table, and there was nothing Hodges could do about it. Not that Lachlan gave a damn what Hodges thought. He had not risked his life at Conjeeveram, and with Hayden's cavalry, to defer to the factor's sense of entitlement.

'Gentleman, here is our position,' he said to the three men gathered around the upturned gunpowder barrel that now served as his map table. 'After the attack this morning, we have one hundred and seventy-three redcoats and two hundred and fifty sepoys fit to man the walls. I calculate that the enemy has around five thousand native infantry. They also have around seven hundred fusiliers and cavalrymen, mostly *Compagnie des Indes* regulars as well as two regiments of sepoy mercenaries. However, to our advantage, their officer corps has been meaningfully reduced.'

'Five thousand!' Hodges said.

'Our scouts tell me that Chanda Sahib is sending a further two thousand irregulars, along with a French artillery battery. They will arrive in the next few days from Trichinopoly. Take heart. That doesn't paint the true picture of our position.'

Silence.

'Even though they have greater numbers, they do not have a force sufficient to successfully storm the walls, as we have demonstrated. We can withstand a protracted siege. There were plentiful provisions left behind when we arrived and, with small rations, we may stretch these to a month, perhaps two. The fort's reservoir is full, and the enemy cannot interfere with that supply, as the channel has been blocked from the inside. We have a large arsenal of powder and shot, and in the two recent actions we have captured a number of enemy muskets and *jezails*.'

Hodges reached into his jacket for his snuffbox. He looked feverish. 'You say we might hold out here for two months. To what purpose?'

'The longer we resist, the greater our chance of turning the opinion of the other warlords in the Carnatic. It is the first time a British force has taken the fight to native territory. Chanda Sahib's rivals will be closely following the outcome.'

'So they can watch us die like dogs?'

'So they will see us fight like men,' Lachlan said. 'You have all heard of Shivaji Ghorpade?'

'He's a freebooter and a bandit,' Hodges said.

'A bandit who commands a sizeable army. I don't know how politics works in Hindustan, but in Africa warlords like him ally with the king they consider the strongest. They have learned not to commit their tribe's destiny to the losing side. Shivaji is a devout Hindu; Chanda Sahib is a Muslim. He may not love him, but he will not oppose him if he thinks he is going to win this war. But the moment he sees weakness he will quickly change his thinking.'

'How many men does this Shivaji have at his back?' Lennox asked.

'Six thousand horse.'

'Six thousand!'

'Enough to sway the outcome if he commits. But at present he is more afraid of Chanda Sahib and the French. That is why we must hold Karimkot.'

'What do you propose?' Jones asked him.

'We will strengthen our defences as best we can and prepare for a long siege. Colonel Douglas made me promise that I will never surrender. I intend to keep my promise.' He looked at the three pale faces in the light of the candle. 'That will be all.'

Hodges did not like being dismissed by a man who had been one of his own clerks, but he had no choice. He frowned and followed the two subalterns to the door.

When they had gone, Lachlan called for Mathieson and asked him if any of their scouts had returned.

'Yes, sir, Rajiv Khao rode in an hour ago.'

'Send him in if you will.'

If he'd met him in a dark alley in Black Town, Rajiv Khao's appearance would have terrified him. His lips had been stained red from chewing betel nut and his hair, under his black pagri turban, was dyed orange with henna. His two front teeth were missing, giving him the look of a predatory animal. In fact, Lachlan knew him as a soft-spoken man with a surprising talent for playing the sitar.

Lachlan sat down with him on the carpets in his makeshift office and offered him cinnamon tea. 'Did you reach Shivaji Ghorpade?' he said.

'I did, *sahib*.'

'And is he disposed to help us?'

A shrug. 'More disposed than before. He told me that he had not believed that the English could fight. But he is not yet convinced. He claims he would like to help us, but he still fears the French guns.'

'So, what do you think he will do?'

'He will wait and watch for now.'

'What will it take to sway him?'

'Don't let Chanda Sahib take back his capital city.'

'I don't intend to.'

This isn't my fight, Lachlan thought. What do I care if the Honourable Company prospers in Hindustan? The politics of the Carnatic are of no concern to me.

There is only one reason I am here.

CHAPTER 61

There were no more attempts to force the walls. The siege settled down to a daily battle of attrition.

The houses of the old town came to within twenty yards of the walls near the Beggar's Tower, and the French deployed their snipers from the upper windows. They fired at anyone careless enough to show their heads above the ramparts. Lachlan placed his own sharpshooters in the tower to return fire and the intermittent crack of musket fire became as natural as birdsong.

Lachlan kept his force there to a minimum, but every day they lost at least one man. Twice, he almost met the same fate. A jemadar standing next to him fell dead with a musket ball between his eyes while they were discussing the weather. A gunner moved in front of him at a critical moment, took the musket ball meant for him and died two days later in the hospital.

Hundreds of Mustapha Sahib's irregulars had been killed in the frontal assault on the first day and they still lay on the *glacis* below the walls, their corpses putrefying in the relentless heat. The black water in the moat was dotted with bloated bodies. The stench was so bad Lachlan could feel it in the back of his throat.

It had been a rare feast for the vultures and crows. Some of them gorged themselves so that they could no longer fly. At night the jackals and curs moved in, snarling and growling, to tear at the corpses. Soon every carrion eater in Hindustan had had its fill, but there were still bodies to be picked clean. The flies hovered in green swarms. Lachlan worried about disease.

Almost a week after the first assault, the French siege guns arrived, two eighteen-pounders. These were at once deployed in an earth emplacement that had been dug for them on the plain. They began to pound the weaker southern wall. Lachlan decided against trying to return fire and instead had his cannons lowered down to the courtyard with ropes and pulleys so they would no longer be exposed to enemy fire.

He had other plans for them.

He had never expected Douglas to live through that first night, but the Yorkshireman was a hard man to kill. For three days he had lain on a table in the makeshift hospital in the cellar, looking for all the world as if he were dead. His adjutant slept on the dirt floor next to him at night. By day, he stood at his side, wetting the colonel's lips with a wet cloth and brushing flies off the bloody sheets.

One day Douglas sat up and demanded that someone fetch Mister McKenzie. He wanted a report on the state of the siege, damn it, and didn't anyone have a glass of brandy for a man dying of his thirst?

'He's still alive?' Lachlan said to the surgeon as he came down the steps into the choking gloom of the cellar.

Thomas wiped his hands on his bloodied apron. 'Only because the Devil didn't want him in Hell, the bad-tempered bastard. He's lost enough blood for ten men. I wanted to take his leg off, but he wouldn't let me. God knows how he's still alive.'

There was a gut-churning thud as another round from the French siege guns landed in the courtyard outside. Lachlan felt it through his boots. The walls shook and a fine cloud of plaster dust rained down from the ceiling.

'I keep thinking we'll get buried in here,' Thomas said.

'You're safe enough, Mister Thomas,' Lachlan said. 'They're targeting the south wall.'

He followed the surgeon past lines of men groaning on stretchers. Not all of them had fallen victim to the snipers; dysentery had begun to take its toll as well, just as he had feared. The smell and the heat were appalling. There were piles of bloodied bandages and soiled linen everywhere. Clouds of metallic green flies buzzed into the air as they passed.

'What about his chest wound?' Lachlan said.

'The ball went straight through, missed his lung by some miracle.'

He had put Douglas in a corner, away from the main press of sick and wounded. He looked bloodless as a corpse and the flesh had wasted off him. Lachlan barely recognised him.

But his voice had lost none of its bite. 'Mister McKenzie. Nice of you to pay me a visit. I am still your commanding officer, you know.'

'Colonel, you put me in charge of the defences, and I am discharging my commission as you ordered. If you wanted someone running in here every five minutes asking you your opinion and begging leave to surrender, you would have promoted Hodges to the job.'

There were few men who had the temerity to stand up to Douglas, and Thomas decided not to wait around to witness the result of Lachlan's belligerence. Douglas's adjutant absented himself also.

When they had gone, Douglas turned on Lachlan the unblinking gaze that had earned him his nickname. His eyes were the colour of stewed prunes. 'How old are you, son?'

'Does it matter?'

'Last month you were a clerk and here you are shouting at your betters and acting as if you've been in the army all your life.'

'This is just my second battle and already I'm tired of killing. Once this is over, I intend not to fire another angry shot the rest of my days. But I promised you I would not surrender the fort, and I won't.'

Douglas grunted. 'What's that damned noise I've been hearing all day? Have they finally brought up some guns?'

'Two eighteen pounders. They're trying to breech the south wall.'

'Will they succeed?'

'The walls are in poor repair but they're stout and they're wide. Still, they are labouring away at it.'

'Do you have a contingency plan if they break through?'

'Of course.'

Douglas smiled, a death's head grimace. 'How are the men standing up?'

'The sepoys are managing the heat, but the Company boys are suffering badly. Many of them have heat boils on their arms and legs. That is not my main concern.'

'What is?'

'Exhaustion. By day they take their proper turns at the pickets, by night I have them repairing the walls, when it's cooler and the snipers are no longer a threat. But with our numbers dwindling each day, fewer men have to bear more of the work. Then there is the mental strain of having to be constantly on the alert for attacks. When they do come at us again, I worry what state our boys will be in.'

'Have you heard from Madras?'

'One of the couriers made it through the lines this morning. Channing has promised to send reinforcements.'

'When?'

'When they arrive from Calcutta. God knows when that will be.'

'Well keep with it, Mister McKenzie. We must never give up hope.'

'Yes, sir. I am glad to see you so much better. I wish you a speedy recovery.'

He left, passing the surgeon on the way out. He was pulling a sheet over another young boy's face.

One less picket for the walls.

Every night, with darkness protecting them from the French snipers, Lachlan set the men to work preparing for the attack he knew must eventually come. The greatest threat lay at the southern wall, where the French eighteen pounders had been working to create a breech.

The moat there was shallow and in poor repair. This was the way they would come.

He had the men dig two deep trenches: one close to the wall, another fifty paces further back. He took his share at the digging, rolling up his sleeves and sweating with the cockney redcoats and native sepoys.

When the work was finally done, they filled the trenches with three-pointed iron spikes. Then they erected palisades from the ends of the ditches to the ramparts, so that there was no way around. He ordered them to pull down stables and use the rubble as a barricade. It was here that he planned to place his fusiliers if the attackers made it past these obstacles.

He didn't think many of them would.

He had positioned one of his nine-pounder field cannons on the flat roof of the hospital, along with his reserve. From here his gunners had a clear field of fire over the killing ground he had created beyond the breech.

The work took the better part of two weeks. By then, the breech in the wall was almost fifty yards wide. But every day the enemy chose to wait, was an extra day for him to prepare.

Douglas suffered a relapse, and his wounded leg was becoming seriously infected, as Thomas had feared it would. He raved and tossed in the grip of a boiling fever. This time the surgeon did not expect him to recover.

Disease had taken hold everywhere. Lachlan's tiny force was down to about two hundred. Thomas sewed the dead into sheets and had details pitch them over the western wall during the night, downwind.

The smell of death seeped into everything. Lachlan could taste it whenever he breathed. His men took to wearing rags soaked in vinegar about their faces. It made them look like bandits.

Lachlan learned to sleep just a few hours at a time and patrolled the walls constantly, to ensure the pickets were alert and to keep up their spirits. His men stared out, dead-eyed, from the walls, waiting, waiting.

The tension was unbearable. What were they waiting for?

CHAPTER 62

Napoleon had moved his headquarters from the plain into Chanda Sahib's own pleasure palace in the town, when it became clear that the quick victory that the Nawab had envisioned would not be forthcoming. They might have to accustom themselves to a long stay.

The *Diwan-i-Khas*, the Hall of Private Audience inside the palace, was a world away from the blood and chaos around the fort. It was nothing less than an earthly paradise.

The pavilion was open on all sides and surrounded by a lacework fence of red sandstone and white marble. There was a garden of cypress and sandalwood with bowers of jasmine and rose. The only sounds were the bubbling of fountains and the occasional screech of a peacock. It appeared serene, except for the bodyguards, who were ringed around the walls in spiked helmets, carrying rounded shields and matchlocks.

It was here that Napoleon held his first conference with his new general staff.

He stabbed his finger at the map in front of him. 'Our guns have succeeded in creating a breech in the south wall. We shall begin the assault at this point. But we shall increase the probability of our success, and better utilize our superior forces, by simultaneously attacking the main gate near the

Beggar's Tower. Last night, nine war elephants arrived from Trichinopoly. They will form the fulcrum of that assault.'

'My uncle is most anxious that this is finished as soon as possible,' Shah Mohammed said.

The Shah was Chanda Sahib's nephew and had only recently arrived from Trichinopoly. Chanda Sahib had sent him to replace Mustapha.

Napoleon looked at the others gathered around the chart table. There was the new artillery captain, Gondet; Fourget, the young fusilier captain; and the three generals in charge of Chanda Sahib's infantry.

'I am aware of the Nawab's problems,' Napoleon said. 'But we cannot throw his army at the fortifications again before we are ready. Another failed assault would only embarrass him and delay the successful conclusion of the siege.'

'We must hurry,' Shah Mohammed persisted. 'I have learned that the bandit, Shivaji Ghorpade, is on the move. He is camped thirty miles from here with six thousand horsemen. His allegiance is as yet undecided.'

'He will not commit himself to a battle until he is sure of the outcome.'

'My uncle has sent a courier asking us to proceed immediately.'

'And we shall. However, my spies tell me the conditions inside the fort are desperate. They are low on food, and they have been decimated by disease and by the expert skills of the *Compagnie's* snipers. Before we waste more of our military resources on an assault, we should at least attempt to achieve our aims through diplomacy. We will offer terms.'

'I say it would be better to annihilate them,' Shah Mohammed said.

'I am partial to annihilation. My record speaks for itself. But I am also a realist. Should our next assault fail, the results could be catastrophic. If you want to take responsibility for that, I shall surrender the command of your uncle's forces to you and leave immediately with my men. What do you say?'

Shah Mohammed thought about it. Finally, he gave a bitter shrug. 'Very well. We parlay.'

It was just after dawn.

Lachlan sat on a chair in the parade ground with his head back and a towel draped across his shoulders. A sepoy barber carefully scraped at the soapy bristles under his neck. Then he rinsed the razor in a bowl of water and ran it along the line of his jaw.

A round from one of the eighteen-pounders crashed into the south wall, and the barber's hand shook.

'Careful now, Mister Das, I didn't survive the French snipers and the Nawab's finest to have you cut my throat at my morning shave.'

There was an appreciative ripple of laughter from the men around the walls.

Mathieson made his way across the courtyard.

'Good morning, Charlie.'

'Good morning, sir.'

'What is our strength today?'

'Eighty redcoats and six score sepoys.'

The barber tidied his work with small precise movements of the razor and towelled Lachlan's face.

'Well, that's plenty. I think I shall only need half that number today. Perhaps we will send the rest back to Conjeeveram to take the waters.'

More laughter from the pickets on the walls. Have to keep their spirits up, Lachlan thought. Especially now when they were in the most parlous state imaginable. They were nearly out of supplies, the south wall was almost down, and their garrison consisted of a handful of dead-eyed skeletons in red jackets shuffling about the ramparts. They had taken to using straw from the stables and stuffing it inside the jackets and helmets of dead men. They had roped these fake soldiers to the ramparts to deceive their enemy into thinking their garrison was twice its number.

Lachlan took the towel and splashed a handful of water from a pail over his face. He and Mathieson strode away and headed back to the main gatehouse. When they were alone, Lachlan closed his eyes and leaned against the wall.

'Are you alright?'

'I'm exhausted. But I can't let them see it.'

'How far are you going to take this?'

'What do you mean, Charlie?'

'This is all futile now. No one's coming to help us. Nothing's going to change. We've held out against a force thirty times our size. What more is to be gained?'

'I won't countenance surrender.'

'Is it worth losing all our lives for this stinking little town? If we surrender now, we can hold up our heads knowing we gave them a damned good fight.'

'I'm in no hurry to go back to the counting house and the ledgers. Listen to me. Every day, every hour that we remain here, our prestige grows, and Chanda Sahib's diminishes.'

'You may be right. But it isn't about that for you, is it?'

Lachlan knew what he was driving at. He didn't answer.

'It's about Gagnon. You're risking all our lives for a personal vengeance.'

'Douglas told me to hold the fort at all costs and I will.'

'Because it suits you to do it.'

'I'm following orders.'

'We're going to get slaughtered,' Mathieson said, 'because of your private war.'

They stared each other down.

Mathieson sighed. 'Very well. I've always admired you, and I won't go against you now. I can't make out if you're mad or incredibly brave. Perhaps both.'

Napoleon strode along the marbled corridor to where he and Adelaïde had their rooms. He drew a breath before he went in.

Adelaïde lay on a divan under a pile of blankets, shivering violently, even though the amber tapers used to light the room made it uncomfortably warm. His nose twitched at the stink of wax and stale sweat.

His adjutant was crouched over her. 'The surgeon has been to see her,' he said. 'He has bled her.'

'That butcher.'

'He left medicine.'

'He might as well feed her muck from the river. It would be as much benefit.' Napoleon jerked his head over his shoulder and the adjutant hurried from the room.

He stared at his daughter. Two days she had been like this. One moment she was burning up, the next shivering as if she were buried up to her neck in ice.

'Dear God,' he said, the beginning of a prayer, but that was as far as it always went. He wasn't a priest, and he didn't believe in their nonsense.

She looked so pale and lost under all the blankets. She whimpered in her sleep. His hands balled into fists at his side, and he felt his fingernails biting into the flesh of his palms. He was unaccustomed to this feeling of helplessness.

There must be something he could do to save her.

'You can't die,' he said.

Rajiv Khao spat a quid of red betel juice out of the window. 'Shivaji has an army of six thousand warriors camped at the foot of the western ghat, *sahib*, not a day's ride from here.'

'What are his intentions?' Lachlan said.

'There is lively debate among his advisers about what to do. The Rajah of Mysore has offered him a bribe to take the part of Ali and you Britishers in the fight.'

'Will he do it?'

'He is still waiting.' He nodded out of the window towards the enemy camp.

'For the next attack?'

Rajiv nodded. 'If the French succeed, Shivaji will proclaim support for Chanda Sahib. If the attack fails, he will learn the words to *God Save the King*.'

Lachlan smiled. 'Thank you, Rajiv.'

Rajiv left. Lachlan closed his eyes for a moment, feeling tired to his bones. He snuffed out two of the candles in the room but left one burning. It was his habit to let his men think he was still awake, no matter what time they looked up at his window in the gatehouse. He drew aside the curtain that screened his quarters and settled himself on a string *charpoy*.

Today he had set the men to making extra cartridges for their muskets, curling scrap paper into tubes and measuring an ounce of powder into each. The powder in the charges was just enough to prime the pan and they could use the paper as extra wadding to stop the musket ball rolling out. This would be crucial on the ramparts when they were firing almost directly downwards.

They had ransacked every ledger and account book they could find among the stores for the wadding. They had even torn all the pages out of Hodges' Bible. Lachlan had told the quartermaster to distribute the entire arsenal, for the next fight would surely be the last.

A supply of primed muskets and captured *jezails* was stacked up beside each man still left on the ramparts. That meant at least three guns to every man, along with a supply of the prepared cartridges.

He kept thinking about what Charlie had said, that his private war could cost them all their lives. Perhaps he was right. But he couldn't go back now. He fingered the cross at his throat. Not for anything.

Madras

Ammani hurried down an alleyway deep inside the *ganj*. Skeletal lepers with toothless mouths pushed their begging bowls at her. There were urchins with streaming noses running everywhere. A near-naked holy man, holding a trident and streaked with white ochre mud, went past her ringing a bell.

She found Mendes's shophouse and went inside, drawing her veil across her nose and mouth while she grew accustomed to the heady miasma of spice.

Mendes appeared from a dark room at the back of the shop. 'Where have you been?' he said to her.

'I couldn't come straight away. The *mem'sahib* needed me.'

'You don't work for your *mem'sahib*,' he said. 'You work for me.' He held out Napoleon's letter. 'This is for you.'

'I can't read it.'

'I know.' The seal had already been broken. Mendes opened it and read it to her, though the letter was short, and he had already memorised the contents. When he had finished reading, he looked up at her. 'Can you do it?'

'I think so.'

'When the job is done you will give half the money to me. What you do with the rest is no concern of mine. You will be free to go. Do you understand?'

'I understand,' Ammani said.

CHAPTER 63

Lachlan was awake again before dawn. He went up to the ramparts and found a shadowed spot out of the light of the flares. Flaming, tar-soaked rags had been wound around stout poles, to blind the French sharpshooters and stop them picking off the men finishing off the trenches and earthworks behind the second breech. The gaps in the wall had been shored up with lumber, sandbags, and the last of the baggage carts.

He trained his spy glass on the inky plain. Pinpricks of light marked out the campfires still burning among the enemy tents. It was broiling, even at this hour, and he wiped a bead of sweat from his forehead. A suffused pale lemon light crept up the sky, silhouetting the distant ramparts of the Mysore Ghat.

Crows and vultures were still looking for scraps on the *glacis* below. Someone fired a musket at them and a few of the birds lazily retreated a couple of paces, but most of them were accustomed to musket fire by now and did not even look up from their breakfasts.

Lachlan winced as the sun broke the horizon and flashed on something moving across the plain. He brought up his spyglass a second time and saw a rider heading towards the gatehouse. He was holding a white truce flag.

'We must accept terms,' Hodges said. 'There are two separate breaches in the walls, we are running out of food, and they outnumber us almost thirty to one. We have done no dishonour to our country or ourselves. Now for pity's sake, enough.'

'My scouts tell me that the governor has sent reinforcements from Madras,' Lachlan said.

'You have been telling us that for weeks. We should consult with Douglas.'

'Of course, if you can find him in a lucid state. He is only now recovering from his latest fever and still sees giant lizards crawling up the walls. He put me in charge of the defence of this fort and he is the only man senior enough to countermand my orders.'

'You are a clerk!'

'Not today.'

'We cannot hold out any longer.'

'We can and we will. As we speak, Shivaji Ghorpade has six thousand horsemen gathering on the plains to the west. It is Chanda Sahib who is running out of time, not us.'

'I have heard our scouts talking among themselves,' Mathieson said. 'The *mullahs* are inciting Chanda Sahib's troops to a sort of religious fervour. They are telling them that whoever dies in a battle against the infidels will go immediately to heaven as a hero of the Faith. And they are giving them hashish. That lot will charge the gates of hell itself without thought of consequence.'

There was a long silence.

'We are facing seven thousand madmen,' Hodges said. 'Is that what you are telling us? And we have three officers, two hundred men and two holes in the walls.'

'Yes, that is how it seems,' Lachlan said. 'Does that scare you?'

Napoleon rode out for the parlay with Ram Singh and a bodyguard of his own cavalry. The iron-studded gates on the western gatehouse swung open and half a dozen riders emerged from the fort. They reined in their horses twenty paces away.

Lachlan stepped his horse out and waited.

Napoleon spurred his horse forward. He tried not to let the surprise show on his face. Surely this could not be the British commander. He looked far too young. He had his left arm in a makeshift sling. He wore neither a helmet nor a wig. His uniform was torn and bloodied.

They studied each other.

'My name is Napoleon Gagnon. I am the commander of Chanda Sahib's army. May I know who I am addressing?'

'You know who I am.'

The reply puzzled him. 'No, I don't think so.'

'It was you that took your band of butchers against my family at Fort Greenock.'

Napoleon had learned to laugh whenever he received a nasty shock. It gave him time to look at ease while giving himself time to think.

'What is so amusing?'

'I have never heard of such a place.'

'Let me refresh your memory. My name is Lachlan McKenzie. I am an Ensign in the British East India Company Army. My father was Hamish McKenzie. You murdered him in cold blood, along with my mother, my brother, my sister and my uncle. You destroyed our home and massacred our entire community. Do you remember me now?'

So, this was the young pup who escaped from him in Delgoa Bay, Napoleon thought. His spies in Madras had been right. What on earth was he doing here? For a moment, he was tempted to draw his pistol, shoot him between the eyes, and forget the conventions of the truce flag.

'Ensign McKenzie, I have no idea what you are talking about. It has nothing to do with our business here this morning. I have come to offer you terms. I will allow your garrison to march out with their arms and baggage if you will surrender the fort to me by sunset today. If you do not, I will storm the fort and put all the defenders to the sword without mercy.'

'Mercy is not something I would ever expect from a man like you,' Lachlan said. 'Besides, it is usual for the terms to be dictated by the man with the advantage. I fail to see how that man could be you.'

Napoleon admired the lad's balls. He said all that with a straight face. 'Ensign, you have a massive breech in your southern wall, and I have seven thousand men at my back. My spies tell me you have two hundred men to defend the fortress and most of them are sick.'

'I will make you a counteroffer,' Lachlan said. 'I will guarantee you and your men safe passage if you leave your guns and your baggage and clear the field immediately. My personal accommodations are up there in the tower, and you are spoiling my view of the mountains.'

'Is that your final answer?'

'It is.'

'Very well. On your head.'

'How did my father die?'

'What?'

'My father and brother. Did they die together, or did you murder them separately?'

Napoleon debated with himself. Should he tell the stripling the truth? He leaned forward on the withers of his horse. 'Perhaps your father abandoned you, boy. Have you ever wondered about that? You must have done. At the end of the day, he was a coward who ran and left you all to it.' There, let him think about that up there in his personal accommodations tonight. He smiled, turned his horse and rode back to his lines.

Lachlan posted double sentries along the walls, and all able men were told to sleep at their battle posts. They huddled in nooks and crannies around the ramparts, restless, exhausted and afraid.

Rain teemed from the parapets and dripped from the rims of their tricorn hats. It ran in rivulets through the newly completed earthworks, turning everything into an ochre swamp. Chanda Sahib's army would not attack in this, Lachlan thought. They would wait until the morning. The challenge now was to keep their powder dry.

He made sure the cannons were ready for tomorrow's business, pouring boiling water down all the barrels to clean out the residues of any charred wadding. He made a final tour of the walls. He found one of his sepoys, the stumps of his legs bound up in white bandages, sitting against the battlement with three loaded muskets. He was smoking an opium pipe to deaden the pain.

By the time Lachlan had finished his rounds, he felt hollowed out with exhaustion. He fell asleep propped against the gatehouse wall.

He came to with a start. The storm had passed, and a huge silver moon rose over the ghats in the sweating dark.

Tomorrow, he promised himself, he would find Napoleon Gagnon on the field and have an end to this.

CHAPTER 64

Lachlan extended his telescope and trained it on Napoleon's camp.

The whole plain seemed to be on the move. Chanda Sahib's army formed up loosely into regiments, a howling, seething mass of turbans, spear points and studded shields. *Mullahs* weaved in and out of the ranks, waving green flags and shouting prayers. War elephants lumbered forward, bellowing as their mahouts goaded them on. Sunlight flashed on their metal plate armour through the heat haze.

An ululation rose from seven thousand throats along with the blast of war trumpets and the sonorous beat of the great kettledrums. His men peered at them over the ramparts. Many of them had rags wrapped around their foreheads to keep the sweat out of their eyes. The only ones up there on the walls not feeling the heat and the tension were his straw soldiers who now outnumbered the real ones.

He jumped down onto the roof of the hospital and climbed onto the barrel of one of the nine pounders. He knew the garrison could all see him from there, though he would have to shout to make himself heard over the din outside the walls.

'Can you see them?' he shouted. 'Our miseries are nearly at an end, for today they will attack us and finally this will be decided. Look at us! Drenched with rain, parched from the heat, exhausted, wounded, sick. We are now almost spent of vigour, of shot, and of powder. Our defences are down on the south wall in two places. We are facing overwhelming odds. What chance do we stand? We have nothing to stop them with!'

There was a long silence. Finally, he drew his cutlass from its scabbard and raised it above his head. 'Except this!'

There were isolated shouts from the ramparts and one or two drew their swords with him.

'And here is what else we have to stop them.' He tore open his shirt and put a hand over his heart above the filthy bandage around his ribs. 'We have heart. The heart to stand here fifty days in this fort and take all the punishment they have given us. We have endured it for one reason. The chance to pay them back! To pay them in kind for every musket ball that claimed one of our own, for every shell, for every miserable day we have spent roasting under this hellish sun at their pleasure. And now today, they will know in return what it is like to suffer!'

Especially you, Napoleon Gagnon.

More ragged cheers. For his next speech he reverted to Tamil, blessing his father for every lesson he spent closeted with his Hindustani tutor at Fort Greenock.

'You sepoys. My first command. Have you seen how every musket ball they have fired at me has not touched me? They have shot their *jezails* at me. They have tried to skewer me with their bayonets. They have slashed me with their swords, and still I stand here. Why? Because the gods are protecting me, because Indra is with me! You have seen this with your own eyes. These same gods are with you too!'

He reverted to English.

'When they write the history of this country, this day will be its first chapter. For we are ready, and they cannot imagine the hell we have prepared for them. They look mighty on the plain but when they enter the trap we have made, they will be like lambs in a slaughterhouse. What do you say?'

They all raised their muskets and their swords and cheered him hoarse.

Lachlan wondered what Sasavona would say if he could see him. He had kept the promise he had made to him that day in the boat. He had survived. He had endured. And now today, somehow, he would exact his revenge in full.

Mathieson heard a chilling cry from the *ganj* beyond the main gate. A turbaned *mullah* stood on a housetop with his arms outstretched, exhorting those below to give their lives for Allah. There was an answering howl from the mob, the streets filling with Chanda Sahib's soldiers - a thrusting, bulging mass of turbans and *jezails*.

At once the drums started. They seemed to come from all around. Men with scaling ladders emerged from the warren of alleyways and ran towards the only section of the wall unprotected by the moat.

There was a trumpeting shriek and one of Chanda Sahib's war elephants emerged from an alley. It was followed by another, then another.

Mathieson shouted the alarm and ran along the ramparts to the western gatehouse to fetch Lachlan.

Lachlan heard Mathieson calling for him. He listened for a moment to the ululation of the Muslim army as they approached the gates. He took a deep breath and closed his eyes, until his mind was calm.

He went up to the roof two steps at a time.

When he got there, he saw someone huddled in the shadows under the parapet wall. It was Hodges.

'What are you doing?' Lachlan shouted at him.

'Get away from me. You're mad.'

Lachlan grabbed him by the collar and dragged him out from his hiding place. 'We need you at the ramparts.'

'I'm not going.' Hodges was shaking.

'Pull yourself together. All the men can see you. Get up!'

The sepoys were staring. One of the Company sergeants shook his head, said something to them, and they laughed.

Lachlan picked Hodges off the floor and threw him against the rampart. 'Musket if you please, Charlie.' He held out his hand. Mathieson found a Brown Bess leaning against the wall and gave it to him. Lachlan pressed it into Hodges's arms. He refused to take it.

'You're a disgrace,' Lachlan said and walked away.

Lachlan stood at the battlements above the main gate, watching the mob stream out of the *ganj*. Chanda Sahib's war elephants were terrifying beasts, gaudily painted, and clad in iron face armour. The infantry bounded between them, carrying siege ladders.

He was not impressed by the apparent formlessness of the attack, for it was immediately obvious to him what Gagnon intended. The assault here at the east wall was a diversion, a feint to draw the greater part of his garrison away from the attack's real focal point. He couldn't let that happen.

'The elephants will try to use their head armour to batter down our gates,' Lachlan told the thirty redcoats gathered around him on the gatehouse roof. 'We cannot let them get that close.'

'What do we do?' one of the corporals said, his musket already at his shoulder.

'Wait for my command. Aim directly at those parts of the elephants that are not protected. Our aim is not to kill them but to turn them.'

The sound was unimaginable. He had never known anything like it. Chanda Sahib's infantry had been whipped to a frenzy by the *mullahs*, and they were howling as they ran. There were nine elephants in the first rank, trumpeting in either terror or rage.

The men waited for his signal.

He had to impose himself on them or they would lose their nerve. He brought down his sword and the air filled with sparks and black powder smoke. He counted one, then two hang fires, and saw the flicker of muskets as they fired their first volley.

The elephants, shot through with musket balls in their forelegs and shoulders, were bellowing in agony. They turned away, trampling anyone in their path. The massed ranks of peasant infantry that were following them were crushed under their massive feet. In moments, it was utter chaos.

Lachlan was stricken with remorse at the sight of what they'd done, but the ploy had worked. It was the only thing that could have saved them. In the next few minutes, Chanda Sahib's elephants did worse slaughter than he could ever have done, as they ran in pain and panic through the army behind them.

The infantry that had run ahead of the animals had not been caught in the mêlée. They reached the bridge and threw scaling ladders against the wall. Not enough of them, though. His men set to work toppling the ladders, using their bayonets on anyone that reached the top of the parapet.

Lachlan looked over his shoulder, to the south wall, where he knew the real attack would come.

The first wave of Chanda Sahib's infantry had succeeded in scaling the rubble at the breech. His fusiliers fired round after round into the mob until their supply of muskets was exhausted. Then they picked up their weapons and clambered back down the fall of masonry. Lennox was with them. A path had been laid out between the trenches, wide enough for one man at a time. Lennox waited until his men were through and followed them.

Moments later the first of the white-robed attackers appeared at the top of the breech. He brought up his *jezail* and loosed a shot at Lennox. He went down, but the man ahead of him heard the shot and turned back for him. He grabbed him by the arm and dragged him the rest of the way to the breastworks on the other side of the courtyard.

Lachlan joined the men at the barricade. Lennox was already back on his feet, supporting his weight on a musket, blood soaking his frock coat and dripping from the fingertips of his left hand. He was white-faced and shivering with shock, but his voice was steady as he directed his fusiliers.

Another volley blasted out, then another. Each time they fired into the screaming, howling chaos, they immediately reached down for another musket, passed up to them by those below. Chanda Sahib's infantry were milling in front of the trenches, hesitating at the spikes. Lachlan guessed there must be two thousand of them out there, as ferocious and terrifying a mob as he had ever seen, urged on by an officer in a yellow turban. He unslung his rifle, aimed, and shot the man through the chest.

It made no difference. Still, they came on. The press of men inside the killing ground would soon become too much. Those at the front were toppling into the pits and the bodies were forming a bridge.

The weight of numbers would soon tell.

Lennox's sepoys had used all their reserve muskets, and precious seconds passed as they were forced to reload. Soon it would be bayonets, and once the fighting was hand to hand their survival could be counted in minutes. They were all looking to him, searching for signs of uncertainty.

'Stand firm, lads!' he shouted. 'We have them as we want them!'

'I do think we need the guns though,' Lennox said.

'Keep them steady, Lennox,' Lachlan said and launched himself across the cobblestones towards the hospital and up the steps to the roof. The gun crews were waiting, crouched down by their nine pounders, which were primed and ready. At his signal they rolled them out to the eaves.

He tried to shout out his orders, but his voice came out as no more than a croak. His throat was parched by the powder-laden air. Chanda Sahib's men were streaming across the ditches. Lennox stood on top of the breastwork, firing his musket into the mob, careless of his own life.

Lachlan finally found his voice. 'Give them a taste of grapeshot if you will, Sergeant Wilkins,' he shouted. The sergeant lit a taper and touched it to the hole of their nine-pounder. The night before, Lachlan had ordered it loaded with langrage: horseshoes, coins, nails. God help me, Lachlan thought, as it roared and jumped on its carriage. When the powder smoke had cleared, the courtyard in front of the barricade was a litter of bloodied white rags.

It was suddenly deathly quiet. He had forgotten to put his fingers in his ears. How many times had he scolded his lads in the *chikunda* about that?

He waited for the clouds of powder smoke to clear. After a few moments, shadowy figures appeared at the top of the breech and the next wave came on. The men at the front of the charge hesitated when they saw the butcher's yard that awaited them at the bottom.

A *mullah* joined them on top of the debris and urged them on. But as soon as they started to scramble down the rubble, they were picked off by the sepoys behind the barricades.

The second of the nine-pounders was loaded and ready to fire. The gunner stood waiting for the order, the fuse smouldering in his hand.

'Sir?'

'Wait,' Lachlan said.

Lachlan brought his rifle up to his shoulder and sighted it on the *mullah* standing at the top of the debris. As you're so eager to send those poor bastards to Paradise, Lachlan thought, you can join them there. He fired. The man threw up his arms, a last appeal to the heavens, and toppled backwards out of sight.

The attackers were stalled by the piles of bodies between them and the barricades. As they ran howling down the scree, they suddenly found themselves trapped. The sight of the nine-pounder rolling to the edge of the hospital parapet sent them into a panic. Those who had not been decimated by Lennox's fusiliers found themselves milling at the bottom of the breach with nowhere to go.

'Fire,' Lachlan said.

This time he remembered to cover his ears.

When the smoke cleared, the second wave had been wiped out by another hail of langrage. Lachlan felt suddenly faint. The morning smelled like a charnel house. How could men do this for a living? He sat down hard on his haunches, fumbling for the pewter pannikin of water at his waist. He gulped at it, trying to clear the paste of gunpowder and dust in his mouth. He wiped his face with his sleeve. The sun was already halfway up the sky. Where had all the time gone?

Napoleon watched as Chanda Sahib's peasant army, screaming defiance and chanting holy verses, poured through the breach in the south wall. They clambered up the shattered masonry and into the fort.

He followed behind the third wave, but it was heavy going through the glutinous mud, which was still littered with half-rotted body parts from the first attack, weeks ago. He had brought with him a squadron of his own sepoys, so that he could direct the final slaughter.

He began composing his victory speech to Chanda Sahib. *In view of the fact that I rescued the situation after your French allies so conspicuously mismanaged it, I suggest we renegotiate my fee for the rest of the campaign...*

He wouldn't like it. The dog would try to wriggle out of payment. Napoleon supposed he might have to assassinate some of his advisers before the Nawab came to appreciate the benefits of being an honest man. Sometimes he felt less like a soldier and more like a debt collector.

But he would bring him to the sense of it. After this showing, Chanda Sahib would realise he could not rely on the French *Compagnie* if he wanted to keep his throne.

Finally, they were at the breach. Napoleon clambered over the shattered stone of the wall, his *subedar* shoving stragglers aside.

He reached the crest and stopped. He couldn't believe his eyes. The rabble were still milling around the courtyard. A runner breathlessly informed him that there were more earthworks beyond the walls and trenches bristling with spikes. He heard the crack of musket fire from the roof of the fort and from the breastworks the British had placed as a second line of defence.

He saw the young pup he had met at the parlay standing on a flat roof overlooking the courtyard. His breeches were torn, and his frock coat tattered, and powder stained. The pup helped his soldiers manhandle a nine-pounder field gun into position on the edge of the roof, the muzzle pointed directly down into the courtyard below. Napoleon knew in an instant what was about to happen. He tried to shout a warning, but his voice was lost in the tumult of the battle.

Besides, it would do no good. Chanda Sahib's men had been goaded on by the *mullahs*. They wouldn't retreat now if the Prophet himself came down to earth and tried to shepherd them bodily back the way they had come.

A red-jacketed gunner held a burning taper to the match hole. The discharge was thunderous inside the narrow canyon created by the fortress walls. The white smoke drifted away in wisps across the dusty square. When it cleared, the grapeshot had cut two swathes twenty paces wide through the howling mob, turning them into offal.

There was a sudden, appalled hush, followed quickly by the panicked screams of the wounded and dying. Knots of survivors staggered back towards the breech. There were enough of them that they could have stormed the breastworks in the time it took the redcoat gunners to reload, but the peasant warriors had lost their eagerness for Paradise. Napoleon supposed they had imagined a glorious death. Having their insides painted up the walls of Karimkot did not tally with the kind of illustrious end their *mullahs* had promised them.

The British had left a gap between the breastworks on one side of the trenches, and the survivors flooded through it, thinking they had found a way through. Just then, the great iron-studded door below the Beggar's Tower swung open, and half a dozen redcoats wheeled a field gun into the courtyard. The gunner touched a smoking taper to the firing hole and there was a roar of flame and smoke.

When the smoke cleared, the courtyard was littered with pulped bodies, scattered every which way. It had been another trap.

Meanwhile the British were lining up on the ramparts of the south wall, reloading their muskets, firing indiscriminately at the handful of survivors inside the fort or those fleeing down the *glacis*. They had a taste for it now.

Napoleon knew he could not allow his own infantry anywhere near this. He turned to Ram Singh. 'Get our men back! Call up Shah Mohammed's reserves!'

The redcoats were still firing volleys from the ramparts at them as they ran. Napoleon felt a musket ball whizz past his face. Ram Singh shouted a warning and pulled him aside, but he slipped on a slick of blood on the raw stone and fell. Ram Singh landed on top of him, blood pouring from the back of his head. He had taken the musket ball intended for him.

The British sepoys were hurling bombs with short fuses down from the ramparts. They were exploding on the *glacis*, driving back their reinforcements. Napoleon realised he had been outmanoeuvred. He should have shot that McKenzie pup when he had the chance.

He had to get away from here.

Lachlan saw a tall, thin man in a white turban scrambling up the rubble in the breach. 'Gagnon,' he murmured under his breath. He quickly unslung his rifle, aimed and fired.

There was a dull click. He remembered he had wasted his shot on the *mullah* and now there was no time to reload. He looked around desperately for another rifle, but the gunners were unarmed. He hurled the Penterman aside and vaulted down the stairs, drawing his cutlass as he ran.

He took the steps three at a time and picked his way through the dead and dying in the courtyard. It was like trying to run through sandbags.

Mathieson went after him. 'What are you doing?'

'I've business to attend to!'

He scrambled desperately up the twisted rubble under the tower. Gagnon had disappeared out of sight over the far side of the breach. He couldn't let him get away.

CHAPTER 65

Napoleon heard one of his men shout a warning. He turned around. A figure charged at him from out of the smoke. He raised his sword to parry the first blow, but the ferocity of the attack drove him back on his heels and he fought to keep his footing among the rubble. His attacker swung again, and he lost his balance and fell back, smashing his shoulder on a jagged block of sandstone. His sabre went spinning out of his hand.

His attacker raised his sword for the killing stroke. Napoleon put up a hand to plead for quarter. It was too late. The sword came down. He threw himself to the side and heard the steel clash and spark on the stone.

He saw his sabre and reached out a hand to grab it. He couldn't. His right hand was gone. Blood spurted rhythmically from his wrist. He stared, frozen in disbelief. He looked up, it was him, McKenzie's pup.

Lachlan raised his sword again. This time Napoleon did not try to wriggle away. He knew in a moment he'd rather die than live without his sword hand.

But the *coup* did not come. The pup suddenly yelled out in pain. His right leg gave way under him, and he fell.

Two of his sepoys ran over, hauled Napoleon to his feet and dragged him away. He tried to wrestle free of them. 'No,' he shouted, 'we have to kill him!'

One of them even scrambled back up the breach to do it. He drew his sword and was about to take off Lachlan's head, but as he raised it a musket ball took him in the throat, and he fell, dead.

Mathieson scrambled up the rubble. By the time he reached the top, his breeches were ripped to shreds. There was blood on his knees and hands, where he had fought for purchase on the shattered stone.

He saw Lachlan attacking one of the Nawab's officers, his sword raised to strike. A mercenary standing fifty feet away raised his musket and fired. Lachlan went down.

Another green-turbaned soldier was about to finish him with his sword. Mathieson raised his musket, fired blind, and was astonished to see the man go down.

The injured officer was roaring at his men, urging them to kill Lachlan, but they were under heavy fire from the ramparts and only wanted to get him down the *glacis* to safety.

Mathieson scrambled down the slope. He thought Lachlan might be dead. Instead, he found him groaning and clutching at his leg.

'Are you alright?' Mathieson said and tore a strip of his own shirt as a makeshift bandage. He wrapped it around Lachlan's thigh to stop the bleeding.

Lachlan was trying to sit up. 'Don't let him get away!'

Two sepoys had followed Mathieson down the sloping rubble, and they helped him lift Lachlan by his legs and arms. A musket ball fizzed past Mathieson's head, throwing chips of stone into his face as it smashed into a chunk of limestone. He shouted at the sepoys to hurry. They half-carried, half-dragged Lachlan up and over the rubble. When they reached cover on the other side, they collapsed among the ruin of bodies and splintered masonry.

Even then, Lachlan tried to scramble back up the slope, shouting that he had to kill the man in the white turban. It took another three sepoys to drag him away.

Napoleon lay on the blood sodden operating table and stared dead-eyed at the dirty canvas roof. The surgeon pulled a bloody rag out of a bucket of water and washed the wound. Someone held his head and forced a teaspoon of laudanum into his mouth.

The surgeon bent to his task, tying off the blood vessels with silk.

'Sear it off, man,' Napoleon shouted at him.

'M'sieur Gagnon...'

'I'm a soldier like the rest of these poor bastards you're butchering. I can take it. Now do it!'

There was a hot iron fizzing in the brazier in the middle of the tent. The surgeon wiped his hands on his apron and brought it over. He nodded to his assistants, who held Napoleon to the table by his shoulders and legs.

Napoleon turned his face away. So, McKenzie's pup had done for him after all. He could even appreciate the poetry of it. Well, this wasn't the end of it. Not yet.

Someone put a rag in his mouth to stop him biting his tongue. His body spasmed and jumped on the table as the surgeon pressed the iron to the stump of his arm. He passed out.

A shaft of light slanted between the bars of the cellar window, picking out the dust motes floating through the gloom. The concussion from the two nine-pounders they had fired from the roof above, had shaken most of the plaster from the walls. In several places it lay in large clumps on the floor.

Lachlan's leg ached mercilessly. Thomas had told him he was lucky - the bullet had gone straight through.

He didn't feel lucky.

He reached into his pocket and took out the cross Catia had pressed into his hand the day he left Madras. He had never put much store in religion. God never took sides in a fight, in his opinion, but he held it to his lips and kissed it anyway. Perhaps Catia knew something he didn't.

There was another volley of musketry from the Beggar's Tower. He had to know what was happening. He tried to sit up, but immediately the room started to spin, and he broke out in a cold, greasy sweat. He retched onto the floor. Thomas hurried over and forced him to lie down again.

'I have to be with the men.'

'No, what you have to do is stay still. You'll be no good to anyone dead.'

Lachlan tried to push him away. Somehow, he got himself upright, but he found he couldn't put weight on his leg. His thigh was swathed in a thick blood-soaked bandage. He clung to the edge of the operating table for support.

'Get Charlie for me,' he said.

Thomas shouted an order to one of his assistants. A few minutes later he came back with Mathieson.

'What are you doing, sir?'

'Help me, Charlie.'

'You're wounded.'

'Never mind. Give me your shoulder, help me up to the roof.'

'I don't know about that.'

'It's not a request, it's an order. Come on, Charlie, don't let me down now.'

He limped up the stone steps, leaning on Mathieson's shoulder. Good God. The bodies of the men they had slaughtered in the breech were still there. They had lain all day in the sun. There were just too many of them for the corpse fires. The stench, after only a few hours, was unimaginable.

He clapped a hand across his mouth and nose and retched a second time.

Hodges was standing at the rampart with an eyeglass.

'Are we ready for them?' Lachlan said.

'Ready for them?'

'How have you deployed the cannon? Why haven't we dug more trenches?'

'Thomas said you were badly wounded. I'm in charge now.'

'I didn't give that order and as you can see, Mister Hodges, I am still conscious and lucid. You will stand down.'

'Stand down? Who do you think you are?'

'I'm the commander of this fort. On Colonel Douglas's orders.'

'Douglas is dead. He died of fever this morning.'

'I am still in charge, and I want more trenches dug tonight.'

'For God's sake, you arrogant fool, after today's bloodbath we're almost out of powder and only one man in three can hold a musket. It's time to talk terms.'

'You may surrender if you wish. There's the gate. I'll have one of the sentries open it for you. Go and talk to them. But we won't be opening the gate a second time.'

'Look at them!' Hodges shouted at him. 'Do you not see them out there? No matter how many we killed this morning there must be five thousand more ready to come at us. Will you risk all our lives for your pride?'

'We are not going to surrender.'

Lachlan hobbled back down the steps and across the courtyard to order the men to boil the cannon barrels and dig more trenches inside the breach. Any man who could stand without assistance was enlisted into one of the burial details.

He dragged himself up the rubble below the southern wall and looked over the *glacis*. How many had they killed today? Hundreds, at least. But Chanda Sahib had thousands in his army, and life here was cheap. They would come again.

He supposed if this was any other fight, he might be tempted to do what Hodges wanted and slip away in the night, let them have the damned fort.

But he couldn't. Not while Gagnon was still alive.

CHAPTER 66

Rabiot stood in the doorway. He was no longer the dapper figure he had been in life. The worms had been at him. The wound in his head was stinking and raw.

'Get away from me,' Napoleon moaned.

Rabiot didn't say anything. His daughter came in, all ringlets and white lace dress. She opened her mouth wide and screamed.

'Stop it,' Napoleon said.

But she wouldn't stop, and the screaming went on and on. Napoleon sat up, suddenly wide awake. Rabiot was gone but the girl was still screaming.

He felt groggy from all the laudanum they had given him. There was sudden, terrible pain in his arm. He looked down at the filthy blood-soaked bandage and remembered what had happened. They had put the stump in a sling.

The onset of pain made him nauseous. He retched over the side of the bed onto the floor. Who was screaming?

Adelaïde.

He stood up, clinging to a pillar for support. A slick of sweat erupted on his skin. The world started to spin, and he had to wait until it stopped. Then he staggered along the corridor. A doctor was sitting beside Adelaïde's bed. He had a priest with him. They both looked up when they saw him.

Dear God, he could feel the heat coming off her from the other side of the room. She moaned and tossed, her eyes rolling back in her head. There were bubbles of froth at the corner of her mouth.

'Can't you do anything?' he said.

'I have bled her three times,' the doctor said. 'The foul humours persist.'

'I have given her unction,' the priest said.

'She's not going to die.'

You should pray for her.'

Napoleon looked at the priest as if he had spoken a foreign language. 'Pray?' he said.

'God is merciful.'

'God is nothing of the kind,' Napoleon said. 'Get out. All of you.'

When the doctor had gone, he sat down on the divan beside her. The fit subsided and she suddenly lay so still, he thought she was dead. He bent over her and put his cheek to her lips to satisfy himself that she was still breathing.

He sat like that for a long time, staring at her, not daring to touch her. She looked so fragile.

'I am being punished,' he said aloud.

Napoleon hobbled his horse and left her to forage outside the gates. The temple had been abandoned for some time by the looks of the place, the jungle fast reclaiming the fallen and mossed stones. There were a few sandal trees and some fragrant bowers of jasmine among this semi-ruin. A thick stand of mango trees provided most of the shade.

It was quiet, save for the racket of the tree beetles and the gibber of a family of monkeys, who were scampering along the ruined walls. He could smell incense. Not all the priests had abandoned it, then.

There was another horse hobbled nearby. He recognised its livery. It belonged to one of Chanda Sahib's regular cavalry.

He went inside. It took some moments for his eyes to grow accustomed to the gloom. He winced as another spasm of pain shot up his arm. His hand itched unbearably, which was illogical because it was no longer there. He could smell the rot from the stump under the bandages.

There were two lamps glowing inside the shrine. He went closer and felt a shiver up his spine. A glossy black statue of a goddess leered at him from the depths. It was a hideous thing; her tongue lolled from her mouth, her eyes were red with rage, and her face and breasts were sullied with blood. She had two red fangs and a necklace of skulls.

Her girdle was made of human hands. Two were held out in blessing, another held a severed head, and the fourth carried a bloodied sword.

Someone had placed a garland of fresh marigolds around the statue's neck.

'Kali,' a voice said from the darkness. 'She represents the force of time.'

Napoleon realised he knew the man. He was one of Shah Mohammed's cavalry officers. 'What are you doing here,' Napoleon said. 'I thought you were all Muslims.'

'Not all of us.'

'You came here to pray?'

'To make an offering, yes. What has brought you here, sahib?'

'The same thing that brought you, I imagine. I am looking for a change in fortune.'

'You think a deity exists only to grant favours?'

'What else is their purpose?'

The man smiled. 'Kali's purpose is to destroy. Does she look at all benevolent to you?' He looked at Napoleon's arm, at the bandaged stump on his wrist. 'That looks like her handiwork.'

Napoleon nodded towards the statue. 'What does this all mean anyway?'

'Kali was born from outrage and a thirst for vengeance. Some things must be destroyed, so that a new good can be created.'

Napoleon had never had time for religion and the impossible nonsense people filled their heads with. You lived, you died. That was all there was to it.

'My daughter is dying,' he said. 'She may already have died while we stand here discussing philosophy.'

'So, the gods are your last resort? They are for most people.'

'I'm here to make a bargain. A contract. The priest told me I should pray for her. I don't believe in begging for favours, but negotiation, this I understand.'

'And what do you have to bargain with?'

'My life. After all, what good is a soldier without his sword hand?'

'Kali ends one cycle of life, so a new one can begin.'

'I do not wish for a new life. I only want to get a fair price for the old one. Your Kali has my right hand on her girdle,' Napoleon said, nodding towards the statue. 'What will she give me for it?'

'What you are talking about has nothing to do with Kali. You are talking about karma.'

Napoleon thought about Rabiot and the little girl with the ringlets. He knew the man was right. Karma was settling with him by taking away the thing he most loved. To save her he must put the debt on his own head.

'I think I have my answer,' he said. 'I will leave you to your devotions.'

'Go in peace, *sahib*.'

Napoleon gave the man a grim smile. Go in peace? He had never gone anywhere in peace, and he didn't mean to start now.

CHAPTER 67

A musket shot echoed around the walls. French snipers in the *ganj* had taken up their task with renewed ferocity. Meanwhile, their artillery had resumed the barrage on the south wall, to try to stop them building new earthworks.

If they came again tomorrow, Lachlan doubted he had enough fit men to withstand another assault. He didn't much care. He just wanted it over with now. He didn't think he could face another day of thirst, flies and fear.

Every time he moved, the pain in his leg made him gasp. The muscles around the wound had seized and he could not bend his leg at the knee. He felt feverish. Thomas had warned him that an infection could kill within a day.

'What are we going to do?' Mathieson said.

'I don't think they'll attack the breach a second time,' Lachlan said. 'My guess is they'll infiltrate the *ganj* and use force of numbers to storm the gatehouse. They don't know we're almost out of powder and shot so they'll be cautious. We have to be patient and use our guns sparingly, lure them through the walls again, create another killing ground.'

'That sounds alright, if we had enough fit men to do it. The truth is we're finished, aren't we?'

Lachlan didn't answer him.

He watched the gun crews using block and tackle to manoeuvre one of the nine pounders off the roof of the main gate and wheel it into position in the courtyard behind the gatehouse. They worked by the light of flares. Even though they had only powder enough to fire it twice more, its presence alone might deter a rushed assault.

The ground shook as another shell hit the walls.

Napoleon crawled on his belly across the *glacis*, a silk scarf wrapped across his mouth and nose. Three times he stopped and pulled aside the scarf to retch. He heard jackals yipping all around him, tearing apart the bodies of the dead.

The moon disappeared behind high, scudding clouds. He felt for the pistol tucked in his belt at the small of his back. Tonight, all debts would be settled. He would put things right.

The broken wall of the fort loomed ahead of him in the darkness. He slowed his pace. He didn't want a sentry to hear him, not when he had come this far. He pushed the rope and grappling hook ahead of him and waited, listening for the pickets on the wall above. Sensing it was safe he stood up and ran the last few yards in a low, crouching run.

He looked up at the ramparts. They were not as high at this section of wall, though the climb would still be difficult with only one good hand.

Lachlan sat at the upturned powder barrel that served as his map table and studied the plans of the fort. No matter how many times he stared at the charts, the answer was always the same. He didn't have enough men.

There was still no word from Madras about reinforcements, but his scouts told him that Shivaji Ghorpade was raiding Chanda Sahib's supply lines, looting at will. He and his bandit tribesmen had not committed to the fight, but that didn't stop them scavenging where they could.

Behind him, the door opened and closed softly.

'Any news for me, Charlie?' He looked around.

But it wasn't Mathieson. Whoever it was had settled themselves on a stool in a shadowed corner of the room. There was a metallic click. He knew that sound only too well. It was the sound of a pistol trigger being cocked. He smelled the coppery taint of blood.

'I should have killed you at Delgoa Bay,' a voice said.

Lachlan felt a thrill of fear and rage. 'How did you get in?' he said.

'I thought you would be pleased. You wanted to meet me face to face. You have your wish.' Napoleon held the stump of his arm in the air, towards the candle. Blood seeped through the rag tied around it. 'You have had your revenge, pup.'

'What happened to my father?'

'He died on my ship. A pistol ball through the heart.'

'Why did you do it?'

Napoleon sighted the barrel of the pistol at Lachlan's chest. 'Why does it matter to you now?'

Lachlan closed his eyes and waited. He wondered if there would be pain.

When he opened his eyes again, Napoleon was sitting with his left hand supporting the stump of his right arm. The pistol lay on the table, the butt turned towards him.

Lachlan stared at it.

'What is wrong with you, pup? It's what you want, isn't it? To kill me. Well, do it.'

Lachlan picked up the pistol, checked the frizzen.

'There is no trick,' Napoleon said. 'It is primed and loaded. If you doubt me, point it at my chest and pull the trigger.'

'Why did you come to Delgoa Bay? On whose orders?'

'I take orders from no one.'

'Why then?'

'It was at the request of a man named Jeronimus Keyser. Is the name familiar to you? He paid me quite handsomely to do it.'

The world yawed on its axis. Keyser had sent him? He had somehow supposed the trail of vengeance would end with Gagnon.

But Keyser? Suddenly he couldn't think. The pistol felt too heavy in his hand. Pull the trigger, he thought. Make this enough. Square the ledger and go home.

The door opened and they both looked around, surprised.

Mathieson stood in the doorway, silhouetted by the lantern in his left hand. 'I thought I heard voices' he said. He saw Napoleon.

'Get the guards,' Lachlan said. Mathieson turned on his heel and walked out.

'That isn't the deal,' Napoleon said. 'I didn't come here to surrender. I want you to kill me.'

'I want you begging me to let you live, not to help you die.'

Napoleon shook his head in disgust and went to the door. Lachlan raised the pistol and for a moment he might have shot him in the back, but the moment passed and then Napoleon was running away down the corridor.

There was a pistol shot.

Lachlan ran to the door. Mathieson was standing in the corridor with a smoking pistol in his hand. Napoleon lay at his feet, his blood streaked up the whitewashed wall. The sulphur stink of the gunpowder hung in the air. Mathieson bent over the body to satisfy himself that he was dead.

'I told you to fetch the guards,' Lachlan said.

'It's easier this way,' Mathieson said.

Lachlan leaned his weight on the cane and stared into the dark. He had thought that once Napoleon Gagnon was dead, he would feel elated, proud and relieved. He felt none of those things. There was just a vague sense of being cheated somehow. Gagnon's death had solved nothing. Instead, it had only opened the door to the grief he had kept locked away since that day. Somehow, until now, it hadn't seemed real. It was as if he'd dreamed it all.

It suddenly hit him with sickening force: he was never going to see any of his family ever again.

And it still wasn't over. The trail didn't end with Mohammed Daoud, or even with Gagnon. Jeronimus Keyser, his own father, had ordered all the killing.

For what - revenge?

If he kept going, if he went after Keyser, what would it serve? This time his luck might run out. Nothing would bring his family back now.

And then there's Catia, he thought. If I walk away now, I can start again. I can be grateful for this second chance.

Yet he had made a promise to Sasavona, and to himself, to avenge his family. If he turned his back on that vow, would he ever find peace again?

The roof was littered with the detritus from the previous day's battle: a shattered ramrod, a sponge pail, torn cartridges, a bloodied bandage. It all seemed so futile now. This was one decision that was easy to make. Now that Gagnon was dead, his reason for being here in Karimkot was gone. Hodges and Mathieson were right. They might as well surrender. There was nothing left to fight for.

Let the French have this stinking town. He wanted to go home.

CHAPTER 68

Mathieson woke suddenly. It took him a few moments to remember where he was. He was lying with his back against a gun carriage. He did not remember falling asleep and realised he must have been too exhausted to even make it as far as his *charpoy*. His neck was sore, his eyes gritty, and his mouth dry as cow dust. He gulped at his water canteen.

The fort was dark, all the flares were out, and a sickle moon hung over the ghats. A dirty stain crept up the sky. Someone was calling his name, an urgent whispering from above. It was one of the Company sergeants on the western rampart. What now?

He stumbled up the steps. The sergeant was leaning over the battlement, pointing at something in the far distance.

'Get down, man,' Mathieson said and tried to force his head down. 'The snipers will get you.'

'No, sir,' the sergeant said and shrugged him aside. 'It's alright. I think they've scarpered.'

'What?' Mathieson peered over the wall. It was true, they were gone. The flood plain was empty. Sometime during the night Chanda Sahib's massive army had slipped away. Their campfires were still smouldering, but the tents and horses were all gone. They must have lit the fires during the night to make them believe they were still there.

'Lachlan!' Mathieson shouted. 'Where's Captain McKenzie?'

Lachlan appeared and Mathieson pointed to the empty plain.

'Why?' Lachlan said. 'We were at their mercy.'

'Ghorpade must be on the move,' Mathieson said.

'But they were shelling us all day yesterday and last night.'

'To cover their retreat.'

Hayden, arrived. He was red-faced.

'Make this good news,' Lachlan said to him.

'We're relieved,' he said. 'One of our scouts just rode in. The reinforcements from Madras are just over the hill.'

CHAPTER 69

Madras

The first reports from Karimkot had called it a glorious victory, but the soldiers who trailed back into Madras that afternoon looked like the pathetic ragtag survivors of a massacre. There was scarcely a man who did not have at least one wound. Barely a handful walked in without help.

There were gasps and cries from around the parade ground as they entered through the Karimkot gate. The wagons carrying the wounded stretched half a mile.

Channing had organized a victory band. But the martial music only made the terrible reality of what they were all seeing appear even sadder. The Company clerks, the wives and the children stood in mute horror as they saw for themselves the brute nature of the victory.

Catia saw Lachlan lying in the back of one of the wagons and jumped onto the tailboard. There was a gasp from some of the onlookers. They'd never seen a woman do that before.

She threw her arms around him. 'Look at you,' she said. 'If my father were here, he would say I should leave you for the vultures.'

'All I need is a good nurse.'

'Is it done?' she said.

He nodded. 'It's done.'

Channing's secretary led Lachlan into the President's office. Mathieson and Hodges followed him in. Lachlan was leaning on the wooden crutch the new Company doctor had given him after he had redressed his leg wound. Lachlan had asked him what had happened to Dunning, but his answer had been curiously vague.

Lachlan was longing for a long bath and a change of clothes. His uniform was stiff with sweat and dried blood, and he needed the barber. But Channing had sent orders that he needed to see him immediately.

'For God's sake, get the man a chair,' Channing barked to his secretary when he walked in.

The secretary pulled up a bentwood chair and Lachlan eased himself down onto it. Mathieson and Hodges remained standing.

'Well, Mister McKenzie,' Channing said, 'it seems you have covered yourself in glory. Mathieson here says you a hero.'

'If it wasn't for Lieutenant McKenzie,' Mathieson said, 'all would have been lost.'

'Every man who took part in the campaign deserves credit, sir. Not just me.'

'He did no more than the rest of us,' Hodges said.

Channing knitted his eyebrows and studied the report in front of him. Lachlan recognised Mathieson's handwriting. He must have made the time to write a full report on the action before they left Karimkot. He realised he had been Channing's eyes and ears during the entire campaign.

The President turned to Hodges. He frowned. 'Mister Hodges, you are also mentioned in dispatches.'

For a moment Hodges looked pleased.

'Most unfavourably.'

Hodges looked nonplussed. 'I served the Company faithfully and helped us secure a great victory.'

'On the contrary, this report says you were neither steadfast nor brave. I am most disappointed. I have decided that you are to be recalled.'

'You can't do that!'

'Mister Hodges, as President of Madras, I assure you that I can.'

Hodges pointed a finger at Lachlan. 'His wife's a French spy!'

'Mrs McKenzie came to see me a few days ago. There was indeed a spy in the fort, and with her help we were able to identify her. She was Mister McKenzie's house servant, a young woman recommended to them by Doctor Dunning. She fled the colony before we could act but thanks to Mrs McKenzie's information we have arrested a Portuguese merchant in Black Town. He has been passing confidential information along to the French, with Doctor Dunning's assistance.'

'Dunning?'

'He is at this moment under lock and key, awaiting transportation to Calcutta, where his case will be heard. He has made a full confession. Apparently, he got himself into a desperate financial position and needed to pay off his gambling debts, which were considerable. The French found out about this and offered him a way out. For myself, I don't understand how any man can betray his country over something as vulgar as money, but there you are. So, your slurs against Mister McKenzie are entirely without foundation. You may leave us.'

Hodges was red in the face. He controlled himself with difficulty, then wheeled around and marched out of Channing's office.

Channing turned to Lachlan. 'They're calling you the Tiger of Karimkot,' he said. 'I have sent a glowing report of your service to the board in London.'

'Thank you, sir.'

'Mathieson here tells me that you even lured that rascal Gagnon out of hiding. We won't have to worry about his interference in our affairs anymore.'

'I didn't really lure him.'

Channing waved away his protest. 'He said you'd be modest about it. Well, I won't keep you. You look like you need a well-deserved rest. I just wanted to congratulate you in person and let you know your excellent service to the Company will be well rewarded. You have a great future ahead of you, Mister McKenzie.'

'Sir?'

'I know you had your sights set on becoming a factor, but I think we can do better than that. I'm going to recommend to the Board that you be given full responsibility for our military operations here in the Carnatic.' He held up a hand, anticipating Lachlan's objections. 'I know you have no formal military training, but you have proved yourself in the field, my lad. I'm going to recommend that you also be made Clerk of the Market, so that you're well rewarded financially. What do you say?'

'So, what did you say to him?' Catia asked him.

'I thanked him, told him how grateful I was for his confidence in me, and said no.'

Catia smiled.

They were sitting on the balcony of their apartments, overlooking the parade ground. Lachlan had his leg resting on a stool. What a luxury it was, he thought, to have on a clean shirt and breeches, not to walk everywhere in a crouch because of snipers, to smell frangipani and frankincense instead of decay and death. He closed his eyes and tried to wrestle the image of the corpses littering the *glacis* at Karimkot from his mind.

'When Gagnon told me about Keyser, my first thought was to go after him, make him pay like I made Mohammed Daoud and Gagnon pay. But what if it's true, that every time you do something, good or bad, something else has to happen to balance it out. What happened to my father wasn't right, but it *was* karma. It all has to stop somewhere, doesn't it?'

'So, what will we do?'

He took her hand. 'We go back to Novo Santiago, look after the plantation, raise a family and watch the sun come up over the ocean in the morning and set at night over the bush. That is going to be enough for me.'

She laid her head on his shoulder. 'Then that's what we'll do,' she said.

Tamil Nagar fort, Trincomalee, Ceylon

A young man in a white jacket and sarong led the girl along the veranda of *Mijn Heer's* bungalow. As she followed him, she thought how peaceful it was. The gardens were ordered and fragrant, a world away from the bedlam of the town outside the fort. She heard a bulbul singing in one of the cannonball trees.

The servant stopped outside two carved sandalwood doors and indicated that she was to go in. As she stepped inside, she realised it was *Mijn Heer's* bedroom. The polished satinwood floor was cool under her bare feet.

There was a carved four-poster mahogany bed against one wall. The mosquito net had been thrown back. Jeronimus Keyser lay on it, wearing only a sarong.

She had not been expecting a man of great physical beauty, and she was not disappointed. His cheeks were rosy from the heat, but the rest of his body was as pale as pig fat. Scallops of fat hung over the tie of his sarong.

He beckoned to her. 'There's not much of you.'

She lowered her eyes. He grunted and flipped back the sarong. 'Get to work, then.'

The girl knelt on the bed between his legs. He was damp with sweat. He closed his eyes and leaned back against the bolster.

She put a wicker basket on the bed between them, opened the lid and took out a small enamel bottle with a cork stopper. 'I want you to drink this.'

He opened his eyes and blinked at her. 'What is it?'

'It is a special potion made from the bark of a fever tree. It will make you as hard as teak. You will see.'

Keyser took the bottle from her. He swallowed the contents quickly and winced. 'It's bitter.'

She took the jar and put it back in her basket. 'Now we will wait for the results,' she said.

Keyser slapped her face. 'No, you do what I paid you to do. Get started.' He closed his eyes again and leaned back against the bolster.

'I thought it would be more difficult than this,' she said.

Keyser sat up, getting impatient now. 'Girl, you don't want to make me angry. I'll have you bullwhipped.'

She smiled. 'A man like you, a man with so many debts. I thought you'd be more cautious.'

Suddenly Keyser looked alarmed. 'What?'

'All these guards everywhere but you are as easy to dupe as a country boy at the market.'

'Who are you?'

'Who I am doesn't matter.'

He tried to grab her but instead he lost his balance and toppled onto his side. He put a hand to his face. There was blood leaking out of his eyes and his nose. Drops fell on the sheet, staining it bright red.

'Gagnon,' he said.

Ammani nodded. 'M'sieur Gagnon has a message for you. He says that all commerce is based on trust and good will. Without it, what will become of us all?'

'Tell him I'll pay him whatever he wants.'

'It's too late for that, I think.

Keyser tried to call for the guard, but he couldn't. He started to choke. He spat blood onto the pillow.

Ammani leaned forward. 'M'sieur Gagnon asked if you knew that one of the young men you sent him to kill at Fort Greenock was your own son. He thought you would appreciate the joke. I can see by your face that you didn't know.'

Keyser reached for her throat, but Ammani wriggled back out of reach, and Keyser slumped onto his side.

By the time the guard realised that something was wrong, Keyser was already convulsing on the floor. Within a few minutes he was dead.

Of the girl, there was no sign.

Pondicherry

Adelaïde stood in the middle of the field, her father's favourite sporting rifle cradled in her arms. Ochre mud had covered her boots and splashed up the front of her white dress.

She had a leather satchel on her back. She reached around and took out a paper cartridge, bit off the end and spat the paper over her shoulder into the mud. She tipped a little of the powder into the frizzen and flicked it shut. Then she poured the rest of the powder down the barrel, followed by the paper cartridge. She pulled out the ramrod, made sure the round was properly loaded, then brought the stock to her shoulder and aimed.

'Time,' she said.

A servant in a white turban stood under the shade of the nearby mango tree with a stopwatch.

'Fifteen seconds, *memsahib*,' he said.

She frowned. Still too slow. The double-tap method was quicker, but a good marksman couldn't take risks with a misfire.

She took a deep breath, nestled the stock into her shoulder and fired. She winced at the recoil. She was already heavily bruised from long hours of practice.

She lowered the rifle and marched through the clinging mud to the target. It was life-size and made of straw. The silhouette of a man had been drawn on a piece of hessian and attached to the figure with rope. Across it, in red letters, had been scrawled the words 'Lachlan McKenzie.'

Her musket ball had entered a little to the left of the chest. Not quite perfect.

The servant pointed to the clouds billowing up the sky. 'It will rain soon, mem'sahib,' he said. 'Perhaps that is enough practice for today.'

'I'll tell you when it's enough,' she said, and went back to her position, pacing out the steps. She reloaded the rifle - fourteen seconds - and fired.

Epic Adventure Series

Colin Falconer's series of historical adventure thrillers draws inspiration from many periods of history.

Visit the fabled city of Xanadu, the Aztec temples of Mexico, or the mountain strongholds of the legendary Cathars. Glimpse Julius Caesar in the sweat and press of the Roman forum, ride a war elephant in the army of Alexander the Great, or follow Suleiman the Magnificent into the forbidden palace of his harem.

Stand-alone stories that can be read in any order.

8000+ five-star reviews.

'A fantastic read' *Wilbur Smith*

Find your next adventure at colinfalconer.org

Special Offers

Colin Falconer books appear in monthly special offers.

To stay in the loop on price drops and new releases, sign up for his mailing list at **colinfalconer.org**. There's no spam and your email will be secure.

Enjoy this book?

You can make a big difference by writing a short book or series review on Amazon.

Honest reviews or ratings help to bring books to the attention of other readers.

About the Author

Born in London, Colin Falconer started out in advertising, then became a freelance journalist. He worked in radio and television before writing his first novel. He has published over forty books and is best known for his bestselling series of historical adventure thrillers – stories on an epic scale, inspired by his passion for history and travel.

He has also written a modern-day crime series featuring London detective DI Charlie George.

His books have been translated into 24 languages.

These days, Colin lives in Australia with his wife and multiple spaniels. He stays in touch with readers via his Facebook Author Page.

Glossary

afterchest — rear of a Cape wagon

baksheesh — money given as a tip

capulana — sarong worn primarily in Mozambique

chikunda — native army

escudo — Portuguese gold coin

glacis
    sloping bank built in front of a fort

godown
    warehouse

hookah
    water pipe

jemadar
    native junior officer

kaffir
    ethnic slur for black people (Afrikaans)

kaross
    rug or blanket made of animal skin

nganga
    witch doctor

FEVER COAST

nullah
                    watercourse or ditch (Hindustani)

prazeiro
                    Portuguese colonist farmer

sepoy
                    native soldier

stoep
                    small veranda

tonga
                    light carriage drawn by one horse

Printed in Great Britain
by Amazon